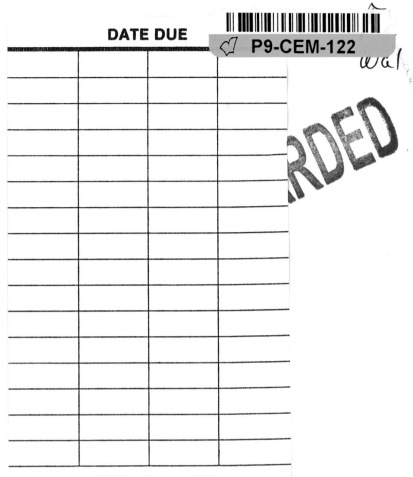

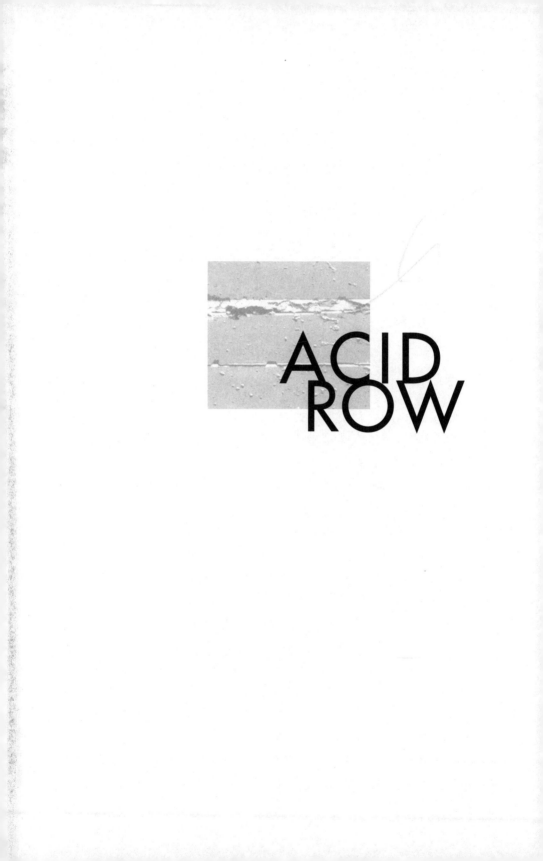

ACID
ROW

ALSO BY MINETTE WALTERS

THE SHAPE OF SNAKES

THE BREAKER

THE ECHO

THE DARK ROOM

THE SCOLD'S BRIDLE

THE SCULPTRESS

THE ICE HOUSE

ACID
ROW

MINETTE WALTERS

G. P. Putnam's Sons
New York

G. P. Putnam's Sons
Publishers Since 1838
a member of
Penguin Putnam Inc.
375 Hudson Street
New York, NY 10014

Library of Congress Cataloging-in-Publication Data
Walters, Minette.
    Acid row / Minette Walters.
        p.   cm.
    ISBN 0-399-14862-0
        1. Women physicians—Fiction.   2. Missing children—
Fiction.   3. Child molesters—Fiction.   4. Poor families—Fiction.
5. England—Fiction.   6. Riots—Fiction.   I. Title.
PR6073.A444 A615   2002   2001059182
823'.914—dc21

Printed in the United States of America
10   9   8   7   6   5   4   3   2   1

This book is printed on acid-free paper. ∞

Book design by Deborah Kerner/Dancing Bears Design

FOR
SHEONAGH
AND
PAT

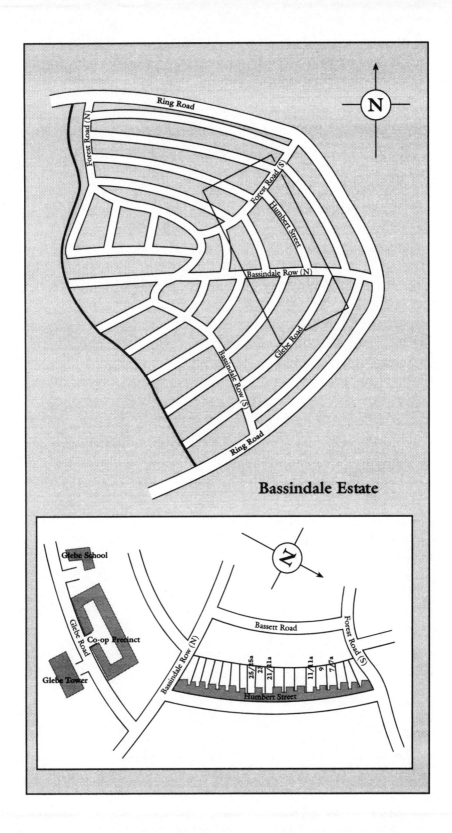

Bassindale Estate

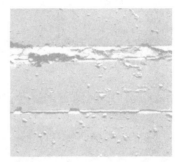

The riot lost momentum as news of the butchery spread through the estate. The details were vague. No one knew how many had been killed or how, but castration, lynching and a machete attack were all mentioned. The streets began to empty rapidly. Collective guilt was felt, if not openly expressed, and no one was inclined to face retribution for murder.

The youths on the barricades who had held the police at bay with gasoline bombs took a similar view. They would argue afterward, and with some justification, that they hadn't known what was going on, but when word of the frenzied attack filtered through they, too, melted away. It was one thing to fight an honorable battle with the enemy, quite another to be accused of aiding and abetting insanity on Humbert Street.

The headlines the next morning—29 July—were lurid. *"Alcohol-crazed lynch mob goes on the rampage"* . . . *"Sex pervert butchered"* . . . *"Five hours of savagery leaves 3 dead, 189 injured . . ."* The outside world gave a shudder of disgust. Headline writers lined up the usual suspects. Government. Police. Social workers. Education chiefs. Across the country, morale in the vocational services reached an all-time low.

But of the two thousand rioters who jostled for a view of the killing spree, not one would ever admit to being there . . .

Official Notification to Health and Social Workers

<u>**Highly Confidential—Not for Public Release**</u>

Rehousing: Milosz Zelowski, 23 Humbert Street, Bassindale—previously of Callum Road, Portisfield.

Reason for move: Targeted by Portisfield residents after publication of photograph in local newspaper.

Status: Registered pedophile. Convicted of sexual assault—3 counts over 15-year period. Released May 2001.

Threat to the community: Minimal. Nature of offense suggests surveillance only.

Threat to offender: <u>Severe.</u>

Police warn that Zelowski may become the target of vigilantes if his identity and status become known.

ONE

Only a handful of staff at the Nightingale Health Center ever read the memo referring to the presence of a pedophile on the Bassindale Estate. It vanished under a pile of paperwork in the central office and ended up being filed by one of the clerical workers, who assumed it had gone the rounds. For those who did see it, it was an unremarkable document, recording the name and details of a new patient. For the rest, it was irrelevant since it wouldn't—or *shouldn't*—affect the way they treated the man.

One of the health visitors tried to have the issue raised at a staff meeting, but she was overruled by her supervisor, who had responsibility for setting the agenda. There was a history of hostility between the two women—neither believing the other was up to her job—which may have prejudiced the way the supervisor handled the matter. It was summertime and everyone wanted to be home at a reasonable time. In any case, even if the doctors agreed that it was dangerous and irresponsible to house a pedophile on an estate full of children, there was nothing they could do about it. The decision to move him had been made by the police.

The same health visitor approached Dr. Sophie Morrison in a blatant attempt to have the supervisor's decision overturned. By that time she was less interested in the pedophile than in scoring points, and Sophie Morrison, being naïve and inexperienced in office politics,

3

imidated. Such, at least, was Fay Baldwin's interpreta-
cheerful young woman who had joined the practice two
e.

aited until the end of evening hours, then gave her signature
ophie's door—a rat-a-tat-tat of brittle nails that produced
l reactions in all her colleagues. "Time for a chat?" she asked
ly, poking her head into the room.

Fraid not," said Sophie, launching herself manically at her key-
d and typing "the quick brown fox jumps over the lazy dog"
etitively into her monitor. "Catching up on some notes . . . and
en home. *Sorry,* Fay. How about tomorrow?"

It didn't work. It never did. The dreadful woman eased herself
inside anyway and perched her scraggy bottom on the edge of the
desk. It was encased, as usual, in an impeccably tailored skirt; and, as
usual, there wasn't a dyed hair out of place. Both were outward and
visible signs that she considered herself a model of efficiency and pro-
fessionalism, but they were in inverse proportion to what was going
on inside her head. It was a Catch-22. She was desperate to cling to the
only thing that gave her life meaning—her job. Yet her hatred for the
people she dealt with—patients and professionals alike—had reached
disastrous proportions.

Sophie had argued that the kindest course would be to retire her
early and set her up with psychiatric help in order to cope with the
emptiness of her life. The senior partner—a great deal less sympa-
thetic toward elderly, frustrated virgins whose only talent was for stir-
ring things up—preferred to let sleeping dogs lie. It was less than
three months before they'd be rid of her for good, was his view. If she
was one of their patients it might be different, but she had coquet-
tishly eschewed Nightingale's doctors in favor of the competition on
the other side of town. "I couldn't *possibly* take my clothes off in front
of people I know," she'd said.

As if anyone cared.

"I'll only be a minute," trilled Fay now in her little-girly voice. "You can spare me sixty seconds, can't you, Sophie?"

"As long as you don't mind my packing up at the same time," said the doctor with an inward sigh. She shut down her computer and slid her chair backward, wondering which of her patients had just had typing exercises added to their notes. It was always the same with Fay. You found yourself doing things you didn't want to do, simply to escape the wretched woman. "I'm meeting Bob at eight."

"Is it true you're getting married?"

"Yes," said Sophie, happy to be on safe ground. "I finally got him up to the mark."

"I wouldn't marry a reluctant man."

"It was a joke, Fay." Her smile faded before the other woman's downturned mouth. "Ah, well, it's hardly earth-shattering news." She pulled her waist-length braid from behind her shoulder and started to comb it out with her fingers, quite unconsciously drawing attention to her unaffected youthfulness.

"It was Melanie Patterson who told me," remarked Fay spitefully. "I would have mentioned it last week, but she said it was supposed to be a secret."

Damn! Damn! Damn! "I didn't want to tempt fate in case Bob changed his mind," said Sophie, concentrating on her braid. It was a gross slander against her amiable fiancé, but if it prevented another row with Fay about Melanie Patterson it would be worth it. They had almost come to blows the week before, and she didn't want a repeat.

"She said you'd invited her to the wedding."

Damn! Damn! And more damns! Sophie stood up and walked across to a mirror on the far wall. Anything to avoid the reproach in the woman's face. "It's not for ages yet," she lied. "The invitations won't be going out for another four weeks." There was a slight softening of Fay's expression in the glass. "What did you want to talk about?" Sophie asked her.

"Well, in fact Melanie's part of it, so it's a good thing her name's come up," said the woman smugly. "Claire simply refuses to listen to me on this . . . keeps saying it's not a matter for discussion . . . but I'm afraid I can't agree with her. First, I take my job rather more seriously than she does—anyone can run a medical practice but it takes training to advise young mothers on the care and health of their families. And, second, in view of the way Melanie lets those children of hers run wild in the street—"

Sophie cut her short. "Don't do this, Fay," she said with uncharacteristic sharpness. "You made your views on Melanie very clear last week."

"Yes, but—"

"No." The young woman turned around, and there was considerable anger in her eyes. "I will not discuss Melanie with you again. Can't you see Claire was trying to do you a favor by making that clear to you?"

Fay bridled immediately. "You can't avoid it," she said. "She's my responsibility, too."

Sophie reached for her case. "Not anymore. I've asked Claire to assign one of the younger visitors to Melanie. She was going to tell you on Monday."

Retirement must have taken a sudden step closer, because the woman's highly powdered face lost color. "You can't reduce my list just because I disagree with you," she said fiercely.

"Calling one of my patients a slut and a whore and then losing your temper when I took you to task about it is rather more serious than disagreement," said Sophie coolly. "It's unprofessional, Fay."

"It's what she is," the woman hissed. "You come from a good family . . . you ought to be able to recognize it for yourself." Spittle flew from her mouth. "She sleeps with any man who shows an interest . . . usually when she's drunk . . . then she swans around like Lady Muck, saying she's pregnant again . . . as if it's something to be proud of."

Sophie shook her head. It was pointless arguing. In any case, she hated face-to-face confrontations with this woman, because they invariably became personal. Fay's life had prejudiced her views. She should have been working in the days when illegitimacy was frowned on and girls "who were no better than they should be" were hidden away in homes for unwed mothers and treated with scorn. That way, her status as a virtuous woman would have counted for something instead of making her an object of pity or amusement. The mystery was why she had ever chosen health visiting as a career, although, as the senior partner was fond of pointing out, lecturing, scolding and training the unwashed masses were probably what health visiting had been about when she started.

Sophie opened her office door. "I'm going home," she said firmly, standing back and making it clear she expected the other woman to leave first.

Fay stood up, her mouth working uncontrollably like an old lady's with dementia. "Well, don't say I didn't warn you," she said tightly. "You think you can treat everyone the same . . . but you can't. I know what these beasts are like . . . seen the kind of damage they do to the poor little souls they abuse. It's all so secretive . . . done behind closed doors . . . filthy, disgusting men . . . silly women who close their eyes to what's really going on . . . and all for what? *Sex!*" She spat out the word like a vile taste. "Still . . . at least *my* hands are clean. No one can say I didn't try." She walked stiff-legged from the office.

Sophie watched her go with a frown of concern. Dear God! *Beasts . . . ? Filthy, disgusting men . . . ?* Fay had lost the plot completely. It was bad enough to accuse Melanie of being a slut. A hundred times worse to accuse her and her men of child abuse.

But then Sophie had no idea that a pedophile had been housed just one door away from four-year-old Rosie and two-year-old Ben Patterson.

▼

The term *sink estate* might have been invented for Bassindale, which stood as a sprawling monument to the social engineering of the 1950s and 1960s, when planners had cut into the green belt to provide subsidized housing for those on low incomes. In this case, two hundred acres of broadleaf woodland bordering Bassindale Farm had been put to the axe and replaced with concrete.

It should have been idyllic. A worthy project in the postwar push for equality and opportunity. A chance for improvement. Quality homes surrounded by open countryside. Fresh air and space.

But all the roads on the perimeter bordering the fields were culs-de-sac. Like bicycle spokes, they ended at a solid rim—houses with block-built garden walls—to protect the surrounding crops and herds from thoughtless estate dwellers and their dogs. The only two thoroughfares, Bassindale Row and Forest Road, looped back on themselves in an unconnected, inverted W to provide four points of access through the concrete belt that kept the estate hidden from the busy traffic on the main road. From the air, Bassindale and Forest looked like the anchoring strands of a section of cobweb, with a tracery of streets and dead ends providing the transverse threads. From the ground—as recognized by the police—they were the potential redoubts that could turn Bassindale into a fortress. The estate was a concrete-clad pressure cooker.

And why not?

Demand for housing following the postwar baby boom had led to poor design and sloppy construction. The inevitable result was costly maintenance with only the most glaring problems being addressed. Ill health was endemic, particularly among the young and the old, for whom the cold wet conditions, coupled with poor diets, weakened constitutions. Depression was common, as was addiction to prescription pills.

Like the road to hell, Bassindale had begun with good intentions but it was now little more than a receptacle for society's rejects. A constant drain on the public purse. A source of resentment to taxpayers, irritation to the police and unmitigating despair to the teachers and the health and social workers who were expected to work there. For the majority of the inhabitants it was a prison. The frail and frightened elderly barricaded themselves inside their flats; desperate single mothers and fatherless children steered clear of trouble by living their lives behind locked doors. Only angry, alienated youth flourished briefly in this barren landscape by stalking the streets and controlling the traffic in drugs and prostitution. Before they, too, found themselves in prison.

In 1954 an idealistic Labour councilor had caused a sign to be erected at the end of Bassindale Row South, the first point of entry off the main road. It said inoffensively: WELCOME TO BASSINDALE. Over the years the sign was regularly vandalized with graffiti, only to be as regularly replaced by the local council. Then, in 1990, during the last year of Margaret Thatcher's premiership, the same council, under pressure to reduce its costs, canceled its budget for the replacement of signs. Thereafter, the graffiti was allowed to remain, untouched by Bassindale's inhabitants who saw it as a truer description of where they lived.

WELCOME TO ASSI D   *ROW*

Acid Row. A place of deprivation where literacy was poor, drugs endemic and fights commonplace.

▼

Fay Baldwin, obsessively replaying Sophie Morrison's dismissal of her the previous evening, wrenched four-year-old Rosie Patterson's arm violently to prevent the child from wiping her dirty hands and nose on Fay's newly cleaned suit. She had come across her in the street, playing with her brother, and she couldn't resist the chance to give their pregnant teenage mother a piece of her mind, particularly as Melanie wouldn't yet know that Fay was to be replaced as her health visitor.

She felt herself vindicated to find the girl curled up on the sofa with a cigarette in one hand, a can of lager in the other and *Neighbours* on the television. It proved everything she had ever said about Melanie's unsuitability as a mother. Rather less easy to cope with was the way Melanie was dressed, in a skimpy top and tiny shorts that revealed long brown legs and a softly rounded tummy with the growing bump of her six-month fetus.

Jealousy ate into Fay's soul while she pretended to herself that she was shocked to see anyone flaunt herself so shamelessly. "It won't do, Melanie," she lectured the girl sternly. "Rosie and Ben are too young to play outside on their own. You really must be more responsible."

The girl's eyes remained glued to the soap opera. "Rosie knows what she's doing, don't you, sweetheart? Tell the lady."

"Down ply rown cars. Down ply wiv neeles," the four-year-old chanted, giving her two-year-old brother a gratuitous cuff on the head as if to demonstrate how she kept him in order.

"Told you," said Melanie proudly. "She's a good girl, is Rosie."

Fay had to use every ounce of self-control not to smack the brazen creature. She had spent thirty years in this hellhole, trying to instill ideas on health, hygiene and contraception into generations of the same families, and the situation was getting worse. This one had had her first baby at fourteen, her second at sixteen and was pregnant with her third before she'd even reached twenty. She had only the vaguest idea who the fathers were, cared less and regularly dumped the children on her own mother—whose youngest child was younger than Rosie—to take herself off for days on end to "get her head straight."

She was lazy and uneducated and had been housed in this duplex because social services thought she might develop into a better parent away from her mother's "unhelpful" influence. It was a vain hope. She lived in unbelievable squalor, was regularly stoned or drunk, and alternated between lavishing love on her children when she was in the mood and ignoring them entirely when she wasn't. The gossip was that "getting her head straight" was a euphemism for an intermittent (between pregnancies) career as a topless model, but as she didn't want her benefits stopped she never owned up to it.

"They'll be taken away from you if you go on neglecting them," the woman warned.

"Yeah, yeah, blah, blah." Melanie flicked her a knowing look. "You'd like that, wouldn't you, Miss Baldwin? You'd have them off me quick as winking if you ever found any bruises. Bet it makes you sick you never have."

Irritated, the woman knelt down in front of the child. "Do you know why you shouldn't play around cars, Rosie?"

"Mum'll 'it us."

Melanie beamed at her and took a drag from her cigarette. "I've never hit you in my life, darlin'," she said comfortably. "Never would. You don't play round cars 'cos they're dangerous. That's what the lady wanted you to say." She flicked Fay a mischievous glance. "Isn't that right, miss?"

Fay ignored her. "You said you weren't supposed to play with needles, Rosie, but do you know what a needle looks like?"

"'Course I do. One of my dads uses 'em."

Annoyed, Melanie swung her legs off the sofa and dropped her cigarette butt into the lager can. "You leave her alone," she told the woman. "You're not the police, and you're not our social worker, so it's no business of yours to quiz my kids about their dads. They're fit and healthy, they've had their jabs and they both get weighed regular. That's all you need to know. *Capeesh?* You've got no right to waltz in here whenever you bloody feel like it. There's only one person from the center's allowed to do that . . . and that's Sophie."

Fay stood up. Somewhere in the back of her mind an inner voice urged caution, but she was too resentful to take heed of it. "Your children have been on the 'at risk' list since the day they were born, Melanie," she snapped. "That means I have the right, *and* the duty, to inspect them whenever I think fit. *Look* at them! They're disgusting. When did either of them last have a bath or a change of clothes?"

"The Social know I love my kids and that's all that fucking matters."

"If you loved them, you'd take care of them."

"What would you know about it? Where are your kids . . . *miss?*"

"You know very well I don't have any."

"Too sodding right." She pulled her daughter close, mingling her beautiful blond hair with the child's. "Who loves you better than anything, Rosie?"

"Mum."

"And who do you love, sweetheart?"

The child put her finger on her mother's lips. "Mum."

"So do you wanna live with Mum or with the lady?"

Tears bloomed in the little girl's eye. "Wiv' you, wiv' you," she howled, flinging her arms around Melanie's neck as if she expected to be torn away from her at any minute.

"See," Melanie told the health visitor with a smirk of triumph. "Now tell me I don't care for my babies."

Something finally snapped inside Fay. Perhaps her sleepless night had taken its toll. Perhaps, more simply, the taunts of an empty life were the last straw. "My God, you're so ignorant," she stormed. "Do you think it's difficult to manipulate a child's affections?" She motioned angrily toward the window. "There's a pedophile in this street who could take your little Rosie away from you with a handful of sweets because she's never learned when love is honestly given and when it isn't. And who will society blame, Melanie? You?" She gave a withering laugh. "Of course not . . . You'll weep crocodile tears while the people who genuinely cared for Rosie—me, and your social worker—get crucified for leaving her with someone so inadequate."

The girl's eyes narrowed. "I don't reckon you should be telling me this."

"Why not? It's the truth."

"Where's this pedophile then? Which number?"

Too late, Fay knew she'd overstepped the mark. It was privileged information, and she'd given it away in anger. "That's not the issue," she said lamely.

"Like hell it isn't! If I've got a sicko living near me, I wanna know about it." She reared up off the sofa and towered over the little spinster. "I know you think I'm a lousy mum, but I've never harmed them and I never would. Dirt don't kill a kid and neither does a bit of swearing now and then." She thrust her face into the woman's. "Sickos do, though. So where is he? What's his name?"

"I'm not allowed to tell you."

Melanie bunched her fists. "Do you want me to make you?"

Terrified, Fay retreated toward the door. "It's a Polish name," she said cravenly before she fled.

▼

She was trembling as she stepped out onto Humbert Street. How could she have been so stupid? Would Melanie give her away? Would there be an inquiry? Had she jeopardized her pension? Her mind was consumed with finding excuses. It was hardly her fault. It was a stupid idea to house a pedophile in Acid Row. There was no way it could remain a secret. Prison was a second home to the men on the estate. Someone was bound to recognize him from his time inside. Her fear began to abate. If anyone asked, she would say she'd heard through the grapevine. Who knew where gossip began in this place? The most ridiculous rumors spread like wildfire. It wasn't as if she'd given Melanie a name . . .

With burgeoning confidence, she set off down the road, glancing sideways as she passed number 23. There was an elderly man at the window. He shrank back as he caught her eye, fearful of being noticed, and she felt herself justified. He was white-faced and unhealthy-looking—like a maggot—and her instinctive shudder of distaste smothered any idea of warning him or the police that his life was in danger.

In any case, she hated pedophiles with a passion. She had seen their handiwork too often on the minds and bodies of the children who called them Daddy.

Death of Innocence

At the end of one of the most horrific murder trials of the last ten years, Marie-Thérèse Kouao, forty-four, and her boyfriend, Carl Manning, twenty-eight, were jailed for life for the brutal torture and murder of Kouao's grand-niece, eight-yr-old Anna Climbie. Anna, born and raised in the Ivory Coast, had been entrusted to Kouao's care by loving parents after the killer aunt, who styled herself to her extended family in Africa as a "wealthy and successful woman," had offered to give the child a better life in England. In truth she was a fraudulent scrounger who needed a "daughter" to work the welfare system.

Little Anna died from hypothermia and malnutrition after being forced to live naked in a bathtub, bound hand and foot, and covered only with a trash bag. She was tethered like a dog and fed scraps, which she had to eat off the floor. Her body showed 128 marks of beating which Kouao, posing as her mother, convinced doctors and social workers were self-inflicted. She also persuaded religious leaders to perform exorcism on the traumatized and tormented child, claiming she was possessed by devils.

During the trial, Kouao, who carried a Bible to persuade the jury she was a religious woman, said she was being attacked by other prisoners while being held in Holloway jail. It was a shameless demonstration of the double standards by which this murderess operated. "They beat me and break my things," she wept. "It's very hard to cope." In response, her cross-examiner demanded angrily: "How easy was it for Anna to cope with what you did to her?"

It is tempting to dismiss Kouao as an evil aberration,

but the statistics of child murder in the U.K. make alarming reading. An average of two children die every week at the hands of their parents or caregivers, thousands more are so badly abused and neglected that their physical and psychological damage is irreparable. By contrast, fewer than five children a year are killed by strangers.

When the *News of the World*, the U.K.'s biggest-selling newspaper, launched its campaign last year to "out" pedophiles, in line with Megan's Law in the U.S., by publishing names, addresses and photographs of known offenders, opinions about the campaign's effectiveness were polarized. The public, shocked by a recent and horrific child murder by a suspected pedophile, largely welcomed it. Police, probation officers and child-abuse lawyers argued that it was counterproductive and likely to force pedophiles to abandon therapy and go into hiding for fear of vigilante attacks.

Their warnings quickly became reality. According to a report drawn up by probation officers, sex offenders in all parts of Britain had already moved, changed their names and broken contact with police, or were considering such action. More alarmingly, following the publication of eighty-three names, addresses and photographs in the Sunday tabloid, angry vigilante mobs attacked the homes of some of these alleged pedophiles and rioted in the streets outside.

In almost every instance the target was an innocent person, either because the newspaper had printed a wrong or out-of-date address or because the vigilantes believed the homeowner looked like one of the photographs. The most bizarre and troubling incident was the vandalization of a female pediatrician's house and car by an ignorant mob who thought "pediatrician"—a doctor who specializes in the diagnosis and treatment of children's diseases—was synonymous with "pedophile"—an adult who is sexually attracted to children.

In the wake of these incidents the *News of the World*

suspended its campaign after promising at the outset to "name and shame" every pedophile in the U.K. "Our job now is to force the government to act [on Megan's Law]," said the embattled editor, "and we'll *name and shame* every politician who stands in our way."

The debate about how to deal with pedophiles rages on, yet the statistics show that thousands of children are more at risk within their own homes than on the streets. Following a recent trial of pedophiles who shared indecent images of children over the Net, a police spokesman pointed to a disturbingly domestic element in the pornography now on display. "Early child pornography was filmed in studios," he said, "but the latest images look as though they've been filmed inside the children's homes. You can see toys in the background. This suggests one or more of the parents was involved in the abuse."

However comfortable the belief that only sadistic strangers prey on children, we focus on the pedophile at our peril. Little Anna Climbie was brutalized and murdered by the people who were supposed to be taking care of her. Countless babies have been shaken to death at the hands of angry caregivers. Childline logs fifteen thousand calls a day from distressed children. Most sexual abuse is perpetrated within the home. Most pedophiles were sexually abused as children. Child pornography exists because parents take part in, sell or abandon their little ones to corruption.

Are we ready yet to "name and shame" the real abusers?

Anne Cattrell

TWO

Suspicion on Humbert Street focused on number 23, not because the occupant had a Polish name but because an adult man had recently moved in. It had been Mary Fallon's house until one of her five children died of pneumonia while awaiting surgery for heart problems. The council denied liability but moved the family hastily to the healthier climes of the newer Portisfield Estate, which was twenty miles away on the other side of the city and a great deal more attractive, having benefited from lessons learned in Acid Row.

After that, number 23 had stood empty for months with its windows boarded up until council workers turned up unexpectedly to air the place out with some warm July sun and paint over the cracks and mold in the plaster. Shortly afterward, the new tenant moved in. Or tenants? There was some confusion about how many were in there. The neighbors at 25 said it was two men—they could hear the rumble of deep conversation through the walls—but only one ever came out to do the shopping. A middle-aged fellow with sandy hair, pale skin and a shy smile.

There was also confusion about how and when they arrived, as no one remembered seeing a van in the street. A rumor spread that the police had escorted them there in the dead of night along with their furniture, but old Mrs. Carthew at number 9, who sat at her window

18

all day, said they came in a van on a Monday morning and helped the driver unload it themselves. No one believed her because her bad days outnumbered her good days, and it seemed unlikely that she was lucid enough to know it was a Monday or even remember the event afterward.

Police involvement was more appealing because it made sense. Particularly to the young, who lived on conspiracy theories. Why were the men brought in under cover of darkness? Why did the second one never emerge in the daytime? Why was the shopper's face so pale? It was a contamination. Like something out of *The X-Files*. Vampire perverts hunting in packs.

Mrs. Carthew said they were father and son, claiming she'd opened her window to ask them. No one believed her because there wasn't a window in Acid Row that a senile old fool could open. It took hammers and chisels to pry them loose from their frames. And even if she could, her house was too far away from 23 for that sort of idle chitchat.

The preferred interpretation was that they were gay—doubly sick, therefore—and mothers with daughters breathed quiet sighs of relief while warning their boys to be careful. Youngsters hung around outside the house for a couple of days, shouting insults and baring their bottoms, but, when nothing happened and no one appeared at the windows, they grew bored and went back to the amusement arcades.

The women were less easily diverted. They continued to gossip among themselves and keep a watchful eye on the comings and goings on Humbert Street. Some of the social workers responded to their questions but few of the women believed the answers, which were unspecific and open to interpretation.

"Of course they aren't going to dump perverts on you just because it's a sink estate. Trust me, if there was a dangerous pedophile in the area, I'd be the first to know . . ."

"Perhaps it's a dastardly plot to get you to keep an eye on your kids . . ."

"Look, these days, convicted pedophiles are under constant supervision. It's the wannabe psychos who come in from outside you really want to worry about . . ."

These answers were repeated endlessly around the community, so no one knew how accurate the reported speech was. However, the fact that there appeared to be no outright denials was seized upon as evidence of what they had always believed: There was one set of rules for Acid Row and another for everyone else.

THURSDAY, 26 JULY 2001—21 HUMBERT STREET, BASSINDALE ESTATE

Melanie offered Sophie Morrison a cup of tea after the doctor had let Rosie and Ben listen to the baby's heartbeat through her stethoscope. She was lying on the settee in the sitting-room, laughing as her toddlers pressed their little fingers to her tummy to see if they could feel their brother or sister moving. "Ain't they sweet?" she said, dropping kisses onto their blond curls before swinging her legs to the floor and standing up.

"I'd love a cuppa," said Sophie with a smile as she saw two teenage boys pause to gape through the window at Mel's naked, swollen belly. "You've got an audience," she murmured.

"I always do," said the girl, pulling down her top. "You can't get up to nothing in this place without the world and his wife watching."

Melanie's was one of the in-between houses in Humbert Street which had been divided some thirty years previously to create two duplexes, one at the front and one at the back. A more sensible solution would have been to convert the properties into single-story apartments, but that would have involved jacking up the façades to create new front doors and installing expensive soundproofing under the upstairs floorboards. Some genius at the planning department had come up with a better idea. It would be quicker, cheaper and less disruptive to existing tenants, ran his argument, to divide the houses across the middle with cinder-block walls, fill in the gaps between the houses on either side with new front doors and stairs for each duplex and utilize the existing corridor, stairwell and landing for kitchens and bathrooms.

It was an unhappy solution for everyone, creating three classes of tenants on the street. Those, like the men at number 23, who were lucky enough to have a whole house and garden. Those, like Granny Howard, who lived in the duplex behind Melanie, who also enjoyed a full-sized garden. And those at the front, with only a patch of grass and a small wall between them and the road. It had turned Humbert Street into a concrete tunnel, and resentment was enormous, particularly among those with no access at all to the gardens at the rear.

"Is Granny Howard still giving you problems?" Sophie asked, lifting little Ben into her arms and giving him a cuddle as his mother went into the kitchen.

"Oh, yeah, she keeps banging her hammer on the wall 'cos of the kids' noise, but we've given up on the garden. She ain't never going to let them have a bit of a play. My Jimmy had a go at persuading her before he got sent down for the thieving, but she called him a nigger and told him to fuck off. I wouldn't mind so much but it's all weeds out there. She don't even go in it herself."

Sophie ran the back of her hand down Ben's cheek. It seemed crazy to her that the Housing Department should keep an old woman, who never went out, at the back, when two little toddlers who yearned to run and play in safety were confined to the front, but there was no arguing. It was written in stone that Granny Howard had held the tenancy of number 21a since 1973 and was entitled to stay there until she died. "How are you doing on the booze and cigarette front? Is it getting any easier?"

"Reckon so," said the girl cheerfully. "I've got the cigarettes down to five a day, and the booze down to a couple of halves . . . one with my dinner, one with my tea . . . sometimes two. No more binge drinking, though. Given that up totally. I still have the odd joint now and then, but it don't amount to much 'cos I can't afford it."

Sophie was impressed. The girl had been smoking two packs a day at the start of her pregnancy, and the highlight of her week had been to get completely drunk and stoned in the clubs every Saturday night. Even allowing for the addict's habit of self-delusion, it was a huge drop, which she seemed to have maintained successfully for the last two months. "Well done," she said simply, sitting down on the sofa and making space for Rosie to join her.

Like Fay, she thought both children in urgent need of a bath, but they were robust and confident toddlers, and she had few worries about their physical or mental health. Indeed she wished that some of her middle-class parents could learn a little about the Patterson way of child rearing. It maddened her how many of them raised their children in disinfected, germ-free environments, then insisted on allergy tests because the kids had never-ending coughs and sneezes. As if bleach were some sort of substitute for natural immunity.

"Yeah, well, I wish that cow Miss Baldwin thought the same," said Melanie crossly as she reappeared with mugs of tea. "She gave me a really dirty look because I was having a cigarette and a beer in front of *Neighbours*. If she'd asked I'd have told her it was my first smoke of the day, but she's not like you . . . She thinks the worst of people whether she needs to or not."

"When was she here?" asked Sophie, lifting Ben to the floor again and accepting a mug.

Melanie plonked down beside her. "Can't remember . . . last week sometime . . . Thursday . . . Friday. She was in a really fucking mood. Snapping away at me like a bloody little terrier."

After Fay knew she was going to be replaced then, Sophie thought with annoyance. "Did she mention that I've asked one of the younger health visitors to take over from her?"

"No. Just gave me a lecture as usual. What's this new one like then?"

"Wacky," said Sophie, sipping at her tea. "Pink hair . . . black leather . . . Doc Marten boots . . . rides a motorcycle . . . adores kids. You and she'll get along like a house on fire."

"Bit of a change from old fart face then." Melanie cradled her mug between her hands, staring into its milky depths and trying to decide how to put the question she wanted to ask. Subtly or bluntly? She chose subtle. "What do you reckon to pedophiles?" she demanded.

"How do you mean?"

"Would you treat one?"

"Yes."

"Even if you knew they'd done stuff to kids?"

"'Fraid so." Sophie smiled at her disapproving expression. "I wouldn't have much choice, Mel. It's my job. I'm not allowed to pick and choose patients. Why are you asking, anyway?"

"I just wondered if you've got any registered with you."

"Not as far as I know. They don't have black marks beside their names."

Melanie didn't believe her. "So how come Miss Baldwin knows about the one on the road and you don't?"

Sophie was genuinely startled. "What are you talking about?"

"I thought maybe you could give me his name . . . the one he's using, anyway. See, everyone's assuming he's a newcomer, but me, I'm wondering if he's been here all along." She waved her hand toward the window. "There's an old geezer in number eight who vanished for about six months last year, then said he'd been visiting his folks in Australia. I reckon it could be him. He's always smarming up to our Rosie and telling her how pretty she is."

Sophie was bewildered. "What exactly did Fay Baldwin say?"

"That there's a pedophile on the road and he'd take our Rosie whenever he got the urge."

God almighty! "What started it?"

"Usual stuff. Lecture . . . lecture . . . lecture. Tried to quiz Rosie about her dad, then tells me what a lousy mother I am when I gave her a bit of my mind. I told her to fuck off more or less . . . then . . . wham! . . . she hits me with this pervert who's gonna seduce Rosie with sweets. Frightened me bloody sick, she did."

"I'm sorry," said Sophie apologetically, visions of lawsuits floating in front of her eyes. "It was after I fired her from your case, so she was probably feeling unhappy. She shouldn't have teased you though, particularly not like that." She sighed. "Look, Mel, I'm not going to excuse her behavior, but she does have some problems at the moment. She's frightened of retirement . . . feels her life's a bit empty. Things like that. She'd love to have married and had babies herself . . . but it didn't work out for her. Can you understand that?"

Melanie shrugged. "She was bugging me something chronic, so I took the mickey about her not having any kids. She got *really* huffy. Started spitting at me."

Sophie remembered how Fay had spat when she'd been talking to her. "It's a touchy subject with her." She stood up and placed her mug on a table. She was careful not to show how angry she was. She could imagine the senior partner's fury if the practice got hit for compensation for "pain and suffering." *The bloody woman ought to have been locked up years ago.* "Do me a favor, Mel. Forget she said anything. She was way out of line . . . shouldn't have done it. You're too sensible to get hung up on anything Fay Baldwin says."

"She looked shit-scared when I said she shouldn't be shooting her mouth off about stuff like that."

"I'm not surprised." Sophie glanced at her watch. "Look, I have to go. I'll have a chat with Fay's replacement, tell her what's been going on, ask her to come out ASAP. You can speak to her about anything—she's a great listener—and I promise she won't give you any lectures. How does that sound?"

Melanie lifted a thumb. "Wicked." She waited for the door to close, then pulled her daughter onto her knee. "See, darlin'. That's a conspiracy. One silly bitch gives the game away 'cos she's a frigid cow, and everyone else makes out they don't know nothing." She recalled Fay's terror as she ran from the house. "But the frigid cow was telling the truth, and the rest're fucking lying."

▼

The message Sophie left on Fay's phone when she got back to her car was a blisterer.

I don't care what your problems are, Fay . . . as far as I'm concerned your mental health would be vastly improved if your milkman fucked you rotten tomorrow . . . but if you ever go near Melanie Patterson again I will personally march you to the nearest loony bin and have you committed. What the hell do you think you were doing, you stupid, stupid woman?

Half an hour later and a mile away in the Nightingale Health Center, Fay Baldwin's hand trembled as she wiped the message from her voice mail. Melanie had betrayed her.

THREE

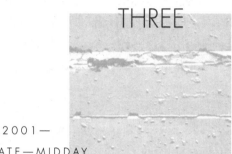

The car was parked for twenty minutes outside the Roman Catholic church in Portisfield. Several people walked past it, but none of them gave it a second glance. One described it afterward as a blue Rover, another as a black BMW. A young mother, pushing a stroller, had noticed a man inside, but she couldn't describe him and, under police questioning, changed her mind and said it might have been a woman with short hair.

When the twenty minutes were up, a thin, dark-haired child opened the car door and slipped onto the passenger seat, leaning over to plant a kiss on the driver's cheek. No one saw her do it, although the young mother thought she might have seen a little girl answering that description turn the corner from Allenby Road a few minutes earlier. Under the same questioning, she vacillated, saying the girl might have been blond.

"All right?" the driver asked.

The child nodded. "Did you get me the new clothes?"

"Of course. When have I ever not kept a promise?"

Her eyes lit up with excitement. "Are they nice?"

"Just what you ordered. Dolce and Gabbana top. Gucci skirt. Prada shoes."

"Wicked."

"Shall we go?"

The child looked at her hands, suddenly hesitant.

"You can change your mind at any time, sweetheart. You know I only want you to be happy."

The child gave another nod. "Okay."

FOUR

The sun was still high in the western sky at six o'clock, and tempers grew short as air-conditioned shops and offices emptied into the sweltering temperatures of that July evening. Tired workers, anxious to be home, boiled in overheated cars and buses, and Laura Biddulph's progress along Allenby Road slowed as she braced herself for another round with Greg's children. She couldn't decide which was more depressing, an eight-hour shift at the Portisfield Sainsbury's or going home to Miss Piggy and Jabba the Hutt.

She toyed with telling them the truth. *Your father's disgusting . . . Don't even think I want to be your stepmother . . .* For a brief and glorious moment, she pictured herself doing it, until common sense returned and she remembered her alternatives. *Or lack of them.* All relationships were built on lies, but desperate men were more likely to believe them. What choice did they have if they didn't want to be lonely?

Outside, the sunlight gave the uniform council houses a spurious glamor. Inside, Miss Piggy and Jabba were closeted in the front room with all the curtains closed and the television tuned at high volume to one of the music channels. The stench of sausage fat assaulted Laura's nostrils as she let herself in through the front door, and she wondered how many visits they'd made to the kitchen that day. If she had her way, she'd lock them in a closet on rations of bread and water until they lost some weight and learned some manners, but Greg was

28

consumed with guilt about his failings so they got fatter and ruder by the day. She peeled off her cotton jacket, replaced her flat shop-assistant's shoes with a pair of mules from under the coat rack and rearranged her baleful scowl into the vacuous, pretty smile they knew. At least if she went through the motions of caring, there was hope of a change.

She opened the living-room door, poked her nose into hot, stagnant air, ripe with teenage farts, and shouted above the noise: "Have you made your own tea, or do you want me to do it?" It was a silly question—greasy plates, smeared with ketchup, littered the floor as usual—but it made no difference. They wouldn't answer whatever she said.

Jabba the Hutt, a thirteen-year-old boy with rampant eczema where his double chins chafed his neck, promptly ratcheted up the volume on the set. Miss Piggy, fifteen years old and with breasts like dirigibles, turned her back. It was a nightly ritual aimed at freezing out the skinny wannabe stepmother. And it was working. If it weren't for her daughter's easy acceptance—"They're okay when we're on our own, Mummy"—she'd have cut her losses a long time ago. She waited for Jabba to mouth "Fuck off" to the air—another routine that never varied—before, with relief, she closed the door and headed for the kitchen.

Behind her, the television was immediately muted. "I'm home, Amy," she called as she passed the stairs. "What do you want, sweetheart? Fish fingers or sausages?" It was the love they hated, she thought, as she listened for the muttered taunts of "Sweety . . . Sweety . . . Mumsy . . . Mumsy . . ." to come from the living room. Terms of endearment made them jealous.

But for once the teasing didn't happen and, with a flicker of alarm, she peered up the staircase waiting for the rush of boisterous feet as her ten-year-old pounded down the steps to fling herself into her mother's arms. Every time it happened, she persuaded herself she was doing the right thing. Yet the nagging doubts never went away, and when there was no response she knew she'd been deluding herself. She gave another call, louder this time, then took the stairs two at a time and flung open the child's bedroom door.

Seconds later she burst into the living room. "Where's Amy?" she demanded.

"Dunno," said Barry carelessly, flicking up the sound again. "Out, I guess."

"What do you mean 'out'?"

"Out . . . OUT . . . Not fucking in. Jesus! Are you stupid, or what?"

Laura snatched the remote control from his hand and killed the picture. "Where's Amy?" she demanded of Kimberley.

The girl shrugged. "Round at Patsy's?" she suggested with an upward inflection.

"Well, is she or isn't she?"

"How would I know? She doesn't call in every hour to keep me posted." The panic in the woman's expression persuaded her to stop teasing. "Of course she is."

Barry shifted uncomfortably on the sofa, and Laura swung around to him. "What?" she demanded.

"Nothing." He gave a shrug. "It's not our fault if she doesn't want to stay with us."

"Except I'm paying Kimberley to take care of her, not send her off to a friend every day."

The girl eyed her maliciously. "Yeah, well, she's not quite the little angel you think she is and, 'cept for tying her up, there's not much I can do to keep her here. It's about bloody time you found out about her. She's been at Patsy's every day since the end of the term, and most evenings she only gets in a few minutes before you do. It's fucking hilarious listening to you make a fool of yourself." She dropped into exaggerated mimicry of Laura's more educated speech. "Hev you been a good gel, darling? Did you prectice your ballay? Air you enjoying your reading? Lovey . . . dovey . . . Mummum's little pumpkin." She pointed two fingers at her open mouth. "It's bloody sickmaking."

She must have been mad to leave Amy with them . . . "Well, at least she's *got* a mother," she spat. "Where's yours, Kimberley?"

"None of your sodding business."

Anger made her vicious. "Of course it's my business. I wouldn't be here if she hadn't abandoned you to have babies with someone else." Her eyes flashed. "Not that I blame her for leaving. What do you think it feels like to be known as the mother of Miss Piggy and Jabba the Hutt?"

"Bitch!"

Laura gave a small laugh. "Snap. But at least I'm a *thin* bitch. What's your excuse?"

"Leave her alone," said Barry angrily. "She can't help being heavy. It's rude to call her Miss Piggy."

" 'Rude!' " she echoed in disbelief. "My God, you don't even know the meaning of the word. *Food*'s the only word you understand, Barry. That's the reason you and Kimberley are *heavy*." She put sarcastic stress on the words. "And of course you can help it. If you used some energy to clean up once in a while you'd have some excuse"—she pointed an angry finger at the dirty plates—"but you stuff your faces all day, then waddle away from the trough as if some servant is going to clean up after you. Who do you think you are exactly?"

She had promised herself she wouldn't do this. Criticism was corrosive, eating away at self-esteem and ravaging trust. In rare moments of accord between her and her husband—distant memories now—Martin had claimed it was a disease. Cruelty's in the blood, he said. It's like a herpes virus. It stays dormant for a period, then a trigger sets it off.

"It's my house. I can do what I want," Barry retorted furiously, his feet thrashing against the carpet as he tried to get a foothold to struggle out of the sofa.

It wasn't clear what his intentions were, but it was funny watching him. Even funnier when she placed a mocking hand on his forehead and pushed him backward. "Look at you," she said in disgust as he fell against the cushions. "You're so fat you can't even stand up."

"You *hit* him," accused Kimberley triumphantly. "I'll phone Childline . . . that'll learn you."

"Oh, grow up!" said Laura dismissively, turning away. "I didn't hit him, I pushed him, and if someone had taught you to speak English properly you'd understand the difference. 'That'll *learn* you' makes about as much sense as Barry saying this is *his* house."

There was a perceptible rush of air as Kimberley surged out of her chair and made a grab at the woman's shirt.

Laura's instinctive response was to deliver a stinging slap to the girl's face and wriggle out of her grasp, but there was a split second of mutually recognized hatred before she had the sense to take to her heels.

"BITCH! BITCH!" the furious youngster roared, pursuing the woman down the corridor toward the kitchen. "I'm gonna fucking KILL you for that!"

Laura slammed the door and leaned her shoulder against it to keep Kimberley out, her heart thumping against her lungs. *Was she mad?* She was no match for the girl in terms of bulk, but she used the strength of her grip to stop the handle from turning, betting on Miss Piggy's fingers being slippery from stuffing chips into her mouth. Even so, it was a war of attrition that only came to an end when the lower panels began to crack under the assault from Kimberley's boots, and Barry shouted that their dad would have her guts if she broke it again.

Gingerly, Laura relaxed her cramped hold as she felt the onslaught die away. She pressed her back against the wood and took a few deep breaths to calm herself. "Barry's right," she warned. "Greg's only just finished painting the door since the last time you two fought over it."

"Shut up, bitch!" howled the girl, with a last, dispirited thump of a beefy fist. "If you're so bloody perfect, why does your daughter call you 'Cunt'? Think about that the next time you 'ooh' and 'aah' when my dad gets his pathetic little dick out. Christ, even your daughter knows you're only sleeping with him to keep a roof over your head."

Laura closed her eyes, remembering Martin's laughter the first time Amy had used the word. Out of the mouths of babes and sucklings, he'd mocked. "Rent is expensive," she murmured. "Sex is free. Why else would I be here?"

Kimberley must have had her ear pressed against the wafer-thin door because every nuance of her voice came breathily through it. "I'll tell Dad you said that."

"Go ahead." She stretched her arm toward the wallphone, but, with her back against the door, it was beyond the reach of her fingers. *Why hadn't Amy told her she went to Patsy's . . . ? Did she use it as a refuge . . . ?* "But he won't be angry with me, Kimberley. He'll be angry with you. He was so damn lonely after your mother went he'd have moved a toothless granny into his bed if she'd been willing. Whose side will he take if you try to force me out?"

"Mine and Barry's when I tell him you're using him."

"Don't be an idiot," said Laura wearily. "He's a man. He couldn't care less why I'm sleeping with him just so long as I go on doing it."

"You *wish*!" the girl jeered.

"How many other women have been here, Kimberley?"

"Bloody loads," she said triumphantly. "We only got stuck with you because you dropped your panties for him."

"And how many of them came back a second time?"

"I couldn't give a shit. All I know is *you* came back."

"Only because I was desperate," she said slowly. "If I hadn't been, nothing on earth would have persuaded me to come here." She listened to the girl's heavy breathing. "Do you seriously think your father doesn't know that?"

There was a perceptible pause. "Yeah, well, he didn't have to make do with a tart," the girl said sullenly. "He's never even asked me and

Barry what we think about it. He *can't* . . . you're always in the fucking way . . . going on about your job . . . getting Amy to show off her
stupid dancing."

"In the kitchen maybe . . . never in the living room. You've made
it clear I'm not welcome there."

"Yeah, right!" There was what sounded like a choked-back sob. "I
suppose you've told Dad he's not welcome either."

"I didn't need to. You and Barry have done that pretty successfully
on your own."

"How?"

"By never turning the volume down . . . never greeting him when
he comes home . . . never eating with us . . . never getting up until
after we've gone to work . . ." She paused. "Life isn't a one-way street,
you know."

"What's that supposed to mean?"

"Work it out for yourself." Laura flexed her fingers to ease the
muscles. "I'll give you a hint. Why did your mother refuse to take
either of you with her?"

Kimberley fired off again. "I *hate* you!" she snarled. "I wish you'd
just piss off and leave us alone. Dad won't like it, but the rest of us'll
be fucking ecstatic."

It was the truth, thought Laura with an inward sigh, and if Amy
hadn't pretended she was happy, they'd have gone sooner. *"Don't worry
about it, Mummy . . . I keep telling you, everything's fine when you and Greg
aren't here . . ."* Laura had believed her because it made her life easier,
but now she was cursing herself for her stupidity. "Why does Amy go
to Patsy's house?" she asked.

"Because she wants to."

"That's not an answer, Kimberley. What Amy wants isn't necessarily good for her."

"It's her life," the girl declared mutinously. "She can do what she
likes."

"She's ten years old and she still sucks her thumb at night. She can't even decide between fish fingers and sausages for tea, so how can she make choices about her life?"

"That doesn't mean she has to do what *you* say . . . She didn't ask to be born . . . You don't fucking own her."

"When have I ever said I did?"

"You behave like it . . . ordering her around . . . telling her she can't go out."

"Can't go out *alone,*" Laura corrected. "I've never said she can't go with you and Barry as long as you stick together." She clenched her fists angrily. "God knows, I've explained it to you several times to avoid accidents. Amy's been here less than two months and still has difficulty remembering the address or the phone number. How is she going to find her way back if she gets lost?"

"She can't get lost going to Patsy's," said Kimberley scathingly. "They only live five doors away!"

"She shouldn't even be there."

"She's a crybaby," muttered Kimberley sulkily. "It gets on your nerves after a while. I figure there's something wrong with her. She's always in the bathroom moaning about her stomach hurting."

Laura pulled the door open abruptly and forced the girl to step back. "Then I want my money back, Kimberley, because I'll be damned if I'm going to reward you for something you haven't done." She checked her watch. "You've got five minutes to have Amy in this house, and another five to put together the fifty quid you've gotten from me for two weeks of nonexistent baby-sitting."

Something in the woman's eyes persuaded Kimberley to take another step backward, closer to her brother, who was watching from the living-room doorway. "I've spent it."

"Then we'll go to the nearest ATM, and you can take it out of your savings."

"Oh, yeah? What if I refuse?"

Laura gave an indifferent shrug. "We'll sit on our cases and wait for your father to come home."

Kimberley's thought processes were slow, particularly when there was no linkage of ideas. "What's 'cases'?" she asked stupidly.

"Luggage?" suggested Laura sarcastically. "Things you pack clothes in?" She lowered her hands to her sides, pretending to lift heavy objects. "What people carry when they wipe the dust of a house off their feet?"

"Oh, that kind of case." Her eyes gleamed suddenly. "Does that mean you're leaving?"

"As soon as I have my money."

Kimberley snapped her fingers at her brother. "Where's that fifty quid Dad gave you for food?" she demanded peremptorily. "I know you've still got it, so give it here."

Barry looked nervously toward Laura. "No."

The girl took an angry swipe at him. "Do you want your fucking arm broken?"

He moved out into the corridor, bunching his fists and preparing to defend himself. "I don't want her to go . . . not till Dad gets home anyway. I don't reckon it's my fault, so I shouldn't have to take the blame for it. Dad went apeshit when Mum left . . . and you just made it worse by saying you were glad she was gone. You're so fucking stupid you'll probably do the same thing again . . . and I wouldn't blame Dad if he lammed into you . . . 'cept he'll lam into me, too, and that's not fair." For a normally taciturn child, the words tumbled out of him. "I told you to look after Amy properly but you wouldn't listen 'cos you're lazy and you're a bully. Do this . . . do that . . . lick my fucking ass, Amy . . . but if you tell your mum, I'll give you a walloping. The kid's frightened of you. Okay, she's a bit of a pain, but the way you carry on it's not surprising she cried a lot. Your trouble is no one likes you. You should try being nicer . . . then you'd have a few friends and you'd feel different about stuff."

"Shut up, creep!"

He inched along the corridor. "I'm going to look for Amy," he said, pulling open the front door. "And I sodding well hope I see Dad on the road because I'll tell him it's your fault."

"Cunt! Prick!" shouted Kimberley after him, giving the wall a violent kick. "Fucking little coward!" She turned a red, angry face toward Laura, shoulders hunched like a boxer's. But there were tears in her eyes, as if she knew she'd just lost the only person who had ever been loyal to her.

➤ Police Message to All Stations

➤ 27.07.01
➤ 18:53
➤ IMMEDIATE ACTION
➤ Missing Person

➤ Laura Biddulph/Rogerson of Allenby Road, Portisfield, reports 10-yr-old daughter missing
➤ Child's name: Amy Rogerson (answers to: Biddulph)
➤ Height: 4' 10" approx. Weight: 60 lbs. approx.
➤ Description: slim, long brown hair, dressed in blue T-shirt and black leggings
➤ Last seen by neighbor leaving 14 Allenby Road at 10:00
➤ May be heading for father's house in Sandbanks Road, Bournemouth
➤ Father's name: Martin Rogerson
➤ Notify all vehicles/beat personnel

➤ Further information to follow . . .

➤ Police Message to All Stations

➤ 27.07.01
➤ 21:00
➤ UPDATE–Missing Person–Amy Biddulph/Rogerson

➤ May be heading for The Larches, Hayes Avenue, Southampton
➤ Resident there with mother for six months until April
➤ Owner/occupier—Edward Townsend—temporarily absent on holiday
➤ Notify all vehicles/beat personnel

➤ Further information to follow . . .

FIVE

SATURDAY, 28 JULY 2001—14 ALLENBY ROAD, PORTISFIELD ESTATE—01:15 A.M.

Relationships inside 14 Allenby Road had broken down completely, and the policewoman in charge of support and counseling suggested moving Laura Biddulph to a vacant "safe" house to prevent war from breaking out. Irrationally, in view of the emerging evidence that Amy had been vanishing every day during the past two weeks, only to return home at night, Laura had clung to the hope that she was with her father. But when she was informed that a search of Martin Rogerson's house had produced nothing and the police were satisfied he had been at his office in Bournemouth all day, hope gave way to fear and she turned on Gregory and his children.

She lashed them viciously with her tongue, and police curiosity about what she was doing there grew. Even the least critical among them could see there was a glaring disparity in age, class, education and physical attraction between her and Gregory Logan and, while there was no accounting for chemistry, her openly expressed revulsion for him and his family gave the lie to any close feeling between them. As the night passed she became more and more distant, sitting huddled against the kitchen door and denying admittance to anyone except police personnel. Red eyed with exhaustion, she cradled a radio in her lap and lifted her head with a jerk every time Amy's name was mentioned. When the counselor suggested she go upstairs for some much-needed rest, she gave a small laugh and said it wouldn't be wise. Unless the police wanted Kimberley Logan dead, of course.

The girl's noise was getting on everyone's nerves. With apparently limitless energy, she had bawled on and off for hours to a second Woman Police Constable (WPC) about how no one loved her, how miserable her life was and how she had never meant to hurt anyone. She refused to leave her room, refused to be sedated and could not, or would not, give any information about where Amy had been during the last two weeks, saying it wasn't her fault if the girl had lied about being with Patsy Trew.

Her brother sat morosely in front of the television, stuffing his face with takeout police sandwiches and claiming it was Kimberley who was lying. According to him, she had known since Wednesday that Amy wasn't with her friend. Patsy had come to the door—a fact borne out by Patsy herself—saying she hadn't seen Amy for days and wanted to know where she was. Kimberley had told her to "fuck off" because it was none of her business. "Amy doesn't like you anymore," she'd told the child, giggling when Patsy burst into tears and ran away. "Jesus, Amy's a sad little bitch," she'd told Barry on her return to the living-room. "I bet she's skulking in a hole somewhere so she can pretend she's got friends. No wonder she's so bloody skinny. She only gets fed when the tart gets back."

A detective sergeant had asked Barry why he hadn't mentioned any of this to Amy's mother. Kimberley would have given him a dead arm, he said, or, worse, kept him out of the kitchen. Did Kimberley give Amy dead arms? He shrugged. Only once. After that, Amy took off every day. Why did Kimberley do it? Guiltily, he wriggled his massive shoulders. "Because Amy cried when we called her mother a cunt," he admitted. "It got on Kimberley's nerves."

Their father, a fifty-year-old bus driver with a beer gut and a bad complexion, did his level best to mend fences. Every so often he called to Laura through the kitchen door to say the police had brought more sandwiches—as if food were the language of love. He seemed incapable of demonstrating any real affection, and the counselor wondered when he had last taken any of them in his arms and given them a hug. He asked few questions about Amy—more out of fear of the answers, she thought, than because he wasn't interested—and preferred to rant about the police wasting their time on speeding drivers when they ought to be tracking down pedophiles. If he had his way the bastards would be "castrated and strung up with their dicks in their mouths"—a medieval punishment for heresy—"because perverts ought to feel pain when they die." She asked him to keep his voice down, fearing the impact such statements would have on Laura Biddulph, but like his daughter he needed to make a noise in order to feel brave.

▼

A search of Amy's room compounded the problem for the police, as nothing appeared to be missing apart from the blue T-shirt and black leggings she was thought to be wearing. She was a tidy child who had a place for everything, and it was doubtful that she had run away because everything she valued—teddy bear, favorite bracelet, velvet hair ribbons—had been left behind. Even her money box, containing five pounds, and the little store of books hidden under her mattress. Why did she keep them there? the police asked her mother. To stop Kimberley from trashing them out of spite, said Laura.

▼

Gregory had been interviewed very thoroughly. How long had Laura been living there? *"Two months."* Where had he met her? *"She traveled on my bus a few times."* Who made the first move? *"Not me. I didn't think she'd give me a second glance."* Who suggested she move in? *"I can't remember. It cropped up in conversation one day."* Was he surprised when she said yes? *"Not really. We'd gotten to know each other pretty well by that time."* How would he describe his relationship with Amy? *"Okay."* How would he describe his relationship with his own children? *"The same."* Had Amy ever traveled on his bus? *"Once or twice with her mother."* Whom did he meet first, Laura or Amy? *"Laura."* Did he know Amy's father? *"No."* Had Laura told him how and where she and Amy were living before? *"Only that she'd been in an abusive relationship."* Was he aware that Kimberley was bullying Amy? *"No."* Had he ever tried to comfort Amy? *"I might have put my arm around her a couple of times."* Did she like it? *"She didn't say she didn't."* Would he describe her as an attractive child? *"She was a good little dancer."* Did she dance for him often? *"She danced for everyone . . . She liked showing off."* Had he ever made excuses to be alone with her? *"What the hell sort of question is that?"*

▼

   Laura's answers confirmed Gregory's except in regard to his relationship with his children. "He can't stand them," she replied. "He's afraid of Kimberley and he despises Barry for being a coward . . . but he's a coward himself, so I suppose it makes sense. He's always been very sweet to Amy. I think he feels sorry for her."

   She was being interviewed in the kitchen by the same inspector, Deputy Chief Inspector Tyler, who had questioned her six hours previously to elicit information about Amy's father. Now, better informed, he sat beside the counselor at the table and asked rather more probing questions about her relationship with her husband. Perhaps Laura knew what was coming, because she refused to get off the floor or move away from the kitchen door, and her almost permanently lowered head with its curtain of dark hair made it impossible to read her expression. It gave a sense of indifference, or, worse, deceit.

   "Why does he feel sorry for Amy?"

   "I told him her father abused her."

   "Was that true?"

   She gave a small shrug. "It depends how you define abuse."

   "How do you define it, Laura?"

   "Exercising power without love."

   "As in bullying?"

"Yes."

"Which is what you've accused Kimberley of doing."

She hesitated before she answered, as if fearing a trap. "Yes," she agreed. "She and Martin are two of a kind."

"In what way?"

"Inadequate people need to dominate."

Tyler recalled his first impressions of Martin Rogerson when the man opened the door in his shirtsleeves and extended a friendly hand. Policemen were used to shock or evasion when they produced their cards—everyone had something to fear or feel guilty about—but Rogerson showed neither of these. He was twenty-five years older than his wife—in his late fifties—a bluff, confident solicitor with an easy manner and a firm handshake. Certainly he gave no impression of being the inadequate bully his wife was describing. "How did Martin bully Amy?"

"You wouldn't understand."

"Try me."

Another hesitation. "He made her beg for affection," she said, "so she thought his love was worth more than mine."

It was such an unlikely answer that Tyler believed it. He remembered seeing an ill-treated dog that had crawled on its belly toward the boy who was whipping it; remembered, too, how when he had intervened the dog had bitten him. "And yours was rejected?" he suggested.

She didn't answer.

He sprang the trap halfheartedly. "If you knew Kimberley was a bully, then why did you leave Amy with her?" he asked.

Laura used the point of a finger to sketch circles on the floor. Each one apart. Each one contained. Tyler wondered what they represented. *Martin? Herself? Amy? Distance?*

"I've been saving for a deposit on a flat," she said shakily. "It's our only way out . . . Amy wants it as much as I do." She opened her other fist to reveal a sodden tissue, which she pressed against her eyes. "She kept promising me Kimberley was different when they were on their own. I knew she was lying . . . but I truly believed the worst that was happening was that she was sitting on her own in her room all day. And that didn't seem so bad . . . not after . . ." She broke off, concealing the tissue inside her fingers again as if it were a piece of dirty laundry that needed hiding.

"Not after what?"

She took time to answer, and he had the feeling she was inventing an explanation. "Just life," she said tiredly. "It hasn't been easy for either of us."

Tyler studied her bent head for a moment, before consulting some notes on the table. "According to your husband, you and Amy haven't lived with him for nine months. He said you left him for a man called Edward Townsend, and as far as he knew you were still with him."

"He's lying," she said bluntly. "He knows Eddy and I split up."

"Why would he lie about it?"

"He's a lawyer."

"That's hardly an answer, Laura."

She waved his remark away. "I was supposed to inform him if our situation changed . . . but I didn't. It's a technical point. Martin can argue that, because he didn't hear it from me, I acted against Amy's best interests by withholding information."

"Who would have told him?"

"Eddy. Martin's still his solicitor. He talks to Eddy more than he ever talked to me." She gave a bitter little laugh. "He's legal adviser to Eddy's company. They're always on the phone to each other."

Tyler let that go for the moment. The vagaries of human nature had long since ceased to surprise him. In Rogerson's shoes, he'd have punched the other man's lights out, assuming of course there was any passion left in the relationship. "Why didn't you inform Martin you'd left Eddy?"

"I was trying to protect Amy."

It was an extreme phrase, he thought. "Is there some other abuse that you haven't told me about?"

"No."

Tyler allowed a silence to develop while he referred to his notes again. It was a very decisive negative, and he wondered if she had prepared for the question. He would have expected a rather more shocked response, a rush to explain why the suggestion couldn't be true. It raised doubts in his mind, particularly as her husband had reacted very angrily to a similar question.

He traced his finger down the lines on the page. "According to your husband, Mr. Townsend's on holiday at the moment. He's gone to Majorca with a girlfriend." He looked up, but Laura didn't react. "Townsend's been a client of your husband's for over ten years," he went on. "A property developer. He and his wife divorced two years ago. You and he began your affair shortly afterward and you moved in with him last October. He lives in Southampton. Your husband agreed to your having custody of Amy while you were living with Townsend. His only proviso was that if the relationship failed, you would return Amy to his care until the issue of your own divorce was settled. He says you returned his child-support checks while you were with Townsend and weren't in a position to support Amy on your own. Is that correct?"

She lifted her hand in a small gesture of protest. "Martin was never as"—she sought for a word—"*reasonable* as that."

"You were sleeping with his friend. He was hardly going to be pleased."

"I didn't expect him to be," was all she said.

"So what happened?"

"It didn't work out with Eddy, so we came here."

"Is there a reason why it didn't work out?"

She fingered the hair in front of her face. "It never had much of a chance. We wanted different things from the relationship."

"What did you want?"

"An escape," she said simply.

"Why did you return the child-support checks?"

"It wouldn't have been an escape."

"What did Eddy want?"

"Sex."

"Is that what Gregory wants?"

"Yes."

"You're a fast worker," Tyler said mildly. "One minute you're with a developer in Southampton, the next you're with a bus driver in Portisfield. How did that work exactly?"

"We stayed in a hotel for five weeks."

"Why?"

"It was anonymous."

"Were you hiding from Martin?"

She shrugged.

"Because he'd have taken Amy back?"

"Yes."

"Who paid?"

"I used my savings." She paused. "I couldn't work because there was no one to leave her with, and we were running out of money. That's why I needed somewhere else."

He glanced about the kitchen. "Why another man? Why not put yourself on the housing list and find a baby-sitter?"

She started drawing circles again. "I couldn't risk Amy telling the housing officer about her father. They'd have taken her away from me if they knew she had somewhere else to live." A tiny laugh fluttered from her mouth. "In any case, Martin's a snob. I knew he'd never come looking for us here. It wouldn't occur to him that I might be willing to live in a council house and work in a supermarket just to be free of him."

"How does Amy feel about it?"

"Even your daughter knows you're only sleeping with him to keep a roof over your head . . ." "I don't know. I've never asked her."

"Why not?"

"You've seen Martin's house." She flicked him a quick, assessing glance. "Which would you choose if you were a ten-year-old girl?"

Rogerson had asked the same question after learning where Amy had been for the last two months. "Your husband's, of course, but if that's what she wants then she should have been given the choice. She has the same rights as you, Laura, and to be a prisoner of war between her parents isn't one of them."

"If she were a prisoner," she flashed back, "she'd be locked safely in her room and you and I wouldn't be having this conversation."

"That's not what I meant, Laura."

"I know what you meant," she murmured, turning up the volume on the radio to shut him out. "But you're using Martin's words, so perhaps you should ask him what *he* means by them."

▼

" . . . two hundred local people joined police during the night to search the surrounding countryside . . ."

". . . police believe Amy may be heading for her father's house in Bournemouth . . ."

" . . . homeowners in the south are being asked to look in sheds, garages, abandoned fridges, derelict houses . . . not given up hope that Amy may have fallen asleep . . ."

". . . NSPCC spokesman said that, while it's an appalling tragedy when any child goes missing, the public should remember that two children a week die from cruelty and neglect in their own homes . . ."

". . . police spokesman confirmed that all registered pedophiles in Hampshire were visited within eight hours of Amy's disappearance . . ."

". . . no leads . . ."

SATURDAY, 28 JULY 2001
10:00–19:00

SIX

Melanie Patterson shared a cigarette with her mother on a bench outside the co-op on Glebe Road. It was an unvarying Saturday-morning ritual during which they caught up on news before doing their shopping together. It was like the old days, when they still lived together. Gaynor would stretch out on the sofa with Melanie curled up against her, and they'd drink a beer and split a cigarette and set the world to rights. They'd always been close and never understood the hassle Social Services gave them about their ever-increasing family.

Gaynor was an older version of her daughter, not so tall, but with the same lush blond hair and sparkling blue eyes. Her fifth child, a little boy, was born six months after his niece, Rosie, but none of the Pattersons found this particularly odd. There was no logic to any of the generations. Melanie's great-grandmother, herself the mother of ten, wasn't born until five years after her eldest brother's death in the First World War, yet she kept his photograph beside her bed and spoke as if she were closer to him than any of her surviving brothers. And maybe she was, because Patterson men were renowned for their feuding—*"It's the Irish in them," Great-Grammer always said, making a tenuous link to some distant ancestor who had crossed the sea to Liverpool during the nineteenth century. "They'd rather be fighting than home in their beds . . ."*—and Patterson women for taking lovers out of boredom—

". . . the good Lord wouldn't have given us wombs if he hadn't meant us to fill them."

It was a view shared by Melanie and her mother. Bossy health visitors could say what they liked about contraception, but childbearing answered a basic need in both of them. As indeed it had for the long line of women before them. There had never been a perception among Patterson women that personal fulfillment lay in taking a regular job and making money. A woman's role was to make babies, particularly when someone else was prepared to pay for them. Indeed, Gaynor's most perfect achievement was this, her eldest daughter, who adored and was adored in equal measure. Men came and went in both their lives, but their constancy to each other was unshakable. They agreed on everything. Loves, hates, beliefs, prejudices, friends and enemies.

On hearing from Melanie the previous Saturday that pedophiles had been housed just one door away from her grandchildren, Gaynor had reacted with predictable anger.

"It makes you sick," she'd said. "The Social's got no business sticking psychos on your road and expecting you to guard your kiddies twenty-four hours a day. That says the perverts are more important than you, Rosie and Ben put together . . . and that's not right, darlin'. Men like that should be locked up for life . . . simple as that." She took a drag and passed the cigarette to her daughter. "I don't want you and the babes in danger," she said with sudden decision. "You'll have to come home. You and the wee ones can take Colin's room, and he can move in with Bry and little Johnnie."

But Melanie had shaken her head. "Jimmy's due out in a couple of days. He'll take care of us. Anyways, I reckon it's the perverts should move, not us . . . which is what I told the cow at Housing—the Social's got a fucking nerve, I said, giving us lectures about"—she drew quotation marks the air—"*'parenting,'* then dumping sodding pedophiles on the street without telling anyone. So she tells me to stop swearing or she'll hang up."

"She never!"

"She fucking did, and I said, if she thought swearing was worse than murdering little kids then she ought to be in therapy. I bet *she* wouldn't like it, I said, if the council stuck perverts next to *her*. So then I get the usual wall-to-wall bull . . . she didn't know what I was talking about . . . it wasn't her responsibility . . . the person to ask was my social worker. I was well pissed off and said if she didn't fucking move them out herself, then us as lives in the street'd fucking do it for her. I mean, they can't rate our kids very high if they reckon it's okay for dirty old men to shaft them whenever they get a fucking itch . . . and that's when she hung up."

Seven days later, fueled by radio and television reports that a child had gone missing in Portisfield, the swell of opinion against the pedophiles had reached fever pitch. It was known, courtesy of a postman who had shown a redirected letter to a neighbor, that the men's previous address had been Callum Road, Portisfield, so late on that Friday night the same neighbor phoned the former occupant of number 23, Mary Fallon, to find out what she knew.

Mary was full of it. Portisfield was crawling with policemen, knocking on doors, showing the kid's photograph, and asking if anyone had seen her or knew where she'd spent the last two weeks. They were talking about a "friend" whom her family didn't know about, but even a moron could work out that "friend" was a euphemism for a predatory pedophile. There were two evicted from Portisfield near on a month ago after one of them was recognized from a photograph, and Mary wasn't the only person who'd told the police to track them down. The kid had been living cheek by jowl with them for God knows how long, and pedophiles being what they are—on the lookout for lonely and vulnerable children—you could bet they'd picked her out for attention. It didn't make sense to assume she'd gone to ground in her own neighborhood, when the chances were she'd been collected and driven somewhere else every day.

Mary was speechless for all of five seconds when her friend told her the Portisfield pedophiles were living in her old house. She couldn't believe it. *Her* house! Home to bloody perverts! What kind of idiot had decided to move them into the Row? The place had more children than adults. It was like putting a junkie in charge of a drugstore. How had they been sussed? Had they tried it on with a kid? Did they have a car? Did they leave the house every day? Had anyone seen a skinny little girl with dark hair there?

The answers to her questions were largely negative, but there was always room for doubt. The men's arrival had been so secret that it stood to reason they could come and go at will. The younger one did the shopping occasionally, scuttling along and never meeting anyone's eyes, but who was to say where he went when he turned the corner out of Bassindale Row or if he had a car parked secretly away from the estate? The older one, white-faced and black haired, had been spotted through the window from time to time, standing in the shadows and scowling at passersby, but who knew where he went at night when decent people were asleep? As for a little girl . . . well, they wouldn't bring her back to the house in daylight, would they?

Plans had been made at the beginning of the week to converge on Humbert Street that Saturday afternoon and force the police to move the perverts out, though there was considerable irritation that Portisfield hadn't had to do anything so dramatic . . . or *energetic*. It highlighted the difference between the way the two estates were per-ceived—the one modern and upwardly mobile, the other a dilapi-dated ghetto for the underclass. The upwardly mobile complained. The underclass marched.

Naturally no one in Bassindale bothered to inform the police of their plan. The idea was to shock the pigs into removing the nonces, those perverts, not give them a chance to order the march banned and arrest anyone who tried to go through with it. In any case, so many of the Acid Row youngsters were serving weekend community sentences that, if the cops got a sniff of trouble, half the foot soldiers would be lost because they'd be locked up in secure detention till the trouble passed. It was a protest of numbers. The more there were, the more powerful the message . . . and the less likely it was to be ignored.

With some justification, Gaynor and Melanie prided themselves on being the leaders. It was they who had brought the perverts to the community's attention. Their resolution that had fired a reciprocal commitment from their neighbors. Their efforts that had translated ideas into action. Also their motivation was entirely unselfish. They believed the council was endangering children by introducing pedophiles into the estate. It was an open-and-shut case. Force the authorities to get rid of the perverts and the kids would be safe.

What they lacked was imagination, for it never occurred to them that their leadership would be secretly hijacked or that a protest march could lead to war. Certainly not in broad daylight on one of the hottest days of the year.

But, as the police could have told them, riots happen when heat frays tempers.

▼

This Saturday, on the bench outside the co-op, Melanie was bringing her mother up to speed on where and when the protesters were meeting that afternoon. "It's mostly women and kids," she said, "but I reckon there's going to be about a hundred, and that's enough to make the rozzers sit up and think. Jimmy'll be there too, and, as long as you and me get there first to keep a bit of order, it ought to work well." She could see that Gaynor was listening with only half an ear. "This is important, Mum," she said severely. "If you and me aren't outside the school in time to organize the sodding thing, then it'll fizzle out. You know what they're like around here. They'll vanish off to the pub if there's no one to tell 'em what to do."

"Yeah, yeah. I'll be there, darlin'." She sighed. "The trouble is, I'm worried about our Colin. That Wesley Barber's been hanging around again, and Col knows I can't stand him."

"Jimmy hates him, too . . . calls him a retard . . . says he gives niggers a bad name 'cos he's stoned all the time on crystal meth. You wanna put your foot down, Ma. Jimmy reckons he's dropping acid as well, and if Col gets into that, he's gonna be real fucked up."

"Oh, God!" Gaynor ran a worried hand through her hair. "What am I supposed to do, darlin'? He was out till three this morning with that little tyke Kevin Charteris. They're up to something and I don't know what it is."

"What they usually do on a Friday night," said Melanie. "Go clubbing and get smashed. Kev's not as bad as Wesley."

Gaynor shook her head. "Col was dead cold sober. I was that mad I waited up for him—he knows he'll get detention if he's caught thieving again—but he wouldn't say where he'd been . . . just fired off and said I was a nagging bitch."

Melanie thought of her fourteen-year-old brother. "Maybe he was getting laid," she said with a giggle. "That's not something a bloke'd share with his mum."

But there was no answering laughter from Gaynor. "I reckon it's joyriding," she said unhappily. "He smelled of gasoline, so he must've been in a car. I gave him a right tongue-bashing . . . told him he'd kill hisself one of these days . . . or *be* killed . . . and he slammed into his room and told me to mind my own fucking business."

"Maybe I should talk to him."

"Would you, darlin'? You know he listens to you. Just tell him I don't want him dead . . . I'd rather see him in the nick than wrapped round a lamppost. At least that way he's got a chance of growing up and making something of hisself."

"I'll do it tomorrow," Melanie promised, "soon as we're rid of the perverts."

PINDER STREET, BASSINDALE ESTATE

W.P.C. Hanson could hardly fail to notice the graffiti as she turned onto Pinder Street. It was sprayed onto a blank wall at the end of the terrace in fluorescent yellows and pinks—DEATH TO PIGS—and underneath was a cartoon representation of pigs' hooves crossed in a Nazi swastika. It hadn't been there the day before, and she forced herself to view it with detachment. *It couldn't possibly be aimed at her.*

She pulled up outside number 121 and climbed out to have another crack at interviewing fifteen-year-old Wesley Barber about a purse snatching in the center of town. It was a long shot. His M.O. fitted perfectly—the target was an old woman coming out of the side door of the post office with her wallet, stuffed with her retirement money, in her hand—but the witness's description, *"a beastly great black boy with staring eyes,"* wouldn't convince a magistrate that sweet-faced Wesley was the culprit.

The boy was educationally subnormal—a juvenile psychopath on acid and meth, according to his principal, who turned a blind eye to his truancy in order to keep him out of school—but he had the face of a saint. Everyone despaired of him, including his mother, who spent most of her time on her knees in church, praying for a miracle. Also, he was never at home when the police came knocking, so the chances of the interview happening were poor.

Hanson heard yelling from the end of the street and looked up to see a gang of youths appear round the corner, wrestling with one another and hurling insults. She dropped her gaze hurriedly, afraid of sparking a confrontation, but the boys beat a hasty retreat when they spotted the police car. Even so, one of them shouted loudly enough for her to catch: "It's a tart on her own, for fuck's sake. We could take her easy."

She put a hand on the car door to steady herself and stared purposefully after the gang as if she were weighing options. She was terrified of Acid Row and always had been. She likened it with being afraid of dogs.

You could follow all the rules about how to behave, but if fear was the only emotion you experienced then fear was what the animals sensed. She'd tried to explain this once to her boss, and he'd slated her for it.

"You'll be spending more time on the Row than anywhere else," he told her. "It's the nature of the job. If you can't hack it, then you'd better quit now, because I'll have your hide if you ever refer to those people as 'animals' again."

She hadn't meant it that way. She used fear of dogs as an analogy, but her boss couldn't or wouldn't understand. She needed help, and the only help he gave her was to make her face her phobia every day. In three months she'd spent so much time alone on the Row that her fear had intensified into paranoia. She believed she was being followed and watched every time she came here. She believed the youths hunted in packs with the specific intention of catching her unawares and unprotected. She also believed, like a typical paranoiac, that her boss was behind the conspiracy to destroy her. He always sent her out alone . . .

▼

"There's that woman copper again," said Wesley's mother, peering through the net curtains. "Are you going to talk to her this time?"

She knew he'd done something bad. She could always tell. Despite all her prayers, she knew in her heart there was no salvation for her son. The pastor had told her he was on drugs, but she didn't believe that. It was the Evil One had hold of Wesley, just as He had hold of Wesley's father.

"No chance. She's trying to pin a mugging on me."

Mrs. Barber glared at her son. "Did you do it?"

"'Course I didn't," he said plaintively.

"You little liar," she said, smacking him across the head with a meaty hand. "How many times've I warned you? Next time you snatch an old lady's money, I'll chase you through the streets myself."

"Leave off," he howled. "It weren't me, Mum. Why can't you never believe me?"

"Because you're your father's son," she said in disgust, turning back to the window and watching W.P.C. Hanson's knuckles turn white from her grip on the car door. "She looks scared," she murmured. "Are you and your friends up to something? What was all that shouting?"

"Nothing to do with me," he lied, tiptoeing toward the corridor and wondering what she'd say if she knew he'd been filling bottles with gasoline. "Tell the copper you don't know where I am." He ran for the back door. "I'll see youse later, Ma."

But Mrs. Barber was more interested in the young policewoman's ashen face. With a sinking heart, she wondered what Wesley had done this time to make this woman so frightened of talking to him.

➤ Police Message to All Stations

➤ 28.07.01
➤ 12:32
➤ Bassindale Estate
➤ Milosz Zelowski, 23 Humbert Street, reports youths causing nuisance in street since interview this morning re. missing child
➤ Patrol car 031 responding

➤ 28.07.01
➤ 12:35
➤ Bassindale Estate
➤ Ms. J. MacDonald, 84 Forest Row South, reports sighting of Amy Biddulph in Bassindale Row at 22:00 yesterday
➤ Reports 25 attempts to make the call
➤ Police lines permanently busy

➤ 28.07.01
➤ 12:46
➤ Bassindale Estate
➤ Patrol car 031 diverted to interview Ms. J. MacDonald re. possible sighting of Amy Biddulph

SEVEN

Jimmy James made a grab for Melanie's waist as she put a plate of food on the table but she was too quick for him, sliding out of his encircling arm in a graceful pirouette. Rosie giggled at the other end of the table. "See, darlin'," said her mother, "I told you he'd only have one thing on his mind when they let him out."

"You shouldn't say things like that to her," said Jimmy. "She's too young."

"She needs to know what blokes are like," said Melanie severely, tapping the edge of his plate with a spoon. "Just eat your dinner so you can get your ass down the road. You're not that drunk you can't understand what's goin' on."

He was a huge, handsome black man with a shaved head who had just spent four months in prison for a string of minor offenses, and who had no intention of going back. He'd told Melanie it was because of his baby that was growing in her belly, but the truth (which he admitted only to himself) was that he was finding it harder and harder to do time. "Yeah, well, I don't, Mel," he said irritably, flicking the spoon away with his finger. "There was a nasty mood on the street this morning, and I don't plan to be anywhere near it if the coppers come in."

"They're not gonna arrest you for marching," she said. "It's a free country. Protests are allowed."

"Depends what kind of protest. You and Gaynor are wrong if you think the acidheads'll do what you tell them. You could end up in the middle of a riot and that's fucking scary, Mel."

"What about the little kid? She was seen in the Row last night, and everyone reckons the nonces've got her."

"Don't be an idiot," he said sarcastically. "What would a couple of gay nonces want with a little girl? Tell me that."

"Perverts are perverts," she said dogmatically.

"Like hell they are. On that basis I'd've slept with blokes in the nick because there weren't any birds available. You fancy what you fancy, and there's nothing you can do about it. The same applies to pedophiles."

"How d'you know?"

"I've got brains, and I use them." He tapped the side of his head. "You and Gaynor'll get yourselves arrested for incitement if you pass on crap-ass gossip and people get hurt."

"Maybe you don't know as much as you think you do."

He shrugged and tilted his chair to look at her. "All right. Who saw the kid and what were they on? Tell me it wasn't that retard, Wesley Barber, who spent five hours on an alien spacecraft, spaced out on acid, having his sperm milked to make a superrace." He grinned at her expression. "Learn a bit of wisdom, babe, and let me eat my food in peace. I don't want my ass busted for some middle-class white kid who's almost certainly dead by now."

She punched his arm. "You've gotta be there, Jimmy. The meet's at Glebe School and if you don't come with me, people'll talk."

"You mean the women'll talk," he said cynically. "So what's new? They do fuck all else except sit on their asses and tear their men to shreds."

"You're such a wimp," she said, trying to rile him. "You make out you're Mike Tyson, but the minute there's any trouble you run the other way."

"Yeah, well, I can't afford trouble at the moment," he said, dropping the chair legs to the floor again and poking a fork grumpily into his food. "I've got some deals going down, and getting nicked for hounding a couple of nonces out of their house ain't part of the game plan."

"Anyone'd think you had a soft spot for them." She was worried about her reputation. What would everyone say if her man failed to turn up after she'd told them what a hard bloke he was? "They'll reckon you got too close to them in jail and started to feel sorry for them."

Jimmy chewed in silence for a while, wondering if she knew how close she was to the truth. He'd had his head done in good and proper by his first cellmate, and he didn't care to be reminded of it. The guy was a music teacher, coming to the end of his sentence, who had taught Jimmy notation during the three weeks they were together. He was a bit of a genius, knew everything there was to know about jazz, and could use his voice to mimic instruments. By the end of the third week he was the backing track to Jimmy's rap, and Jimmy was beginning to plan a legitimate career in music. They even had a demo tape under way. It was looking good till word leaked out that his mate was banged up for giving hand jobs to some of the boys in his school. Two days later he had all his fingers broken in the showers.

It took Jimmy awhile to get over it. The motherfucker had tried to tough it out on the open wings after being transferred from an all-Rule prison on the Isle of Wight. He claimed he was in for check fraud, which was the kind of thing an educated man might have done, but someone snitched—probably an officer—and he ended up in the vulnerable-prisoner unit for protection. Jimmy never saw him again, although he thought about him from time to time. He was the only bloke he'd ever met in prison whom he actually liked, and it struck him as pretty sad that his pleasure came from *giving* hand jobs when most guys preferred to be on the receiving end.

"Let them think what they like," he told Melanie, pushing away his barely touched plate. "I've got better things to do than shout insults at weirdos."

GLEBE SCHOOL, GLEBE ROAD, BASSINDALE ESTATE

Gangs of drunken youths were already milling around the school forecourt, downing lager and psyching themselves up for a confrontation with the perverts. In among them, Wesley Barber pranced like an idiot, mouthing off about how he was going to roast nonces . . . firebomb the school . . . raid the co-op . . . stick pigs. He twitched with excitement like a dog scenting a bitch in heat, and there was jeering from the other boys as he karate-chopped the air in imitation of Wesley Snipes in *Demolition Man* and *Blade*.

"Jesus, you're a fucking retard, Wesley!"

"What you on, meathead?"

Colin Patterson and Kevin Charteris dragged him away. "Calm down, for fuck's sake," said Colin angrily. "My mum'll go apeshit if she hears you talking like that. She'll call the cops if she thinks you're gonna do something stupid. It's supposed to be a march, you spastic." He felt brave because he was drunk, never mind the thicko was hyped to the eyeballs on every bit of crap the dealers were selling. Even on a good day, Wesley was as crazy as a dog with rabies, and most times Colin steered clear. But today was different. Today, as Kev said, they needed a psycho to do the business for Melanie.

Wesley tried to jerk them off their feet to break their grip. "You said we was gonna do war on vampire perverts," he roared like a child in a tantrum, "teach the motherfuckers a lesson. Was you lying?"

"Jeez, his head's shot to pieces this time," said Colin. "Look at his eyes. They're like a fucking zombie's."

Kevin, the only one of his friends who had any control over Wesley, hooked an arm round the boy's neck and wrenched his wrist up behind his back. "Are you gonna keep your mouth shut, you stupid moron?" he hissed into his ear. "'Cos if you don't, you won't get nowhere near the pervs. None of us will. Col's right. If his mum gets a sniff of trouble, there won't be no march and no fucking war. Geddit? The fun'll be over . . . 'n' you'll get wasted for ruining everyone's day."

The madness died in Wesley's eyes as suddenly as it had flared. A slow, peaceable grin spread across his face. "I'm okay," he said. "Youse don't have to call me a moron, Kev. I got it. It's just a march." His face fell into the sweet lines that had already fooled a number of magistrates. "We just gonna let the vampires know we've sussed 'em, right?"

"Right," said Kevin, letting Wesley go and gripping his hand in a raised salute. "Go on, Col, give him a high five," he ordered the younger boy. "We're mates, ain't we?"

"I guess," said Colin, taking a stinging slap on the palm. But he wasn't so drunk that he didn't notice the switchblade that Wesley was twirling in his other hand.

FLAT 506, GLEBE TOWER, BASSINDALE ESTATE

"I have to go now," said W.P.C. Hanson to the senile old man in the dingy fifth-floor flat in one of Bassindale's tower blocks. "I'm sorry I haven't been able to help." Depression weighed upon her like Sisyphus's stone. It had been a wasted visit, just like the others she'd made that day. Nothing she did was valuable. She was a cipher . . . an officer without authority.

The air in the flat was claustrophobically stale, as if the windows and doors were never opened. Mr. Derry sat in permanent gloom, with the curtains closed to keep out the sun, his eyes fixed on the flickering images of the muted television in the corner as if soap-opera characters were his only point of reality in a confusing world. Talking to him had made her depression worse, because whatever spark of lucidity had encouraged him to phone the police that morning had died the minute he hung up.

He fiddled with his hearing aid. "What's that?"

She raised her voice. "I have to go now."

"Did you find the boys?"

She'd answered the same question patiently for thirty minutes, but this time she ignored it. It was pointless talking to him. He had reported the theft of £200 in cash from the tea caddy in his kitchen, but he had no idea when it was taken or who was responsible. All he could tell her was that three boys had rung his doorbell one day but, as he hadn't liked the look of them, he hadn't let them in. She pointed out the discrepancy—if they weren't allowed in, they couldn't have stolen the money—but the old man was insistent. He could spot a wrong 'un a mile off.

She made a pretense of investigating by poking around the filth in his kitchen. But there was no tea can—just a cardboard box of Tetley bags that had passed their sell-by date months ago—and no evidence that there had been any money or that anyone other than she had disturbed the dust in this place for months. He might have been talking about something that happened yesterday . . . or fifty years ago . . . because his brain was shot and his memory locked in a tiresome dementia that made him replay his obsessions in loops.

How did he look after himself? Who cared for him? She felt swamped by misery as she stared at the accumulated years of grease on the stove and the tidal mark of scum in the sink. She wanted to cleanse her hands, but the smell from the drain nauseated her. There were germs everywhere. She could feel them burrowing under her skin, attacking her brain, undermining her resolve. What was the point of living like this? *What was the point of living at all?*

That thought had circled in her head all the time she was speaking to him, and now she wondered if she'd voiced it aloud, because he assailed her impatiently. "What's that?" he demanded, saliva shooting from his mouth in droplets. "Speak up, girl. I can't hear you."

"I have to go," she repeated, pronouncing her words as carefully as a drunk.

He frowned. "Who are you? What are you doing here?"

How many times had he asked her that? How many times had she answered? "I'm a police officer, Mr. Derry."

"Did you find the boys?"

It was like listening to a cracked record. She shook her head. "I'll be putting in a request for a health visitor to come and talk to you," she told him. "She'll assess your circumstances and probably recommend a move to assisted living, where you'll receive more care and protection than you have here."

He turned back to the television. "They should have sent a man," he said scathingly.

"I'm sorry."

"I wanted a real cop . . . not a namby-pamby creature who's scared of her own shadow. It's no wonder there's so much crime in this place."

It was the last straw. Her head had been splitting since she came onto the estate, and shouting through Mr. Derry's deafness had made the pain worse. She wanted to scream at him, tell him what she really thought, but she was too repressed to do anything so dramatic. "A man wouldn't have bothered to listen to you," she said tightly, preparing to stand up.

"You think so, do you? Well, maybe I'm not bothered about lazy little chits who'd rather sit around than do their jobs. What do you say to that, eh?"

She hated him with a passion. He was senile, he was rude and he was filthy. Everything she'd touched in this disgusting place had left its mark on her. "What do you expect me to do?" she asked. "Go out and arrest the first three boys I find just because you say your money's been stolen? There's no proof you even had it." She stood up abruptly and swept a trembling arm around the room. "You wouldn't be living like this if you'd had two hundred pounds in a tea caddy."

Her sudden movement frightened him. He seized the heavy, antiquated telephone on the table beside his chair and brandished the receiver at her. "Get away from me!" he shouted. "I'm calling the police. Who are you? What are you doing here?"

She knew she was going to faint, but there was a moment of clarity when she saw the funny side. "I *am* the police," she heard herself say with a laugh in her voice, before her knees gave way and she fell toward him.

FLAT 406, GLEBE TOWER, BASSINDALE ESTATE

The elderly woman in the flat below Mr. Derry paused in the middle of her telephone call to listen to the noisy banging from upstairs. "That senile old bugger's up to something again," she told her friend crossly. "He's going to bring my ceiling down if he's not careful. What do you suppose he does? Throw his furniture about whenever he has a tantrum?"

The friend wasn't interested. "Oh, for goodness' sake, Eileen!" she wailed anxiously from five stories up. "Why won't you listen? There's something terrible going on. I've been looking through Wally's binoculars, and there are boys everywhere. Do you think they've been drinking?"

"How would I know?"

"I wish you'd look out of your window. There're hundreds of them. They're turning cars over at the entrance to Bassindale Row."

Eileen Hinkley was curious enough to peer around her curtain, but she was lower down and her view was obscured by roofs. "Have you called the police?"

"I can't get through. The lines are jammed."

"Then dial nine-nine-nine."

"That's what I've *been* doing," her friend protested, "but every time I get transferred to the police, there's a message saying they know about the disturbance in Bassindale and not to bother reporting it."

"Good heavens!"

"Exactly. But I can't see any policemen through the binoculars." Her voice rose in fear. "We're all going to be killed. What do you think we should do?"

Eileen glanced toward the ceiling as a slamming door set her china rattling. "Lock ourselves in and wait for the trouble to pass," she said firmly, crossing her fingers for luck. "You never know . . . we might hit the jackpot. Maybe the thugs'll kill each other . . . and give us a bit of peace."

➤ Police Message to All Stations

➤ 28.07.01
➤ 13:55
➤ Bassindale Estate
➤ Milosz Zelowski (a.k.a. Nicholas Hollis), 23 Humbert Street, requests protection or removal to safe house
➤ Advised police resources stretched

➤ EMERGENCY LINES AT FULL CAPACITY

➤ 28.07.01
➤ 14:01
➤ Bassindale Estate
➤ Anonymous call—barricades being erected on Bassindale Row
➤ Believed intention—to prevent access to patrol cars

➤ EMERGENCY LINES AT FULL CAPACITY

➤ 28.07.01
➤ 14:08
➤ Bassindale Estate
➤ URGENT
➤ Patrol car 031 reports all access routes to Bassindale blocked

➤ EMERGENCY LINES AT FULL CAPACITY

EIGHT

The two policemen in patrol car 31 watched the blockade building from a safe distance. They had exited the estate on Forest Road South with the intention of driving along the main road and coming back up Bassindale Row North to check on Zelowski on Humbert Street. But it was too late. Bassindale was already impassable, and a retracing of their steps showed that all four points of entry to the estate had been blocked.

"Serves them right," said the older officer, switching the radio to standby. "I said it could be turned into a fortress if the bastards got angry enough." He lowered the window and spat onto the grass shoulder. "I blame the planners, myself. They should've asked the police what they thought before they built a concrete jungle and filled it with villains."

"Yeah, yeah," said his partner, who'd heard it a thousand times. He was scanning the scene through a pair of binoculars. "It's well organized . . . must have been coordinated for two o'clock." He whistled through his teeth. "I reckon we got away lightly . . . five minutes longer with the MacDonald woman and we'd have been trapped." He lowered the glasses. "What the hell's going on?" he demanded. "I mean, if Amy *is* in there, why are these idiots trying to keep us out?"

His partner gave an exasperated sigh. "She's not in there. If the woman had been able to tell us something about the style of T-shirt the kid was wearing, I might have been convinced"—he shrugged—

70

"but what sort of answer is: 'It was blue'? She was giving us what she'd heard on the telly."

They'd been over this once already. "What we think isn't the issue, George. The issue is what does *that* lot"—he nodded at the youths manning the barricade—"think? Assuming they think at all, of course." He raised the binoculars again. "Shit! Get on to the guvnor and tell him to shift his arse if he doesn't want the whole estate burning down. The stupid sods are siphoning petrol into bottles, and half of them've got fags in their mouths. *Jee—sus!*" He watched a child—no more than twelve years old—toss a bottle toward his friend. "What the *fuck* do they think they're doing?"

The same thought was in Sophie Morrison's mind as she braked sharply to avoid a gang of drunken youths on Glebe Road. One of them raised a finger at her as if it were her fault that he was too drunk to negotiate the road properly, and she mouthed *wanker* at him through the windshield. She half expected him to retaliate by bringing his fist down on her hood—a standard response in Acid Row—but one of his friends pulled him toward the sidewalk and she drove on, waving a finger of her own. She saw the friend grin amiably in her rearview mirror and turned the finger into a salute of acknowledgment as she recognized one of her patients.

She had a healthy respect for the inhabitants here—as did all professionals—but she wasn't intimidated by them. Of course she took precautions. She drove with her windows closed and her doors locked, secured her cell phone in a medical case, made it clear to her patients that she never carried drugs or credit cards or large amounts of cash, always parked in brightly lit areas and never walked down dark alleyways at night. She also carried a slimline pepper spray in her pants pocket which, to date, she hadn't had to use.

In the two years since she'd qualified and joined the practice, she'd grown surprisingly fond of Acid Row. At least the people here were open and unashamed about their ailments—usually depression, lone-liness, alcohol-, drug- or prostitution-related—while the wealthier end of the catchment area insisted on claiming that its alcoholism, Valium dependency and STDs were symptoms of "stress." She found the waste of time pandering to their respectability both tedious and irritating, and preferred the more straightforward approach of the estate dwellers.

"Give us some Prozac, Doctor, my man's in jail and the kids are driving me crazy . . ."

It didn't make them any easier to treat, though. As with all patients, most of her effort went into persuading them that a change of lifestyle would be of greater benefit than drugs, but positive responses in Acid Row were more rewarding because they were harder for the patients to achieve.

By the laws of nature most of her older patients were women, and when she first arrived she'd heard the same thing from all of them. Their husbands were dead. Their friends were in homes. They never went out because they were disabled or afraid. Or both. Their only conversations were with caregivers who were too young to know what they were talking about, or too impatient to listen.

She had realized very quickly that all they wanted was a little gossip with their peers from time to time, and by persuading three of the most active to compile a list of well-guarded telephone numbers, she had created a growing network of chat lines that allowed them to do it. It was known as "Friendship Calling," and interest in the scheme had now crossed the Atlantic with the most recent inquiry coming from a housing development in Florida.

Her telephone rang twice, and she gave a groan of irritation before pulling onto the side of the road. Two rings were the practice, three were her fiancé. She spun the case's combination lock, flicked the mobile open and pressed the "1" button. "It had better be good," she said to the receptionist at the other end, "because I promised Bob I'd be in London by six."

"It depends whether you're still in Bassindale," said Jenny Monroe at the other end. "If you're not, I'll try to reroute John. The chap sounded pretty desperate."

"What's wrong with him?"

"It's his dad, says he can't breathe. He's an asthmatic and he's turning blue. Mr. Hollis at twenty-three Humbert Street. They're new patients, only registered a couple of weeks ago, so we don't have any notes yet. The son says he's seventy-one and not in the best of health. I told him to call an ambulance, but he said he's already done that and no one's turned up. He's obviously panicking. Can you do it?"

Sophie glanced at her watch. Her shift had been over two hours ago, but Humbert Street was around the corner. It was one of the transverse roads that linked the two through routes, Bassindale Row and Forest Road. She worked out directions in her head. Left at the end of Glebe onto Bassindale North, right onto Humbert, then right onto Forest South at the end. She'd be halfway home. Not much of a delay, then, assuming the visit didn't take too long. "Where's John?"

"Western Avenue. Twenty minutes away."

"Okay." She propped the receiver under her chin and picked up a pen. "Give me the name and address again." She wrote it on her pad. "Why do you think the ambulance hasn't turned up?"

"Overextended, I suppose. Their response times are getting worse and worse."

Absentmindedly, Sophie reached into her pants pocket and pulled out the pepper spray that was digging into her thigh. "I wondered if there'd been an accident or something," she said, dropping the spray into her case. "There were a hell of a lot of people milling around the school earlier."

"Not that I've heard."

"Righto. I'll blame you if I'm late and Bob gets cross."

"You always do," said Jenny cheerfully before she hung up.

➤ Police Message to All Stations

➤ 28.07.01
➤ 14:15
➤ Bassindale Estate

➤ EMERGENCY LINES AT FULL CAPACITY

➤ Occupants of 105 Carpenter Road report crowd gathering on Glebe School courtyard
➤ Rumor that child matching Amy's description was seen on Humbert Street last night
➤ Possible target—Milosz Zelowski, 23 Humbert Street
➤ Zelowski not responding to telephone
➤ Situation unstable

➤ EMERGENCY LINES AT FULL CAPACITY

➤ 28.07.01
➤ 14:17
➤ Bassindale Estate
➤ EXTREME URGENCY
➤ W.P.C. Hanson believed to be in Bassindale
➤ NOT RESPONDING

➤ 28.07.01
➤ 14:23
➤ Police helicopter on standby

NINE

The man shielded himself behind the half-open front door and muttered apologies for calling the doctor out on a Saturday afternoon. His father was having difficulty breathing, he said, jerking his head toward the interior of the house. He spoke in a whisper, forcing the young woman to lean forward, and she caught something about "a panic attack" and "asthmatics being drama queens." It was a belittling description for a man, and Sophie assumed the whisper was to prevent his father from hearing what he was saying.

From the sun-drenched street behind her, a child's voice yelled: "Hey, youse dirty sicko! Go screw yourself!" but such words were commonplace in Acid Row, particularly from the mouths of children, and Sophie ignored them. Apart from a handful of kids on the opposite sidewalk, the road had been empty when she arrived, and her only concern was to get this last call over with as quickly as possible. She stepped across the threshold and waited for the door to click behind her.

The man looked unhealthily pale in the gloom of the hallway, where his face hung like a moon in the shadows. Unwilling to catch his eye, she looked down the hall and was therefore unconscious of the way he assessed her. He thought her as small and slim as a prepubescent girl, and shrank against the door in a desperate attempt to avoid contact. Why had they sent a woman? She stood with her back to him,

75

waiting for directions, but he was tongue-tied by the narrowness of her hips and the glossy braid that hung between her shoulder blades. It would be easy to mistake her for a child if it weren't for the confident way she carried herself or the adult expression in her eyes when she turned to him impatiently and asked him to lead the way.

"You're new patients," she reminded him. "I don't know which room your father's in."

He opened a door to the right, where the curtains were drawn and a table lamp offered scant illumination. The atmosphere was fetid with body odor from the elderly, overweight man who lay gasping for breath on a sofa, his constricted throat wheezing with the effort to draw in air, frightened eyes bulging from his head in fear that each breath would be his last. Oh, good grief! thought Sophie impatiently. Was the son subnormal? Or a father killer? God knows, it didn't take Einstein to work out that asking an asthmatic to breathe in an oven was a bad idea.

She squatted beside the sofa. "I'm here to help you, Mr. Hollis," she said encouragingly, placing her case on the floor and releasing the catches. "My name's Dr. Sophie Morrison. You're going to be fine." She spoke to ease his fear and inject a sense of normality into an abnormal situation, then gestured briskly to the son to pull back the curtains. "I need more light, Mr. Hollis, and perhaps you could open the windows to let in some fresh air."

The father raised an anguished hand in protest.

"He doesn't like people looking in," said the son, switching on the overhead lamp. "That's what started this attack . . . seeing a face at the window." He spoke hesitantly as if unsure how much information to impart. "He has an inhaler," he told the doctor, pointing to a blue plastic tube in his father's fist, "but it's worse than useless when he's in this kind of state. He can't hold his breath long enough for the drugs to take effect." He could smell the scent of her skin over the stench of his unwashed father. Apricots, he thought.

"How long's it been going on?" asked Sophie, touching the old man's face. Despite the heat in the room, the skin felt clammy and cold, and she knelt beside the sofa, reaching into her case for her stethoscope.

"An hour on and off. He was beginning to calm down till the children started shouting—" He broke off.

"Has he complained of pains in his chest or left arm?"

"No."

"When did he last use the inhaler?"

"When he was calmer. Thirty minutes ago, I'd guess."

"Any other medication? Sedatives? Tranquilizers? Antianxiety drugs?"

He shook his head.

The old man was dressed in a loose white shirt that someone—presumably the son—had had the sense to unfasten, exposing fleshy, hairy breasts. With ironic thoughts about inappropriate touching, Sophie released the waistband of his trousers to make space for his diaphragm, then placed the stethoscope among the curls on his chest. It was like listening for a heartbeat beside a pneumatic drill. All she could hear were the grating rasps in the throat. She smiled into his panic-stricken eyes. "What's his Christian name?"

"Franek. He's Polish."

"Does he understand English?"

"Yes."

She placed both hands on the man's jawline and gently massaged behind the neck, breathing deeply through her nose and encouraging Franek to do the same. She spoke softly while she did it, calling him by name, soothing fears, instilling trust, and slowly but perceptibly the frantic, hyperventilated breaths began to lengthen and a calmer pattern prevailed. It was a piece of pantomime, a learned technique to relax a patient, but a drop of water slid from Mr. Hollis's right eye as if kindness were a rarity in his life.

"He won't do that for me," said his son bitterly. "All he ever wants is a doctor. I suppose he doesn't trust me enough."

Sophie smiled at him sympathetically while she warmed the stethoscope's chest piece between her hands then placed it over the old man's heart. She listened with relief to the steadying beat, then rested against her heels. "It's not that he doesn't trust you," she said, watching her patient drift into exhausted sleep like a toddler after a tantrum, "just that he knows doctors have alternative remedies if relaxation fails." She folded her stethoscope and packed it away in her case. "Does he often have attacks like that?"

"Once in a while. Normally he can control his asthma with the inhaler, but when he starts to panic—" He gave a helpless shrug. "That's when I have to call a doctor."

"You said it was a face at the window that brought it on," she reminded him. "Why? Is he worried about being burgled?"

There was a small hesitation before he ducked his head in a nod.

Sophie pushed herself to her feet and took a surreptitious glance at her watch. She needed to be home by three-thirty if she had a realistic chance of meeting Bob in London by six. "Have you been burgled before?"

"No, but he's frightened of shadows. It's a rough area."

There was no arguing with that, thought Sophie wryly. Even her beat-up old car was a target when she wasn't in it. In daylight hours, she parked outside the homes of her elderly Friendship Calling women patients in the hope that they were nosy enough to stand by their windows to see whom she was visiting and watch over her car at the same time. Today's guardian was Mrs. Carthew—mild dementia and rheumatoid arthritis—although Humbert Street, usually lined with bolshy adolescents, had been strangely quiet today and she'd been sorely tempted to park outside the Hollises' front door. Only the caution of experience had stopped her.

"Is there a place we can talk without disturbing him?" she asked, reaching for her case. "I'll write a prescription for a mild sedative to help him through the weekend, but I suggest you bring him to the office on Monday so we can review his medication. Also I can teach him some breathing techniques that might help."

The son looked resigned, as though he'd heard it all before. "There's the kitchen."

She followed him down the corridor and sat herself at the table. "How long have you lived here?" she asked, opening her case again and taking out her prescription pad.

"Two weeks."

"Where were you before?"

"Portisfield," he said reluctantly.

Sophie was immediately curious. "Did you know this poor little kid who's missing—Amy Biddulph? It's been on the news all day. I think they said she lived on Allenby Road."

"No." He had an Adam's apple that leaped uncontrollably around his throat. "We were on Callum Road . . . about half a mile away."

"Some parents are so irresponsible," said Sophie unsympathetically as she filled out the prescription. "According to the radio, she vanished yesterday morning but the police weren't alerted until the mother got home. It makes me mad. Who'd allow a ten-year-old to wander around the streets these days?"

There was a moment of silence. "Her father was on TV earlier. He was in tears, begging whoever has Amy to let her go." The Adam's apple made another violent lurch. "It's not always the parents' fault," he said in a rush. "There's no way you can control every minute of a child's day."

He sounded as if he knew what he was talking about, and Sophie wondered if he had children of his own. If so, where were they? "What made you move to Bassindale?"

Another hesitation. "We were getting on each other's nerves in Portisfield, and the council said we could have more room if we agreed to move here."

"You're lucky not to have been given a duplex. They're awful."

His eyes roamed toward the window. "We said we wouldn't come if it was likely to be smaller. But this is all right."

She only half believed him. The tone of his voice suggested nothing about the place was "all right." Certainly, Bassindale wasn't the sort of estate that anyone moved into voluntarily. "I'm sorry," she murmured with genuine sympathy. "Adult men rate low on the housing list. I suppose you were ousted for a family with school-age kids?"

He was grateful for her naïveté. "Something like that."

"Then I'm not surprised your father has panic attacks. It can't be easy for either of you."

Her kindness unsettled him. "It's not all that bad," he said defensively. "At least we have a garden here."

She nodded, studying him carefully for the first time. He was one of those nondescript people who lack anything out of the ordinary for the eye to seize upon—except the bobbing Adam's apple—and she wondered if she'd recognize him again if she met him on the street. Even his hair lacked color, a faded ginger that bore no resemblance to the thickly sprouting dark curls that covered his father. "What's *your* name?" she asked.

"Nicholas."

She gave him a friendly smile. "I was expecting something Polish."

"I was christened Milosz."

"Is that Polish for Nicholas?"

He nodded.

"So where does Hollis come from?"

"My mother. It was her maiden name." He spoke curtly, as if he found her curiosity intrusive, and Sophie was left to wonder why he and his father eschewed a Polish surname in favor of an English one. Easier for people like her to pronounce, perhaps?

She tore off the prescription and handed it to him, advising him to let his father sleep as long as possible. "If you can persuade him to have some windows open, it'll help," she said. "Fresh air will do him more good than that oven he's in at the moment." She prepared to stand up. "When he wakes up, you might think about moving him to a back room."

He glanced at the prescription, then placed it on the table. "Don't you have drugs in your case?"

"We never bring them into Acid Row. We'd be jumped every time we opened our car doors." She watched as he darted nervous glances along the corridor. "What's the matter?" she asked.

"Can't you hear them?"

She listened to the sound of distant voices on the road outside. "It's a bit noisy," she agreed, "but it usually is around here. The kids have nothing better to do with themselves than yell at one another, particularly on a Saturday afternoon when they start drinking at midday."

He didn't say anything.

"It's school vacation," Sophie reminded him. "They're bored."

He took a breath as if to argue the point, but instead gave a dispirited shake of his head and retrieved the prescription from the table, tucking it into his trouser pocket. There was no point keeping her any longer. "I'll see you out."

She closed her case and stood up. "One of my colleagues will be on call throughout the evening," she told him, "but if your father has another attack, then you might do better to phone for an ambulance. In normal circumstances their response time is quicker than ours. The only reason I was able to come so quickly was because I was around the corner." She felt sorry for him suddenly. "But I don't think you've much to worry about. Fear's exhausting. He'll probably sleep through the night and by tomorrow, when the street's quieted down, he'll wonder what all the panic was about."

"I expect you're right."

"If he takes a sedative before he goes to bed, I honestly don't think you'll have any trouble," she assured him, leading the way from the room. She checked her watch again. "The drugstore on Trinity Street stays open till six o'clock, so you have plenty of time to get there before it closes." With an impulsive gesture she stopped before the front door to offer her hand in farewell.

It was like a little bird alighting in his palm, and Nicholas stared at it with a strange fascination. He wanted to hold on to it, fill his nostrils with the scent of someone clean, but his hand trembled under hers and he pulled it away. "Thank you for coming, Dr. Morrison," he said, reaching past her to open the door.

▼

There was a moment, Sophie always thought afterward, when she could have walked out of that house as innocent and undamaged as when she'd gone in. But the time for thinking was so brief—a heartbeat to make a decision that she didn't know she needed to make. A fraction of silence as the door opened, when she should have walked out but didn't—because a patient's son said thank you and she paused to smile at him.

> Police Message to All Stations

> EMERGENCY LINES AT FULL CAPACITY

> 28.07.01
> 14:35
> Bassindale Estate
> EXTREME URGENCY
> Anonymous call—mobile phone—reports 200-plus crowd entering
  Humbert Street
> Armed with stones and bottles
> Possibly Molotov cocktails
> NO ACCESS
> SITUATION OUT OF CONTROL

> EMERGENCY LINES AT FULL CAPACITY

> 28.07.01
> 14:37
> Police helicopter airborne

TEN

There was no preparing for what happened next. No defense against the blast of sound that beat against them like a tidal wave as a hundred throats let out a howl of triumph. No protection from the sharp-edged flint that scythed through the air and sliced the skin on Sophie's right arm. It was so unexpected, so shocking, that her automatic reaction was to slam the door and lock herself inside a prison.

She could hear herself swearing, but the words were drowned out by a hail of stones that thundered against the wooden panels and sent her into a scrambling crouch as she backed away from the danger. She saw the door shudder under the assault and shouted at Nicholas to run. He stared at her, his mouth working as if he were trying to say something. For an awful moment she thought he was going to pass out before instinct kicked in and he scurried crablike toward her. They evinced the most visceral reflexes, hunching their bodies like animals, reducing themselves as targets, heads down, facing the predator beyond the door. Even if either of them had had time to rationalize what was happening, the sound of the fusillade beat against their ears and numbed intelligence.

Sophie looked to the open doorway of the living room as sanctuary, failing to recognize that the windowless corridor was a thousand times safer. With heart thudding, she pushed herself upright and spun into the room, ready to slam the door behind Nicholas. She was aware that Franek was on his feet, she was even extending a supportive hand toward him, when the window exploded inward and shards of glass ripped through the flimsy curtains to let in dappled streaks of sunshine. It happened in a split second, but she saw it with such clarity that the tableau became indelibly printed in her mind. Beautiful in the way the light pierced the room. Tragic in the inevitability of what must happen next. An old man's murder.

She remembered it as bloody in her dreams because the terror of anticipation created a more powerful memory than the reality. But it was a false memory. Even while she was screaming a high-pitched warning—"Get away, get away, get away!"—and Franek was turning to look at her, the glass daggers were falling harmlessly to the floor, their momentum absorbed by the cloth of the curtains. He must have been visible to the crowd outside because they raised their voices again, and this time individual words were recognizable.

"*Animal . . . !*"

"*Fucker . . . !*"

"*Pervert . . . !*"

Nicholas caught him by the arm and bundled him into the corridor, calling to Sophie to close the door. "The kitchen," he told her, herding his father past the staircase. "There's a phone in there."

▼

It was all happening too fast. Sophie's sense of reason clamored that they were running into a trap, but the impetus of the frightened men swept her toward the kitchen. Franek slumped to the floor beneath the sink, shouting at his son in Polish and gesturing angrily toward Sophie. Nicholas answered in quick, rasping phrases, motioning to the old man to move away from her. He grabbed at the telephone, rattling the cradle for a dial tone, then abandoned it to barricade the kitchen door with the table.

"What are you doing?" Her voice shook nervously.

"The phone's dead."

She gestured toward the door. "Yes, but I don't understand what's going on. Why are the people outside? Why were they shouting at your father?"

Another burst of Polish from Franek.

"What's he saying?"

"That there's no time for talking," said Nicholas, shifting a small microwave to the table to add some weight to the flimsy obstruction. "We need to make the barricade stronger."

Franek spoke from the floor, this time in English. "This keeps us safe till help comes, yes?"

"I'm not sure." She struggled to control her voice. "Why are they there? Why isn't the phone working?"

Nicholas gave an uncertain shrug. "I suppose they've cut the line."

"Why?" She reached for the receiver herself, pressed it to her ear. "Why would they *do* that?"

"Why? Why? Why?" said the old man from the floor. "You ask too many questions. Be useful. Help Milosz block the door."

"But—" Sophie forced herself to think. "Perhaps I should try to talk to them? If I go back to the living room and shout through the window, I can tell them who I am. Most of them will probably know me. I have several patients on Humbert Street. One of them's just next door. There might be a policeman out there."

"No." The fat old man laid a hand on his chest and drew in a noisy breath. "You stay." He added something in Polish.

His son gave a rueful shrug. "He's afraid he's going to die."

"He's not the only one," Sophie countered with spirit, "and, frankly, I don't think hiding in here is a solution. We'll be sitting ducks if they break down the front door."

"He says he can feel another attack coming on."

She shook her head angrily. "There's nothing wrong with him," she snapped. "He ran in here like a two-year-old. In any case, I dropped my bag in the hall."

If Nicholas was surprised by her lack of sympathy, he didn't show it. "The police'll be here soon. We'll be all right then."

Sophie listened for sounds in the corridor but all she could hear was sporadic and muted shouting that seemed to be coming from the direction of the window. "Can the crowd get around the back?"

Nervously, he followed her gaze. "It's gardens. They'd have to break down the fences to reach us." He broke off to listen. "It's an echo from the road," he said.

Sophie grabbed the edge of the table and slid it away from the door. "Yes, well, I'm not prepared to bet on it . . . and this bit of rubbish wouldn't keep a child out." With an irritated gesture toward Franek, motioning to him to get up, she turned the handle and peered through the gap. Ominously, the shouts from the street seemed to have quieted, but the doors were still closed and there was no one in the hallway. "Take your dad upstairs and I'll get my bag. I'll check through the mailbox to see what's happening."

Another burst of Polish from Franek, followed by Nicholas's grip on her arm, dragging her backward. "I'll get the bag," he said. "You look after Dad."

She shook him away. "Get off me!"

With a muttered "Sorry" he released her immediately, only for his father to clamp a filthy palm over her mouth and grab her around the waist with the other. He urged her toward the stairs, the heat of his naked breasts pressing against her shoulder blades. "Be good, little girl," he whispered in her ear, "or I break your back like a twig. You keep us safe till the police get here. Yes?"

ELEVEN

Amy had been missing for over twenty-four hours, and the phones in the incident room had rung nonstop since her photograph was shown on television news broadcasts. She had been seen the length of Britain, from Land's End to John O'Groats, and each report had to be painstakingly investigated. The most promising were those describing a little girl in the company of a man, but at the height of the holiday season this wasn't unusual. Fathers regularly escorted their daughters to buy food at mini-markets in service stations or stood outside the ladies' room while the child went in. There was a sense of growing frustration as each new lead faltered.

In contrast to this scattershot approach, which such investigations invariably generated, the focus of Inspector Tyler and his team's efforts was on finding out where Amy had been during the last two weeks. The pattern that was emerging was a strange one. According to Barry, she had left every morning at ten o'clock—he always woke when the door banged—and returned every evening at quarter to six, saying she'd been with Patsy. But when Kimberley called her a liar on Wednesday evening, Amy had turned into a "right little bitch."

The boy looked puzzled as he described the scene. "Normally she was a bit of a spastic—cried a lot—didn't like telly—then Kim calls her a liar and she goes fucking ballistic. She was kicking and fighting, and it was only when Kim promised she wouldn't tell her mum that

Amy backed off. The deal was that she had to get back before Laura, otherwise Kim'd lose her baby-sitting money."

"This was Wednesday?" Barry nodded. "And she stuck to the bargain on Thursday night?" Another nod. "Did either of you try to find out where she was going?"

"Sort of. Kim kept needling her about crawling into a hole because she didn't have any friends."

"Did she react?"

"Just said we'd be jealous if we knew."

Relatives of Laura Biddulph and Martin Rogerson had been interviewed overnight to no effect. Rogerson's parents were living in a retirement home in Brighton and hadn't seen their granddaughter for almost two years. *"She only came once. Martin wanted to mend fences . . . we hadn't spoken since his divorce . . . but Amy was very trying . . . cried all the time. We think she was ill . . . kept going to the loo with a stomachache but wouldn't be helped. Strange child . . . very irritating . . . takes after her mother, we think . . . She certainly irritated Martin. We asked him not to bring her again. No, we had no idea he and Laura were separated."* His sons from his previous marriage had never met her. *"We warned him before he married that we'd take Ma's side . . ."* What sort of father was he? *"Distant . . . uninterested . . . We never had the feeling he liked us very much . . ."* Did he beat you if you were disobedient? *"Hardly . . . he never came home till late . . . that was Ma's job . . ."*

Biddulph's parents, retired and living in Oxfordshire, near their eldest daughter, had also seen Amy only once, when Laura had brought her on a surprise visit during the summer of the previous year. Like the Rogerson family, they presented a picture of alienation from the child who had disappointed them in marriage. Mr. Biddulph did most of the talking.

Did Laura mention any problems in the marriage? *"She wouldn't . . . too afraid of hearing 'we told you so' . . ."* They didn't approve of Martin? *"Of course not . . . little better than a pedophile . . . taking a child-bride as a trophy . . ."* Did they know Laura was planning to leave him? *"No . . . it came out of the blue when she phoned to say she was with someone else . . ."* Did they ever meet Townsend? *"No . . ."* Did Laura talk about him? *"I think she said he was a builder . . ."* Did Amy talk about Martin while she was staying with them? *"No . . . it wasn't encouraged . . ."* Was Laura's relationship with her daughter a loving one? *"If you mean, were they all over each other all the time, then no . . . We're not a demonstrative family . . ."* Did they see anything to suggest Amy was being physically abused? *"By whom . . . Martin or Laura?"* Either. *"Certainly not Laura . . . she wouldn't harm a fly . . . As for Martin . . . the man's capable of anything . . ."*

Laura's sister put a different gloss on the answers. "My mother was forty-eight when Laura was born. She assumed she was going through menopause, and out pops a bouncing baby daughter. I was eighteen and my brother was sixteen. We thought it was a spare tire . . . you know, fat moves south after forty-five . . . and instead we get presented with Shirley Temple. All singing, all dancing and three times as cute as we ever were. She was spoiled rotten. Dad was approaching retirement and suddenly discovered the joys of fatherhood, while poor old Mum got relegated to second place. Dad has only himself to blame that she married Martin. He taught her how easy it is for pretty girls to wind old men around their little fingers."

"Do you get on with her?"

"I hardly know her. She's more like a distant cousin."

"Are you jealous of her?"

The sister was a stocky farmer's wife with wind-blistered cheeks and work-hardened hands. "Used to be," she admitted. "Not anymore. She lost her glitter when she married Martin."

"Did you meet Amy when they came up?"

"Oh, yes. Laura brought her over one evening."

"What did you think of her?"

She smiled rather cynically. "She's her mother's clone. All singing, all dancing, if she thought the routine would get her something . . . quiet as a mouse if she didn't. She seduced my husband in two seconds flat for a fifty-p tip. He thought she was the most adorable child he'd ever met."

"And you? Were *you* seduced?"

She considered for a moment. "In a funny sort of way I suppose I was. She was like an organ-grinder's monkey . . . all over you whether you wanted it or not. That's Laura coming out in her, of course. We just peck each other on the cheek from time to time, but Laura's incredibly tactile. It's very un-Biddulph of her." She paused. "Or *was*," she said with a touch of surprise. "Thinking back, I don't remember her being at all demonstrative last summer."

The neighbors in Portisfield were eager to help—too eager in some cases—but disappointingly uninformative. Those who knew Amy hadn't seen her during the two-week period; those who didn't sent the police after red herrings.

"You wanna search the house at the end of Trinity Street . . . There's a bloke in there hangs around the playgrounds . . . deserves a right kicking if you ask me . . ."

"I've seen the mother a few times . . . I said to my friend: 'What's that eejit Gregory want with a woman half his age?' 'Dirty old man,' she says back to me. Kimberley'll be jealous as sin. You just wait. They'll be killing each other before long."

"I did see a child very much like this photograph . . . pretty little thing with long dark hair . . . She was with a man in a car . . . they stopped beside me at the traffic lights . . . it was a black car, I think . . . not a Mini or a Rolls . . . those are the only ones I can tell apart . . ."

▼

The police had taken over the church hall next to the Catholic church in Portisfield as their incident room. In one corner, D.C.I. Tyler briefed his superintendent early on Saturday afternoon. "There's something damned odd going on . . . I can't get a handle on it at all. Biddulph's clearly distraught . . . swings between screaming and yelling at Kimberley Logan and sitting like a zombie . . . then refuses to leave the house or make a plea for Amy. Rogerson's the opposite . . . levelheaded, polite, composed, ready to do anything we ask . . . then bursts into tears the minute the cameras point in his direction."

"Why does that surprise you?"

"He was cracking jokes before we went into the press conference. Antiwomen by and large." He rotated his hand to encourage a response. "What happens when your dishwasher breaks down?"

"I don't know."

"Kick her."

"*Mmm.*" The superintendent stroked a thoughtful hand down the back of his neck. "It may be his version of screaming and yelling at the Logan girl. We can't all do and say the right thing at the right time." He paused. "You say the parents hate each other."

Tyler nodded. "Rogerson's quite forthcoming about it, says the age barrier meant they had nothing in common . . . claims he was a fool to marry her . . . should have recognized what was likely to happen . . . Townsend was an affair waiting to happen. He admits that some of the blame was his because he spent too much time at work, but he says he doesn't bear any grudges, even suggests he's quite pleased to be rid of her." He smiled cynically. "That's what he *alleges,* anyway."

"You don't believe him?"

Tyler thought about it. "I don't know. He's too insistent that his only concern is for Amy's welfare when, by his own admission, he doesn't pay child support and hasn't seen the kid in nine months. He explains it away by blaming Laura for returning his checks when she was living with Townsend, then vanishing completely. He says she's manipulating the child's affections to give herself a bargaining chip when it comes to the divorce. You haven't supported her, she doesn't like you, won't want to live with you . . . that sort of thing."

"It happens. Children become footballs in these situations. It's sad, but not unusual."

"But that's the point, sir. I can't see that there is a situation. It's rare for a father to be awarded custody, particularly one who works the hours Rogerson does, so why is Laura convinced she's going to lose the kid? It doesn't make sense. They should be looking for joint custody, then everyone's happy." He paused to collect his thoughts. "Something else that doesn't make sense is Rogerson's house. You wouldn't think a kid had ever lived in it. There are no toys . . . the TV's about six inches square . . . no videos . . . no jungle gym in the garden . . . valuable pieces of china all over the place. Amy must have been scared of breaking something every time she went into a room." He shrugged. "I'm questioning whether he wanted a child at all, let alone custody of her if the wife took off."

Another drawn-out *"mmm."* People who didn't know the boss well assumed he was humming to himself. Those who did were accustomed to these verbal ellipses by which he gave himself time to think. Most of his subordinates had picked up the habit themselves, although they were careful never to mimic him to his face. "Interesting. Did you put any of this to Rogerson?"

Tyler nodded. "Before the press conference. I asked him why they'd been fighting over the child when joint custody would have solved the problem, and he said he agreed but there was nothing he could do about it if his wife wouldn't talk to him."

"What was Laura's reaction?"

"He's plausible, therefore he's a lawyer. Or vice versa."

"She's right. They're all bloody sharks."

The D.C.I. smiled. "There has to be something else, though, sir. One of them's got a stranglehold on the other, but I don't know why and I don't know which. My gut feeling says Rogerson has some dirt on his wife—possibly having to do with Townsend—otherwise she wouldn't have sold herself to Logan to put a roof over her head."

"What do we know about Townsend?"

"Not much. He's on holiday in Majorca with his new girlfriend. Rogerson's still acting for him, which strikes me as a bit bizarre. You'd have expected him to trash him when he stole his wife." He looked up with raised eyebrows.

"In what capacity? Personal? Business?"

"Both. Laura says they're always on the phone to each other."

The superintendent looked thoughtful. "Maybe you should turn the question on its head and ask why Townsend would want a man he'd two-timed as his lawyer. That's more interesting, don't you think? It suggests that they have more things in common than just Amy and her mother."

"Like what?"

"Secrets? Perhaps it's the men who have a stranglehold over each other? Where's he based? What's this business?"

"Southampton. It's a building company called Etstone. Rogerson gave us both addresses. We've had a car outside Townsend's house since nine o'clock last night in case the kid turned up, and we've talked to the neighbors. One or two of them remember Laura and Amy, but none was particularly friendly with them. They all described Townsend as a player—"pretty tasty" was the way one woman described him—and said he was often away. He's been married twice. The first wife lasted three years, the second only twelve months. He's had a multitude of affairs, but Laura's the only girlfriend who was allowed to move in. According to the same woman, he's far more interested in one-night stands than in relationships. Gary Butler, who interviewed her, said she was definitely one of the one-night stands, and wasn't too happy about it."

"A bit of a bastard then?"

"Sounds like it. We've had no success talking to anyone at his office. It's closed for the weekend and the answering machine doesn't give contact numbers. He left his hotel address in Majorca with his immediate neighbor in case of emergencies, so we're trying to get hold of him there. The manager told us he has a rental car and disappears off to a nudist beach farther down the coast. He's expected back this evening. I'll have another go then."

"Do you think he's involved?"

Tyler shook his head. "I don't see how he can be. He's been out of the country since Tuesday, and Amy's been vanishing every day. I'm just tying up loose ends. He might be able to throw some light on what's going on between the parents."

"*Mmm.*" The superintendent studied him closely for a moment. "You're chasing wild geese, son. Rogerson was at the office all day, Biddulph was at the checkout counter and Logan was driving his bus. Rogerson might have paid someone to snatch her and hang on to her till the heat dies down . . . but he has nothing to gain by it. It's not as if he can produce her after a week or two and say it was all a mistake. There's no record of abuse, and the kid's teachers describe her as well-balanced and above average." He made an impatient gesture. "We're looking for a psycho. It's the only explanation."

Tyler shook his head in frustration. "Then where's the wretched kid been going every day? Who's she been with?"

▼

One of the incident room computers was routinely reporting police messages from other divisions. "There's a riot going on in Bassindale," said its operator to Tyler as he paused on his way out.

"Why?"

"They seem to be targeting a pedophile."

"What's his name?"

"Milosz Zelowski." He scrolled through the messages. "He was moved from Portisfield two weeks ago . . . interviewed this morning . . . house searched . . . requested protection . . . advised police resources stretched . . . rumor that Amy was seen on his road last night . . . two hundred–plus crowd after him with stones and bottles . . . barricades going up . . . W.P.C. on the ground not responding . . . Zelowski's phone out of order . . . situation out of control." He looked up. "That's a hell of a choice, sir."

"What?"

"Do we look for the kid or protect the pedophile? We haven't got the bodies to do both."

➤ Police Message to All Stations

➤ 28.07.01
➤ 14:43
➤ Bassindale Estate
➤ UPDATE—Missing officer—W.P.C. Hanson

➤ Hanson's scheduled visits this A.M.—W. Barber, 121 Pinder Street—M. Furnow, 72 Harrison Way—J. Derry, Flat 506, Glebe Tower
➤ 4′ automatic calling ... Barber 729431/Furnow 729071/Derry 725600
➤ —No response
➤ —No response
➤ —No response
➤ —No response
➤ —No response

TWELVE

Jimmy James stared angrily at the OUT OF ORDER sign on the elevator doors in Glebe Tower and then, for good measure, landed a heavy fist on the pockmarked metal where an airgun had stitched a V into the gray paint. He was after a guy on the eighth floor who owed him money, but he drew the line at climbing the stairs. The creep had been dodging him since Thursday, so ten to one he was out anyway. Probably on the street with the rest of the morons.

The block was eerily quiet. On a normal Saturday, the metal stairwell echoed with the shouts of children, but today they were locked in their flats or trailing after the mob like camp followers. Earlier in the afternoon he had passed a group of seven-year-olds chanting outside the school where Melanie's foot soldiers were gathering. *"Beef eyes out . . . beef eyes out . . ."* They didn't even know what they were supposed to be saying—*"Pedophiles out"*—let alone what it meant, and he doubted if the adults were any better informed. It depressed him. Ignorance always did.

He lit a cigarette and pondered his options. There was no avoiding what was happening. Melanie had talked about "a protest march," but the smell of gasoline in the air suggested something else. He had made a detour to look at one of the exit routes and found it blocked with cars, some on their sides, all with the gas-tank caps off and the gasoline siphoned out or spilling across the tarmac. He watched boys fill bottles with gasoline and girls stuff rags into the necks, and he didn't have to be Nostradamus to predict the war that was coming. A solitary police car was visible on the far side of the barrier and the anxiety on the faces of the two officers mirrored his own.

The pedophile was just an excuse for the boiling resentment of Acid Row's underclass. They were the Jews in the ghetto, the blacks in the townships, the people without a stake in the affluence beyond their boundaries. And the irony was that they were mostly white. Jimmy could sympathize with them up to a point—as could every black in the land—but he also despised them for their unwillingness to change. He had plans to take Melanie and the kids out of this . . . find somewhere in London where he could go straight and make something of himself . . . or *did,* he reminded himself gloomily, until he discovered that none of his contacts was doing business that day.

At least two had had the sense to get off the Row before the barricades went up, and a third refused to open his door. For different reasons none of them wanted a brush with the law, and that meant keeping their heads down until the trouble passed. Out of sight was out of mind, and tomorrow was soon enough to resume negotiations. Jimmy was rapidly coming to the same conclusion. He should have been on a train by now with money in hand and something to sell, but, in the absence of either, his only choice was to lie low in Melanie's house. Time enough to go straight when his deals were done, but now he was beginning to worry. Maybe it hadn't been such a good idea to leave Mel and the babes to go on the march on their own? Who knew what the fuckers of Acid Row were planning for Humbert Street?

He ground the cigarette out under his heel and jabbed his finger viciously against the elevator button. All he'd needed was for one thing to go right, but nothing worked in this godforsaken place. It was a slap in the face to a useless piece of machinery but with a metallic clunk the doors juddered apart. He thought his luck had changed until he saw the body on the floor. *Ah! Jesus! Jesus! Jesus!*

He didn't stop to think . . . just took to his heels and ran.

INSIDE 23 HUMBERT STREET

Sophie retreated into a corner and felt in her pocket for a tissue to wipe the taste of the old man's hand from her lips. She was so frightened her fingers wouldn't respond, and she pressed them against the wall to stop their trembling. The room was cluttered with odd pieces of furniture, and Franek stood guard in front of the doorway, his head cocked to one side, listening for his son who was moving something heavy on the landing. His eyes never wavered from her face, a long unblinking stare that forced her to stare back. What if he moved? What if he attacked her again? The crowd's words echoed in her mind. *"Animal . . . fucker . . . pervert . . ."*

Nothing made sense. Where had the crowd come from? What had started it? The street had been virtually empty half an hour previously. Fear for herself colored her thinking and dashed all thoughts of Melanie's pedophile from her mind. Had she been lured there? Had someone seen her come in and guessed she was in danger? *"Animal . . . fucker . . . pervert . . ."* Then why attack her when she tried to leave? And where were the police?

It was like groping her way through a fog. Her thinking was paralyzed by the old man's malignancy. Nothing she imagined about him could be worse than the reality. She knew he was reliving his hands on her breasts as they reached the top of the stairs and his stabbing erection against her ass, felt him suck the juice out of her every little tremor that told him she was reliving it, too. He took a sudden step forward.

"I'll *kill* you," Sophie warned, her voice croaking with dryness. She felt for the pepper spray in her pocket, couldn't believe that on the one occasion when she needed it it was locked inside her case along with her mobile. *Where was her case? Had Nicholas retrieved it, or was it still beside the front door?*

Nicholas must have heard her speak, because he called out sharply in Polish, and his father turned away reluctantly to look through the doorway. It was a sudden awakening—a release from hypnosis. She cast around wildly for a weapon, seizing upon a couple of hardback chairs and arranging them in front of her, pulling the backs tight against her legs.

Franek heard the scrape of the wood across the floorboards. "What is this for?" he demanded angrily. "You think chairs will save you? You do better to help Milosz move weighty things to protect the door. He try to push the armoire through from my room. That is useful"—he pointed at the chairs—"this is not."

She ignored him to reach for a glass vase and an old cricket bat, which she put on one of the seats in front of her, followed by some hardcover books and a worn enamel plate with a curved lip.

"You do what I say. You help Milosz."

She shook her head and lifted the vase in both hands. Beyond him, she spotted her case resting against the banister.

He gave a throaty chuckle. "You think the glass will break my head?" He tapped his forehead. "Hard as iron. You think you can fight Franek? Look at these"—he clenched his fists and danced toward her like a boxer, feinting at her cheek—"one hit and I put you to sleep."

Her automatic reaction was to step back, withdraw, avoid a confrontation, but she couldn't because the wall was pressing against her shoulder blades. She moistened her lips. "Go on then," she said in a voice husky with fear, "because I'll smash your fucking head in if you even try."

He was clearly tempted, because his nasty little eyes glittered with excitement, but he shook his head. "There are more important things to do."

She licked her lips again.

"This is good," he said approvingly. "You very scared now. You do as Franek say."

"Not until you give me my case," she managed, jerking her head toward the banister.

He followed her gaze. "Always you want this case. What is in it?"

"Antiseptic wipes. I have to clean this cut on my arm."

He was interested enough to retrieve it, his fingers feeling immediately for the catches. "First help Milosz, then I give you your case."

"No."

He frowned as if he wasn't used to disobedience. "Do what I say."

"No."

"You want me to hurt you?"

She gave a creditable shrug. "I'll live, but you won't if those
people break in." She watched him tug at the catches. "You're wasting
your time. It's a combination lock."

Frustrated, he let it fall to the floor. "It's you who wastes time
with your refusing."

"Then go and help Milosz yourself," said Sophie, wondering how
much longer her legs would hold up. "It's your neck he's trying to
save."

"You want a chance to get away? Out the window maybe?"

She shook her head.

"Okay. Stay there." He left abruptly.

Sophie lowered the vase to the seat again and put a trembling hand
on one of the chair backs. Was it a trap? Was he waiting for her out of
sight? She steeled herself to dart forward and snatch up her case . . .
but fear held her back. Surely obedience was better? She could protect
herself in this corner, lash out with the cricket bat if he came too close,
cut his face with the glass. It took a powerful exercise of will to move
out from behind the chairs. Every instinct argued against it. *Obey . . .
submit . . . placate . . .* But he'd done what she wanted him to do—left
her alone with her case—and the sound of dragging furniture on the
landing gave her courage.

She was out and back again in half a second flat, crouching behind
the chairs and flipping the wheels on the locks. *Hurry . . . hurry . . .
hurry . . .* She seized her mobile phone and punched the "1" button.
"Jenny," she whispered, staring over the seats at the landing, "it's
Sophie. No, I can't. Just listen. I need help. Phone the police. Tell them

I'm on the last call you gave me. Yes—the patient—Hollis. He's taken me prisoner. There are people outside. It's all mad. *He's* mad. I think he wants to rape me—" She broke off as she saw a shadow slide across the banister. She hurriedly pushed the "Off" button in case Jenny rang back, shoved the phone into the case, grabbed an antiseptic wipe and slammed the locks closed. She didn't have time to retrieve the pepper spray.

Franek, face gray with effort, heaved the edge of an oak wardrobe through the doorway. "What you doing?" he asked suspiciously.

She tore the wipe from its package and pressed it to her arm. "Protecting myself from your filth." She saw Nicholas on the other side of the wardrobe. "You've no right to lock me up like this," she told him. "That crowd outside doesn't want me. Most of them know me. I'm their doctor. It would make more sense to let me talk to them on your behalf. If you take me into a front bedroom, I can speak to them from the window. I might be able to persuade them to call the police."

"The police are to blame," said Franek angrily, forcing out the words between heavy, rasping breaths. "They cause this trouble for us when they hammer on our door to make interviews about missing girl." He left his son to swing the rest of the wardrobe inside, muttering something in Polish before collapsing against the wall.

"You'll have to help him," said Nicholas, pushing the door to and manhandling the wardrobe in front of it. "He can't breathe."

Sophie concentrated on cleaning her arm. She needed time to think. *"Missing girl . . . ?"* Amy Biddulph?

"Please, Dr. Morrison. He shouldn't have lifted this. It was too heavy for him."

She glanced across at Franek, who was watching her from beneath veiled lids. "No," she said flatly. "Your father forfeited his rights as my patient when he took me prisoner. That entitles me to put my own safety before his."

Nicholas flicked her yet another apologetic smile while he pushed more pieces of furniture in front of the wardrobe to clear a space in the middle of the room. "He was scared you were going to leave us. He wouldn't have done it otherwise."

"That's no excuse."

He nodded agreement, helping his father into the space and settling him on the floor against some chair cushions. "He doesn't think straight when he's frightened." In a surprisingly tender gesture, he smoothed the hair from the old man's face. "None of us does."

There was some truth in that, thought Sophie, remembering her frantic retreat down the corridor. If she'd had her wits about her, she'd have run the other way and taken her chance at the front door. Surely she had more allies outside than inside? Did she have *any* inside? "Your father put his filthy hands all over me and rubbed his erection against my pants," she said bluntly. "Is that what you call 'not thinking straight'?"

He sighed, more in resignation, she thought, than any real surprise. "I'm sorry," he said inadequately.

She expected an explanation, but it seemed an apology was all she was going to get. For the moment, anyway.

From downstairs, muffled but audible, they heard the sound of more glass breaking.

GLEBE ROAD, BASSINDALE ESTATE

Jimmy slowed down as he reached the end of Glebe Road and turned into Bassindale Row North. To his right was one of the four barricades, heavily manned by drunken youths shouting taunts at the police cars beyond. To his left lay Humbert Street, some hundred yards distant, with children spilling excitedly around the entrance. *Jesus wept!* If he holed up in Mel's house he'd be dragged into the war on the pedophiles, and if he tried to leave the Row he'd be dragged into the war on the police.

What to do? He retreated back the way he'd come and leaned

against a wall to catch his breath. Across the road he could see an old woman watching him from her window. A couple of kids at another. There were eyes everywhere. It made him wonder if anyone had seen him charge out of Glebe Tower like Ben Johnson on steroids. He must have looked guilty as sin. *Shit!* He shouldn't have panicked like that. He remembered touching the elevator button. A cigarette butt with his DNA was lying among the litter on the floor. That would be enough to pull him in for attempted murder.

Swearing copiously, he took out his mobile and flipped it open. He didn't want to do this. He couldn't afford it. None of his contacts would come near him if they knew he was talking to the cops. And it was all for nothing anyway. The ambulance wouldn't be able to get through the barricades.

He dialed 999.

➤ Police Message to All Stations

➤ EMERGENCY LINES AT FULL CAPACITY

➤ 28.07.01
➤ 14:49
➤ Bassindale Estate

➤ Jennifer Monroe, Nightingale Health Center, reports female doctor taken hostage by Hollis, 23 Humbert Street
➤ Possible rape
➤ 23 Humbert Street currently occupied by Milosz Zelowski
➤ Believed alias Hollis

➤ EMERGENCY LINES AT FULL CAPACITY

➤ UPDATE: Patrol car 031 still reporting all access denied
➤ Negotiations continuing

➤ Police Message to All Stations

➤ 28.07.01
➤ 14:53
➤ Bassindale Estate
➤ Anonymous caller requesting help with injured policewoman
➤ Paramedic on line
➤ W.P.C. Hanson believed to be only policewoman in area

THIRTEEN

Word circulated that someone had seen a child at the pedophile's door just before the first stone was cast. Like a game of telephone, "a little woman with a black case" rapidly became "a little girl in black leggings," confirming the rumors that Amy had been seen on Humbert Street the previous day. Also, it was logical. Where else would she be but in the home of a man who had been her neighbor in Portisfield until two weeks ago?

There were plenty of indications that they were wrong. The kids who had been chanting "sicko" for days and who had seen a woman go inside at half past two. The appearance of a police car outside number 23 that morning, seen by the neighbors, when Milosz Zelowski had been interrogated and his house searched from floor to attic with no result. Another car with a doctor's sticker in the window, parked down the road, still there over an hour later. The unlikelihood of a convicted pedophile revealing his victim to public gaze.

But the crowd lacked direction. There were too many factions and too many leaders. Everyone wanted a voice. Youth called for war. Age for respect. Women for security. "Getting rid of perverts" was their only battle cry, and the loudest proclaimers were the teenage girls who had been drinking pint for pint with their boyfriends but whose slighter bodies were less able to absorb the alcohol. Like drunken fishwives, they harangued the boys to ever wilder acts of aggression.

106

In the aftermath, "protecting Amy" would become the catchall defense for what they did. No one doubted that the pedophile had her in his house. It was a fact. She was seen in the street. She was seen at his door. If anyone was to blame, it was the authorities. There wouldn't have been any trouble if pedophiles hadn't been foisted onto the already beleaguered inhabitants of Acid Row. No one wanted them. Why would they? The Row was home to single mothers and kids. Who, but the women, could or would protect their children from perverts?

Certainly not the police, whose idea of rescuing youngsters was to arrest them.

▼

Melanie pushed people aside to storm across the road and confront her fourteen-year-old brother and his friends, who were prying slabs and bricks from the low wall that bordered the tiny garden in front of her duplex. "What do you think you're doing?" she yelled, grabbing Colin by the arm and trying to drag him away. "That's the only bit of garden the kids have to play in. Who the fuck's going to rebuild this afterward? None of you, that's for sure."

"Leave off," Colin said crossly, shaking himself free. "It's what you wanted, isn't it? Giving the perverts something to think about." He grinned in satisfaction as Wesley Barber dropkicked the bricks and dislodged another three. "Good one, Wes."

Melanie smelled the lager on her brother's breath and saw the wild look in Wesley's eyes that suggested speed or worse. She looked around wildly for Gaynor. She couldn't believe what was happening. It was supposed to be a peaceful march of mothers and kids with placards, but those who didn't live on Humbert Street had dropped out at the end of Glebe Road when they saw the barricade on Bassindale Row. Someone was going to get killed, they warned fearfully, seizing their little ones' hands and heading for home. Gaynor had gone after them to try to persuade them to go back, and that was the last Melanie had seen of her.

Where was she now? the girl wondered desperately. Had she deserted, too? The thought panicked her. What about Rosie and Ben? She had taken them with her to the gathering on the Glebe School courtyard—Ben in a stroller, Rosie on foot—but by the time the "march" reached Humbert Street it was out of control and she had thrust the kids through her front door and told them to watch TV till things quieted down outside. It was vain optimism. The crowd was getting bigger and more boisterous by the minute, and the duplex was just one door away from number 23. If drunken idiots like Colin started hurling bricks around . . .

She punched his arm. "You're frightening Rosie," she hissed furiously, seeing her daughter's white face in the window. "I had to put her and Ben inside because it was too dangerous out here."

Startled, he followed her gaze. "Jeez, Mel! They're supposed to be over at our place. Mum said Bry was gonna look after them. What do you wanna bring them on a thing like this for?"

She wriggled her shoulders unhappily. "Everyone brought their babes . . . we wanted to embarrass the council . . . but the others all left . . . and Mum's vanished. I've been looking everywhere."

"You're such a tit," he said scathingly, looking at the mass of people blocking each end of the road. "You'll never be able to get them through that lot. These guys're all rat assed. It just needs one of youse to trip and you'll all get trampled."

She felt tears stinging at the back of her eyes. "I didn't know this was going to happen. It was supposed to be a protest march."

"It's you started it," he told her. "Nonces out, you said."

"Not like this," she protested. "It's all gone wrong." She caught his arm again. "What'm I going to do, Col? I'll kill myself if anything happens to my babes."

The terror in her face sobered him. "Find Jimmy," he suggested. "I reckon he's big enough to push a way through and get youse all to safety."

INSIDE 23 HUMBERT STREET

Sophie stood motionless in her corner, listening. There had been no more breaking glass, and she guessed the sound they heard must have been the remains of the living-room window falling in. A quick glance at her watch told her it was a good thirty minutes since she'd been hit by the stone and ten since she'd called Jenny, but all she could hear was the continuous muted rumble of the crowd.

No police sirens. No megaphones barking orders. No shouts of fear. No stampeding feet as the rioters fled.

She watched the men from beneath lowered lids, her brain weary with the endless thoughts that kept circling inside her head. Nicholas was studying his watch as if he, too, was wondering what had happened to the police, but Franek had eyes only for her. What did he want from her? *"You keep us safe till the police get here . . ."* Was she a hostage? Was she a victim? Was she both? Did Franek care what shape she was in as long as her presence kept his persecutors at bay? *"Animal . . . fucker . . . pervert . . ."* How dangerous was he? Did he think if he raped her she wouldn't find the courage to try to escape? Was she right? What would happen if the minutes of waiting became hours? Questions . . . questions . . . questions . . .

She wished she hadn't hemmed herself in so tightly that the only way she could relax was to prop one shoulder at a time against the wall. She tried to keep her movements to a minimum, aware that every time the silk of her camisole stretched across her breasts it excited him more, but she was becoming exhausted and knots of anxiety tightened in her stomach as her indecision about what to do grew worse. His raking gaze—a horrible perversion of a normal man's admiration—made her feel dirty . . . and guilty . . . and she folded her arms across her chest in a vain attempt to cover herself.

She should never have worn a sleeveless top . . . she was exposing too much flesh . . .

Melanie was wrong... he couldn't be a pedophile... he wouldn't be looking at her like this if he were a pedophile...

The silence in the room was unbearable. So was the heat. The smell of the old man's body odor filled her nostrils and made her want to puke.

She forced herself to speak. "Something's wrong," she said, her voice grating with dryness.

Nicholas glanced nervously toward the window. "What?"

"There ought to be sirens by now."

He thought so, too, because his Adam's apple lurched violently in his throat. "Perhaps no one's bothered to tell them what's going on."

Sophie ran her tongue around the inside of her mouth. "Why wouldn't they?" she said on a more even note.

Nicholas glanced at his father but the old man continued to stare at Sophie, refusing to be drawn into explanations.

"They don't like us," said Nicholas.

She attempted irony. "I guessed that."

He didn't answer.

"I'm not too keen on my own next-door neighbors," she went on, desperate to keep the conversation going, "but I wouldn't stand by while a mob threw stones at them."

"It would have been all right if they'd sent an ambulance. Dad and I could both have gotten out, and none of us would be in danger."

"Did you know this was going to happen?"

He gave a small shrug, which she could interpret as she liked. "Why didn't you call the police?"

"I did," he said wretchedly. "Several times. They never came."

"So you called my office?"

He nodded. "I told them not to send a woman . . . but they didn't listen."

"You said it was an emergency," she reminded him, "and the nearest male doctor was twenty minutes away." She shook her head in bafflement. "What would a man have been able to do that a woman couldn't?"

"Nothing. I just didn't want a woman involved . . . not one like you, anyway." He made a despairing gesture with his hand. "But it's too late now . . . there's nothing I can do."

Oh, God! Fear wrenched at the knots in her stomach. What was he trying to tell her? *Involved with whom? The crowd outside? His father?* Instinct told her it was Franek because her flesh crawled every time she looked at him. He reminded her of a sewer rat—unpredictable, vicious, a carrier of disease, something repellent and evil. She tried to persuade herself it was a reaction to the way he'd thrust himself against her, but she knew that wasn't true. He frightened her because she had no control over him . . . and neither, she believed, did his unnaturally submissive son . . .

"There's nothing I can do . . ."

OUTSIDE 23 HUMBERT STREET

Melanie pressed the redial button on her mobile for the tenth time in as many minutes and listened to the computerized voice asking her to leave a message on Jimmy's voice mail. "It doesn't make sense," she told her brother. "He never talks this long even when he's on a land-line."

"Then he hasn't got it with him."

She took a deep breath. They'd had this discussion several times before. "I already told you. I saw him put it in his pocket," she repeated patiently.

He shrugged. "Then it's turned off."

"He wouldn't *do* that, not when he's got deals in the works."

"Then it's been stolen and whoever has it's doing the talking."

Stress got the better of her. "How many times do I have to tell you?" she snapped. "Nobody steals anything from Jimmy. Something bad's happened, so why the fuck can't you get that into your skull instead of blathering rubbish at me?"

It was the excuse Colin had been waiting for. It was no fun hanging around his sister—all she ever did was lecture him—and the call of his friends was stronger than the unwanted responsibility of a niece and nephew. He shoved a finger under her nose. "You've gotta be wrong sometime," he told her. "If it hasn't been stolen . . . if he didn't leave it in the house . . . if he ain't got it turned off . . . if it ain't lost . . . then he's gotta be talking to someone." He turned away. "But I've fucking well had it, Mel. It's your mess . . . *you* sort it out."

INSIDE 23 HUMBERT STREET

The old man could read Sophie's mind. "You think I fake the panic to make a prisoner of you," he said suddenly. "It make you angry to be fooled. Maybe you not so good a doctor, after all."

She forced herself to look at him. "Did you?"

His eyes glittered spitefully. "You so clever, little girl. You work it out for yourself."

She shrugged as if to demonstrate that his browbeating had no effect on her. "I already have. You may have exaggerated it a bit, but most of what I saw was genuine. You're certainly asthmatic. Your breathing's troubling you now . . . has been since you moved the wardrobe." She smiled slightly. "You should use your inhaler before it gets any worse, Mr. Hollis." She watched him pat his trouser pockets and allowed herself a momentary thrill as his eyes flicked nervously toward the door. It was a small triumph—his son had hustled him out of the living room too fast to remember his inhaler—but a big step on her route to wresting back some control. "I think you'll find you left it downstairs," she said.

"So? I manage without."

"If you can."

He smacked his chest. "Sound as a bell. Nothing wrong. You try to frighten Franek."

Too bloody right! "I don't need to." She jerked her chin toward the front of the house. "What do you think's going to happen when half a ton of angry men burst through your front door? You'll be so scared, you'll die of respiratory failure."

He gave an amused snort as if he enjoyed her spirit. "You help me if this happens," he told her. "It's your job. You swear the oath of Hippocrates."

Sophie shook her head.

"I take you to court . . . sue you for negligence." He rubbed his thumb and forefinger together. "Get you sacked . . . win lots of money."

"You won't be able to," she said.

"How you make that out?"

"I'll scream 'rape' the minute I hear footsteps on the stairs. If it's the police, you'll go to prison. If it's your neighbors, they'll tear you apart."

"You try . . . I snap your neck . . . like this." He wrenched imaginary vertebrae between his muscular fingers.

Nicholas shifted unhappily. "Is this necessary?" he asked.

His father ignored him.

"We don't know how long we're going to be here," Nicholas told Sophie. "Shouldn't we try to get along?"

The sweet voice of reason, she thought. "Then let me negotiate for you. That's far more sensible than sitting in this oven and dying of dehydration. We don't have any water," she pointed out.

"It won't be long. The police will be here soon. We can be friends till then."

"Friends . . . ?" Was he mad, too? "Your father threatened to kill me."

"And you threatened to have him ripped apart," he reminded her.

"It's not that I blame you . . . you're frightened . . . we're all frightened. I just can't see what good it's doing. We'd do better to sit in silence than keep sniping at each other. At least that way we can hear what's going on outside."

Her inclination was to agree with him because her temperament was naturally amenable. Also, she was desperate to sit down and relax her guard. Perhaps he saw the indecision in her face, because he reached for one of the chairs to pull it away.

"No!" she snapped, clamping her hand on the chair back.

"You'll be more comfortable out here," he said persuasively.

It was a seductive invitation, and one not lost on Franek, who gave his son's shoulder an approving pat. Suspicions flowered wildly in Sophie's mind. Was Nicholas his father's procurer? Was this a variation on the good cop–bad cop routine? Was the son the seducer? Did that explain his submissiveness? Somewhere in the turmoil of her mind, common sense told her it would be the other way around. *It was the customer with dirty secrets who was vulnerable . . . the procurer with power to blackmail who was in control . . .* "I prefer it where I am," she said tightly.

He didn't press the issue. "Okay," he said, taking his hand away. "Let me know if you change your mind."

"I won't."

"You not so tough," said Franek. "Soon you fall over—poof "—he chopped his hand toward the floor—"then your mind goes to sleep and Franek makes the decisions."

She didn't say anything.

He studied her lasciviously, grinning when she clamped her arm across her breasts again. "Now *you* scared," he jeered.

She was. She couldn't bear the way he knew what she was thinking. It was as if he understood the trigger points of a woman's terror and recognized their signatures in every tiny shift of expression. It was an invasion. A brutal assault on resolve, setting her at war with herself about whether to keep standing up to him or appease through silence.

She needed desperately to run her tongue across her lips—there was no moisture left in them—but she forced herself not to. He'd see it as another sign of fear . . .

. . . and fear excited him . . .

The thought ripped through her mind like a lightning bolt. *Fear excited him.* God, she'd been slow! People had written books about fuckers like this. She could even remember the definition in her medical dictionary. *"Sadism—sexual pleasure and orgasm derived from the infliction of pain or suffering on others, specifically humiliation and torture."*

It wasn't her breasts that were exciting him, it was the guilt he read in her face every time she covered them. It wasn't his penis against her ass he was remembering, it was the terrified way she'd wiped the taste of his filth from her lips. The little shit was getting his rocks off by abasing her. *"You not so good a doctor, after all . . ."*

She *had* to stand up to him. Oh, God! Oh, God! *But was she right?* If only Bob were there. *He* would know. He was an expert when it came to bastards like this. He treated them, for God's sake. Her eyes flooded suddenly at the memory of her fiancé. She was supposed to be meeting him, and he wouldn't even know why she'd let him down.

Do it! She moistened her lips and dropped her hands to the chair back, staring Franek down. "Tell me about Nicholas's mother," she invited him. "Tell me how scared she had to be before you could get an erection?"

He frowned at her angrily and said something to Nicholas.

"He doesn't understand what you mean," said the younger man, lowering his eyes and refusing to look at her.

"Yes, but *you* do," she said, "so translate for me. Ask him what he had to do to her to get himself in the mood? Tie her up? Beat her black and blue?"

Nicholas shook his head.

"Okay. I'll do it. I'll spell it out for him in words of one syllable. He's thick as pig shit, but he ought to be able to understand the word *sadist.*"

A tiny narrowing of the old man's lids told her he did. "You stop now before Franek get angry," he ordered.

She laughed, terrifyingly complacent, thrilled to have scored so easily. "So where is Milosz's mama now?" she asked, leaning forward and aping his accent. "Fucking someone else?"

Of course she wasn't ready. Nothing in her life could have prepared her for the speed with which Franek launched himself from the floor and smashed his fist into her face.

FOURTEEN

D.C.I. Tyler was in his office at headquarters when a call came through from the Bella Vista hotel in Majorca. There was a gabble of Spanish from an operator, then: "The manager said I could call you on his phone," said a girl's tearful voice. "He says you might give me some money because you were asking about Eddy."

Tyler sat up immediately and reached for a pen. "Do you mean Edward Townsend?" he asked.

"Yes," she wailed. "He's such a bastard. The manager says I have to pay the bill . . . but it's huge . . . and I can't . . ." The voice broke into racking sobs.

"Who am I talking to?" he asked patiently. She sounded too young to pay bills.

"Franny Gough. He said he loved me," she wept. "He said he was going to marry me. I don't know what to do . . . I don't have a plane ticket because he never gave me one . . . and the manager won't let me leave till the bill's paid. He's taken the rental car . . . and there's no way for me to get to the airport . . . and if I phone my mother, she'll kill me. She kept telling me he was no good . . . but I just thought she was jealous because Eddy's the same age as her and she can't get a man . . ."

He listened to the pathetically immature voice at the other end, spilling the same woes and misconceptions that girls had been

117

spilling for centuries, and he wondered if she was as gullible as she was pretending or if she thought naïveté was a way to win a man's sympathy. But whose? *His or the manager's?* "When did he leave?"

"Yesterday. I did everything he wanted . . . you know, got dressed up . . . but he said I didn't look right because my hair was too short . . ."

Tyler tried to speak over her voice. "What time yesterday?"

But she was in high gear and didn't hear the question. ". . . so I said I'd wear a wig, and that made him really mad because he said kids only wear wigs when they have leukemia. I said he was picking on me for nothing . . . it's only a video . . . but he said men don't fancy kids who look sick . . . and now I really hate him because he's left me here . . . and the manager says I could go to prison." She came to a halt in a burst of weeping.

He waited for her to calm down. "How old are you, Franny?"

"Eighteen," she muttered.

"You sound younger."

"I know." She spoke hesitantly as if she were weighing her words. "I look it, too . . . that's why Eddy likes me. I turned eighteen in May. You can ask the manager if you don't believe me. He's taken my passport and says he won't give it back till the bill's paid."

"I'll talk to the manager later. What time did Eddy leave yesterday?"

She blew her nose noisily into the receiver. "I don't know. He was gone when I woke up."

"What time was that?"

"Midday," she said reluctantly as if sleeping until noon was a crime. "We didn't get back to the hotel till two in the morning, and I went to sleep pretty soon after. I reckon that's when he left, because the sheets on his side were still tucked in."

Tyler did some rapid thinking. How early did flights leave Majorca on a Friday? Could Townsend have made it to Portisfield by lunchtime the same day? Assuming, of course, he was the man seen in the car outside the Catholic church . . . and Amy was the child seen rounding the corner. Too many imponderables. "What kind of car does Eddy drive in England?" he asked the girl.

"A black BMW."

Close . . . "The manager told me this morning that you and Eddy were at a nudist beach along the coast. Why did he say that if you've been on your own since yesterday?"

More sobs. "I didn't know what to do . . . I hid in the room because I knew there'd be trouble if he found out Eddy'd gone. He was really suspicious . . . kept asking me if I was Eddy's daughter . . . so this morning I pretended Eddy was waiting for me in the car, then sneaked around the back and got in through the fire escape . . . I thought maybe I could find someone else to pay . . . you know, a bloke on his own . . . but I was so hungry I called room service . . . and then the manager comes knocking on the door saying the police in England want to talk to us . . . so I told him Eddy went yesterday and he goes apeshit because Eddy didn't give him a credit card when we arrived . . . he said it was in his case and he'd bring it down later . . . but he never did . . . so the manager hauled me down here to talk to you . . . and I haven't got any money . . ."

Tyler held the telephone away from his ear, waiting for her high-pitched wailing to diminish before he spoke again. *If he'd followed the gist of what she was saying, and she was telling the truth . . .* "I'll sort it out for you. All right?"

She rallied immediately. "I suppose."

"But," he went on firmly, "I want answers to some questions before I do."

"What sort of questions?" she asked suspiciously. "Maybe I shouldn't talk to you without a lawyer listening."

Not completely naïve then . . . "It's up to you, Franny. I'm investigating a child's disappearance, and I'm not prepared to waste time helping you if you're not prepared to help me."

"What child?"

"Her name's Amy Biddulph. She's been missing since yesterday."

"Shit!"

"Did Eddy ever mention her?"

"Never fucking stopped," she said, sounding very adult suddenly. "It was Amy this, Amy that. You don't look like her, you don't talk like her. Who is she then?"

"The daughter of your predecessor. She's ten years old and has long dark hair."

"Shi-i-it!"

"What color's your hair?"

"Brown. He only likes brunettes. That's what he says, anyway."

"Amy's mother's a brunette. And very pretty. Like her daughter."

"*Fuck* him! I said he was a bastard."

"Are you going to answer my questions?"

Another long pause while she considered her options. "Yeah, okay. He hasn't done me any favors."

Those were the truest words she'd said. "Where did you fly from?"

"Luton."

"Which airline?"

"Easyjet."

"Are they the ones that sell tickets over the Internet?"

"Sort of. You don't get a ticket, just a number that confirms your seat. Eddy got a good deal because the plane wasn't full."

"Which day was this?"

"Tuesday."

"And he was gone again by Friday morning?" said Tyler in surprise. "How long were you expecting to stay there?"

She started to wail again. "He never said . . . and I never asked because I thought it was a vacation . . . you know, two weeks or something. Okay, I know it was a bit last minute . . . Like, Sunday we're mucking around at my place and Tuesday we're jetting off to Majorca . . . but I didn't reckon he was going to leave after three fucking days. Otherwise, I'd have made him hand over his credit card. I mean, that sucks, don't you reckon?"

"Did he book a return flight?"

"I don't know." She paused to think about it. "Probably not, because he brought his laptop with him. He said the system's supposed to be flexible, so you pay for each flight separately. It means you can book wherever you are."

"Does he use the Net a lot?"

"All the time," she said crossly. "He's really boring about it."

"Do you know what his e-mail address is?"

"I only know the business one—townsend@etstone.com—all lower case."

"How many does he have?"

"About six . . . maybe more. He uses codes so people can't read them by accident."

"Why is he worried about that?"

"It's confidential business stuff. He gets really twitched about people finding out what contracts he's got on the go."

Tyler warned himself against jumping to easy conclusions. It was one of the perils of the job, something policemen had referred to in the past as a "hunch" or "having a nose for a villain." Too often it had resulted in large settlements for miscarriages of justice when alleged villains proved to be innocent, and the "hunch" was based on nothing more than a series of unfortunate coincidences. Nevertheless . . . an attraction to young-looking women . . . videos . . . the Internet . . . ?

He didn't want Franny making similar connections, so he changed the subject by asking her a series of unalarming questions about how much luggage Townsend had brought with him and whether he'd left anything behind. Then: "You said something earlier about it 'only being a video,'" he said idly. "What was that about?"

She hesitated. "Nothing much. He's always filming things."

"What sort of things?"

She didn't answer.

"You mentioned wearing a wig," he said lightly, "so presumably he was filming you."

She was less willing to go into detail now that she'd calmed down. "It's just stuff he does for himself," she said reluctantly.

"Pornography?"

"Christ, no!" She sounded genuinely shocked.

"What then?"

"He likes watching me on video when I'm not with him."

"Dressed or undressed?"

"Which do you think?" she asked sarcastically. "He's a bloke, isn't he?"

Under other circumstances Tyler might have defended his sex, but perhaps her experience of men was as limited as the cynicism behind her remark suggested. If so, he felt sorry for her. "Is that why he took you to the nude beach?"

"I guess."

"Did he film anyone else there?"

"No." Unexpectedly she giggled. "He said they were all too old and fat. In any case, most of them were men and men don't turn him on. The nudie beaches are where they go to pick each other up."

Tyler switched tack again. "Why did he leave? Did you have a row?"

"Not really. He was a bit ratty on Thursday afternoon."

"In what way?"

"Your tits are too big . . . your ass is too big . . . you've got too much makeup on . . . you look like a tart . . ." She spoke in a chant as if she'd learned her faults by heart. "I got really smashed Thursday night, so maybe I turned him off," she finished sadly.

Tyler heard the beginnings of self-recrimination in her voice and injected a little sarcasm of his own. "Why do you still believe anything he said?" he asked. "He's a con artist. He's taken the manager for a ride and left you to clean up his mess. Is that the kind of—uh—*bloke* who attracts you? Because you haven't got much of a future if it is."

"He's so good-looking, though," she said, "and he was really *sweet* at the beginning."

"Good-looking men always are," said Tyler unsympathetically, fingering the lines on his forehead, "until they get inside your knickers and find you're no more exciting than the last girl they had."

"You sound like my mother."

"Is there anything else you can think of that might help me? Did he get any phone calls?"

"There was a message for him when we got back to the hotel. It was in an envelope that had been pushed under the door . . . he seemed quite excited about it. He made me take a shower so he could call someone . . . it might've had to do with that. He told me to go to sleep after . . . said he wasn't interested in sex."

"And this was two o'clock in the morning?"

"Yes."

"What did the message say?"

"Dunno."

"Did you try to find it after he'd left?"

"Maybe."

"And?"

"It wasn't in the trash."

"Did you answer the phone for him while he was there?"

"They were all on his mobile."

"Did you hear any conversations that might have been with a child?"

"He used to go out of the room." A pause. "Most of them sounded like business. He's got problems with some of his houses."

"What sort of problems?"

"Dunno. He went ballistic every time I asked . . . said people were stealing from him. He said it would all be sorted out next week."

Tyler stared at his office wall. "Who was he talking to? Customers? Partners?"

"Dunno," she said again.

"Can you remember him using a name? Perhaps at the beginning, when he said hello?"

"I didn't listen."

"Try to remember, Franny," Tyler said patiently. "It's important."

"But it was all so boring," she whined. "There was some stuff about contracts and dates one time. I think that might have been his lawyer."

Tyler wrote *Martin Rogerson* on his pad and followed it with a question mark. "Does the name Martin ring any bells?"

"Oh, yes," she said in surprised recollection. "He said, 'Hello, Martin.'"

"Which day was that?"

"Thursday, I think."

Tyler held his breath for a moment, then asked her to give him her mother's telephone number and address. She refused until he pointed out that he had no intention of paying her hotel bill himself, and neither would the British taxpayer. "You're an adult and, under the law, that makes you as responsible as Townsend for the debts you incur. It's a clear-cut choice. Either you sort it out yourself or I'll ask your mother to do it for you. Now where does she live?"

With bad grace, the girl gave an address and telephone number in Southampton. "She'll kill me," she said again.

"I doubt it, but I'll do what I can to make her go easier on you." He thought about telling her to show some maturity for the first time in her life, but decided against it. If she couldn't learn the lesson for herself then nothing a stranger said down the phone would persuade her. Instead his instruction was to stay put in Southampton when she returned as he wanted to interview her face-to-face, then he spoke to the hotel manager for five minutes to check out the truth of what she'd told him and sort out a few details. He thanked him for his assistance and asked him to give the girl something to eat while he contacted her mother.

"I am not hopeful that this woman wants Miss Gough back," said the manager in good, but heavily accented English.

"Why do you say that?"

"In this country no mother would allow her child to do what this one does. Señora Gough cares nothing for her daughter, I think."

NIGHTINGALE HEALTH CENTER

It was rare for Fay Baldwin to go into the center on a weekend but she had been brooding over Sophie's high-handed dismissal and her scathing message on the answering machine, and by Saturday had worked herself into a fine fury. The fact that other doctors had similarly dismissed Fay, leaving just a handful of clients to see her through to retirement, was conveniently forgotten. This time she planned to make an official complaint, accusing Dr. Morrison of negligence toward Melanie's children.

In her twisted logic, the presence of the pedophile on Humbert Street was tightly interwoven with the conspiracy to remove her. She had even persuaded herself it was courage that had led her to reveal his presence on Humbert Street. Dr. Morrison had no concern for the children. She had proved it by banning all discussion of the man's existence and then accusing Fay of insanity when she dared to mention it. Fay, by contrast, was *only* concerned with dear little Rosie and Ben. As she *should* be. It was her job as their health visitor. How dare a doctor override her authority? Who—*above everyone*—had fought to preserve the safety—*and sanctity*—of the Patterson children?

She didn't particularly want her presence noticed in case Sophie had spread the word about what she'd done—she needed time to prepare her case—so she planned to sneak into the health visitors' office when the receptionist was busy with a patient. But she was startled to find the door to the main reception area blocked by a policeman. Even more startled to see the waiting room empty of patients and Dr. Bonfield, the senior partner, in a T-shirt and shorts, standing behind the reception desk with Jenny Monroe. Harry Bonfield and Fay did not get along, and she would have left immediately, had the officer not drawn attention to her presence.

"Let her in," Harry called. "She's one of ours." He waved Fay forward with a rolling arm movement, staring hard at Jenny's computer. "Have you heard about Sophie? It's a nightmare. The police have been caught flat-footed . . . so we're trying to find someone to get a message through to whoever's in charge of the bloody thing. If only the silly girl hadn't turned off her mobile . . . we could talk directly . . . sort it out sensibly." He nodded at the computer. "Jenny's going through the list to see if she can find anyone on Humbert Street we can talk to . . . but it's hopeless . . . The patients are filed by name, not street . . . it's like looking for a needle in a blasted haystack. The nearest one of mine is on Glebe Road, but she's deaf as a post and not answering." He flicked his hand to get her up. "It's a crisis, Fay. Any ideas? *Humbert* Street. You must have some customers there."

Fay might have been a little more circumspect had Harry not referred to Sophie as a "silly girl." As it was, she leaped to the conclusion that Sophie was in the wrong. "I *did,*" she said primly. "Not anymore. Courtesy of Dr. Morrison."

Harry frowned at her. What the hell was the stupid woman talking about? "Has the patient moved?"

"Not that I'm aware of."

"Could we have a name?" he suggested silkily. "When you're ready, of course."

Fay pursed her lips into a tight little rosebud. "Melanie Patterson."

He tapped Jenny's shoulder and leaned forward to watch while she scrolled through to P. "Got it," he said. "Twenty-one Humbert Street. Okay, Sophie's her registered practitioner. What do you think?" he asked Jenny.

The woman chewed her lip. "She's only nineteen," she said, pulling up Melanie's notes. "Six months pregnant . . . two toddlers . . . but it looks as if she knows Sophie pretty well. She's seeing her every two weeks for prenatal care." She shook her head. "I don't know, Harry," she said worriedly. "We could scare her stiff and start a miscarriage."

"Young women aren't usually that fragile, still . . ." He pointed to the next-of-kin box. "What about her mother? Gaynor Patterson? She's just two streets away. How about calling her and seeing if she can give us the names of any of Melanie's neighbors?"

"Okay." Jenny tapped Gaynor's number into the phone. "Hello," she said. "Am I speaking to Gaynor Patterson? . . . Briony . . . Yes, it's important." There was a long pause while she listened to the voice at the other end. "All right, darling, then how about you give me both numbers and let me have a try . . . No, I'm sure she won't be angry. Do you come to the health center? Do you know who Dr. Morrison is? That's right, Sophie . . . Well, I'm the lady who sits at the desk and calls your name when it's time to go in." She chuckled. "You've got it . . . the old one with glasses. Good girl." She wrote on her pad, then listened again. "No, sweetheart, promise me you won't go looking for Mum. It's dangerous out there, and you might get knocked over. If I get through, I'll tell her you're worried and you want her home. Is that a deal? . . . Sure, I'll call back in about twenty minutes. Yes, my name's Jenny. Bye, now."

She raised stricken eyes to Harry. "The poor little kid's frightened out of her wits. She says it was supposed to be a protest march, but she thinks something awful's happened because gangs of boys keep charging up their road and all she can hear is screaming and shouting. She's worried that her mum and Melanie have been hurt because they were leading the march." She pointed to her pad. "She's given me their mobile numbers, but she says she's been trying for half an hour and can't get past their voice mails. I promised I'd give it a try for her."

Harry ran a worried hand through his thinning hair, sending it heavenward in wisps. "Do that," he said distractedly. "They're probably the people to talk to, anyway. They must have some clout if the march was their idea." He paused. "I can't believe this," he blurted out. "Kids on their own in the middle of a damn riot. Who started it? Tell me that. I'll wring their bloody necks myself. Did this kid say if she tried Melanie's house?"

Jenny nodded. "She says Rosie answered, but there was so much yelling she couldn't hear what she was saying . . . so she hung up and tried again. The second time the phone was busy, and she thinks Rosie hasn't put it back properly, which means they're probably on their own as well."

"How old's Rosie?"

Jenny checked the computer. "Four."

"Dear God!" He raised his voice. "Have you heard any more on your end?" he asked the policeman.

"Sorry, sir." The young man held up his radio, which crackled intermittently with messages. "Same as before. The helicopter's still reporting all cars held outside the barricades. It's not looking good. There's a W.P.C. down as well—head injuries—and we can't get to her either."

"Christ, what a mess!" said Harry. "Couldn't you chaps have seen this coming? What the hell induced you to put this man in there in the first place? You must have realized that most of the people on that estate would automatically assume pedophile meant monster." He glared angrily in Fay's direction as if he held her responsible.

Her mouth opened and closed like a goldfish's, but no words came out.

Harry focused on her for a moment, then ignored her. "What was he convicted for, anyway? You say he's not dangerous, but what sort of pedophile is he?"

The policeman gave an unhappy shrug. "All I know is what we were told in the briefing before I came out. He was a teacher at a private school and got sent down for three counts of sexual assault . . . It was a long time frame . . . The first one happened about fifteen years ago . . . the last fairly recently. He's only interested in boys and didn't get much of a sentence because his first victim was seventeen, the last two sixteen, and all said they consented to what was going on. I reckon the assumption was he'd get his head kicked in if he tried the same thing in Acid Row."

"What did he do?"

The youngster cast an embarrassed look at the two women. "Stimulated them," he muttered.

"What sort of stimulation?" demanded Harry, with a doctor's insensibility. "Oral or masturbation?"

"Masturbation."

"In return for what? The same or penetration?"

"Nothing."

"What do you mean, 'nothing'? How did he achieve orgasm himself?"

The policeman shrugged. "None of the boys was asked to do anything. That's why his sentence was only eighteen months."

Harry shook his head in bafflement. "So his pleasure was in giving."

"I guess."

"He sounds too passive to be a rapist."

"That's what my guvnor said. He wonders if Dr. Morrison's got the wrong end of the stick. Let's face it, she's bound to be scared . . . I mean, we know there's a big crowd on that road . . . and one of the callers said they were armed with stones.

"Let's say the guy put his hand on her arm to reassure her . . . and let's say she assumed more than he intended because she knew he was a sex offender."

Jenny stopped redialing the numbers. "But I don't think she did," she protested. "*I* certainly didn't." She paused to order her thoughts. "In any case, which one's the pedophile? The father or the son? Sophie was very specific. She said the *patient* had taken her prisoner and wanted to rape her . . . and the patient, according to the information I had, was the father."

The policeman made a face. "I thought there was just the one."

"We've definitely got two of them registered."

"Bring up their notes," Harry told Jenny. "Let's see their ages."

"I already did. They're new patients, and their records haven't come through. All we've got is Francis and Nicholas Hollis, Twenty-three Humbert Street, with an asterisk beside the names and 'Zelowski' in brackets." She scrolled through to prove it. "But I do remember the son saying his father was seventy-one . . . and that would make him well past retirement age for a teacher, wouldn't it?"

Harry looked inquiringly toward the policeman. "How old's your pedophile?"

"Not that old. I've seen a photo of him. Mid-forties, I'd reckon."

Harry swore under his breath. "Keep phoning," he told Jenny. "And you," he instructed Fay, "tell me anything you can remember about Melanie . . . names of boyfriends, girlfriends, fathers of her kids, anyone we can contact."

"What are you worried about?" asked the constable.

"I'm wondering who taught your pedophile that giving pleasure was an aim in itself. Forget the age and sex of his victims; it's very unnatural behavior . . . incredibly docile. It suggests that his needs must always be subservient to someone else's."

"The father?"

"Almost certainly. There's too much evidence showing that abused boys become abusers themselves . . . and the most likely abuser is the father or stepfather." He shook his head. "The way this guy does it suggests that sex frightens him. And if he learned that from his father . . ." He looked very old suddenly.

Jenny touched his hand briefly while she listened to yet another playing of Melanie's mail. "Sophie's a tough girl," she said. "She won't submit that easily." This time she left a message, asking for her call to be returned as a matter of urgency. "We'll have to leave this phone free now," she said. "There's no point having it tied up if Melanie does ring back. That leaves just one line operational out here, plus the direct

lines in the offices. I think we need to spread out and work separately."
She glanced at Fay. "Thought of anyone yet? You can use the computer
in Sophie's office to track down their numbers. It might be better if
you let me make the call, though. The police don't want us saying too
much and making the situation worse."

"But . . . I don't understand . . . *what* situation?" Fay protested.
"It's all very well to say do this . . . do that . . . but how can I do anything if I don't know what's going on?"

"Neither does anyone else," said Jenny, "except that Bassindale's
rioting. The police think it's targeted at this man Sophie's with, but
no one knows how his identity was revealed. He was convicted as
Zelowski but was registered as Hollis when he moved to Bassindale."

"Some idiot with a big mouth and no brain," said Harry grimly,
stalking off toward his office. "They ought to be shot . . . putting
people in danger like this."

"I agree," said Jenny equally grimly, turning back to the telephone and trying Gaynor's number again. She noticed that Fay's face
suddenly got blotchy, but she paid no mind to it because this time the
phone was answered.

FIFTEEN

Tyler instructed one of his sergeants to locate Martin Rogerson and deliver him to headquarters ASAP. "Paula Anderson drove him to the press conference, so get hold of her and see if they're still in the area. I want him here where I can see him, so tell Paula not to accept any excuses. If she's already returned him to Bournemouth or is still en route, ask her to bring him straight back again. Understood?"

"She'll need a reason, boss."

"New lead . . . promising this time. I'll interview Laura at Gregory Logan's house first"—he checked his watch—"which gives Paula about an hour's leeway. The earlier the better, though, tell her. It won't do Rogerson any harm to twiddle his thumbs for half an hour in an interview room."

He beckoned over the sergeant who'd interviewed Townsend's neighbor and ran through the notes he'd made on flights. "See if Easyjet has a record of him traveling back on Friday morning. It'll be the Palma to Luton route. And get them to check for a Ms. F. Gough. She flew out with him on Tuesday but doesn't know if he organized a flight home for her. Find out if he had a reservation that he changed to Friday. That'll tell you the day he was intending to return. If she's lucky, he booked her in on the same flight."

The sergeant was curious. "Is this the new girlfriend?"

"You tell me. Did you get a name or a description when you spoke to his neighbor?"

He shook his head. "She never met her, just said the new girl was probably the reason for the break with Laura."

"Or with Amy," said Tyler. "We're all assuming it was the mother he was interested in."

The sergeant frowned. "I don't get it, boss."

"According to the hotel manager, Franny Gough looks and sounds like a twelve-year-old. She's dark and petite and 'pretty cute.' The manager's words, not mine. Remind you of anyone?"

"Jesus!"

"Right. Townsend's been making videos of her on a nude beach, but he buggered off early Friday morning after talking to someone called Martin and then getting a message—possibly a fax." He pointed to the e-mail address Franny had given him. "Try mailing Townsend and see if he bites. Tell him you need to talk to him about Laura and Amy Biddulph. Nothing heavy. Just say you need the names and addresses of anyone they became friendly with during the time they were living with him."

"Do I put in a contact number?"

Tyler nodded. "Give him my mobile . . . tell him it's yours."

"What do you really want from him?"

"What he's been up to for the last twenty-four hours," said Tyler, going back into his office and closing the door behind him. He dialed the number Franny had given him.

"Hello?" said a woman's voice.

"Mrs. Gough?"

"Yes."

"This is Detective Chief Inspector Tyler of Hampshire Police. I'm phoning on behalf of your daughter."

There was a small silence. "What's she done this time?"

No concern for the girl's welfare, he noticed. No *"Is she all right?"*

which was the usual reaction to such a call. "She's been abandoned in a hotel in Majorca, and the manager won't let her leave until the bill's been paid. The manager confirmed that her companion's rental car and possessions are gone, so I think you can be sure she's telling the truth."

"Edward Townsend, I suppose?"

"That's the name she gave me."

He heard the flick of a cigarette lighter at the other end of the line. "How did the Hampshire Police become involved?"

"We've been trying to contact Mr. Townsend on another matter. When the manager discovered he'd already left, he asked Franny to talk to me."

"What was the other matter?"

There was no reason not to reveal it as she'd shortly be hearing it from Franny herself. In any case, he needed information. "The missing child, Amy Biddulph, lived in his house for six months."

She let out a long sigh . . . or a lungful of smoke. It was hard to tell from her steady voice if she was reacting emotionally. "I warned Francesca," she said, "but she wouldn't listen to me. It's her age. She thinks she can control everything." She sounded disinterested, as though she were talking about a stranger.

"Do you know Townsend well?"

"Hardly at all. I'm friendly with his first wife."

He pulled forward another piece of paper. "Could you tell me what you do know, Mrs. Gough? Perhaps you could start with why you warned your daughter against him."

"He's forty-five. She's eighteen. Do I need any other reason?"

Tyler noted the sharpness of her tone. "*Is* there another reason?"

"Nothing I'm prepared to say to someone I've never met."

"I'm a policeman, Mrs. Gough, and anything you tell me will be treated in confidence. This is urgent. Amy's been missing for over twenty-four hours, and if you know something that can help her we need to hear it."

"Except you can't prove you're a policeman over the phone, and I can't afford a libel suit. For all I know, you could be a journalist."

She was right, but he wondered how anyone could be so detached about the fate of a child. *"Señora Gough cares nothing . . ."* "Then let's deal with one thing at a time. I'll give you the number of the Bella Vista in Puerto Soller. The manager's English is good, and he's prepared to take your credit card number over the phone to settle the account and organize travel home for Francesca. I'll also give you the number of the operator here. When you call, you can check on my credentials and leave a message for me to return the call. Is that acceptable to you?"

This time the sigh was unmistakable. "Not really."

"She *is* your daughter, Mrs. Gough."

There was a quiet laugh at the other end. "I know, and I wish I could say she wasn't. I might feel less guilty about my shortcomings. Do you have children, Inspector? Do they steal? Do they drink? Do they sleep around? Do they take drugs?" The questions were rhetorical because she didn't wait for answers. "I paid out five thousand pounds for Francesca on her eighteenth birthday to settle mobile phone and mail-order bills, and to reimburse the parents of two of her friends whose credit-card numbers she'd been using to order things off the Net. I've written off her thieving from me, and I've set her up in a flat of her own to give her a chance to prove she's responsible. The quid pro quo for all of this was that she would never expect me to bail her out of a problem again, and she would take up the university place she's been offered. Instead, she takes off for Majorca with my best friend's ex-husband and claims the reason I'm angry is because I'm jealous." She paused. "So, tell me, Inspector. What would you do in my shoes if a policeman called you and told you your daughter was in trouble . . . *again?*"

Tyler answered honestly. "Stick to the rules I'd laid down."

"Thank you."

"But I'm not in your shoes, Mrs. Gough. I've been divorced longer than I was married, and I don't have children. My entire experience of girls of Francesca's age was arresting them for theft and prostitution when I was a cop on the beat."

There was another short silence. "And?"

"I can't remember a single one whom I didn't arrest at least twice, though the average number of arrests per girl was more like five or six. They all said they were never going to do it again . . . but they were all back on the streets within days of being released because getting stoned on the money they made out of theft or prostitution was quicker and easier than saving up the pittance they could earn as a supermarket checkout girl."

She wasn't a woman who rushed into speech. "I don't understand the point you're making," she murmured after a moment.

He was irritated by her silences. "I'm saying that habits are hard to break without a strong incentive, and few of us succeed the first time. How many times have you tried to give up smoking?" he asked bluntly. "Once? Twice? Do you wake up every morning and say today's the day?"

She gave another sigh. "I hoped that making her responsible for herself would be an incentive."

"She's not ready for it."

"She's eighteen."

"But sounds and behaves like a twelve-year-old, and you don't hand a twelve-year-old the keys to a flat." He glanced at his watch. He didn't have time for this. Franny and her problems would have to wait. "Look, I'm going to give you the numbers, anyway, and it's up to you what you do about them. Whatever you decide, will you please call your daughter and explain? There's an outside chance she has a flight home, which one of my team is checking at the moment. I'll ask him to call you with the result. Also, I do need to talk to you again. If you haven't left a message by six o'clock this evening, I'll come out to Southampton to interview you . . . either tonight or tomorrow morning."

"Do I have any choice in this?" she asked after he'd given her the numbers.

He ignored the question. "One last thing. You said you were friendly with Townsend's first wife. Presumably you're not going to give me her name and address until you've checked me out, so would you be good enough to contact her and ask her to call the incident room?"

She hesitated so long that he wondered if she'd hung up.

"Mrs. Gough?"

"I hoped she'd never find out that Francesca's been sleeping with Edward," she said unhappily. "I thought it would all blow over and she wouldn't need to know."

"Why would she care?"

"She has a daughter of her own," she said before cutting the line.

NIGHTINGALE HEALTH CENTER

Harry Bonfield was reluctant to phone Sophie's parents until he'd spoken to her fiancé, Bob Scudamore, but her parents' address was the only next-of-kin detail recorded in her file. He remembered a psychiatrist friend in London whom Bob had mentioned over dinner one night as being a close colleague, and a phone call to him produced Bob's home and mobile numbers. Not for the first time, Harry blessed the clubby nature of the National Health Service. It was the biggest employer in the country, but it was still like a village where someone knew someone who could put you in touch in an emergency.

The long-distance relationship that Sophie and Bob had conducted throughout her time at the Nightingale Health Center had worried Harry considerably. Bob, five years older than she, was well up the ladder in the psychiatric department of one of the London teaching hospitals, and Harry had assumed it was only a matter of time before he popped the question and Sophie returned to London. It was becoming harder and harder to recruit young doctors into general practice, and he was pessimistic about the chances of keeping one of the best they'd attracted in years.

His worst fears had been realized two months ago when Sophie had wagged a diamond ring under his nose. "What do you reckon?" she'd asked. "Am I wise or am I wise?"

"Bob?"

She laughed and gave him a punch on the arm. "Who else would it be? God damn it, Harry, I don't have a closetful of secret lovers, you know!"

Belatedly, he stood up and pulled her into a warm hug. "Of course you're wise. He's a splendid chap. I just hope he appreciates how lucky he is to have you. When's the big day?"

"August."

"Mmm," he said gloomily. "Is this your way of telling me you're about to hand in your resignation?"

"God, no," she said in surprise. "Bob's been given a consultancy at Southampton. He's been angling for it for ages. It means we can finally live together. That's why we're making it official." She lifted her eyebrows in perplexity. "What on earth made you think I'd want to leave?"

The blinkered stupidity of age and ingrained habit, he thought wryly as he sat down again. It had never occurred to him that the man would move for the woman, even if this was the twenty-first century.

He reached Bob at his flat in London. "What can I do for you, Harry?" said the other amiably. "Are you calling because Sophie's going to be late?"

"Not exactly." Harry told him baldly and succinctly what he knew. "I didn't want to call her parents until I'd spoken to you . . . It's better, anyway, if you talk to them." He paused for confirmation.

"Good. Also, we need your help. Jenny says Sophie's very conscientious about keeping her cell phone charged, so we're assuming she's turned it off because she doesn't want these men to know she's got it. That means there's a good chance she'll call again as soon as she has an opportunity . . . and I'd be happier if I had someone here who was qualified to talk to them and negotiate her release."

"I'm leaving now," said Bob. "I'll call her parents on the way."

"We may not be able to wait for you," said Harry urgently. "We need someone closer. The police have been caught flat-footed . . . say they couldn't have predicted it . . . the riot's blown up out of nowhere . . . and they're overextended with this kid missing twenty miles away. We have a young constable trying to help us, but he can't even raise the probation office at the moment. It's complete bedlam. It would be useful to locate the psychiatrist who wrote Zelowski's pre-sentencing report, or anyone who saw him while he was inside. I can give you the two prisons he spent time in. They're both fairly local. Would that help you find a name for me? Even better, a copy of the report itself?"

Bob didn't waste time. "Give them to me," he said. "Also your direct line and the health center's fax number. I'll get back to you as soon as I can." He paused just before he hung up. "Harry?"

"Yes."

"If she calls before I get there, tell her not to provoke them . . . particularly the one who wants to rape her. If he's as dangerous as you think he is, it will only excite him."

OUTSIDE 9 HUMBERT STREET

Gaynor Patterson was terrified. She was trapped against the wall of a house on Humbert Street, unable to advance, unable to retreat. There was no freedom to move, just a press of humanity all around her, jostling to stay on its feet between the houses and the cars parked along the curb. Down the middle of the road, phalanxes of youths were charging in chaotic scrums to get to 23 and join the fun, but with each thrust of their powerful bodies, a compensatory ripple spread through the encircling crowd driving it backward.

Youngsters had sought escape on the roofs and hoods of vehicles, but they were precarious refuges. Every time a wave surged against them, the cars rocked on their suspensions and footing was lost. It was only a matter of time, she guessed, before the idea of turning the cars over and spinning them on their roofs would appeal to the wilder element in the crowd, and then people really would be hurt.

Her frantic 999 call on her mobile fifteen minutes earlier had increased her fear when a computerized voice informed her that the emergency operators were overwhelmed with callers reporting the disturbance in Bassindale. The police were unable to respond immediately. Callers with other emergencies should stay on the line. The advice to anyone in Bassindale not involved in the disturbance was to remain inside their homes.

Gaynor, who had seen footage of the Hillsborough Stadium disaster, when football fans had been mercilessly crushed by a stampede of people behind them, was terrified that a sudden catastrophic surge would cause the people against the wall to be suffocated. She was doing her best to protect those around her—mostly young girls who had fled to the edge to find safety—but it was getting harder and harder. She had shouted herself hoarse in a vain attempt to alert the people in the middle to their plight, but her voice was drowned out by the youths' shouting.

Desperate to find out what had happened to Melanie, and after her own attempts to raise her daughter had failed, she had handed her mobile to a girl at her side and told her to keep pressing the "1" button until someone answered. "Give it back to me when it rings," she said, while she shielded the youngster with her body. She tried to attract the attention of a man some twenty yards away who was big enough to make his way through to them, but he remained stubbornly deaf to her shouts.

Tired and tearful, the girl gave up after ten minutes. "It ain't no fucking use," she wailed. "No one's answering." She started hitting at Gaynor as claustrophobia overwhelmed her. "I wanna get out!" she screamed. "I wanna get out!"

Gaynor smacked her hard across the face. "Sorry, sweetheart," she murmured, folding the child in her arms as she burst into tears, "but it's too dangerous. You must stay here till I can work something out." *But what, for God's sake?*

The phone began to ring.

She grabbed it from the youngster, pressing a palm to her other ear so that she could hear above the din. "Mel? Is that you, sweetheart? I've been calling and calling. Are you all right? What about Rosie and Ben?"

"Mrs. Patterson?"

"Oh, shit!" swore Gaynor in disappointment, close to tears herself. "I thought it was my daughter."

"I'm so sorry. It's Jennifer Monroe at the Nightingale Health Center. Briony gave me your number. I need to talk to you very urgently."

Gaynor shook her head in disbelief. "You've got to be joking. Listen, love, whatever it is, it can wait. Even if you're going to tell me I've got terminal cancer, it's no way as urgent as what's happening here. Everything's out of control . . . there's no sign of the fucking police . . . and I'm trapped against a wall with some young kids who're shit-scared. It's like Hillsborough, for Christ's sake. There's got to be over a thousand people squashed into this area alone. I'm going to hang up. Okay?"

"Don't!" said Jenny sharply. "I probably know more than you do at the moment. Keep talking to me, please. This has nothing to do with medicine, Gaynor. I'm trying to help you. The police can't enter the estate because all the roads are barricaded. That means you and

Melanie *must* find safety for yourselves, and I might be able to help you if you let me."

"Go on then."

"Can you tell me where you are?"

"Humbert Street."

"Whereabouts exactly? You said you were trapped against a wall."

"Down at the end. Number nine. We've tried banging on the door . . . but the lady inside's brain's shot and she won't let us in . . . I guess she's frightened, poor old cow."

"Do you know what her name is?"

"Mrs. Carthew."

"Okay, hang on. I'm going to check to see if she's on our list." There was a few seconds' pause. "Got her. She's one of Sophie's and she's in the 'Friendship Calling' scheme." Another pause while voices were muffled by a hand over the receiver. "All right, Gaynor, this is the plan. I'm going to phone Mrs. Carthew and, while I'm doing that, I want you to talk to a police officer who's here with me. He's been listening to you on the speakerphone and he's going to advise you about what to do when Mrs. Carthew opens her door."

"You're wasting your time, love. She's been gaga for years."

"Let's see, shall we?"

Another voice came on the line. "Hello, Gaynor. Ken Hewitt. Right, the important thing is not to start a stampede. If everyone's frightened they'll pile in after you, and that's going to make the situation worse. What we need is a controlled exit. Can you tell me first how many youngsters you have with you?"

Gaynor did a quick head count. "Ten or so."

"Good. First, I want each one of those kids eased carefully through the door so that people around you don't know it's happening. Keep it very quiet. Okay?"

"Yes."

"Pick the two biggest kids, and tell one of them to create a throughway to the garden by clearing any furniture from the hallway and opening Mrs. Carthew's back door. Tell the other one to stand by the front door. The one by the front door *has* to be strong—if there's an adult close by, all the better. He or she will give you the signal when the way's clear and also act as your regulator, because I need you to be the marshal on the outside when the exit's established. If too many people try to push through when the door opens, then you and whoever's inside *must* close it and drop the latch. If you don't, people will be trampled in the hallway and the exit will jam. Stand in the doorway and only let one through at a time. It *must* be controlled. Do you understand?"

Gaynor was five feet four and weighed a hundred and ten pounds. How the hell was she supposed to hold back a stampede? "Yes."

"All right. Now, I've looked at the layout of Humbert Street, and there are gardens running back-to-back with the gardens of Bassett Road. The kid you pick for the back door needs to start breaking down fences to open up space. We're looking to create spillover areas for anyone who wants to escape. Tell the kid to break out toward Forest Road South. We need people to head for home . . . take some steam out of the situation . . . not mill around in the gardens at the back."

"Okay."

"Last, don't attempt to advertise the exit. As people start to feel the pressure easing behind them they'll move into the vacant space and come to it of their own accord. That'll make the job of controlling them much easier." He fell silent for a moment, listening to Jenny relaying instructions. "Excellent. Mrs. Carthew says she'll unlatch the door, but she needs time to go upstairs before you open it. She's frightened of being knocked over. She has a portable phone, so she'll confirm to Jenny Monroe when she's safe and I'll give you the go-ahead. Understood?"

"Oh, Jesus Christ!" Panic leaped in Gaynor's chest. "But I haven't explained any of this to the kids yet."

"Take your time," he said calmly. "It's important that they all understand what they're doing. Tell me when you're ready."

She knew one of the girls already, Lisa Shaw, a bright child in the same class as Colin. She wasn't big enough to act as a regulator, but she could certainly clear the hallway and lead the way out to Forest Road. She nodded immediately when Gaynor explained what she wanted her to do. More nods when Gaynor impressed upon all of them the importance of a "controlled exit" to prevent people from being hurt. A complete blank when she tried to make the biggest child understand her role. She was an immature giant with a slow brain and her eyes swam with tears when Gaynor asked her to man the front door.

"I'll do it," said Lisa. "She can help me. The others can clear the hallway." She smiled at Gaynor. "Don't worry. I'll see that they do it right. Col'll kill me if you get flattened. He reckons you're Supermum."

➤ Police Message to All Stations

➤ 28.07.01

➤ 15:33 ***

➤ Missing person investigation—Amy Rogerson/Biddulph

➤ ALERT ALL COUNTIES

➤ Wanted for questioning: Edward Townsend

➤ Registered address: The Larches, Hayes Avenue, Southampton

➤ Last seen: Hotel Bella Vista, Puerto Soller, Majorca 03:00, 27.07.01

➤ Returned to London Luton Friday A.M. on Flight EZY0404, arriving 08:25

➤ Registered vehicle: Black BMW—W789ZV V

➤ Believed to be somewhere in the south

➤ May be traveling with a child

SIXTEEN

Jimmy James was losing patience with the paramedic on the other end of the line. He'd had to wait five minutes before the ambulance operator answered, and now his battery was running out. What the hell kind of service were these shysters operating? Every time he followed an instruction, the man demanded more. He'd eased the policewoman into the recovery position and checked her airway for blockages. Confirmed all the major life signs—breathing, heartbeat, pulse. Tried to bring her around—without success.

And now the idiot was asking him to locate her wound.

"Look, mate, how am I supposed to talk to you and find out where she's bleeding at the same time?" he snapped, staring at his right hand, which was gory with the woman's blood. He felt bile rise up his throat. "It's okay for you . . . you're used to it . . . but it's not fucking okay for me. There's blood everywhere. I'll have to move her hair out of the way and I can't do that with a fucking phone in my hand. Okay . . . okay . . . I'm putting you down."

He laid the mobile on the floor behind him and, with a groan of disgust, used both hands to part the stained blond hair at the back of the woman's head where the already crusting blood seemed thickest. He picked up the phone again and felt it slip in his hand. "FUCK IT!" he roared. He heard the paramedic's alarmed inquiries through his own swearing. "Of course something bad's happened," he snarled.

146

"I've just smeared blood all over my sodding mobile. Yeah . . . yeah . . . I'm sorry, but it's making me sick, this is. I've got a thing about blood, okay? All right . . . all right . . . she's got a gash on the back of her head . . . I don't know . . . two inches maybe. I can't tell if there're any more . . . not without rolling her over . . . she's got long hair, for Christ's sake, and it's all over her face." More alarm. "No, of course, I'm not going to turn her over . . . you've already told me about pushing bone into her brain." He made a face. "Listen, pal, there's more of a problem with dirt . . . This sodding elevator's so filthy she'll die of blood poisoning if any of the germs get into her. Guys around here piss in it, you know. It's the fucking council's fault . . . If they pulled their finger out once in a while and sent some cleaners in . . . Okay . . . okay . . . I'm doing it now."

He put the phone down again and lifted hanks of hair from the woman's face. He hadn't seen it before, and he was startled by how pretty she was—pale and fine boned, like a Victorian china doll, with faint flushes of rose in her cheeks as if to prove there was blood left in her. With gentle hands he felt beneath the part of her head that was lying against the floor, but his fingers came out no bloodier than they were before.

"There's just the one cut as far as I can tell," he said, retrieving the phone, "and it looks like it's scabbing over . . . No, of course I haven't got a fucking bandage . . . Where would I get a bandage in a sodding elevator?" He rolled his eyes to heaven. "What do you mean, go look-ing for a first-aid kit? Listen, mate, I'm black as the ace of spades and I'm covered with blood. Think again, okay . . . There's no way I'm knocking on doors in this dump. Half of them're in their eighties and'll be scared witless if a bloody, wild-eyed nigger bursts in on them . . . and the other half're teenage Nazis who'll stick a knife in my ribs as soon as look at me. I'm in Acid Row, for Christ's sake . . . not the fucking Seychelles. Yeah . . . yeah . . . yeah . . . If you're that brave, then put some shoe polish on your face and tell those bastards on the barricades you're my cousin. Let's see how far *you* get."

He checked the battery level on his mobile. "I've got about another five minutes," he warned, "so you'd better come up with something fast." He listened, then raised his eyes to the elevator buttons. "The doors are opening and closing all right, so I guess it's working. No, pal . . . never heard of it . . . What the hell is 'Friendship Calling'? Mrs. Hinkley . . . flat four oh six . . . fourth floor . . . Yeah, I reckon I could live with that . . . so long as you talk to her first and she knows the score." He reeled off his mobile number. "I'll turn it back on in five minutes . . . Just don't forget to tell her I'll run if she starts screaming . . . I'm feeling sick as a dog here . . . and I don't need any more hassling." He listened some more. "Why can't I stay anonymous? What the hell difference does a name make? Okay . . . okay . . . Tell Mrs. Hinkley it's Jimmy James, and I live at Twenty-one Humbert Street. No, she can't look me up in the fucking book. I've only been there two days . . . Jesus! Because I've just come out of fucking prison. That's why."

OUTSIDE 23 HUMBERT STREET

Colin appeared suddenly at Melanie's elbow and shouted into her ear that she'd better do something quick because Kevin Charteris and Wesley Barber were handing out Molotovs to their mates. "I can't stop 'em, Mel. They're well lagered up. I've told 'em Rosie and Ben are in the house, but they just ain't interested."

She stared at him in alarm. "What are you talking about?"

"Gasoline bombs," he said. "The riot's been planned for days . . . ever since you and Ma said you was gonna march. Kev 'n' Wes 'ave been fillin' the bottles since Tuesday . . . Reckoned the only way to get rid of perverts was to burn 'em out. I told 'em the fire'd spread to your place, but they just said fuck off. Wes is stoned out of his head. He's such a dick . . . He's been droppin' acid 'n' speed and he's talking about burning the whole fuckin' road down."

It was a wake-up call. Like icy water being poured over her head. She couldn't keep looking to Jimmy for help, she realized. If her children were to survive, then it was up to her to protect them. "Where are they?"

Colin jerked his head toward a huddled group at the edge of the semicircular space outside number 23. "Over there."

In contrast to the bottlenecks at either end of the road, the space in front of the pedophile's house, and those beside it, had remained relatively clear, almost as if an invisible cordon were holding the crowd back. In a sense this was true, since those at the front, unwilling to be ousted from their grandstand view, were constantly pushing backward to counter the pressure from behind.

It had allowed Melanie to stand guard over her front door, hitting out at anyone who tried to encroach, but she drew no comfort from it since the reason for this jealous guarding of the space was excitement. It had become the gladiatorial arena where the more bullish of the youths launched their bricks and stones into the pervert's living room, destroying everything of value to the exultant "oohs" and "aahs" of the crowd.

"Stay here," she said, shoving her mobile into Colin's hand.

"What are you going to do?"

"Stop them," she said fiercely.

She charged across the tarmac and grabbed one of the youths by his collar. "Where's Wesley?" she demanded.

The boy tried to shake her off, but as he moved aside she saw Kevin Charteris squatting on the ground and flicking an unresponsive lighter to a gasoline-soaked rag in a bottle. "Oh, my God!" she stormed, seizing him by his ponytail and hauling him to his feet. "What d'you think you're doing, you stupid bugger?" She smacked the lighter out of his hand. "My house is next door, and my kids're in there."

"Fuck off," he said furiously, twisting to get away from her.

She hit him across the head with her other hand and swung him around in front of his friends. "Are you crazy or what?" she demanded.

"Where d'you get these bottles from? Whose fucking idea was it?" She jerked Kevin's head back. "It had to be yours and Wesley's, Kevin. You're the only ones stupid enough."

"Why d'ya always pick on me?" said the boy sullenly, his face flushed with alcohol. "Everyone's doin' it."

Melanie cast about wildly to see if he was telling the truth. "The whole place'll go up and who's going to put it out? You reckon those idiots on the barricades'll let fire engines through?"

"It was your idea, Mel," he said, yanking his hair from her hand and backing away from her. "You said you wanted to get rid of the perverts and that's what you're gonna get." He nodded to Wesley, who was standing behind her, and grinned when the boy tossed over another lighter. "We're gonna burn 'em for you."

She lunged at him but was held back by Wesley. "What about Amy? D'you want to burn her, too?"

"She ain't in there."

"She was seen at the door."

"It don't make no difference," he told her carelessly. "Stands to reason, she'll be dead meat under the floorboards by now. That's how it works, Mel. Perverts kill kids. We kill perverts." With another broad grin, he set fire to the rag and shifted the bottle to his right hand in order to lob it toward the shattered window of number 23.

He knew very little about how to construct a Molotov cocktail, and because he was drunk his reactions were slow. He did not know how quickly the neck of a bottle would heat up when the gasoline inside it ignited, or how dangerous a Molotov cocktail could be to the thrower. The principle behind such an incendiary device—to keep the gasoline contained in the bottle until it shattered against its target— was little understood by amateurs. Certainly Kevin had no idea of the value of screw-top lids or tying the rag around the neck of the bottle rather than stuffing it inside.

There was a frightened bellow from the crowd around him as, with a cry of pain, he dropped the bottle from scorched fingers and it broke on the road at his feet, engulfing him in flames. Like the ripple effect on a pool after the surface has been disturbed, the stampede to get away from him eddied out in frantic waves. His friends, ablaze themselves from their proximity to the exploding bottle, lurched backward, beating at their arms, chests and hair; women and children screamed as they were pressed into the solid wall of people behind.

Only Melanie, protected by the bodies of his friends, remained where she was, her attention focused on the fireball in front of her. She had time to think that she didn't even like Kevin Charteris. He was the evil influence that had caused Colin to be arrested twenty times for petty theft and vandalism, and he was so far out of control that he'd helped Wesley Barber put his mother in the hospital twice.

But she knew him—it wasn't some stranger on fire—and the tug of kinship was powerful.

She was screaming, too—she couldn't help herself—but in the midst of the bedlam she had the sense to take off her jacket and throw herself on Kevin, wrapping the leather around him and using her own weight to force him to the ground. She rolled him from side to side to smother the flames, gagging on the smell of his burning hair, eyes stinging from the heat of the blazing gasoline on the tarmac. She was aware of people coming to her assistance, dragging the boy away from the source of the fire, adding more clothes to the rolling body, before she was hauled backward and someone was beating at her head.

"You stupid bitch," her brother sobbed as he pushed her face down on the ground and threw himself on top of her. "Your sodding hair's on fire."

INSIDE 23 HUMBERT STREET

Franek's fist caught Sophie high on the cheekbone, rattling her brain. The blow was powerful enough to knock her off her feet, but the wall behind her kept her upright. Instinct made her fight back when there was no reasonable hope that anything she did would be effective. A second blow would knock her out. She responded with the only thing at hand—the chair—shoving it hard against him and bringing the seat into contact with his knees.

There was no logical thought behind it—she was too dazed for that—but when he grunted in pain she remembered the vase. Hit back or die. She seized the vase by the neck and smashed it against the wall, scything it toward his head in a desperate piledriver of a forehand. "You FUCKER!" she screamed, slashing the razor-sharp edges across his face.

He groped for his eyes, blood streaming, and she swung the vase again, slicing the skin on his fingers like the serrated fat on pork. "Get AWAY from me!" she roared, adding her other hand to the neck of the vase and balancing it for a double backhander. "GET AWAY!"

This time she missed him completely and the vase flew from her hand to shatter against the far wall. She was like a madwoman. Cursing. Bellowing. "FUCKER! FUCKER! FUCKER! I hope you DIE!"

She was reaching for the cricket bat to bring it down on his head when she was grabbed around the waist by his son and dragged away. "Stop! Stop!" yelled Nicholas. "Do you want to kill him?"

Sophie cradled the bat in one hand and drew the chair against her with the other, rearranging her defenses, crouching like a kestrel on a post, watching like a ferret. She couldn't speak because she couldn't breathe. Like Franek earlier, adrenaline and panic had collided in her chest to rob her of oxygen. But in her head a scream of hatred circled: Yes! Yes! YES!

Nicholas tried to pull Franek's hands away from his eyes but the old man resisted, rocking and keening to himself. "I think you've blinded him," he said, turning toward Sophie.

She lifted the bat above her head, ready to bring it down in a chopping blow if he took a step forward.

"I don't want to hurt you," Nicholas protested, spreading his hands in a pacifying gesture. "But this is all so crazy. Why do you keep provoking him?"

She didn't move, just kept watching him.

Outside, people started screaming in terror.

9 HUMBERT STREET

Gaynor heard the screams from her place in Mrs. Carthew's doorway. She looked up for a moment, half thinking she could hear Melanie, but the sound of an engine somewhere in the distance distracted her. "Something's happening," she told Ken Hewitt into her phone, as people squeezed past her one at a time.

"What?"

"People are screaming," she said fearfully, "and I can hear an engine. Could that be the police coming?"

"I don't think so." There was a short pause while she heard the sound of his radio. "I can't get through at the moment," he told her calmly. "Just keep going, Gaynor. How many have you got out so far?"

"I don't know. Fifty maybe. It'd be quicker if we let them through two at a time. They're starting to push."

"Don't," he said urgently. "You won't be able to control it."

The warning came too late.

Cries of alarm from the crowd farther down as they stampeded from the burning gasoline spread panic like wildfire at Gaynor's end of the street. Frightened people in front of the door pushed to get through and, unable to keep her feet, she was carried in with them. She clung desperately to the handle to pull herself in behind the door, then shoved Lisa and the big child toward the garden. "Get out now," she ordered. "Go home."

They were ripped away by the flood, and she saw Lisa's face turned toward her as she was carried along. "Look where you're going!" Gaynor screamed after her, flattening herself against the wall. "Stay on your feet!" But the child was already out of sight.

There was nothing Gaynor could do except stand and watch. She felt bruised and battered from the flailing hands that shot out to find support as bodies thrust through the doorway, but she knew there was no way she could close the door on her own if a catastrophe happened. No way she could prevent the pushing and shoving as desperate people struggled to stay upright. No way she could slow their impetus.

She was responsible. If she hadn't insisted on the march—even been proud to be one of its leaders—none of this would be happening. She found herself praying: "Dear God, please don't let anyone die." She repeated it over and over again without pause, as if continuous intercession were the only way to hold God's attention. But she knew He wasn't listening. At the back of her mind lurked the awful guilt of the lapsed Catholic. If she'd been a better person, listened to the priests, confessed her sins, attended church . . .

COMMAND CENTER—
POLICE HELICOPTER FOOTAGE

The video link from the air to the command center ten miles away gave an alarming overview of what was happening on the ground. Activity was concentrated around Humbert Street and the barricades at the four entrances to the estate. It was estimated that some two to three thousand people were massing in and around Humbert, with spillovers in Bassindale and Forest, while the barricades were attracting a river of recruits as word spread of their existence. The police were powerless to act. Events had taken them by surprise, and they lacked the manpower to respond.

The watchers in the center stared in disbelief at the aerial pictures of Humbert Street, wondering what malign fate had placed the pedophile on a road where the short-term policy of filling in gaps between properties to create more accommodation had turned it into a solid-walled maze. It would lead to argument and recrimination afterward, with the police blaming council officers for refusing to take their warnings about access seriously, and the council blaming the police for not doing their jobs properly. For now, all anyone could do was watch as the ignorant mob, unaware of the danger it was in, squeezed relentlessly into a space that was too small to take it.

The sheet of flame as Kevin Charteris's gasoline bomb exploded, followed by the thrust of panic as the crowd surged away from the flaming tarmac, was caught vividly on camera. It was as if a giant magnet had suddenly reversed its poles and impelled people outward like so many iron filings. There was terror in the upturned faces of women and children as they were slammed into one another or forced against the constraining walls of houses. Sickening pictures of youngsters falling under trampling feet. Only the exit through Mrs. Carthew's house offered any hope of a lifeline as a stream of wildly stampeding people fled into the tablecloth-sized garden in the back, crashing through fences to reach the relative safety of Forest Road.

A separate focus of activity was the Co-op Supermarket and the shops surrounding it. Rightly or wrongly, the managers had chosen to close when the first rumors of trouble reached them, and the security grates across the windows were now under heavy assault from axes as a fifty-strong band of thieves attempted to plunder the goods. This activity, too, was attracting recruits, and groups of youths, wearing baseball caps to disguise themselves from the hovering helicopter, were pouring toward the area to pick up any scraps the axe wielders left.

Evidence that there was some preplanning of the riot showed most clearly in the organized way the cars had been positioned at the entrances. This was no random overturning of vehicles where they stood, rather solidly built fortifications, shaped like arrowheads and angled out toward the main road in a deliberate attempt to frustrate any push by police armored vehicles to ram through them. Fires were being lit in the gardens to either side, piles of tires and green-wood branches, saturated with gasoline—further evidence of preplanning—driving thick black smoke toward the slowly assembling riot squads on the other side of the main road.

Even as officers in the command center were watching the pictures, they were already questioning why there had been no prior warning that something of this magnitude was brewing in Acid Row. The assumption continued to be that news of a pedophile in their midst had roused the estate to anger—a view bolstered by reports from social workers and housing officers—but it wasn't at all clear from the video pictures whether the masked youths on the barricades were linked to what was taking place on Humbert Street or had taken advantage of the estate's discontent to launch a war of their own.

It was a female officer who summed up what most of them were thinking.

"We'll be crucified when the press get hold of this."

GLEBE TOWER, BASSINDALE ESTATE

Jimmy James and Mrs. Hinkley stared at each other suspiciously as the elevator doors opened. Neither was impressed. *She* looked ancient. *He* looked shifty. *She* had a bad-tempered mouth like an inverted horseshoe. *He* was a dandy, covered with gold jewelry. *She* was like his aunt . . . fond of lecturing. *He* was a crook . . . who had never come by that jewelry honestly.

Her face softened as she looked at the policewoman. "Can you lift her into this?" she asked, pointing to the wheelchair in front of her. "Our friend the ambulance man said you must keep movement to a minimum . . . If she has a skull fracture, the important thing is to avoid slivers of bone going into her brain."

"I do know that," said Jimmy through gritted teeth.

"Then don't do anything in a hurry . . . and you must support her head very carefully . . . like a baby's."

He bared his teeth in a wolfish smile. "Sure thing, baas."

"It's Mrs. Hinkley."

She looked him straight in the eye, daring him to continue playing the fool, and the likeness to his aunt intensified. But she was far too thin—his father's sister was a barrel of a woman—and there was a suggestion of slovenliness about Mrs. Hinkley, with her lank white hair, ill-fitting shoes and old cardigan with frayed cuffs and darns in the elbows, which implied poverty or carelessness.

He relented slightly. She was doing him a favor by agreeing to help him, and it wasn't her fault that they came from different generations and different cultures. He offered a bloodstained hand. "Mr. James . . . Jimmy to my friends."

He hadn't expected her to shake it—it wouldn't have worried him if she hadn't—but she surprised him by taking it warmly between her two. "Splendid. I'm Eileen to mine. Shall we proceed? I have bandages in my flat. Also washing facilities."

The wheelchair was obviously hers, because she clung to his arm, walking with a dragging limp, as he pushed the policewoman to the flat. "I broke my hip two years ago," she explained, "and I haven't been steady on my pins since. In here," she said, pushing open the door to her bedroom. "Put her on the bed, and I'll see what I can do about cleaning some of this blood out of her hair. Did the ambulance man explain how you were supposed to lay her down?"

"Yes." He looked at the frilly cream bedspread with matching pillowcases. "I'd better take these off first," he said, reaching down to pull the spread back.

She smacked his hand. "No."

"They'll get ruined," he warned. "Look at me." He gestured at his clothes. "All my decent threads fucked to blazes."

She tut-tutted at the obscenity. "I have to sleep in this bed," she told him. "I'll throw the spread away if necessary."

He couldn't see the logic. "It's a good one. Why don't we just put her on a sheet, then all you have to do is make the bed again afterward?"

"Because I can't," she said crossly, holding up arthritic claws. "I have a home helper who comes in every week to do it, and she's not due again till next Friday. It's the reality of old age, I'm afraid. Dependence on others to do—rather badly—what you did so well yourself just a few years ago. It's deeply frustrating. It makes me want to scream sometimes."

He eased her aside and stripped the bed down to the bottom sheet. "I'll do it for you," he told her as he lifted the policewoman carefully out of the chair and eased her into the recovery position on the flat surface.

"Hah! You'll be long gone before the ambulance gets here," said Eileen shrewdly. "Now that you're rid of the responsibility, you'll be off like a rocket."

She was right, of course. "My pregnant lady and her two kids are out there," he said. "I need to know what's happened to them." He saw the disillusionment in her eyes. "What time do you usually go to bed?" he asked.

"Nine o'clock."

"Then I'll be back before nine. Is that a deal?"

"We'll see," she said, bending over the young woman and feeling the pulse in her neck. "A deal's only a deal when it's honored." She pointed toward a bathroom on the left. "There's a tin bowl in there and a tray with some cotton and disinfectant. There's also a roll of bandages in the cupboard over the basin. I need the bowl filled with warm water and everything brought out here. If you clear the bedside table first and pull it forward, we can use it as a work surface."

He did as she asked, and watched while she set about cleaning the matted hair. "Are you a nurse?" he asked.

"Once upon a time till I started a family. Then I became a volunteer with St. John Ambulance."

"Is that why the paramedic knew you'd help? He talked about something called 'Friendship Calling.'"

"It's a telephone club for people who can't get out," she explained, rinsing the cotton in the tin bowl. "Among other things, we take turns calling all those who're poorly, and if we don't get an answer we alert the ambulance service. I'm one of the organizers, which is how they knew my number."

"You're a bit of a saint then?"

"Good Lord, no, I just like good gossip." She looked up for a moment and chuckled at his expression. "Yes, yes, all about the good old days and how dreadful modern youth is. But I expect you're the same. Everyone over seventy's senile. Isn't that what you think?"

"Sometimes," he admitted. "They're pretty rude, that's for sure . . . Act as though everyone has to respect them whether they deserve it or not."

"In our day, we respected our elders without question."

"Yeah, but things have moved on. You can't demand it anymore. You've got to earn it." He gave an Ali G flick of his fingers. "Like I have no trouble respecting you—you're working with me—but there're others who wouldn't have opened their doors."

"I doubt I would if they hadn't phoned to tell me what was happening. You're hardly an old lady's dream, Jimmy." She carefully swabbed around the long cut in the policewoman's head, her gnarled fingers curled around the cotton. "Poor child. Who on earth could have done a thing like this?"

"Is she going to die?"

"I shouldn't think so. Her pulse is strong."

"She's lost a hell of a lot of blood."

"Head wounds always bleed, but they generally look worse than they are."

He envied her calmness. "You're very relaxed about it."

"We can't make her better by screaming and shouting. In any case, skulls don't fracture easily." She nodded toward the bathroom. "Go and clean yourself up," she ordered, "while I put a pad on the wound to protect it. When you're finished, bring me the smelling salts from the second shelf of the bathroom cabinet. They're in a green bottle. We'll see if we can bring her around."

Jimmy always thought of it afterward as a little miracle. One pass of the bottle under the young woman's nose, and she opened her eyes and asked where she was. Why did people do that? he wondered. Was awareness more about *where* you were than *who* you were? Did you need to be sure you were safe before you could acknowledge anything else?

Whichever, his relief was intense. He hadn't wanted her to die. He didn't approve of people hitting women, not even policewomen.

Eileen watched the fluctuating emotions show themselves in his face and, with a hoarse *"harrumph,"* tapped the back of her hand against his leathered arm. "She has you to thank for this."

"I didn't do anything."

"You could have left her."

"I did," he admitted honestly, "till I remembered I'd left my fingerprint on the fucking elevator button." She frowned disapprovingly. "Sorry. I get a bit lippy when I'm stressed."

She gave another little chuckle. "The ambulance man told me to expect a big nigger with blood all over him who had just come out of prison and couldn't speak without uttering obscenities." Her eyes twinkled at his look of surprise that the description had been so blunt. "He said he didn't know how true it was because he was simply passing on your own description of yourself . . . but in his opinion you were a hero and he'd put money on the fact that I could trust you." She watched a blush darken his cheeks. "Give me a kiss," she said gruffly, "then go and look for your lady friend and her kiddies. I hope they're all right."

He planted a smacker on the wrinkled skin.

"And make sure you're back by nine," she finished severely, "or I'll never make a deal with you again."

OUTSIDE 23 HUMBERT STREET

Complete mayhem followed Kevin Charteris's self-immolation. People scattered in all directions, crashing into one another, fighting to get away from the flaming tarmac. Spread-eagled on the road beneath her brother, Melanie saw Kevin being carried away by his friends, using her leather jacket as a stretcher, the skin of his head red and raw where the flames had fed on his glossy auburn ponytail. She flung Colin off and touched her hands frantically to her own head.

"It's all right," he told her. "Most of it's still there."

Her teeth started to chatter with shock. "They ought t-to leave K-Kevin where he is," she said urgently. "C-call an ambulance. I s-saw this p-program that said p-people can d-die of shock."

"I guess they reckon it's better to take him to the barricade," said Colin uncertainly. "There're cops up there can get him to the hospital."

She shook her head. "Why d-did he do it? I t-told him not to. D-didn't I, Col?"

"Yeah, yeah, but we've gotta get out of here," said Colin, hauling her to her feet. "They've all gone fucking mad. Jesus!" He fended off a hurtling body, dropping Melanie's mobile unnoticed beneath stamping feet, and dragged her toward the sidewalk. "There's gonna be a fight in a minute."

She was trembling from head to toe. "I don't know what to do," she wailed. "What about my babies?"

"You're gonna lock yourself in with the kids while I go looking for Jimmy," he said purposefully.

"He's g-going to be mad at me," she wailed. "He said this would happen."

"Yeah, but he won't be mad till after you're safe," said Colin. "And that don't matter a fuck. Come on, Sis, get a grip. I know it ain't no picnic, but you've gotta be strong for Rosie and Ben. The poor little bastards'll be scared shitless by now." He gripped her arms to imbue her with some of his steel, but she wasn't looking at him. He watched her eyes stretch wide in horror, turned to see what she was looking at and saw Wesley Barber launch another flaming Molotov at the pedophile's door.

"Oh, *shit!*" he said in tearful despair. "Now we're *really* fucked!"

- Police Message to All Stations

- 28.07.01
- 15:43
- Bassindale Estate
- MAJOR ALERT
- Riot squads in place
- Entry to Bassindale imminent
- Orders awaited

- UPDATE—W.P.C. HANSON
- Situation secure

- UPDATE—HUMBERT STREET
- Controlled exit operating
- Panic reported
- Possible attack on 23

- UPDATE—DR. MORRISON
- No new information

SEVENTEEN

Nicholas cradled his father on the floor, supporting him across his knees in a surreal parody of Michelangelo's *Pietà*. The old man lay unmoving, face turned toward his son's chest, tiny rivulets of blood crusting on his neck. No one spoke. In the extraordinary stillness of that back bedroom, cluttered with unpacked boxes and small bits and pieces of unwanted furniture—relics of the Zelowski family history— Sophie had a sense that for these men conversation was a rare interlude in the silence that dominated their lives.

In another place, at another time, she might have mistaken Nicholas for a monk. There was something very ascetic about his thin, expressionless face that seemed inured to passion, and she wondered if he'd schooled himself to hide his feelings or if he lacked feelings altogether. He was *hiding* them, she thought, remembering his shocked reaction to the determined way she'd attacked his father. Raw emotion frightened him.

But did that make him an ally or an enemy? She couldn't decide as she listened to the screams of the crowd still echoing outside. *Would he support her version of events or his father's?* In the distance she could hear a helicopter, and she relaxed slightly at the thought that rescue was imminent. *Did it matter whom Nicholas supported? Would she still want to prosecute when this was all over? Did she hate Franek that much? Weren't they all in the same boat? Terrified out of their wits?*

164

"I can hear a helicopter," she said, recognizing from Nicholas's expression that he could hear it, too. "Do you think it's the police?"

"It has to be."

"Oh, God, I hope so," she said fervently.

He began to make excuses. "Life would be easy if we never did anything we regretted. But things happen . . . accidents . . . people in the wrong place at the wrong time. It doesn't make you evil . . . just unlucky." He raised his eyes. "Do you know the Aesop fable about the scorpion and the frog?"

Sophie shook her head.

"The scorpion wants to cross a river, but he can't swim so he begs a frog for a ride. The frog begins by refusing because he's afraid the scorpion will sting him. The scorpion laughs and says he's not that stupid. 'If I sting you, you'll die,' he tells the frog, 'which means I will die, too, because I can't swim.' This persuades the frog to do as the scorpion asks, but halfway across the river the scorpion stings him anyway. 'Why did you do it?' asks the frog as he's dying. 'I couldn't help myself,' says the scorpion. 'It's my nature.'" He touched his father's head. "Talk of my mother always makes him angry," he went on. "If you'd done as I asked and stayed quiet, he wouldn't have hit you."

"You mean submit . . . like you?" She smiled sarcastically. "It's not in my nature."

"It's easier."

"You're worse than he is," she said. "He's brutish . . . uncivilized . . . disgusting . . . but *you*"—she shook her head in disbelief—"you let him do it. What sort of person does that make you?"

He gave a small shrug, metaphorically washing his hands. "I did try to warn you."

"How?" She raised her fingers to her cheek and touched the puffy flesh. It was aching all the way down to the bone, and she wondered if it was broken. "All I recall is being told to shut up . . . do as I was ordered . . . let your father believe he could control me."

"It's the same thing."

She searched his face, looking for something—*anything*—that would persuade her he didn't believe what he'd just said. She found nothing. In his philosophy, it seemed, the victim took responsibility. The aggressor none.

"He wouldn't have hit you if you hadn't made him lose his temper," he said, as if to prove the point.

Sophie took a firmer grip on the cricket bat. "Why didn't you warn *him*? Why didn't you tell him you'd break his arms if he touched me again?"

He flexed the fingers of his right hand and watched them with a strange sort of fascination. "It wouldn't have stopped him," he said.

"Why not?"

"He's not afraid of me."

Sophie was appalled, watching the son keep the father quiescent by stroking his fleshy breasts. She couldn't have spoken, even if she'd wanted to.

NIGHTINGALE HEALTH CENTER

A call came through on Harry Bonfield's direct line five minutes after Bob Scudamore had phoned to say he was in his car and hoped to be at Nightingale within an hour and a half. He told Harry that a Dr. Gerald Chandler—*"good bloke . . . works closely with my future boss at Southampton"*—would be phoning in the next few minutes.

"I'm on the Isle of Wight and it's the holiday season," said Chandler regretfully. "Even if I managed to get my car onto one of the ferries, I still can't reach you any quicker than Bob can. I'm attached to all three prisons here in various capacities, but my work is principally with sex offenders in Albany." He was silent for a moment while he gathered his thoughts. "I remember Milosz Zelowski well. I liked him, as a matter of fact. He's a shy, rather pleasant man . . . fantastic musician . . . retreats inside his head all the time to listen to jazz.

Imaginary, of course . . . he plays it out entirely for himself . . . things he's composed or things he's heard. The danger for Bob's fiancée is that he's severely emotionally repressed . . . and deeply introverted. I can fax through my notes on him. They're not particularly easy to read . . . they're a handwritten transcription of the tapes I made of my interviews with him . . . but they'll give you an idea of the sort of person you're dealing with. The full typed report's at my office . . . I'm willing to drive there, but it'll mean another thirty minutes before you get them."

"Fax the notes," said Harry, "but give me a quick rundown first. Does this repression make him dangerous? Would he rape Sophie?"

Chandler considered the question carefully. "Under normal circumstances, no," he said. "He's not very highly sexed and his predilection is very definitely young men. He finds the whole idea of penetration deeply disgusting and prefers not to ejaculate if he can help it. It's like anal retention in children who refuse to perform on parental demand. Shedding his seed gives him the heebie-jeebies. That's not to say he isn't interested in orgasm for himself . . . but it's a very private thing. He uses masturbation of others as a form of manipulation. In simple terms, anyone he pleasures is under his control as long as they continue to derive pleasure from what he does. The three boys he was convicted of molesting were engaged in homosexual activity already . . . they all admitted to it. They also admitted to being in love with Zelowski and plaguing the life out of him . . . so he gave them what they wanted in order to control them. They all described him as an unemotional man, which doesn't mean he wasn't attracted to them, merely that he keeps his feelings well hidden."

"But he *is* a pedophile?"

"Yes. Insofar as he suffers from a psychosexual disorder that predisposes him to find adolescent boys attractive. But I'm doubtful he'd have done anything about it if the boys hadn't found him attractive first. He's a likeable man. Says very little . . . listens a lot. He was a Samaritan in prison. Used to sit for hours with suicidal men, hearing their problems. He understands internalized fear and pain rather better than most."

"Why did the boys betray him?"

"They didn't. He was caught *in flagrante* with the most recent one, and confessed to the other two under questioning. It was the parents who insisted on the prosecution—they wanted someone to blame for their sons' homosexuality—and the judge made an example of him. It's a common story. We live in a puritanical society that refuses to acknowledge that children have sexual feelings. No court today would dare accept that a kid could be a seducer, despite the statistical evidence that shows the U.K. has the highest number of teenage pregnancies in Europe." He sounded irritated. "It's sexual curiosity, for God's sake . . . Been going on for centuries, and arbitrary laws putting ages on when it's legal to indulge don't make a blind bit of difference. You have to persuade . . . not coerce."

Harry, who had to deal with the consequences of teenage pregnancies for girls and their distraught parents, agreed with him, but now wasn't the time to discuss it. "What about exceptional circumstances? Would he rape her in the situation they're in at the moment?"

"Difficult to say. If I understood Bob right, they're trapped with Zelowski's father inside a house with a riot going on outside."

"Yes."

"And the police think Milosz is the target?"

"Yes."

"It's a potent cocktail. They'll all be very frightened—for different reasons—and fear is a powerful emotion. How will Sophie react do you think?"

"I don't know. She's a levelheaded girl, but she's got quite a temper when she's aroused. I can't see her giving in easily."

"That's what Bob said."

"Is that good or bad?"

"It depends on how the two Zelowskis react to it. I certainly agree that the father is the more dangerous to her, but Milosz may be aroused to see her fight back, particularly if his emotions are already in turmoil because he's afraid of the crowd. He's had very little experience with women. His mother left when he was five and, as far as I could discover, he was a complete loner at school and music college. At the moment I'm struggling to understand the logic of why his father's with him when one of the recommendations in my report was that Milosz should sever all links with him as his primary abuser. I assume he was too frightened to live on his own—a lot of them are—which is why the recommendation was ignored, but it was damn stupid of his probation officer. What's worrying me is that Milosz won't do anything to *prevent* a rape . . . and may even feel emboldened to take part if he's excited enough. It depends on what combination of stimuli are needed to release his emotions."

Dear God! "What do you know about his father?"

"Only what he told me himself. It's all in the notes. I asked him why he hadn't cited his father's abuse in his defense or mitigation plea, but he said it wouldn't have been fair because his father didn't know that what he was doing was wrong. It's probably true, too. He claimed his father's family was of Polish Gypsy origin and he was brought up in a culture where the dominant male sets the rules of behavior within the family. From what Zelowski told me, it seems pretty clear the man has a strong sadistic streak. He says he remembers his mother being flogged one day because her cooking wasn't good enough . . . so I imagine the sex was pretty brutal, too. Certainly Milosz was subjected to considerable violence as a child until he learned to use masturbation as a method of deflecting his father's anger."

Harry felt queasy. "At the age of five?"

"Yes. It's sickening, isn't it? But we're looking at a very low grade of intelligence. There was no attraction to children per se; the son was simply expected to fill the sexual void after the wife left. A frightened child is always an easy mark, and it's a lot simpler than going out and making new relationships. According to what Milosz told me—so I've no independent evidence of this—his father took to curb-crawling and picking up prostitutes. That's when his abuse of Milosz stopped. He was questioned several times after women ended up in the hospital with battered faces, and Milosz was always expected to provide an alibi. He did it, of course, because it was the only way out of his own abuse, but he said he felt bad because it reminded him of what used to happen to his mother. The police may have records of the questioning. Could be worth a shot?"

Harry made a note. "Was the father employed?"

"On and off as a laborer." A sarcastic note entered Chandler's voice. "More off than on, I gather. According to Milosz, he suffers from asthma so he was usually too sick to work, but it didn't sound very convincing to me. I'd say he was working the system."

"Mmm." Harry wondered how genuine the panic attack was that the son had given as the reason for needing a doctor. "Was the mother Polish?"

"No, English. Milosz remembers very little about her except that she was blond. His father won't have her name mentioned. All he ever told the boy was that he spent the war in Spain to escape the Nazi persecution of the Gypsies . . . made his way to England in the early 1950s . . . and married Zelowski's mother in order to obtain residency rights. He said she was a prostitute when he met her, and went back to it when he kicked her out after finding her in bed with another man."

"Why didn't she take the son with her?"

"Who knows? Wasn't allowed to? Couldn't afford him?"

"What does he feel about that?"

"According to him, nothing . . . and in a sense he's right. He's been so successful at repressing his emotions that his mother's rejection seems no worse than anyone else's. He's learned to cut people out of his head . . . puts music in their place. As a matter of fact, he registered higher emotional disturbance at the memory of being fired from his music department than he ever did talking about his mother."

"In what sense is he wrong?"

Another pause for thought. "He tried to cut off his penis when he was first convicted . . . sawed away at it with a plastic knife. It didn't work, of course, but he told me afterward that it was a serious bid to castrate himself. He wouldn't explain why, except to say he was ashamed, but it does suggest he has some fairly powerful emotions that he's not admitting to."

"What about his father? How does Milosz feel about him?"

"Neutral. Neither loves him nor hates him—though I imagine it's the most comfortable relationship he's ever had. He's been controlling his father since he was five years old, so the old man holds no surprises for him. That's why I felt it was important to break the dependency . . . not because the abuse continues—it stopped when Milosz went to secondary school—but because he needs to externalize his feelings instead of masking them inside his head with jazz tunes."

Harry rubbed his hair anxiously into a bird's nest. This was well beyond anything he understood about the human psyche. "So how do I handle them? What do I do if Bob isn't here and Sophie passes her phone to one of them and leaves the negotiating to me?"

There was a long pause. "In different ways, they're both dangerously egocentric—the one extroverted and probably sadistic, seeking his pleasure outside . . . the other introverted and repressed, seeking his pleasure inside—which suggests that neither of them will be seeing Sophie as a person. Merely as a means to an end."

"What end?"

"Whatever they've decided . . . together . . . or separately. To one she may be an object of desire. To the other she may simply be the hostage who keeps them safe. Perhaps one sees her in both guises. Perhaps both do. There are several permutations, Harry. You'll have to listen to what they say and try to work it out."

14 ALLENBY ROAD, PORTISFIELD

Little had changed in the Logan house, except that Kimberley had ceased her crying. Barry and Gregory still sat morosely watching television in the front room, and Laura remained closeted in the kitchen. There was no question of any of them going outside. Photographers, their long lenses focused on the front door, were camped behind barriers at the end of the street, hanging like leeches on the family's misery.

Laura had moved to a chair at the table, her strained, white face showing her exhaustion. Tyler shook his head gently as he opened the door and saw hope leap into her eyes. "No news of her," he said, pulling out another chair, "but that's a good sign, Laura. We really are optimistic that she's alive."

"Yes." She placed a hand on her heart. "I think I'd know if she was dead."

He smiled encouragement, leaving her with her illusions. He'd heard the same sentiment expressed a hundred times, but the link between people who loved each other was in the mind, not in the body, and real pain only began when death was certain.

"I need to ask you some more questions about Eddy Townsend," he explained.

She dropped her head abruptly to shield her eyes, and he cursed himself for letting her off the hook earlier. He should have realized that her obsession with hiding was too pathological to be confined to Rogerson alone. But he wondered what secrets could be so bad—*or criminal?*—that she would gamble on her daughter's life by not revealing them. What lever would pry them out of her now?

"We suspect Amy might be with him," he told her bluntly. "He returned early from Majorca, and a car similar to his was seen in Portisfield yesterday with a child answering Amy's description in the passenger seat."

She stared at him with such a bleak expression in her dark eyes that he knew she had been afraid of something like this from the beginning.

"I need to know what happened, Laura."

She dropped her face into her hands and ground the heels viciously into her lids as if she were driving out her devils. When she spoke, it was like an emotional dam bursting. "He was so handsome . . . so sweet . . . completely different from Martin. He really *cared*—about me . . . about Amy. It was all so different . . . so *attractive* . . . he called us his little princesses." Her voice broke on a half sob, half laugh. "Can you imagine how that felt after being treated like Martin's hired help for ten years . . . making excuses for the fact that we were in his precious house . . . walking on tiptoe so he wouldn't know we were there . . . never opening our mouths so he couldn't find something to criticize? I should have listened to my father . . . he said Martin only wanted a trophy . . . a bit of fluff on his arm that proved he could still get it up . . ." She lapsed into silence.

Tyler waited. He wanted the story in her words, not his.

"Martin went completely berserk when I told him I was pregnant," she went on at last, "accused me of doing it on purpose. I knew the deal . . . no children . . . why hadn't I taken precautions? He tried to force me to have an abortion . . . said if I didn't he'd throw me out without a penny." A very hollow laugh. "So I went to a rival lawyer to see if I could get the house if we divorced."

This time the silence was interminable, as if she were replaying the entire episode in her head.

"What happened?"

"They were in the same lodge. I should have known they would be . . . As far as I can see, the whole profession works on dodgy handshakes. You scratch my back; I'll scratch yours." She tugged her hair across her face. "Give my client a break . . . if you want a blind eye turned, I know this judge . . . I know these policemen. The law is corrupt."

He felt he had to defend his colleagues. "It really isn't like that, Laura. Masons are bound by the rules just like everyone else."

"Are you one, too?"

"No."

"Then don't apologize for them."

He didn't want to lose her. "Fair enough. What did this lawyer do?"

"Told Martin why I'd consulted him . . . said I seemed to have a pretty good knowledge of how much he had and where he'd stashed it . . . warned him he could lose a lot more than the house if he didn't mend fences." Her voice rose. "He wasn't acting for me, he was acting for my husband. I could have been free . . . had a home . . . brought my baby up the way I wanted"—a shudder ran through her body—"but it wasn't my lawyer who told me that, it was Martin . . . afterward . . . when he said what a fool I'd been. He *loved* that, you know. It made him feel powerful . . . getting back at the pathetic little woman who *almost* got away."

"What did he do?"

"Martin?"

"Yes."

She dropped her hands beneath the table. "Offered a reconciliation before the divorce papers could be filed . . . said he couldn't live without me . . . claimed it was shock that had made him react the way he did. God, I was stupid. I actually *believed* him. He said he wanted to do the right thing by his baby . . . and I was *glad*." She couldn't keep the hands hidden for long. She was too expressive. She smacked the knuckles together in recrimination. "I used to blame it on being pregnant . . . you know, hormones out of kilter making you so desperate for security that you'll do anything . . . now I know it's me. I'd rather delude myself than face the truth."

Tyler wondered suddenly if he'd been misjudging her. He had thought her an intelligent woman—calculating, even—who had some control over the events in her life. Now he saw her as a piece of

flotsam, directionless, passive, waiting for events to change her. It would explain her tirade against Gregory and his children, he thought. She had been willing to bottle up her hatred and frustration indefinitely, until Amy's disappearance allowed a confrontation.

"Why didn't you pursue the divorce when you realized the reconciliation wasn't genuine?"

She shook her head. "You keep trying . . . hoping things'll get better. In any case, I felt guilty because I loved the baby more than I loved him . . . and he knew it. The same thing happened in his first marriage."

"Is that why he didn't want any more children?"

"Yes."

"It's a different kind of attachment, though, isn't it?"

"Not to someone like Martin. He needs to be the center of attention."

"What does he do when he isn't?"

"Makes life hell," she said simply.

He watched her for a moment, recalling her words of last night. "By exercising power without love?" he suggested.

"Yes." A sigh. "It's verbal abuse. A constant drip-drip-drip of insults. You're stupid . . . you're slow . . . you're an embarrassment. He used to tell Amy how thick I was . . . then get her to say something clever to prove she took after him and not me. You end up believing it after a while." She gave an unhappy shrug.

"Did Amy believe it?"

"I didn't blame her. All she wanted was her father's approval. Sometimes I wished he'd hit me so I could prove he was abusing me . . . Confidence is very shallow."

"Is that why you liked Eddy Townsend? Because he gave you your confidence back?"

She nodded. "It was so easy for him. He used to come to our house regularly on business, so he knew what Martin was like." Another hollow laugh. "All he had to do was be pleasant, and I turned him into a saint. It's pathetic, isn't it? Maybe Martin's right . . . maybe I am thick."

"Or lonely," said Tyler. "We've all been there at one time or another. You shouldn't put yourself down."

She pressed the heels of her hands into her eyes again, and he guessed she was holding back tears. "He started coming around when Martin wasn't there . . . that's how the affair began. Then he said he wanted to take videos of me because he couldn't stand being away from me . . . needed something to remind him that I loved him." Her voice faltered. "Oh, God! I was so flattered. Can you believe that? What sort of sad little bitch flaunts herself naked in front of a camera because a man says he loves her?"

Franny Gough, thought Tyler soberly. It was one hell of an M.O. Persuade a woman you loved her, then make movies of her masturbating. Did any of them ask what happened to those images? Did it cross their minds that they might end up on the Internet to be drooled over by millions?

"Thousands every day," he said unemotionally. "Men do it, too. It's no big deal. We're fascinated by our bodies. We love them. We hate them. Most of all we want to know what they really look like . . . and you can't tell that from a mirror."

His kindness destroyed her. It was awhile before she was composed enough to speak again. "I should have known, though."

"What?"

"That he didn't want me . . . he wanted *her*. He was forever asking her to dance for him or sit on his lap and tell him stories. She loved it . . . it's all she ever wants to do . . . make people smile. And I thought what a fantastic man he was . . . so patient . . . so kind. Martin just got angry when she showed off. It took the limelight away from him."

"When did you first start to worry about Eddy?"

She threaded her fingers through her hair, yanking at it. "When I found him making a video of her in the bath," she admitted. "He'd been bad tempered for weeks—nothing I did pleased him—then I saw him looking at her . . ." She lapsed into silence again.

"When was that?"

"Two weeks before we left."

"Why didn't you leave immediately?"

"I couldn't be sure. He'd filmed her everywhere, you see . . . playing in the garden, playing in the house . . . always with her clothes on. I thought maybe I was overreacting, because I knew the sort of videos he'd made of me. And she wasn't a bit upset . . . rather the opposite, really . . . she liked being filmed . . . so I didn't think he'd asked her to do anything bad." She raised haunted eyes. "I should have known," she said again.

"What happened then?"

"Nothing much for about a week, then he started being unkind to her. He wanted her to sit on his lap one evening after school, but she refused and he smacked her. After that, he just kept picking on her for no good reason."

Sexual frustration? wondered Tyler. Did he find children more attractive than the girly-looking substitutes? Or was a child who masturbated on film more profitable? "Did you ask him why?"

"No." It was a whisper.

"Why not?"

Her eyes filled with tears. She opened her mouth to say something, but the words seemed to stick in her throat. Instead she shook her head.

"You were too frightened?"

She nodded.

"Of him or of what he was going to say?"

"I thought he'd try to keep us there," she managed.

"How could he have done that?"

She shook her head again, but whether because she didn't want to say or didn't know wasn't clear. Tyler allowed the silence to lengthen.

"Amy loved him," she said at last. "If I'd said I was taking her away, he'd have told her."

"What would she have done?"

"Made life unbearable . . . like Martin. They're very alike." Another long pause. "I lied to her. I said Eddy was bored with her and had told me to take her away before he started hitting her."

"Which is when you went to the hotel?"

She was on surer ground. "Yes."

"How did Amy feel about that?"

"She was difficult for a few days, but only because she was unhappy about leaving school without telling anyone. She was worried that if we kept moving she'd never make any friends . . . kept asking why we couldn't go back to Bournemouth."

"Not Southampton?"

"No. She never mentioned Eddy."

"What explanation did you give?"

"I said if she wanted to go back to Bournemouth it would mean her living on her own with her father . . . and she said she'd rather be with me." She looked at Tyler for reassurance. "She wasn't lying, you know. In all the time we were living with Eddy, Martin made no attempt to see her or contact her. She phoned him a few times . . . but he was always busy. She knows he doesn't love her . . . didn't want to be with him . . . not on her own anyway . . . even if this"—she gestured around the kitchen—"wasn't what she wanted either."

Whatever Tyler's feelings for Amy before—more objective than involved, as he would admit himself, if he was to do his job successfully—he was appalled by the terrible turmoil the child must have been suffering. What was love? Her mother's resigned dependence on men? Her father's indifference? Townsend's lust? Ephemeral school friends? Was a smile synonymous with affection? Did she dance and tell stories to feel wanted?

"Did Eddy try to contact you after you left?" he asked Laura.

"He couldn't. He didn't know where we were."

"Nor did Martin?"

Laura shook her head.

"Would Amy have given either of them the number here? Did she write letters? Did she have the means to pay for a call or buy a stamp?"

She clasped her arms across her chest and rocked in misery. "I told her not to," she said.

"But you didn't ask?"

"I was too— I hoped . . ." Her eyes filled with tears again. "She thinks I'm stupid . . . and I truly can't bear it when she lies to me."

No, thought Tyler, you'd rather delude yourself than face the truth. At least to that extent she understood herself, although whether she would ever be able to forgive herself for it was another matter.

▼

Barry said he didn't remember Amy receiving any calls at the house, but agreed that, as he and Kimberley slept until noon, they might have come through in the mornings before she left the house. He said she'd made at least three calls from a public telephone in town during the first week of vacation.

"It was before she started disappearing," he said. "The three of us went down to the center a couple of times. She made one the first day and two the next."

"How did she pay for them?"

"Called collect."

"Did you listen to what she said? Hear the name of the person?"

"Nope."

"Where were you standing?"

"Close the first time. Miles away the second."

"Then you'd have heard the first call. Try to remember, Barry."

He shrugged. "I wasn't interested. You don't listen when you're not interested. She was crying, anyway, so it was embarrassing." He quailed before the inspector's irritated frown. "It might have been someone whose name began with 'M,' 'cos Kim said afterward it was fucking rude to call someone by his initial."

▼

Tyler went upstairs to check with Kimberley, then returned to the kitchen. "What does Amy call her father?" he asked Laura.

"Daddy."

"Not 'M' for Martin?"

"No," she said, rather shocked. "He'd never have let her."

Tyler had guessed that. "Does 'M' mean anything to you? Barry and Kimberley both say she called someone from a public phone and called him 'M.' She called collect, so she must know him well. At the moment I can only think of Em . . . short for Emma. Did she have a school friend in Southampton or Bournemouth with that name?"

The final vestiges of color drained from Laura's face. "She swallows her *D*s," she whispered. "She was saying 'Ed.'"

EIGHTEEN

Sophie had lost track of time because her watch had stopped. Whenever she looked at it, it read the same as when she'd been trying to work out how long she'd been a prisoner. There was so much silence in the room she felt as if she'd been there for days. The beat of the helicopter blades came and went. The screams from the street rose and fell like a Mexican wave. She strained to pick up anything that would give a hint as to what was going on.

"It wasn't the police," she murmured at last. "They'd have broken in by now."

"They'll have to clear the street first," said Nicholas.

It was true, she told herself determinedly. These things *did* take time. How long was a piece of string? How many policemen were needed to quell a riot? Nicholas returned to staring at the wall in front of him, with only the odd flicker of his eyes toward the door betraying any kind of concern. Franek appeared to be asleep.

She couldn't understand Nicholas's composure. Was his habit of submission so ingrained that he accepted everything without question? Did he lack imagination? Or was hers too active? She made an effort to clamp down on the endless hypotheses that took turns bedeviling her brain, but it was like trying to stop a runaway horse. There was nothing to do in the oppressive silence inside that room except replay her fears.

Why was the response so delayed when she'd told Jenny she was afraid of being raped? Was something worse happening somewhere else? Suppose the police couldn't get through? What would happen? How long would they have to remain like this? What if men from the crowd banged on the door and claimed to be officers? How would Nicholas and Franek know the difference? How would *she* know? Should she call out? Should she stay quiet? What if the room was stormed? What did the people outside want? To frighten? To kill?

She had to talk to remain sane. "Do you have a job?" she asked Nicholas.

Reluctantly, he shifted his attention back to her. "Not anymore."

"What was it when you had it?"

"Teaching," he said flatly.

"What kind of teaching?"

"Music."

"What made you give up?"

"I was fired."

It signaled the end of the conversation unless Sophie was prepared to ask him why he'd been sacked. Which she wasn't. It was an area that she'd rather leave unexplored. She had no idea if Fay had had any real knowledge about a pedophile in the street, or whether it was a rumor that had spiraled out of control, but she had to assume there was a connection between what Melanie had told her and what was happening outside.

She recalled Nicholas's discomfort when she'd asked him if he'd known Amy Biddulph in Portisfield and Franek's remark about the police causing trouble for them "by banging on the door and conducting interviews about the missing girl." The fear that the child's body was somewhere in the house kept trying to intrude, but she blotted it out to avoid panic overload. The police would have searched for Amy, she told herself, and they certainly wouldn't have left the men unguarded if there was any suspicion that one or both of them were involved in her disappearance.

But which of them had been interviewed? That question could not be blotted out so easily. She wanted it to be Franek, but reason told her it was Nicholas, and she had no wish to hear him confirm it. It could only make the situation worse—once secrets were out they lost their shame—and she would rather keep Nicholas as an ally, however imperfect, than force him to reveal that he was as bad as his father.

Again, silence prevailed. Again, she found herself concentrating on the sounds from outside. The direction had shifted. Some of it seemed to be coming from the gardens. "There are people shouting at the back now!" she exclaimed fearfully.

Nicholas heard it, too, because he glanced nervously toward the window.

"You said they couldn't get around without breaking the fences," she accused him.

"I expect that's what they've done."

His refusal to understand implications enraged her. "Then where are the police?" she hissed. "You keep saying they're out there . . . but *where*? They wouldn't let the crowd run riot in the gardens. That's not how it works. It's all about containment and controlled channels of escape. They seal roads, designate safe exits. I've taken courses in this . . . it was part of my training in hospital emergencies."

"What difference does it make?" he said quietly. "There's nothing we can do except wait."

She stared at him in disbelief. "Is that it? We hide our heads in the sand and hope the problem goes away?"

He smiled slightly. "Nothing's ever as bad as you think it's going to be," he murmured.

"No!" she snapped, stress getting the better of her. "It's usually worse. Do you know what the pain of cancer's like? Do you know how brave a person has to be to suffer the agonies of having their organs eaten away by tumors?" She jabbed a finger at him. "Do you know how many of them want to kill themselves? *All* of them. Do you know how many of them stick it out for the sake of their families?" Another ferocious jab. "*All* of them. So never . . . never . . . never . . . say to me again that nothing's as bad as you think it's going to be."

"I'm sorry."

"Don't keep apologizing," she stormed. "*Do* something!"

He hadn't intended it as an apology. He had spoken with genuine sympathy. Her fear was a physical thing that needed constant expression, and there was nothing he could say that would allay it. She hadn't experienced real terror before, didn't know that the mental torture of anticipation was a thousand times worse than the brief pain of reality. But it wasn't something he could teach her. She had to learn it for herself. "We could board up the window in case they start throwing stones again," he suggested.

She glanced around the room. "What with? How would we attach it anyway? We need nails . . . a hammer. That's a *stupid* idea." She paused to gather her thoughts. "We need to know what's going on," she said desperately, "and that means we'd be better off in one of the front bedrooms. At least we'd be able see if there are any police out there. We're going to be in danger from broken glass wherever we are."

He must have agreed, because he eased his father into a sitting position and half rose with an indecisive move toward the wardrobe. "It's a trick," Franek muttered, gripping him by the arm to hold him back. "Don't listen to her. She confuses you with lies so she can escape." His face was streaked with blood where the vase had scored a cut across his forehead, but there was nothing wrong with his eyes, which fastened again on Sophie.

Nicholas spoke sharply in Polish.

Franek answered him, then tightened his grip on his son's arm so that his knuckles stood out sharply. "We do as I say. We wait here, where it's safe."

There was no more argument. The old man's authority was too strong. Nicholas settled back beside him, rubbing his arm vigorously when Franek released him. "We'll be all right," he reassured Sophie. "This is England. The police will come."

GLEBE ROAD, BASSINDALE ESTATE

When Aunt Zuzi had asked Jimmy at fourteen years old, following his first police warning for shoplifting, who was the most important person in his life, he had answered: "Me." Her response had been tart. "Trust you to admire a fool," she had said.

He had always been a disappointment to her—average at school; preferring white girls to black girls; bringing shame on the family with his tangles with the police; refusing to go to church—but it never occurred to Aunt Zuzi that she was partly to blame for his behavior. She had taken the place of his dead mother in his father's household, and had run a regime of disparagement from the day she moved in. Nothing her three nephews did was good enough.

Jimmy's two younger brothers had become withdrawn and compliant, struggling to conform to the Aunt-Zuzi view of what men should be—hardworking, God-fearing nonentities who abnegated their authority to the women who ran their homes. It was a *black* thing. Which (abnegation) was precisely what Jimmy's father did. Relieved to be rid of the responsibility of his growing family, he had tamely handed his paycheck to his sister each Friday, then vanished for the weekend with whatever he'd managed to steal from it without her noticing. She would belabor him viciously when he finally came home, smelling of women and booze, and only succeeded in confirming his view that the less time he spent with her and his children the better.

It was a vicious circle from which neither of them could break free. Aunt Zuzi resented her unmarried state, for which she blamed men—either directly, because none had shown an interest in marrying her—or indirectly, because her brother and nephews cramped her style. Jimmy's father resented her presence in his house but understood that it was a necessary evil if his children were to be cared for. It had led to unhappiness for everyone, particularly Jimmy, who was old enough to remember his mother and whose rebellion against her supplanter's merciless belittling had led him inevitably to prison. As, of course, Aunt Zuzi had predicted it would.

How different it was in Melanie's family, where children were loved unconditionally and every transgression excused with "he/she didn't mean to do it." Jimmy had argued many times with Melanie and Gaynor that this kind of unthinking love was just as bad as no love at all. "Look at Colin," he would say. "He's just as bad as I was at his age, but where I got beaten for it and told there was no way Aunt Zuzi would appear at the nick on my behalf, you both go running off at the drop of a hat to berate the cops for arresting him. What kind of message are you giving him . . . that it's *okay* to get himself in trouble?"

"Being beaten didn't stop you from stealing, though, did it, darlin'?" Melanie would say. "Just made you worse. So why d'you want my mam to beat our Col? Can't you see it's better to let him grow out of it naturally . . . knowing his mam will always be there for him?"

"Col's a rebel," was Gaynor's response. "There's no legislating for it. Some of us are . . . some of us aren't. I'm one . . . Mel is . . . We don't like being told how we're supposed to live our lives. And if that kind of thinking is in your nature, then it don't make a darn bit of difference whether you're loved or hated . . . You'll still be a rebel. The difference is, if you're loved, there'll always be a place where you're welcome."

Jimmy remained convinced there was a middle way—something between the heavy-handed rod and liberal, unconditional love—but the Patterson lifestyle was seductive. He hadn't seen or spoken to his father or Aunt Zuzi for five years, although he kept in irregular touch with his brothers, but he couldn't imagine a future without Melanie and her extended family.

Which was why he was worrying about them now. He skirted the shopping district, where looters were ripping off every last item, and made his way toward the intersection of Glebe Road and Bassindale Row North. The smell of burning was heavy in the air and distant shouting seemed to be coming from Humbert Street, but he decided to take a quick detour up to the Bassindale entrance to see how close the police were to breaching the barricade.

According to what he had been told by Eileen Hinkley, whose friend was watching through binoculars from her ninth-floor flat in Glebe Tower—"*a bit dippy . . . lost her husband a year ago . . . thinks anyone who comes to her door wants to rob her . . . a bit like the senile old fool upstairs who throws his furniture around whenever he gets it into his head he's been robbed*"—Armageddon, or something very like it, was being fought in broad daylight on Acid Row's streets.

"She's a great believer in sinners being held accountable on the Day of Judgment," Eileen told Jimmy, "but that can only happen after the battle between good and evil." Mischievously, she tapped a claw against her temple. "She's completely potty, of course, and very hazy about how it's supposed to work. She keeps telling me she's going to be saved because she's booked her place among the righteous, and I keep telling *her* she's living in cloud cuckoo land. It's the nature of religion that we're all damned—we'd have to worship every god to be sure of a place in heaven—but she won't believe me."

Jimmy grinned. "So you might as well be an atheist and enjoy yourself?"

"That's my view," she said cheerfully. "You're damned if you do . . . and damned if you don't . . . so make the best of it while you can."

He waved at her. "I'll see you later."

With sudden concern, she placed a claw on his arm. "Be careful, Jimmy. My friend said she wished it was nighttime."

"Why?"

"Because the police are losing the battle . . . and she wouldn't know that if she couldn't see it. Apparently they're camped on the main road, unable to enter the estate. The goons are setting fire to everything in sight. She's frightened out of her wits . . . thinks we're all going to be murdered in our beds . . . and that despite her confidence in her own salvation."

"Are *you* frightened?" he asked her.

"Not yet," she said drily. "But at the moment I've only got her word for what's happening . . . and she always exaggerates."

Not in this case, thought Jimmy in dismay, as he stared at the scene of devastation in front of him. Armageddon wasn't a bad description. All that was needed was for the Four Grim Horsemen of the Apocalypse to spur their steeds through the driving smoke, and fantasy would become a horrible reality.

Overturned cars in the jaws of Bassindale Row were violently ablaze, sending an oily, choking, black pall into the air from the melting rubber tires and the latex foam of the seats inside. It had started with a misdirected Molotov cocktail that had landed short of its target—a police vehicle—to spray the upturned bottom of an ancient Ford Cortina instead, exploding its leaking gas tank. The wind blowing off the rolling fields behind the estate and down the concrete-lined draft of Bassindale Row had sent the dense fumes away from the youths on the barrier into the eyes of the police, and the idea of blanketing the "pigs" in blinding smoke was promptly adopted.

Jimmy wasn't the only one to recognize that it was a shortsighted policy. The barricaders had tied scarves across their noses and mouths, ready for when the wind changed direction and swung the advantage the other way. It wouldn't help them—the smoke was too thick and cloying to be filtered by fabric—and the police would argue afterward that the masks were employed to disguise and not to protect.

There on the ground, Jimmy foresaw only that the arrest of anyone caught in the open when the barricade was breached was inevitable. A swirling gust punched a hole in the black pall of smoke, giving him a momentary glimpse of the police armory and serried ranks of black-uniformed riot officers beyond. *Jesus!* he thought, sliding back into the shadow of a doorway. It was like something out of *Star Wars*.

As he backed away, a small kid raced down the road toward the barricade and, to a crescendo of whooping and hollering, lobbed a flaring gasoline bomb through a gap in the smoke. The flame flickered in its arc like a will-o'-the-wisp before igniting in a sheet of flame across the tarmac in front of the police. It had a tenth of the beauty of a firework, but a thousand times the excitement.

This was war.

OUTSIDE 23 HUMBERT STREET

Wesley Barber's Molotov had also found its target. A sheet of flame roared up the front door of the pervert's house, feeding on the oil in the gloss paint and melting it in glowing strips from the door. To Melanie, who had seen fires only in the movies, this was a catastrophe. Such a blaze could never be contained. Once it took hold of number 23 it would pass within minutes to Granny Howard at 21a and Rosie and Ben at 21.

"Oh, my God! Oh, my God!" she screamed, running toward it. "Do something, Col! Do something!"

He tried to hold her back, but she was too strong for him, and he watched in desperation as she stamped at the outer fringe of burning gasoline on the path in a vain attempt to get closer to the door and kick the fire out. If she'd still had her jacket she'd have had some protection, or could have used it as a blanket to smother the flames. As it was, she was wearing only a T-shirt and shorts and the heat was too much for her.

With a howl of despair, she turned away to shield her face and sank to her knees in front of the crowd, sobbing hysterically, her hands clasped in appeal in front of her.

A hush fell. Wesley Barber, about to light a second bottle for another attack, had it snatched from his hand by one of his friends. "That's Col Patterson's sister," he snarled. "D'ya want her to burn, too?"

Wesley, slow-witted and pumped up on drugs and adrenaline, bellowed furiously into the silence: "Who fucking cares? It's only a white bitch."

Everyone heard him. Melanie certainly did. She rose unsteadily to her feet and wiped her tears away with the back of her hand. She carried more authority than she realized, not only because she and her family were well known on the estate, but also because she was so obviously pregnant. As usual, her dress, or lack of it, revealed more than it covered, and no one could misinterpret the way her hand dropped to protect her naked, swollen tummy.

"My baby's black!" she shouted at Wesley. "Do you wanna murder blacks, too?" She raked the crowd with a scathing glance. "Is this what you came for? To watch wasted retards like Wesley Barber kill people? How's anyone gonna get out if these houses start burning? There're old people and kids on this street. Are you gonna be proud of yourselves when dead kiddies're brought out on stretchers? Is it gonna make you feel good?"

It was a message that wasn't lost on the women. Or on Colin. With more courage than he knew he had, he walked the ten yards to stand beside his sister and take her hand, publicly fixing his colors to her mast and ranging himself against his friends. It was a poignant symbol of what had set all this in motion—love of family and a desire to safeguard children—and these two slight figures, looking pitifully young with their tear-streaked faces, restored some sanity.

A middle-aged black woman pushed out of the crowd to join them. "You keep going, love," she told Melanie. "You're doing the right thing." She raised her voice. "Come on, sisters!" she bellowed in a deep, throaty roar, which carried farther than Melanie's higher pitched voice. "Let's have some solidarity here. This ain't nothing to do with race." She stared Wesley down. "And you'd better get your black ass home, boy, before I decide to tell your ma what you called this lady. Mrs. Barber's a fine woman, and she'll whop your hide for it."

A former school friend of Melanie's slid away from her boyfriend. "I'm up for it," she called, shaking herself free of his clutching hand and running to stand by Colin. "Youse'll all get charged with murder if you don't back off," she scolded the crowd. "This whole bloody thing's just crazy. My gran's only three houses down, and she ain't done nothing to any of youse. It ain't her fault there're perverts on the road but if you burn them, you burn her, too."

Others joined them, making a brave little line in front of the burning door. It stopped any more gasoline bombs from being thrown, but Wesley wasn't the only one to lick his lips excitedly as the pine beneath the gloss caught fire and began to shower their backs with sparks.

▼

Jimmy dropped back down Bassindale Row but made no attempt to push his way through the bottleneck at the end of Humbert Street. Instead he bypassed it and turned right into Bassett, which was the next parallel road. This, too, was thronged with people, most of them women, standing on the sidewalk outside their houses, desperately asking for news of the police. Where were they? Why weren't they doing something? Did Acid Row not matter? Rumors of gasoline bombs were rife. As were stories that houses were being left to burn because fire engines couldn't get past the barricades.

Jimmy steered a path down the middle of the road and pretended ignorance whenever he was addressed directly. If they were that concerned, they could do what he had done and take a look for themselves. The more the better. If even half of these women decided on positive action instead of wringing their hands and complaining about police inaction, the kids on the barricade would be caught with an army behind and an army in front and the chances were they'd slink away with their tails between their legs.

Forest Road South was in flux when he reached it, with frightened people, mostly teenagers, forcing their way down the middle to get away from Humbert Street and others pressing up the sidewalks to reach it. There was shouting from the ones in the middle.

"Go home, for Christ's sake . . ."

"It's out of control . . ."

"Kids are being trampled . . ."

Jimmy caught a girl by the arm. "What's going on?" he asked her.

She smacked at him in fear. "Let go of me, you bastard!"

"I don't want to hurt you," he protested. "My girlfriend's in there. Melanie Patterson. She organized the march. Do you know her? Have you seen her?"

She took a breath. "Her mum's helping people get out," she stuttered, pointing toward a gap in the fence fifty yards away. "She's in there."

"What about Melanie?"

She tried to pull away from him. "I don't know," she wailed, beating at him again with panic in her eyes. "This has nothing to do with me. I just wanna go home."

He released her immediately and shouldered his way toward the broken fence. It was becoming increasingly obvious to him that there was no shelter anywhere in this lunatic asylum. Anarchy ruled. But what did they want? he wondered. To bring the house down on top of their heads? Destroy the little they had for a few hours of glory? Leave the Mrs. Hinkleys of this world to pick up the pieces after the tantrum was over? Did they even know?

It was all mad. As many youngsters were forcing their way in through the fence from the road as were desperately struggling to get out, and Jimmy guessed that the frightened warnings of the escapees, far from acting as a deterrent, were stimulating a rubbernecking curiosity. He pushed his way inside, using his bulk to force a passage, and looked across the bobbing heads to see what was going on. It was pandemonium, bodies jostling for position in the confined space of the

first garden, some pushing one way, others pushing another. He saw a friend of Melanie's brother, Lisa, thirty feet away in a gap in the next fence along, angrily remonstrating with a group of youths. She was in tears, desperately trying to use her negligible weight to stop them from forcing a way in.

As Jimmy watched, one of the boys made a lunge at her, grabbing at her shirt to dislodge her. Jimmy started forward, his towering figure sweeping youngsters aside like confetti, watching while the child fought like a tigress to hold the gap. Good for you, girl, he thought, as he saw her brace herself against the fence posts on either side of the gap, kicking her sharp little feet at the boy's shins.

Jimmy hooked an arm around her attacker's neck, chopping at his hand to break his grip on Lisa's clothes. "What's going on?" he demanded, using his full two hundred and fifty pounds to hold back the press of bodies behind him.

"She's already let loads through," said one of the other boys sullenly, "so what's the fucking deal about us?"

"I couldn't stop them," Lisa sobbed hysterically, pulling her shirt across her flat chest. "You're all so fucking ignorant. You think it's fun."

Jimmy looked past her to the chaos in the gardens behind her. "What's the plan?"

She took a deep breath to hold back her sobs, realizing the urgency of making him understand. "Make an exit to Forest Road. Persuade everyone to go home. We've got a door onto Humbert Street open. Melanie's mum's there. She said to make sure this side stays open. But it's not working 'cos people keep pushing through the fence."

"Okay." Jimmy squeezed his arm tighter around the neck of the boy he was holding and shot out his other hand to grip his sullen friend by the throat. "Nod if you know who I am," he instructed.

The youth nodded.

"Then don't mess with me, because I'm pretty pissed off already about what's been going on. This is the deal. My lady and her family are on Humbert Street, and I want them out. You and your friends are gonna help me. Do you understand?"

Another nod.

"Good." He loosened his hold on them both. "How many of you? Six? Seven?"

"Seven."

He selected the four biggest by putting his hands on their shoulders and stationing them in front of Lisa in the gap. "Guard it," he ordered them. "If anyone gets through from this side, I'll come after you and beat the fucking shit out of you." He bared his teeth in a wolfish grin. *"Capeesh?"*

More nods.

"Lisa will send people out behind you. And you three"—he touched the heads of the remaining boys—"will help get them out onto Forest Road. That means you've got to clear this area first. I'll start you off, then it's up to you. All right?"

"They won't listen to us," said the boy whose throat he'd grabbed.

"Sure they will. Gimme that piece of fencing." He nodded toward a sharp-pointed slat that had splintered when the panel had been pushed over to create the exit. "This is Armageddon," he told them, "and you're on the side of the angels for the first time in your miserable lives." He worked saliva into his mouth, seized the slat in a meaty hand and turned around, his eyes bulging from his head and froth foaming at his mouth.

"WH-AAH-AH!" he roared, brandishing the spear above his head like Cetshwayo in *Zulu*. "WH-AAH-AH!"

It was the stuff of legend. A huge, mad black geezer putting the horde to flight. The retreat was instantaneous. No one wanted to confront a madman.

Jimmy's eyes were still bulging when he turned toward the youths. "You'd better be here when I bring my lady out," he warned them, "or you're all fucking dead."

There was no dispute. Only an idiot would argue with a total maniac.

He gave Lisa's shoulder a comforting squeeze as he edged past her. "Give me a shout if they try to run away. I'll be listening." She stared back at him with frightened eyes, and he gave her a quick, encouraging wink. "Don't worry, darlin'. Everything's going to be fine."

She believed him and drew confidence from it . . . but she might have felt differently if she knew how often Jimmy James had been wrong.

He wouldn't have been in prison so often if he'd occasionally been *right* . . .

NINETEEN

There was a sudden drop in the noise from outside as a single voice—a girl's—rose above the crowd. Franek tapped his chest in satisfaction. "It is the police," he said. "First they frighten . . . then they bring order. It is the way of things."

"We'd be able to hear megaphones," said Sophie, listening.

"You always argue," said the old man angrily. "Why not just accept that Franek is right? Is this so hard for you? Where is your courtesy toward the elders?"

"You've done nothing to earn it," she said fiercely. "And what sort of crap is"—she dropped into mimicry of his accent again—'First they frighten . . . then they bring order'? You talk as if they're the Gestapo. What do you think they've just done? Shot every tenth man to encourage the others?"

A sharp flurry of Polish.

"It would be better if you don't mention the Gestapo," said Nicholas uncomfortably. "Many of his family died during the war."

"A fair number of mine did, too," she said dismissively. "There isn't an Englishman alive today who didn't lose grandparents or uncles or aunts. It doesn't pass the 'so what' test. Trying to embarrass me into silence isn't going to make what he says any more sensible. There still haven't been any sirens," she reminded Nicholas.

"Perhaps they don't want to aggravate the situation."

She shook her head. "There'd be *something*," she insisted. "They know you're in here. They wouldn't leave you in fear unnecessarily." (She meant "me," of course. They wouldn't leave *me* in fear unnecessarily.)

Franek gave a snort of irritation. "Enough of this! Who cares what they do if it sends these"—he gestured contemptuously in the direction of the street—"*animals* back to their cages?"

A scream bloomed in Sophie's head, and she had to fight to control it. "I thought *you* were the animal," she snapped back. "*Animal . . . ! Fucker . . . ! Pervert . . . !*" She emphasized each word. "Isn't that what they called you?"

"What do you know of anything?"

"I know *you're* the one in the cage, Mr. Hollis."

Nicholas laid a restraining hand on his father's arm. "Please don't do this," he begged Sophie. "It isn't necessary."

"It is to me," she said angrily. "Your father's wrong, and you know it. Something terrible's happening outside . . . and we're sitting here like idiots waiting for it to happen because you haven't the guts to confront him."

He raised a placating hand. "He needs to believe what he's saying," he murmured. "It stops him from panicking. As a doctor, you should understand that."

"Yes, but as his prisoner, I don't," she said curtly. "As far as I'm concerned, the sooner he has another asthma attack the better . . . and you can bloody well do the honors this time, because I'm not going to lift a finger to help him."

Another silence fell. They were invariably dictated by Nicholas's refusal to answer, and Sophie wondered if his unwillingness to talk was a form of apathy or a form of manipulation. He surprised her by speaking suddenly.

"It's wrong to abandon your principles," he said quietly, "whatever the circumstances."

She might have accused him of being patronizing if he hadn't said it so gently. "What are *your* principles?" she asked.

He thought for a moment. "Tolerance . . . conciliation . . . under-standing. I'm not persuaded that provocation and anger achieve any-thing."

Neither was Sophie, nor was she persuaded that sitting on his hands while his father launched an assault on her came under any of those headings. It was her privilege, as the victim, to turn the other cheek; not his, as the passive bystander who hadn't even been hurt.

"Conciliation isn't about doing nothing," she said. "It's proac-tive . . . positive . . . hard work. You have to get between people to prevent confrontation, not look idly by while confrontation is happen-ing. It's what I want to do with that crowd out there . . . but you won't let me because you'd rather keep me as a shield to hide behind. And that's not 'understanding' or 'tolerance.'" She paused. "It's cow-ardice."

He wouldn't meet her eyes, but Franek chuckled. "You more use to us in here," he said. "You keep us amused with your little tantrums. You so scared you can't keep your mouth closed even for a minute." He held up his hand and worked his fingers and thumb like a duck's beak. "Quack . . . quack . . . quack. Your mamma should have taught you to keep it closed. You'll drive a man mad with your nagging. But maybe you don't have one, eh? Maybe they all run away because you so bossy."

Briefly, she closed her eyes, inhaling deeply through her nose. *God, how she hated this old man . . .* "The world's changed since you last had anything to do with a woman, Mr. Hollis."

"What is this supposed to mean?"

She caught the warning glance that Nicholas flicked in her direc-tion and took a firmer grip on the cricket bat. "The only woman who would come near a Neanderthal like you," she spat at him, "would be one you had to pay . . . and a whore would say or do anything as long as you gave her money up front. So don't tell me how to make a suc-cessful relationship . . . You haven't even been able to do that with your son."

His eyes bored into her. "Milosz gets on fine with his dada . . . always has. You ask him if you don't believe me."

"There'd be no point," she said. "He's already made it clear he believes in tolerating people, and presumably you fall into the category he's prepared to tolerate, otherwise he wouldn't be living with you."

"There you are, then. You wrong."

"Except I wouldn't describe an uneasy truce between an ignorant, violent bully and a man who sits in silence as a successful relationship." She raised a sarcastic eyebrow. "It works for you because you need to believe in the fantasy that you have some control, but it isn't working for Nicholas if he has to turn off his feelings in order to live with you." She stared him down. "So don't tell me I'm wrong, Mr. Hollis, when you don't know any better than I do what your son really thinks about you."

He jabbed his finger at her again. "You be quiet now . . . you no longer amusing."

"The truth never is," she said with a small laugh, "particularly if you're prone to panic attacks."

"I make Milosz shut you up," he warned.

Sophie studied the son's bent head and the way his thin hands writhed in his lap and decided not to test him. She kept thinking about her telephone call, wondering if Jenny had understood what she said. Her thoughts were an unconscious echo of the question the women in Bassett Road were asking. *Did Acid Row not matter? Did rape not matter?*

She felt a terrible guilt for her own self-deprecating sense of humor. It must be her fault. Jenny had thought she was joshing. She was always making stupid jokes about sex. *"What do you mean it's big? You should see an elephant's . . . they're so big they dangle on the ground . . ."* *"If you don't give it a rest occasionally, it'll drop off . . ."* *"My mother always said a man could be turned on by the backs of a woman's knees . . . but I didn't believe her . . ."*

She should have called the police directly. No policeman would have considered a woman's cry of "rape" a joke. Perhaps she still should? Indecision racked her again. *What to do? What to do?* The mobile was her one trump card. Her only lifeline with the outside world. If she revealed that she had it, Franek would certainly take it away from her to prevent her from giving her version of events. If she didn't reveal it, how would anyone know what was happening here?

GARDENS BETWEEN HUMBERT STREET
AND BASSETT ROAD

With Jimmy cajoling and threatening all intruders to join the exodus toward Forest Road, the gardens between it and Mrs. Carthew's house began to clear. Some of the elderly householders, emboldened by his authority, emerged to lend a hand. One old boy, sporting a tin helmet and a fearsome-looking machete—relics of his war service in the Far East—stood guard over the broken fence between number 9 and number 11 while Jimmy pursued a gang of boys who were making their way to the back of 23.

They weren't much over ten or eleven years old, and he caught up with them as they started throwing stones at the windows of a house with a jungle gym in the garden. He waded in, cursing them. "What the hell do you think you're doing?" he roared. "You can't count, you stupid little bastards! This isn't twenty-three! What does the jungle gym tell you?" He jabbed a finger at the house. "There are *kids* in there. You don't even know who you're looking for, do you?" He rounded them up and herded them back the way they'd come, thumping them on their shoulders when they didn't move quickly enough for his liking.

"I'll have my dad on you," said one. "You're not allowed to hit kids."

"Tell me where you live and I'll save you the trouble," snarled Jimmy, giving him a shove toward the gap where the old soldier was standing. "Your dad can pay for the damage you've done to my neighbor's windows. In fact, you can all give me your names and addresses. Someone's gonna pay for these broken fences, and it sure as hell ain't gonna be the people who live here."

They took to their heels and ran for the exit.

He touched the old man on the arm. "Will you be all right, pal? I need to get through to the front. My lady and her babes are caught up in the middle of this, and I wanna make sure they're safe."

"You can't go through Dolly Carthew's house," he warned. "The traffic's flowing the wrong way." He was a dyed-in-the-wool racist with strong views about polluting his Anglo-Saxon heritage, and he eyed the big black man suspiciously. "That looks like blood on your jacket."

"It is." Jimmy took note of the wariness. "There're people being badly injured and no way to get ambulances to them. Do you know Eileen Hinkley? Glebe Tower . . . used to be a nurse . . . runs 'Friendship Calling'? We're using her flat as a first-aid center."

He must have used the magic words—"Open, Sesame"—because the old soldier nodded. "I'd let you through my house if I lived on Humbert Street, but I'm over there on Bassett." He nodded toward the garden backing onto Mrs. Carthew's, which had been laid waste by trampling feet. "You'd better let me have a word with young Karen at number five. She won't open her back door if you go knocking, but she'll listen to me." He beetled his brows into a fierce line. "You'll have to swear you won't let thugs barge in when you go out the front, though. She's disabled . . . Can't have her knocked over by louts."

Jimmy nodded. "I understand."

The man handed him his machete. "Stay here. I'll see what I can do."

Jimmy propped the weapon against a fence post, then flipped open his mobile, hoping the battery had had time to build up a small charge. He assumed at least an hour had passed since he left Glebe Tower, but when he checked his watch he was amazed to find it was barely thirty minutes. There wasn't a flicker of life in the phone, and he tucked it back in his pocket while he considered his options.

There'd been no time to work out a plan but, judging by the fear on the faces of the people running out of Mrs. Carthew's back door, all hell had broken loose on Humbert Street and the sensible course was to get themselves as far away as possible. How easy would it be to extract Melanie and the kids? And what about Gaynor? If it was true that she was working Mrs. Carthew's front door, then he and Mel could hardly abandon her to take off in the other direction.

The simplest course would be for them all to find a way into the gardens and meet up there. They could head for Gaynor's house and safely lie low there until the rioting died down. But there was no rear exit out of Melanie's duplex unless he broke through the cinder-block wall into Granny Howard's living room . . . and the miserable old bitch would probably be waiting for him on the other side with a meat cleaver . . .

A woman with a toddler in her arms sank to the grass at his feet, tears streaming down her deathly white face. "I've l-lost my l-little Anna," she stammered before her eyes rolled up and she toppled side-ways, smothering the baby beneath her.

He plucked the child out from under her and cradled it in his arms, looking around for a little girl. "ANNA!" he yelled. "MUMMY'S HERE! AN-NN-A! AN-NN-A!"

He didn't want to be here . . . he'd planned to get Melanie out and start again . . . he was supposed to be on his way to London with merchandise! Who had appointed him his brother's keeper?

"AN-NN-A! I'M LOOKING FOR A LITTLE GIRL CALLED ANNA! HAS ANYONE SEEN HER?"

"Here," said a boy with a tearstained face, pushing a filthy little girl in front of him. "She fell over." His lower lip trembled. "I don't know where my mum is either, mister." A big tear rolled down his cheek.

With a sigh, Jimmy stretched out a large palm and drew them both to his side. "You're safe now," he told them.

Five minutes later, his friend, the soldier, was surprisingly amenable to taking the pathetic little flock under his wing. It had swelled by three more grubby urchins who had become detached from friends or parents and were too frightened to wander alone in the crowd. "As soon as it calms down, I'll take them to my kitchen and give them a cuppa," he said gruffly. "You get on now. Young Karen's waiting for you. Just remember to close the front door after you. She's frightened enough as it is."

"Will do." Jimmy stuck out his hand. "Thanks, mate. I owe you one."

The old man took it. "It's like the war," he said wistfully. "Adversity brings out the best in people."

"Yeah," said Jimmy with gentle irony, "that's kinda what Eileen Hinkley said."

▼

"Young" Karen was sixty, give or take ten years, and suffering from Parkinson's disease. She was in a wheelchair and couldn't speak, but she smiled and nodded when Jimmy thanked her and said he'd make sure the front door was firmly closed behind him. He wanted to ask her if she was frightened . . . ? Who looked after her . . . ? Was she lonely . . . ?

But there wasn't time. And she wouldn't have been able to tell him, anyway.

People were beginning to lie like lead weights on his heart. Money debts he could understand. Emotional ones were a killer. It was the six-degrees-of-separation syndrome. Invisible threads linking him to the whole damn world. Policewomen . . . paramedics . . . feisty old ladies . . . disabled ladies . . . mad soldiers . . . kids . . . babies . . . He preferred anonymity.

Gaynor threw another silken loop around his neck by bursting into tears when he appeared at her side. "Oh, Christ, Jimmy," she wept, clinging to him. "Thank God . . . Thank God. I prayed for a miracle."

The crush had slackened after the first onslaught because the breathing space created in the street by the sudden exodus of two or three hundred had persuaded the others to remain where they were. It couldn't last. There was too much traffic pressing in relentlessly from Forest Road for claustrophobia not to strike again, and Jimmy, a head taller than Gaynor, could see it coming.

"Time to go," he told her, nodding toward the hallway. "Make your way home and I'll bring Mel and the kids as soon as I find them."

She shook her head. "I can't," she said stubbornly. "Someone's gotta stay here, and it has to be me because it's my fault it ever started." She showed him her cell phone. "I've got a cop on the other end. He says we need to keep this exit open . . . get more to operate if possible . . . either that or stop people from coming into Humbert." She thrust the phone at him. "You talk to him, Jimmy," she begged. "*Please.* Maybe he can tell you how to stop it before anyone gets killed."

"What about Mel?"

Gaynor's eyes clouded with anxiety. "I don't know. We got separated. I just keep telling myself to have faith in her. Your lady's not a fool, darlin', and she'd never let anything happen to the bairns." Tears began to well. "To be honest, I'm more worried about our Col." She laid a hand on her breast where the pain was. "He's such an idiot when he's lagered up . . . but I do love him something chronic, Jimmy."

OUTSIDE 23 HUMBERT STREET

Colin had never been more sober. Or afraid. His skin was beginning to scorch through his T-shirt, and he knew the fire had to be put out or the heat would force them to abandon their stand and the house would go up anyway. He kept glancing around to see how fast the wood was being consumed. He had a clearer idea of how combustion worked than his sister, recognizing that the flames would need to burn through the door before they could take hold of carpets, baseboards and furniture inside, but he couldn't see how to prevent that from happening.

He kept wondering why the perverts weren't doing anything. Didn't they realize what was going on? Smell the burning? If he was them he'd be pouring kettles of water through the mailbox while the going was good. Surely they understood that this meager line of people couldn't protect the door indefinitely?

Insidious thoughts wormed inside his head. Were the nonces even in there? Maybe they'd slipped out the back. Were he and Mel guarding an empty house?

"I'm gonna climb through the window and put the fire out from inside," he shouted into Melanie's ear. "But you've gotta make sure the line sticks it out while I do it 'cos I don't want Wesley chucking a bomb in after me. D'you understand?"

Perhaps she had come to a similar conclusion, because she nodded immediately. Her bare arms and shoulders were glowing red from the heat, and all she said was: "Just be quick, okay?"

He dropped behind her and took off his shoe to knock the remaining shards of the windowpanes from their frame. A frisson of curiosity ran through the crowd as he hopped across the sill. What was he doing? Protecting the perverts by siding with them? Or trying to make them surrender?

Wesley Barber's voice rose into the air. "Your bruvver gonna get fried if he don't bring them sickos out, bitch."

Melanie forced saliva into her dry mouth. "It's you gonna get fried, Wesley, if anything happens to our Col. I'll pour the gasoline over you and light the match myself."

INSIDE 23 HUMBERT STREET

Colin, who was no stranger to burglary, had to support himself against the doorjamb as he poked his head into the corridor. His knees were shaking so much he thought he was going to fall over. It was one thing to use a sledgehammer on a back door when you knew the owners were out, another to walk in on a couple of gay pedophiles when you were pretty sure they were waiting for you. He'd acted without thinking. Supposing they took him hostage? Supposing they buggered him?

Shi-i-it!

His ears strained to pick up any sound of voices, but it was impossible to cut out the noises from outside. The smell of the burning door was strong, and he couldn't believe they'd just leave it. *Where the fuck were they?* He crept past the door of the back downstairs room, listening acutely when he noticed it wasn't fully closed, but if anyone was in there he couldn't hear them. A quick glance up the stairs showed no one lurking at the top, but he wasn't inclined to investigate. His head was full of movie images of vampires in coffins.

The kitchen door was ajar, and he tiptoed up to it. He could see the edge of a table protruding behind it and guessed correctly that the table had been used to jam it closed before someone decided to open it again. But why? Because they were still in there and wanted to know what was going on? Or because they weren't?

And if they weren't . . . then the open door meant the fuckers were somewhere behind him . . .

He swung round, his heart leaping around his body like a rat in a trap. He would have run away if he hadn't seen smoke spilling through the mailbox. He had to do something quickly or Wesley and his gang would torch the place the minute Mel was forced to abandon the door, but fear of perverts clashed with fear of fire inside his head, and he stood in petrified indecision. Like his mother down the road, he started to pray. *Oh, God, please don't let the perverts be in the kitchen . . . Oh, God! Oh, God!*

▼

In the back bedroom all three prisoners heard the water tank in the attic above them fill as Colin turned on both the taps in the kitchen sink and set the system running.

"There's someone in the house," said Sophie.

Franek started to rise.

"Don't come near me," she warned, lifting the cricket bat. "I'm not going to be your shield. I'm not going to let you touch me again."

He took no notice but pushed himself into a crouching position, gesturing to his son to widen the distance between them and make it harder for her to attack them both at the same time. There was a moment as Nicholas rose to his feet when Sophie thought he was going to obey, but instead he turned on his father, pressing his weight hard on the back of Franek's neck to force his face down to his knees and squeeze the oxygen from his lungs. There was a brief struggle before the old man collapsed sideways on to the floor, sucking air noisily through his mouth.

"He panics very easily" was all Nicholas said.

TWENTY

Police Constable Ken Hewitt recognized the name as soon as Gaynor told him her daughter's "fella," Jimmy James, would be coming on the line in her place. Hewitt had been one of the arresting officers responsible for putting James behind bars for his most recent stretch, and he wasn't optimistic that the man would want to deal with him. The arrest related to burglary offenses in 1998 and was based on information received from James's ex-girlfriend, who had been ditched, as Hewitt now realized, for Gaynor Patterson's daughter. In typical woman-scorned fashion, the ex had set out to knife her lover.

James had fought like a devil to resist arrest, flicking policemen off his arms like troublesome insects, claiming he'd been straight for twelve months and that his new lady was pregnant. None of which cut much ice with the law. He was lucky when it came to his lawyer, who managed to keep the case in the magistrates' court by persuading James to plead guilty to three charges in return for having five others, including assault on police officers, dropped; and lucky when it came to the judge, who accepted flimsy evidence that he had been in paid employment for twelve months, had settled down to start a family with his new girlfriend and was making a genuine attempt to turn his life around. Even so he had still been sentenced to eight months, of which he would have to serve half, despite his lawyer's optimism that community service was a more likely outcome.

208

"Hi, Jimmy," said Ken now, squeezing his eyes ruefully at Jenny Monroe, "P.C. Ken Hewitt."

Jimmy's voice came clearly over the speakerphone. "I remember you. You're one of the blokes who arrested me last time. Young geezer . . . dark hair."

"That's me. You damn near broke my arm."

"Yeah, well, no hard feelings. Listen, it's not that easy to hear you . . . there's a hell of a racket going on around me . . . so speak loud and slow, okay. Tell me what you want. Gaynor talked about opening up some other exits."

"I need you on a landline, Jimmy. Can you go into Mrs. Carthew's house and find her upstairs? She's in her bedroom. We'll tell her you're coming. Just don't let anyone else follow you up. She's not very strong. Understand?"

"Sure. I'm getting pretty good at this stuff. But I reckon the frailer they look the tougher they are inside."

"What did he mean?" asked Jenny as the cell phone lost his voice to pick up the noise of the crowd.

Hewitt shook his head. "Search me."

INSIDE 9 HUMBERT STREET

Mrs. Carthew had rather vacant blue eyes and pinkly tinged cheeks. She was sitting in an armchair by her window and smiled sweetly at Jimmy when he appeared in her bedroom doorway. She held out the telephone to him and gestured happily toward the scene outside. "Is everyone enjoying themselves?" she asked, as if she were presiding over a street party.

"Some of them are," he agreed, putting the receiver to his ear to tell Ken Hewitt he had arrived. He found himself thinking that here was another old lady who seemed to be living in poverty. Glimpses through the open doors on the landing when he was trying to find her had shown the extra rooms to be all but empty, so why she was living alone in a house that was big enough to house a family was inexplicable. Most of her possessions seemed to be packed into this one room, though there was nothing of value—Jimmy's automatic assessment on entering someone else's house—just utilitarian furniture, an old television and some ornaments and photographs.

"Don't mind Mrs. Carthew," Ken Hewitt was saying. "She lost the plot about half an hour ago . . . thinks it's the end of the war . . . V.E. Day. She obviously comes and goes because she was *compos mentis* at the beginning . . . but we think it's better to agree with her so she doesn't get frightened."

"She's all on her own in here," said Jimmy, turning away slightly and covering his mouth with the large hand holding the receiver. "I'm not surprised if she comes and goes. There's no furniture in any of the other rooms, and it doesn't look like she has many visitors. I guess memories are all she's got . . . and that's pretty sad."

"She told us her children emptied the house two years ago when she went on a waiting list for assisted living, and she hasn't seen any of them since. But it's best to avoid the subject. It was talking about her kids that made her regress."

"No problem," said Jimmy, giving Mrs. Carthew an encouraging wink. "As I said, I'm getting used to it. They're all at it. I've got an old geezer out back guarding the fence with a tin helmet on his head, yelling about the war and waving a machete around."

Hewitt promptly reverted to being a policeman. "I don't think you should have encouraged that. It doesn't sound very safe."

"It's not supposed to be safe. He's a deterrent."

"He could find himself in court if someone gets hurt . . . so could you for—"

"Cut the crap," Jimmy hissed angrily, turning his back on Mrs. Carthew so as not to alarm her. "Do you think I care a fuck at the moment what you pricks are gonna do after this is over? It's you cops' fault this is happening. I'm only here because I want my lady out. And

I'll tell you this . . . we ain't got many choices here . . . and a guy who's willing to persuade people to go home strikes me as a better bet than having people trampled to death back and front of this sodding street. So don't start laying your responsibility on me. I'm not the sodding police . . . and I'm not taking any of the blame because you idiots couldn't see this war coming. My old geezer's guarding some kids and doing his best to keep the exit flowing . . . and if anyone gets sliced because they go too near him, then that's their sodding fault. *Capeesh?*"

A woman's voice came on the line. "Jimmy, this is Jenny Monroe," she said calmly and evenly. "I'm the receptionist at the Nightingale Health Center. Your Mel and her kids are patients here . . . so are Gaynor and her family. May I explain to you why the health center's involved and what we're doing? We're trying to use a network that one of our doctors set up to find people on Humbert Street who might be prepared to open their doors as Mrs. Carthew did. Unfortunately, Mrs. Carthew's very hazy about names—"

Jimmy broke in. "What's this network called?"

"Friendship Calling."

"Okay. I know about it. There's a lady in Glebe Tower called Eileen Hinkley, flat four-oh-six. She's one of the people who has the numbers. If she's not listed, the ambulance service knows how to get hold of her. She'll be able to help you."

There was a brief pause while Jenny passed the information to someone in the background. "That's fantastic," she said warmly. "One of my colleagues is calling her now. Thank you so much."

"Is that it?" said Jimmy, surprised to be let off so lightly. "Because I'd sure as hell like to find out what's happened to Mel and the kids. Get them out, if possible."

"No," said Jenny sharply, afraid he was going to hand her back to Mrs. Carthew, "please don't go! We're so desperately in need of help." Her voice rose. "Someone has to take the lead out there . . . make them see sense. We need marshals at the exits. We need— Are you still there?"

"Yeah."

He heard the policeman murmur away from the speaker: "You need to think about how much you're prepared to tell him . . . she could end up dead if they decide to storm the house."

"What's he talking about?" Jimmy demanded. "Who's 'she'? Who could end up dead?"

"Please wait, Jimmy." Jenny half muffled the speaker by placing her hand over it, but she was close enough for her higher, very agitated tones to carry. Nothing of what the policeman said was audible.

"This is crazy . . . We've got to trust someone . . . Yes, but the police aren't doing anything . . . Oh, for God's sake! . . . Of course she'll feel more confident if we can get a message to her . . . *anyone* would . . . No, I couldn't give a tuppenny damn about his record . . . If Gaynor approves of him, then so do I . . . ."

Her voice came back so suddenly and so strongly that Jimmy jerked the receiver away from his ear. "Can I trust you? Gaynor seems to trust you. She said over and over again, 'If only Jimmy was here.'"

"You don't need to shout, lady. The volume's on bellow, so I reckon Mrs. Carthew's deaf"—he saw the old woman looking at him—"as well as a house without an attic—if you get my drift." He paused. "You'll have to tell me what you want before I'll say whether you can trust me. I'm not doing nothing that'll take me back to jail."

Jenny made a supreme effort to bring her fluctuating emotions under control. "I'm sorry. Everyone's so worried here. I need assurance that you won't repeat what I tell you to anyone, Jimmy . . . not even to Melanie or Gaynor. Ken's worried that if word of it leaks out, then the crowd will go mad and attack the house . . . and that'll make the situation even more dangerous. Apparently some kid has already set himself ablaze with a gasoline bomb, and the police helicopter says there are more lining up. According to them, it's only a matter of time before the house goes up . . . and that means everyone inside will go with it . . . including Sophie."

Jimmy struggled to make sense of this by superimposing the knowledge he already had. "I thought the kid's name was Amy," he said.

A baffled pause. "I'm talking about Sophie . . . Sophie Morrison." He heard Ken Hewitt murmur again in the background. "Oh, God, no! This has nothing to do with the missing child, Jimmy. Sophie's one of our doctors. She's the real reason we became involved. She made an emergency call to me saying the men at number twenty-three had taken her prisoner. She sounded incredibly frightened—talked about being"—she paused as if selecting a word—"attacked—then turned off her phone."

"Is she the one getting married in a couple of weeks? I'm sure that's the name on the invitation Mel and me've been given."

"Yes."

"Mel's always going on about how great she is . . . Sophie this . . . Sophie that."

"Almost all her patients are in Bassindale, and a lot of them are elderly. She's the doctor who started Friendship Calling because she recognized how lonely some of them were. I know you're probably thinking I'd say anything to make you help her, but she's a truly good person, Jimmy, the kind who makes a difference in other people's lives." Her voice quavered. "She wouldn't be in that house now if she didn't care about her patients. She was supposed to quit at midday but was running late because she thinks talking's more important than handing out pills. Then I asked her to make that one extra call because the man was panicking—" Her voice broke completely.

"I guess you're pretty fond of her."

There was the sound of nose blowing at the other end. "I can't bear to think of anything bad happening to her."

"You said she'd been 'attacked,'" he reminded her. "Was she talking about the men in the house or the people outside?"

"Hang on." There was a long silence before she spoke again, and he suspected that this time she had pressed the "mute" button. "She said one of the men wanted to rape her," she told him, "and she's not the type to imagine a thing like that."

Jimmy frowned to himself, remembering his conversation with Melanie earlier. "I thought these guys were pedophiles, so why would they want to rape a woman? Plus, they must be scared shitless themselves with half of Acid Row screaming for their blood?"

He waited for an answer that didn't come, because the policeman's voice spoke again in the background.

NIGHTINGALE HEALTH CENTER

Jenny muted the speakerphone, and glared angrily at Ken. "Don't keep telling me to watch what I say to him!" she snapped. "At least he's *there*. At least he's listening. What are the police doing to rescue Sophie? *Nothing* . . . except sitting on their backsides and keeping a lookout because they're afraid of making the situation worse. Well, here's what I think." She jabbed her finger at him. "If Harry explains to him the sort of danger he's likely to face . . . and if he agrees to help . . . then we should all get down on our knees and be grateful that *someone* in that godforsaken place has more courage than the bloody police have."

INSIDE 9 HUMBERT STREET

Jimmy made a face at Mrs. Carthew as the receiver came alive again. "Listen, I'm not trying to knock the doctor," he said by way of explaining his skepticism to Jenny. "I bet the poor lady's scared out of her wits, but it doesn't make much sense whichever way you look at it. I mean, you'd have to be a fucking moron to rape your hostage when the reason you're under attack is because you're a deviant. You'd do the opposite . . . you'd be nice to her . . . get her to speak for you . . .

persuade the acidheads you were framed. That's something everyone in Bassindale can relate to."

A man's voice answered. "This is Harry Bonfield, Jimmy. I'm the senior doctor at Nightingale. Believe me, we've been having these same thoughts ourselves, so we took advice from a psychiatrist. What you're describing is a *reasoned* reaction to a problem . . . and that isn't necessarily the way these men will behave. We're getting some feedback from the police helicopter, and they're telling us there's no sign of anyone at the windows . . . which is the opposite of what we'd expect if the men wanted Sophie to plead for them. They'd make her very visible, encourage her to call out and say who she is, use her as a deterrent—*your* word—against gasoline bombs."

"Maybe she's too frightened to do it."

"We don't think so. Sophie's an intelligent woman, and a tough one, too. She knows that a lot of people in that crowd will recognize her or have knowledge of her, particularly if she talks to them. It makes no sense that she isn't being allowed to negotiate. She's one of the few people who might be able to take some steam out of the situation."

Jimmy couldn't fault his argument. "So what do you reckon's going on?"

"It's a guess, but we think the older man is running the show. He's not the convicted offender—that's the son—but there's evidence that the father is a serial sexual abuser. Both his wife and his son suffered at his hands—he wields a whip, which suggests he has a strong sadistic streak. He's also a habitual user of prostitutes—he's been arrested and fined in the past for curb crawling, and questioned several times after women were admitted to the hospital and gave a description matching his. There was never enough evidence to convict—he uses false names, and none of the prostitutes would face him in court—but he's definitely not the kind of man you'd want as jailer of a pretty young woman."

Jimmy was reminded of Eileen's remark about her friend being prone to exaggeration. The doctor was making this guy out to be a full-blown psychopath, but if that were the case, then why the hell wasn't he behind bars? Jimmy had a strong suspicion that these people in the safety of the health center were manipulating his sympathies to make him do something he wouldn't want to do.

"You sure you got this right, Doc?" he asked cynically. "I mean, one minute you're telling me he likes tender boy meat . . . the next you're saying he's trawling the streets for women. That don't add up. Why would he fancy his little son, if his real taste's for full-grown bitches?"

There was an amused laugh at the colorful language. "Do you want the three-year course or the one-minute sound bite? Don't answer that, Jimmy. I'll do my best with a sound bite. Someone with the kind of personality disorder that this man seems to be suffering from has no forward thinking and can't anticipate the negative consequences of what he does. Also, he never blames himself. It'll be the victim's fault for triggering his aggression or frustration. If, as we believe, his particular paraphilia—that's a sexual disorder—is sadism, then other people's fear is a major turn-on for him, and, once aroused, he won't be remotely interested in them as people, only in his immediate gratification. This would have meant that his son, who must have lived in permanent terror, was both the reason for the father's arousal and the satisfier of it. Does that sound logical to you?"

"It fucking sucks," said Jimmy in disgust. "Why the hell wasn't the kid given some protection?"

Harry sighed. "Because forty years ago people didn't know this kind of thing went on."

"Jesus! How old is this bloke?"

"The father? Seventy-one."

"And you reckon he's still dangerous?"

"Unfortunately, yes . . . particularly to someone like Sophie. If she's arguing with him and trying to protect herself—which is what we think she'll be doing—he'll rationalize that whatever happens is her fault."

"Won't he be worried about being punished for it afterward?"

"It depends on how excited he becomes, and how much he thinks she's responsible. This isn't a stable personality, Jimmy, or a particularly bright one. The best adjective would be *complacent*. The fact that he's never been convicted of abuse will almost certainly have persuaded him in his own mind that he has a right to behave as he does. He may even imagine that the police agree with him. A man is stronger, therefore a man's authority should be obeyed." Harry paused. "You had it right at the beginning when you called him a moron. Put *deviant* in front, and you've got some idea of what Sophie's dealing with."

INSIDE 23 HUMBERT STREET

Sophie watched the old man writhe on the floor, fighting for breath. If she could move the armoire, or persuade Nicholas to move it for her, she could get out of that dreadful room. "Let me go downstairs and talk to whoever's in the house," she urged Nicholas. "Now . . . while your father can't stop me. I promise I won't leave. I'll stand at the bottom of the stairs and make sure no one comes up."

He glanced undecidedly toward the door. "You won't be able to prevent them."

"Of course I will, if you give me a chance to speak with them. We must start trying to help ourselves. Can't you see that?"

"It's safer to wait for the police."

A terrible apathy nudged at her brain, because part of her agreed with him—the hesitant part that exists in all of us and makes us braver with the danger we can see than with the one we can't. She almost persuaded herself it would be safer to stay where she was—cocooned by the spurious protection of four brick walls. Who knew what was going on outside? Was she really so sure that anyone would bother to listen to her? What if she made the situation worse?

She felt Nicholas's gaze on her and remembered how his gentle manner had almost seduced her before. *Damn it! Damn it! Damn it! She wasn't this feeble! What would Bob say if she told him she decided to take her chances with rape because she was too afraid to walk out of a room* . . .

"It's not safer for me," she countered with spirit, stamping her foot to fire him up. "I have friends out there . . . people who *care* about me . . . unlike you . . . and this"—she jerked her chin at Franek— "low-grade piece of *shit*!"

"I'm sorry."

Oh, ple-ease! "Find some courage!" she snapped. "If the police were coming, they'd be here already . . . and you *really* need to ask why the only thing we've heard is a helicopter. Doesn't that say to you that they're trying to find out what's going on? And why do they need to do that, Nicholas, if the streets are full of policemen? You're an educated man, for Christ's sake. Use your brain . . . *think* . . . work it out for yourself. We're more likely to be attacked than we are to be rescued."

He didn't say anything but watched Franek's movements begin to calm as his breathing steadied.

Sophie spoke more urgently. "Your father isn't going to let me go," she said. "We both know that . . . and we both know why. I think you're gambling that we'll be rescued before he loses control completely, but he's already assaulted me twice." She raised a hand to her puffy cheek. "The only reason I haven't got two of these is because you intervened the third time, but he won't let you get that close again. So what's going to happen if we're here for another five hours, Nicholas? Are you going to offer yourself as a punching bag to protect me? Or bury your head in the corner and leave your father to get on with it?"

He put his hands in his pockets and stirred the toe of his shoe in the dust on the floor. "You don't think much of me, do you?" he said.

What answer should she give? Yes? No? Should she be truthful or should she lie? What was his psychology? Schizoid? Paranoid? Borderline?

"I believe he's abused you so badly that you're terrified to do anything without his permission. I can't pretend to understand it—you're a grown man and you shouldn't even be living with him—but it *is* a fact." She made her tone as unemphatic as she could. "So, yes, you're right, I don't think much of you." She studied his bent head for a moment. "The danger to you is outside, Nicholas, and hiding in here, hoping we're going to be rescued, is crazy. Do you know anything about the people who live on this estate? You said earlier it was a rough area . . . so give me your best guess on what they'll do to a pedophile if they catch him before the police do."

He didn't seem surprised that she knew why the crowd was outside. He even looked relieved that he didn't have to pretend anymore. "Cut off his dick," he said dispassionately. "I think they're right, too. I tried to do it myself in prison, but I was stopped before I did any serious damage. No one's allowed to mutilate themselves these days . . . not even pedophiles."

Dear God!

"You really do need help," she said, equally dispassionately. "What the hell is going on inside your head that makes you think it's *your* dick that should be sacrificed?"

Telephone Message

For: D.C.I. Tyler
From: Mrs. Angela Gough
Taken by: P.C. Drew
Date: 28.07.01
Call timed at: 15:46

Mrs. Gough has paid her daughter, Francesca's, bill and has arranged for her to be flown home this P.M. *N.B. Townsend's original booking was for next Saturday 08.04.01.* Mrs. Gough asked for the following information to be given to D.C.I. Tyler.

1. She doesn't want the responsibility of involving Edward Townsend's first wife but is prepared to pass on what her friend has told her re. Townsend.
2. He has been divorced twice. In both instances his wives divorced him. In the case of her friend's divorce (second wife, too, she believes) he was represented by Martin Rogerson.
3. The official reason for the first divorce was Townsend's adultery with the woman who became his second wife. The *unofficial* reason was Townsend's obsession with his stepdaughter (9 at the time of the divorce, now 17). No evidence that he abused her sexually—the child denied it—but mother was distraught to find videotapes of her daughter in the nude. Similar tapes had been made of the mother before he married her, as Townsend said he liked to watch her when she wasn't with him. She found two other tapes of children she didn't know.
4. Rogerson and the wife's solicitor brokered a settlement that resulted in the video issue being dropped and an agreement of silence imposed. Mrs. Gough believes Martin Rogerson threatened the wife with exposure of the tapes, although her friend has never actually said so. The wife continues to feel guilty about her silence as she believes Townsend to be a pedophile.

5. Mrs. Gough has seen the photograph of Amy on TV. She says the child looks very like her friend's daughter at the same age.

6. Townsend's second wife had an 8-yr-old daughter. The only knowledge Mrs. Gough has of that marriage is that it lasted less than a year.

7. Mrs. Gough warned Francesca that Townsend had an unhealthy interest in young girls. Francesca accused her of being jealous because she couldn't attract men herself. Mrs. Gough now regrets that she didn't use the word *pedophile.*

G. Drew

TWENTY-ONE

Martin Rogerson looked up angrily when D.C.I. Tyler entered the interview room. He had a mobile telephone clamped to one ear, and it wasn't clear whether his anger was directed at Tyler or the person on the other end. With a curt "good-bye" he snapped the instrument closed and placed it on the table in front of him. Frustration was etched into the aggressive set of his jaw, and Tyler had a glimpse of the bully Laura had described in the early hours. Certainly there was no bluff friendliness in his expression now.

Tyler pulled out a chair and sat opposite him. "I'm sorry to have kept you waiting, sir," he said with a pleasant smile. "I assumed you'd be halfway to Bournemouth before you received the call, but I understand you asked W.P.C. Anderson to take you to Southampton instead?"

He put an upward inflection into his voice, but Rogerson was in no mood to respond to the question or the smile. "She told me it was extremely urgent—something to do with a new lead," he said, his educated accent clipping the words impatiently, "but it can't be that urgent if you're happy to leave me staring at a blank wall for twenty minutes." He tapped his watch, wielding his finger like a club. The alpha male attempting to dominate. "You've got my mobile number. Why couldn't we have done this by phone? I have a meeting in Southampton in two hours."

"Then you've plenty of time. It's less than thirty minutes away." Tyler studied him curiously, felt the heat of his impatience. "Surely your daughter's more important than a meeting? Your wife won't even take a rest in case something comes on the radio while she's asleep."

"That's below the belt, Inspector. Your sergeant's already told me you haven't found a body, and he said it was cause for optimism." He made an effort to relax. "I've been a solicitor too long to worry about things until I have to . . . unlike my wife, who frets herself sick, and invariably finds it was a waste of energy." He folded his hands over the telephone and leaned forward to bridge the gap between them. "Tell me about this new lead. Of course I'll do anything to help."

"Thank you." Tyler paused, wondering who Rogerson had been talking to on his mobile, and if the conversation was the reason for both his optimism and his impatience. "I need to ask you some questions about Edward Townsend, sir."

The lawyer's eyes narrowed slightly. "What sort of questions?"

"How would you describe your relationship with him? Is it a personal one or a business one? Or is it both?"

"What does this have to do with my daughter?"

There was no reason not to tell him. "We believe Mr. Townsend may have been involved in Amy's disappearance."

"That's impossible." It was a very decided statement.

"Why?"

"He's been out of the country since Tuesday."

Tyler looked at the mobile. "Have you just been speaking to him? Is he part of this meeting that's taking place in two hours?"

Rogerson shook his head. "I'm not prepared to discuss my client's business affairs, Inspector—not without the proper authority."

"So the meeting involves Mr. Townsend's business?"

The lawyer folded his arms but didn't say anything.

Tyler watched him for a moment. "Did you handle both of Mr. Townsend's divorces?"

"Is this relevant?"

"I'm merely asking for confirmation that you acted for him, sir."

Rogerson didn't answer.

"Fair enough." The DCI stood up. "In Townsend's absence, the only other person who can confirm it is his first wife, but it'll mean another long wait while I try to contact her, I'm afraid."

Rogerson pointed impatiently to him to sit down. "Yes, I represented him. That's all I'm prepared to say, however. If you have any other questions relating to my client, you must put them directly to him."

"We will as soon as we locate him," said Tyler, resuming his seat. "Do you know where he is, Mr. Rogerson?"

"No."

"Do you have a number where we can contact him?"

The man moistened his lips. "No. The only number I have is not being answered."

Tyler wondered if he was lying, but decided not to pursue it for the moment. "The questions relate to you, Mr. Rogerson, and what you knew about your client. Edward Townsend made some highly questionable videos of his stepdaughters that led at least one of his wives to suspect he was a pedophile. As his lawyer, you knew they existed. Would you care to explain to me why under those circumstances you allowed your daughter to live with him?"

His composure was definitely rattled. He was taking time to answer. "I am not going to comment on that, except to say that your version of events is as questionable as you claim these alleged videos were."

"And why," Tyler went on implacably, "you insisted that she be returned to your care if and when Townsend grew tired of her?" He watched the other man's face smooth itself of expression. "Was she on loan, Mr. Rogerson?"

Rogerson picked up his mobile and tucked it into his jacket pocket. "You have no grounds whatsoever for this line of questioning,

Inspector, and I have no intention of answering. I suggest you establish some facts before you attempt to pursue it again."

"I believe I have strong grounds," said Tyler mildly. "Strong enough to detain you, in fact, should you try to leave." It was his turn to lean forward. "Your client, Edward Townsend, left Majorca at six o'clock yesterday morning, and a car similar to his was seen in Portisfield seven hours later with a child matching Amy's description in the passenger seat. Would you care to comment on that?"

The man's mouth opened briefly, but whatever it was he was planning to say remained unspoken. Even to Tyler's unsympathetic gaze, he looked shaken.

"He has a very unhealthy interest in young girls . . . particularly your daughter. We think you knew this before Amy went to live with him. His bent is making nude videos of prepubescent children. He has several e-mail addresses—all encrypted—with only his legitimate business address being open for scrutiny. He was in Majorca this week filming an Amy look-alike, and someone called Martin telephoned him on Thursday. Their discussions were so sensitive that the girl with him wasn't allowed to listen, but following the call Townsend returned to England. Do you want to tell me what you said to him, Mr. Rogerson? Particularly anything relating to Amy."

Rogerson considered for a moment. "This is absurd. You're completely on the wrong track. Even if I were the Martin he spoke to, how could I have said anything about my daughter when I haven't talked to her in months?"

"Do you deny phoning Edward Townsend in Majorca?"

"I am certainly denying that I am in any way connected with my daughter's disappearance."

Tyler took note of the politician's answer. "Don't play games with me, Mr. Rogerson," he said sharply. "This is a child's life we're talking about—*your* child's life. Have you spoken to Townsend in the last twenty-four hours, either in person or on the telephone?"

The man paused before he answered. "I have tried to contact him," he said. "His mobile is either turned off or out of power." He read the other man's expression correctly. "I had—and *have*—no reason to believe that Amy is with him," he said firmly. "I wished to speak to him in relation to business."

Tyler found his expression less easy to read. Was this another evasive answer when a simple "No" would have sufficed? "Which one?"

"As far as I'm aware, there is only one. Etstone, his building company."

"We believe he may have Internet businesses. Do you know anything about them?"

Rogerson frowned. "No."

"Were you aware that he returned to England yesterday morning?"

"No."

"When were you expecting him back?"

A small hesitation. "I don't believe he mentioned a date to me."

That was a lie, thought Tyler. "Our information is that he booked a return flight for next Saturday."

The man looked away. "I wasn't aware of that."

Tyler switched tack abruptly. "Amy made a collect call two weeks ago to someone she referred to as 'Em.' Was that you, Mr. Rogerson?"

"No.

"Do you know who it might have been?"

"I've no idea. As I've said several times, I haven't seen or heard from the child in months."

"Your wife suggested she was saying 'Ed' because she swallows her *D*s. Was that something you heard Amy doing when she was living with you?"

"No."

"Meaning you didn't notice it or she didn't do it?" he asked.

"Both. The demands of my work meant she was usually in bed by the time I came home, but if I'd heard her doing it I would have corrected her."

"Were you close to your daughter, Mr. Rogerson?"

"Not particularly. She was always her mother's child."

Tyler nodded, as if the statement were reasonable. "Then why threaten to take her away?" he asked. "Why frighten Laura with a custody battle?"

Rogerson breathed deeply through his nose. "I've answered that question twice . . . once last night and again before the press conference."

"Answer it once more, please."

He flicked another glance at his watch, containing his irritation with difficulty. "The agreement Laura and I reached was that the quid pro quo for my not putting obstacles in the way of her taking Amy last September was a promise that if her circumstances changed, the issue of custody would be settled in court . . . with Amy's wishes being paramount. I felt it both reasonable and responsible that the child be given the choice."

"And you were happy to have her back if she chose you?"

"Of course. She's my daughter."

"Then why didn't she know that?"

The man frowned. "I don't understand the question."

"If she knew you loved her, why didn't she call you and ask to come home when Laura left Townsend?"

"Presumably because she wasn't allowed to." Perhaps, like his wife, he feared traps, because his voice took on a persuasive note. "Let me put the question another way, Inspector. Why wasn't Laura prepared to test the issue in court? Wouldn't you say that's pretty good evidence she knew Amy would choose me?"

"Not really," said Tyler bluntly. "I prefer my evidence simple and straightforward. If Amy had wanted to be with you, she'd have called you up. There's a telephone in the Logans' house. It was freely available for her to make private calls after Laura and Gregory left for work each morning. This was a child in torment. Insecure . . . lonely . . . being bullied by her baby-sitters . . . lying to her mother so that Laura could keep on working to find a way out of the mess they were in. You're her father. You were the obvious person to come to her rescue. So why didn't she turn to you for help?"

"Perhaps she tried and I wasn't in. Perhaps she didn't want to upset her mother. Children have complicated reasons for the things they do. Perhaps it was me she didn't want to upset."

Tyler agreed with the last remark, which was almost certainly true, although he would have substituted "arouse" for "upset." It was the nature of this man's arousal that remained obscure. "I have two takes on this so-called 'agreement.' Mr. Rogerson," he said frankly. "One is that the only use you've ever had for your daughter was as a stick to beat your wife with. Edward Townsend came at you out of the blue—you had no idea Laura had been having an affair with him or was planning to leave you—so you bought some time to conceal your assets. As long as the threat to take Amy away hangs over her head, Laura's too frightened to go near a lawyer because she knows from past experience that the deck is stacked against her."

Rogerson shook his head. "Why can't you just accept that I take my responsibilities as a father seriously? It wasn't my choice that Laura have an affair. Nor was it Amy's. While they were with Edward Townsend—and despite Laura's ridiculous insistence on returning my support checks—I was satisfied that my daughter was being properly cared for. I knew the man, knew the standard of living he enjoyed. There was no such guarantee in a second relationship . . . as has been amply demonstrated. I question whether Amy would be missing today had my wife not broken the conditions of our agreement."

Tyler made no reaction at all to this remarkable statement. "My *second* take," he went on, as if the man hadn't spoken, "is that you were prepared to lend Amy to Townsend for a period of time—probably to keep his business. To that end you allowed him to seduce your wife— a woman you no longer had any interest in—with the sole intention of exploiting your daughter. The only proviso was that Amy should be returned to you when Townsend's infatuation had run its course . . . either to abuse her yourself or to offer her to other clients. Whichever the case," he went on firmly, overriding Rogerson's indrawn breath, "you actively connived in handing guardianship of a ten-year-old child to a man you knew to be a pedophile."

Rogerson's eyes glittered with suppressed anger. "You're on very dangerous ground," he warned. "What basis do you have for an allegation like that?"

"You were Townsend's lawyer at the time of his first divorce. You helped suppress the evidence of his pedophilia."

"I deny that absolutely."

"Do you deny that tapes of his naked nine-year-old stepdaughter existed and that no mention of them was made during the divorce?"

"All I will say is that certain issues were dropped on the instruction of the wife, who did not want pieces of compromising material, concerning her, made public. I had no reason to believe from this material that Edward Townsend was a pedophile. I did—and do—believe that he is only interested in women."

Tyler stared him down. "Why did Amy cry when you took her to see your parents?"

The sudden switch ratcheted up the other man's irritation. "What's that got to do with anything?" he snapped.

"It was an occasion when Amy was alone with you . . . without her mother."

His face closed immediately. "What are you implying?"

"I'm just wondering why Amy was so unhappy that day that your parents asked you not to bring her again."

"The child cried. Is that so unusual? The occasion was too much for her."

"Why?"

"How the hell—" He broke off to take another calming breath. "Because my parents live in a nursing home, and a fair proportion of the patients have Alzheimer's," he said in a more even tone. "That's frightening to a little girl."

"I thought it was a retirement home."

"Nursing home . . . retirement home . . . they're much of a muchness."

"Retirement homes don't cater to Alzheimer's patients."

There was a short silence. "Then it's my daughter's nature to be shy. What do you want from me? A detailed analysis of a single day in a child's life?"

Tyler eased back his chair and stretched his legs. "No one else describes her as shy, Mr. Rogerson. All singing, all dancing is the description that seems to fit her best. I'm told she likes to make people smile."

This time the silence was a long one.

"I don't see the point you're making," said Rogerson finally.

"The only other people who say she cried all the time are Kimberley and Barry Logan . . . and they were bullying her mercilessly. They also say she was forever locking herself in the bathroom because her stomach was hurting. Your parents said the same thing: '. . . kept going to the loo with a stomachache but wouldn't be helped.'"

"I don't remember." Tyler watched the man's eyes drop to his watch again, as if the only thing that worried him was his meeting in Southampton.

"It's a common symptom of abuse, Mr. Rogerson, particularly in girls. Endless trips to the bathroom . . . a refusal to let anyone help because they don't want the evidence of their abuse to be seen. On a physical level, the pain in the stomach may be due to infection of the urinary tract or genitals. On a psychological level, it's a probable indication of stress . . . possibly anorexia or bulimia, where secretive vomiting is commonplace. Your daughter's very thin. She's also obsessively anxious to please."

Rogerson stared him straight in the eye. "Are you accusing me of child abuse?"

"I'm interested in the timing of your visit to your parents, which falls within the period when Laura and Townsend were having their affair."

"Then I suggest you take it up with Laura. As you've very successfully established in the last ten minutes, my contact with my daughter has been negligible since she was born." He put his palms on the table, preparatory to standing up.

Tyler stabbed a finger onto the table. "Stay where you are," he ordered curtly. "I haven't finished with you yet."

Rogerson ignored him. "You certainly have," he said, pushing himself to his feet, "unless you can produce some evidence of what you've been saying." He started to turn away.

Tyler stood up. "Stop there, please, Mr. Rogerson. I am arresting you for conspiracy and incitement to commit indecency with children. You do not have to say anything, but it may harm your defense if—"

The lawyer swung back at him, his face ugly. "It's you who should stop," he commanded, using his finger like a club again. "I insist these charges be properly explained before you read me my rights."

"—you do not mention when questioned something that you later rely on in court. Anything you do say may be given in evidence." He stared the other man down. "As a result of your arrest, the police will exercise their right to search any property you occupy or have control over . . . including your personal computer files and hard disk. Do you understand what I've just told you?"

The man's face was devoid of expression, except for a tic that made his left eyelid flicker uncontrollably. He chose to remain silent.

Tyler smiled slightly as he held out his hand. "Your telephone, please, Mr. Rogerson."

9 HUMBERT STREET

Jimmy listened with increasing dismay to what Harry Bonfield was urging him to do. In effect, to enter number 23 through the back door and negotiate Sophie's release. Either by his own efforts or by taking over Sophie's mobile to start a dialogue among the Hollises, Harry Bonfield and the police.

"Are you still there?" Harry asked when Jimmy didn't reply.

"Yeah, yeah, I'm thinking." Another pause. "Okay, this is how I see it. You've got a psycho and a nonce shitting themselves because half the estate's camped outside their door, and the only thing that might stop them from being ripped to pieces is this doctor they've taken prisoner. They haven't done the sensible thing, which is to use her as a mouthpiece, therefore they're planning to stick her in front of them and hold a knife to her throat if anyone bursts in. Plus, they may have raped her already—either because they're so deviant they can't help themselves, or on the basis that the more frightened she is, the less likely she'll be to try to save herself when the standoff happens. How's that for a summary?"

"Right on, I'd say."

"Right, so what's gonna be different when I burst in? I don't see it makes much difference whether it's one guy or a thousand guys. These Hollises are still gonna be twitched as hell, and the lady's still gonna have a knife to her throat. I don't know nothing about this kind of shit, Doc. If I do it wrong, your friend could be dead. Are you sure it wouldn't be better to wait for the cops?"

There was some background conversation again. "Ken Hewitt says the riot police have been ordered to hold back from storming the barricades to avoid the houses along the entrance routes being set on fire. There are two squads circling the fields behind the perimeter wall at the back of the estate, but they estimate another hour before they can assemble a large enough number to make an effective attack. You're

232

our best shot, Jimmy." Harry paused. "You're our *only* shot. I don't want to put any more pressure on you than I already have, but the word from the helicopter is that some youths in Humbert Street have started gasoline-bombing the Hollises' house. They've been stopped for the moment by a small line of people who are trying to protect it, but it doesn't look as if it's going to hold very long."

"Who's in the line?"

"Mostly women." Harry broke off to listen to Ken Hewitt. "It's being led by a tall, blond, pregnant girl."

"Shit!"

"Is that your Melanie?"

"Sounds like it."

"Then you should go to her assistance," Harry said immediately. "Sophie would expect it . . . so would I."

Jimmy didn't answer.

"I think he's gone," said Harry's voice at the other end.

"Jesus, Doc, give me a break, okay! I'm thinking. Is that *allowed?*" He didn't expect an answer, so he didn't wait for one. "Right, this is what's gonna happen. Forget negotiations. Instead I'm gonna make these two bastards an offer they can't refuse. Do you reckon Sophie's got the balls to come with me if I offer to protect them and get them off the estate? See, it strikes me, the trouble'll die down quicker if the crowd can go inside the house and find it empty. All they'll do is trash the place."

"How will you take them off the estate?"

"Meet up with the cops who're coming around the back." He took a tremulous breath, which told the listeners at the other end how frightened he was. "It's gotta be safer heading into the estate than trying to go around the barricades. All the action's up toward the main road, and not many people are gonna know what these fuckers look like. It'll just look like three guys and a girl, heading home. What do you reckon?"

It sounded flaky, even to his ears, but all Harry said was: "It's better than anything we've come up with. Good luck."

Jimmy returned the telephone to Mrs. Carthew, then dove down the stairs toward the garden.

HAMPSHIRE POLICE HEADQUARTERS

"He's using initials to store his numbers," said Tyler's sergeant as he ran through the menu on Rogerson's phone, jotting down letters and figures. "You'd better be right about him, Guv. He'll take us for every last penny if you're wrong . . . and you'll be on gardening leave."

"I'm not wrong," said Tyler, looking over his shoulder. "You didn't see his face when I mentioned his hard disk. He's downloaded something that he's ashamed of, and he knows we're going to find it."

"Okay. E.T. This looks like it." Gary Butler wrote the numbers on the pad and swivelled it toward his boss. "What are you planning to do with it?"

"Try it," said Tyler, reaching for the landline. "If Rogerson was telling the truth, Townsend isn't going to answer anyway." He let his hand drop. "On second thought," he said, "I'll use Rogerson's phone. The bastard might be more forthcoming if his lawyer's number flashes on."

"You'll kill the case if you don't tell him who you are, Guv."

"We don't have a case," said Tyler grimly.

INSIDE 23 HUMBERT STREET

Colin's attempt to pour water through the letter box from inside the house was worse than useless. The top of the kettle jammed against the door as he tilted it, and most of the liquid ran down inside. He took a quick peek through the gap, burning his fingers on the metal slot, and saw with alarm that Melanie and her line had been forced by the heat to move away from the house toward their tormentors.

He ran back to the kitchen and ripped open the cabinets, looking for a bucket or anything else that would hold a substantial amount of water. He found a metal pail beneath the sink, which he shoved under the running taps while he continued to search. A mixing bowl. A large Tupperware box. He substituted them for the overflowing bucket then heaved the two gallons of water down the corridor.

He had come to the conclusion that the only thing to do was open the door and empty the bucket directly onto the flames. But his hands were trembling as he reached for the latch because he knew it would be an irresistible invitation to Wesley Barber to charge the house or, worse, throw another gasoline bomb.

With Colin as the target . . .

Ambulance Service Report

Ambulance No:	512
Date:	07.28.01
Time of Collection:	5:55
In Attendance:	K. Parry, V. Singh

Patient Details:	(supplied by Andrew Fallon, friend)
Name:	Kevin Charteris
Address:	206 Bassindale Row, Bassindale
Age:	Fifteen
Next of Kin:	Mother—Mrs. M. Charteris, 206 Bassindale Row (unavailable when paramedics tried to contact her by telephone)
Status:	Patient was brought to the ambulance outside barricade
	Dead on arrival
	Estimate of 75% burns (2nd & 3rd degree) to head and body
	Attempt at resuscitation failed
	Death due to shock—estimate of time: 10 minutes prior to arrival
Destination:	Southampton General Hospital

TWENTY-TWO

The phone was answered after the first ring. "What do you want, Martin?" It was a man's voice and the sounds of an engine and passing traffic told Tyler he was in his car, almost certainly using a headset. The fluctuating volume and intermittent breaks suggested the signal wasn't good.

Tyler was a reasonably good mimic and Rogerson's deep, cut-glass tones weren't difficult to ape in short bursts. "Where are you?" he asked.

"In England. About an hour away . . . you can thank John Finch . . . told me what was . . . the wind . . ." It was a London accent, and he was angry. The chewed vowels were accentuated by the airwaves, his irritation strong enough to put an edge on them.

Tyler put his hand over the mouthpiece, then raised it slightly. ". . . Amy."

"The signal's bad. I can't . . . you properly. What about her?"

"Police . . . questioning me."

The man's voice came in a sudden strong surge. "Yeah, well, I'm sorry about the kid, but it doesn't change anything. I'll have your guts if you're not at the Hilton in an hour." The line was cut abruptly.

Tyler switched off the mobile and handed it to his sergeant.

"Well?" the other man asked.

The D.C.I. pressed his thumb and forefinger to the bridge of his nose. "If that was Townsend, then he's on his way to the Southampton Hilton. And he's mighty pissed off."

"What about?"

"Christ knows," he said.

"Do you think he has Amy?"

Tyler rubbed a tired hand across his face. "It didn't sound like it."

GARDENS BEHIND HUMBERT STREET

There was nothing Jimmy could say to the soldier other than to ask him to go on guarding the fence and stop anyone from coming through behind him. He saw distrust in the old man's eyes, as if he thought Jimmy were saving his own skin by escaping through the empty gardens toward Bassindale Row, but there was no time for explanations and no sense in making them either. The truth would be repeated to others, and a lie wouldn't be believed.

He ran along the path of broken fences that the boys had made earlier, searching the backs of the houses for Granny Howard's duplex at 21a. She had let him into her downstairs room once when he'd tried to make peace with her, and he'd noticed the ornaments she kept on her windowsill. One in particular had seized his attention because it looked valuable. A sizeable bronze statue of a rearing horse. He hoped to God it was still there, or that she was sitting in her window, because if he couldn't locate the back of Melanie's house then he was going to have trouble finding number 23.

He found the horse in a window two properties on from the garden with the jungle gym, and caught a glimpse of Granny Howard's ill-tempered face as he crossed the overgrown patch of weeds that she guarded so jealously but never entered. That made the next fence the boundary with number 23. He ducked into the shadow of a small apple tree and took deep, steadying breaths as he squinted at the windows of the back room and kitchen, searching for signs of movement behind the glass.

He knew it had to be laid out like Mrs. Carthew's house, which meant his only access was through the kitchen, but he could stand there indefinitely trying to find out if the men were on the ground floor. Logic told him to go carefully, climb the fence near the house and crawl along the wall beneath the windows, gambling that a quick look into each room to see if it was occupied wouldn't give him away. His temperament urged the exact opposite. Take the problem head-on, vault the fence and charge the door, for even if he took the cautious option, the door was almost certainly locked and would require a shoulder thrust to break it down.

He groaned to himself. Whichever he chose would be wrong.

Life was like that.

HAMPSHIRE POLICE HEADQUARTERS

A similar thought was running through Tyler's head. Life was a poker game. Play the cards? Or cut his losses? He couldn't see Martin Rogerson accepting an apology, so cutting his losses wasn't much of an option and, like Jimmy, his nature urged action.

"To hell with it!" he told his sergeant. "I want Townsend held for questioning. Get on to Southampton and ask them to pick him up when he arrives at the Hilton. They'll need to be in place within the next half hour. Tell them we're on our way and we'll talk to him there. If he asks what it's about, they're to say our interest relates to the six-month period Amy spent in his house. I don't want him spooked. Also, ask them to hold anyone who arrives for a meeting with him and Rogerson. Let's be sure they're kosher before we let a group of pedophiles loose."

"What about Rogerson?"

"Hang on to him."

Butler looked troubled. "Are you sure you're doing the right thing, Guv?"

Tyler smiled slightly. "No."

"Then shouldn't—?"

"Townsend's M.O. sucks, Gary. I've got two women and five kids who've all been captured nude on video." He counted them off on his fingers. "First wife . . . first stepdaughter . . . Laura . . . Amy . . . Franny . . . and two unknowns. And those are the ones we know about. Both women believed the tapes were for his own private enjoyment when he was away from them. So why does he start filming their daughters the minute he gets them into his house? And why does he use encrypted e-mail?"

"Why move women into his house at all? Why bother to marry? Why pretend with Laura?"

Tyler touched a finger to a paragraph in Mrs. Gough's message. "She says Amy looks like the first stepdaughter at the same age. Perhaps it's a personal thing. Perhaps he can't resist a certain type of child. Slim, dark and age about ten. He was angry with Franny Gough because she was too well developed."

"Or Rogerson's right and it's the women who attracted him. The fact that he made videos of them tends to support that. Maybe he's a bit of an artist . . . likes the female form . . . pre- and postpuberty. Lots of us do, Guv."

"You telling me you like leering at little girls, Gary?"

Butler shrugged. "Neither of the women said he abused their kids, just that he made videos of them."

"In order to exploit them. I'll put money on his being a pedophile. Even more on Rogerson's knowing it."

"Yeah, but not the pedophile who's taken Amy. Don't forget, she was with someone else while he was in Majorca. Kimberley and Barry said she was out of the house the same as usual on Tuesday, Wednesday and Thursday. You'll dig a bigger hole for yourself if you don't release Rogerson now. He told you she wasn't with Townsend, and he'll have your hide if she turns up dead on the other side of the country while you're busy hounding him and his client."

"He's going to have it anyway." The D.C.I. rubbed the back of his neck, eyes narrowed in thought. "Who's 'Em' if it's not 'Ed'? Whose black car was it if it wasn't Townsend's? Who was the kid seen getting into it if it wasn't Amy? Why did he come home early? Why didn't he go back to his house? Where's he been for the last twenty-four hours?"

"A better question would be why did he take Franny Gough to Majorca if he had Amy on tap? It doesn't add up . . . not to my mind anyway."

Tyler stared past him, lost in thought. "Perhaps having her 'on tap' is right," he said then. "He knew where she was, knew she'd still be there when he came back." He brought his gaze back to the sergeant. "He'd need a constant supply of girls if he's running a pornography site," he pointed out, "and Franny said the trip was a spontaneous one."

"But why go all the way to Majorca? Why not film Franny in her flat?"

"Change of pace? Didn't want Mrs. Gough running to the police because of what the first wife had told her?"

"Those are all shots in the dark, Guv. You can't hold people on sketchy guesswork. The super'll be on your back before you know it. Rogerson's already working up a storm in his cell." He paused. "Tell me this. Why would Townsend jeopardize everything by abducting the kid? What was Amy planning to do that forced him to ditch Franny and come home? How did he *find out* what she was planning to do? A kid couldn't have afforded to call a cell phone in Spain from a phone booth in England. It doesn't make sense. There are too many flaws."

"Do you have any better ideas?" Tyler demanded crossly. "We've got a missing child and a suspected pedophile who knows her intimately. He also has a bloody close and bloody strange relationship with the father . . . bearing in mind that he seduced the man's wife. Wouldn't you say it's worth investigating?"

He saw only skepticism in the other man's eyes, and nodded irritably toward the door. "Just do it, Gary. If I'm wrong, I'm wrong. At the moment, I couldn't give a damn one way or the other . . . just so long as the kid ends up alive. The truth is she sounds like an uppity little brat whom I won't like if I ever meet her. I'm not into all singing, all dancing. I like children who are normal . . . a bit shy . . . keener on being with other kids than adults . . . but I've never been in Amy's position. It can't be much fun having to beg for love."

GARDEN OF 9 HUMBERT STREET

The old soldier watched the black man's antics from where he was standing. None of the fences were so high that Jimmy's ducking and weaving were hidden from him. He put the worst interpretation on what he saw. There was only one reason for a man to stare into windows as he slipped past the backs of the houses before taking cover behind a tree to case one of them. The Negro was using the opportunity of the riot to break into any property that looked empty.

The old soldier's indignation at being an unwilling abetter to crime was colossal. Did the man think he was stupid? Or a coward? Did he take it for granted that a retiree would turn a blind eye while his neighbors were robbed?

As he saw Jimmy jump the fence, he stooped to retrieve his machete from where it was propped against a post and set off after him.

INSIDE 23 HUMBERT STREET

For Colin, who was fumbling for a grip on the hot metal latch through the baggy hem of his T-shirt, the sound of the splintering doorjamb in the kitchen was the last straw. Fear paralyzed him. Every horror that he could possibly have imagined was coming true. He was caught in a trap . . . couldn't run . . . couldn't hide . . . and the only thought he had in his head was that none of this would be happening if he hadn't helped Kevin and Wesley make gasoline bombs.

▼

Upstairs, Sophie and Nicholas froze as the crash of the door flying open below them shook the floorboards on which they were standing. All their energy was concentrated on listening, heads tilted to catch sounds that could be translated into meaning. It's said that a thousand thoughts can race through the brain in seconds. In both their minds was just one.

Who . . . ?

The back of Sophie's head cracked against the wall before she was even aware that two strong hands had gripped her ankles and jerked her off her feet. She had a confused impression of a chair being swung at Nicholas's face, before she felt herself being dragged into the middle of the room and Franek's filthy hand clamping itself across her mouth to stifle the scream that was rising in her throat.

She stared up at him, eyes like saucers.

He lowered his mouth to her ear. "You want Franek to fuck you now, little girl?" he whispered.

▼

Jimmy was alarmed by the running taps and overflowing bowls in the sink. He didn't attempt to work out what they were for, merely accepted that it meant someone was nearby. He shrank against the wall beside the door and tried to calm his breathing. He became aware of sounds from upstairs. Something heavy dropping to the floor. The scrape of wood on wood, like furniture being moved. The shouts from Humbert Street carried through to him as if a door or a window were open somewhere. Also a smell of burning wood and gasoline.

He glanced at the taps again, putting two and two together. Gasoline bombs. Running water. It wasn't difficult to guess that someone was trying to put a fire out, or that whoever it was must have heard him. But which of the Hollises was it? The psycho or the pervert? And were they waiting for him in the hallway?

In one fluid movement, he yanked the table into the middle of the room, kicked the door wide and grabbed the microwave oven with both hands, ready to bring it down on the head of whoever was out there.

He was greeted with a wail of fear, which was cut off in mid-breath. "Oh, *fuck* it, Jimmy!" bellowed Colin as he burst into tears again. "You scared the shit out of me! I thought you was the pervert come to bugger me."

Such was Colin's reputation for thieving that Jimmy's first thought was that he was looting the place, until he saw the bucket at the boy's feet. He lowered the microwave to the floor and walked past the back room and the stairs, taking a quick glance at both as Colin had. He had a clear view of the front room, saw the devastation caused by the bricks, took in the broken window and the waiting crowd outside.

"What's going on?" he asked, grabbing the boy by the shoulders and pulling him into a hug.

"Everyone's gone crazy," wept Colin. "The sodding door's on fire, but the kettle don't work." He wiped his tears on his sleeve. "Mel's on the other side, trying to stop them from making it worse, but she's being forced away 'cos it's too hot. I was gonna open the door and chuck water on it, but I'm shit-scared Wesley's gonna bomb me. Kev's already gone up like a fucking torch . . . half his skin's burnt off."

Jimmy made what he could of this. "How d'you get in?"

"Through the window."

"Okay." He didn't waste time on further explanation. "They'd have fire-bombed the living room by now if that's what they wanted," he said. "You open the door. I'll work the bucket. Are you up for it?"

"Yeah."

Jimmy seized the handle of the pail. "Just don't open it too far," he warned, "or we'll both get fried. Ready? Go."

But he knew as soon as the door began to open and flames licked around the jamb that the fire was too well established for one pail of water. He kicked it closed again and threw the water against the crack between the door and the frame. "It's too late," he said. "We can't put it out from this side."

Colin started to wail again. "Oh, Jesus, Jesus! What we gonna do? If this place goes up, Mel's'll go, too . . . 'n' Rosie 'n' Ben're in there. That's why she's trying to stop the fuckers throwing any more bombs."

Jimmy thought rapidly, then steered him toward the living-room door. "Shift your ass back out there and I'll feed you buckets through the window. Get Mel and her line to help you. When the fire's out, tell them all to stand in front of the door and the window till I give you the signal it's okay to leave." He put his hand on the back of Colin's neck and gave it an encouraging squeeze. "Can you do that, mate?"

"Sure." He was so relieved to have Jimmy take over that it never occurred to him to ask what he was doing there or how he knew that Melanie had established a line in front of the pervert's house.

COMMAND CENTER—
POLICE HELICOPTER FOOTAGE

Faces weren't recognizable from the air, but hair and clothes were. The co-op vandals had the sense to wear caps and dispose of their clothes immediately after the riot. The barricaders wore balaclavas and scarves, and did the same. None of them was ever identified.

Video footage of what went on on Humbert Street was a different matter. Few believed that vigilantism was a crime, and the hovering helicopter attracted upturned faces and gestures of defiance as if to say: This is how justice should be administered. Perverts out. The same rule for Acid Row as for Portisfield. An eye for an eye. A tooth for a tooth. Fear for fear.

Despite their denials afterward that they were there, had a part in or incited murder, over one hundred people were identified from still photographs reproduced from the tape. It was a long and painstaking process that took over two years to complete, but that came to nothing when a jury failed to recognize the first defendant to come to trial from the grainy black-and-white mask of hatred that was presented to them. In their judgment, there was no resemblance between the clean, well-dressed, smiling eighteen-year-old on the stand and the vicious-looking adolescent in the picture. All subsequent cases were dropped.

In the end, the only people who admitted their part in what happened were the brave handful who had formed Melanie Patterson's line. Everything they did was captured by the helicopter's camera, from holding the gasoline bombers at bay to putting out the fire and trying to hold off the assault when it finally came. But none of them would give evidence of incitement against particular individuals. They were too frightened of Acid Row's violent gangland culture of retribution.

The single exception to this was Wesley Barber.

Everyone named him.

TWENTY-THREE

Jimmy kept his ears open every time he returned to the kitchen to fill the bucket and bowls. Once, there was a muffled thump as if some-one's head had been slammed against the floor; another time, he thought he heard voices. There was certainly no one downstairs. On his passage through to the living room he pushed the door of the back room wide open, and a quick glance showed it to be empty. Of people.

It was full of other things. An Aladdin's cave of sound equipment and instruments. Computers. Synthesizers. Mixers. Amplifiers. Key-board. Guitars. Drums. Even a saxophone. To a man like Jimmy, it was heavy temptation. A studio in the making. Everything he needed to go straight. It prejudiced his thinking from the moment he saw it. He didn't want it trashed or stolen. He wanted it for himself.

On his third trip past, he checked the lock and found a key on the inside of the door. It was half a second's work to shoot the bolt and zip the key inside his pocket. It wasn't much of a deterrent if the idiots outside decided to charge it, but it might hold long enough for him to hoof it back and stake a claim.

Afterward, of course, he regretted locking the door because it took away the only hiding place in that dreadful house.

But it's easy to be wise in retrospect . . .

▼

247

Sophie had grown bolder as the afternoon wore on. If Franek managed to catch her again, she had told herself, she would scratch his eyes out, drive her knee into his testicles, bite, claw, cripple. She certainly wouldn't give in. Better to fight to the bitter end than let him think a woman was easy. Such brave thoughts. Taken from fiction, not from real life. Designed to bolster confidence while she was on her feet and holding a weapon in her hand. Impossible to implement when she was flat on her back on the floor.

She was pinned like a butterfly to a board, unable to break free. The weight of his body was holding her down, his hands clamping hers to the floor above her head, his fleshy breasts and thick black curls smothering her mouth and nose and preventing her from crying out. He stank of dirt and sweat and she could feel the bile of disgust and defeat rise in her throat, threatening to choke her. She didn't know if it was her fear or his strength that had stolen her energy. All she knew was that if she didn't want to be punched again, the sensible thing was to lie quiet and not provoke him.

He laughed against her ear. "You like the rest," he gloated. "You rather Franek fuck you than spoil your pretty face. But maybe I do both. How will that make you feel, little miss? Ugly? Dirty? Will you run away and hide because Franek make you frightened? This is good. You not respect a man the way you should."

She felt him force her hands together so he could grasp them both in one of his. She felt his other hand move down to her pants and tear at the waistband. And all the while she could hear the sound of someone moving downstairs. She wondered if it was Nicholas. Had he gone away and left her to his father? Did he think that if he wasn't in the room it made his responsibility less?

Tears of anger pricked behind her eyes. She hated the son with a passion. He was a coward. A two-faced creep. Why had he listened to her if he had no intention of standing by her? How *dare* he abandon her? How *dare* he allow his father to empty his filth into her?

Later, she would ponder the irony of misdirected anger. She had torn strips off Bob once because a patient had been rude to her but, instead of tackling the patient, she had taken her fury out on Bob. He had waited calmly until the storm blew over, then murmured that if she planned to make a habit of anger transference then she ought to take up boxing. "We all know it's safer to beat up on people who won't retaliate," he told her, "but it's a quick way to lose friends. You need to find ways of dealing with confrontation when it happens."

"I'd rather avoid it."

"I know. It's a woman's thing. You're afraid of making a fool of yourself."

Perhaps her subconscious remembered the conversation. Perhaps, more simply, the reality of Franek's groping hand ripped through apathy and reawoke determination. She had promised herself she wouldn't submit.

But what was this if it wasn't submission?

She twisted her face sideways and let out a scream—a piercing, high-pitched sound that carried to Jimmy downstairs—cut short by a sudden blow to her face as Franek let go of her hands and punched her in the teeth.

"Shut up, bitch!" he growled, face contorted in fury, blood running down it where her nails had clawed the scabs from his wounds. "You want Franek to do what he do to Milosz's mamma?"

He chopped at her face with his fist, over and over again, as if she were a piece of meat that needed tenderizing and, as consciousness began to drift, she understood that Milosz's mother was dead.

▼

Jimmy heard the scream as he lifted the bucket across the sill, his chest heaving with the effort of running back and forth to the kitchen. "That's gotta be the last one, Col," he panted. "You'll have to take over now. I need you to keep those bastards at bay for another five minutes. You reckon you can hold out that long?"

Colin's face fell. "What'ya gonna do?"

"You don't wanna know, mate. Just trust me, okay." He looked beyond the boy to Melanie, who was rearranging her line to a rain of insults from Wesley Barber and his friends. He'd remained largely hidden to the crowd by the body of Colin, but word had spread that a black man was inside the pervert's house. The taunts had been endless as they'd struggled to put out the fire. *"That your man in there, Mel . . . ?" "What's a brother doing with perverts . . . ?" "How come you let him put a black bastard in your belly if he's a shirt lifter . . . ?" "Maybe you gotta yen for sickos yourself . . . ?"* "Just keep the retard off my back," he said grimly, "because I'll tear his head off if he comes anywhere near me. Can you do that?"

Colin looked panic-stricken. "What happens if I can't?"

"Lock yourself and Mel into the duplex with the bairns. I'll be back for you as soon as I can." He smacked the boy's palm. "You're a good bloke, Col. You've got more guts and brains than that nigger'll ever have."

GARDEN OF 21A HUMBERT STREET

The old soldier heard Sophie's scream from his place in the shadow of the apple tree, but with only a vague idea from his neighbor of why Acid Row was rioting—*"They've been moving queers onto Humbert Street"*—he assumed the Negro was responsible for the woman's terror. He didn't like homosexuals any better than the next man but, sure as eggs were eggs, they didn't use women in their perverse practices.

Savages did, though. No white woman was safe with a buck on the loose. He clambered over the fence and gripped the machete with two hands as he crept toward the kitchen door. It swayed drunkenly on its hinges from when Jimmy had burst it open, and was evidence, if the old man needed it, that a strong man was inside.

INSIDE 23 HUMBERT STREET

For all his bulk, Jimmy trod softly on the stairs, sliding his back up the wall and watching for movement on the landing. The house was an exact replica of Mrs. Carthew's, with every door open except the back bedroom's. He slid around the banister and gripped the handle with meaty fingers, listening for sounds.

He heard a man's voice, but he couldn't make out what he was saying. It was a croon. Soft and sweet and lyrical in a language he didn't understand. He eased the handle and put pressure on the door, but it was locked and wouldn't budge. He swore under his breath. What to do? Tell them he was there and waste time on explanations? Or charge another door?

His shoulder was bruised from his last effort and there wasn't much room in the confined space of the landing, but the sound of the woman's scream still echoed in his head and he couldn't see what option he had other than to take them by surprise. As if to prove the point, there was a sudden flurry of noise in the room, shoes scrabbling against the floor, a piece of furniture moving as if a foot had caught it, a woman's voice, muffled by a hand, saying: "No . . . no . . . no . . . !," the sickening squelch of a fist hitting soft tissue. Then the crooning again.

Ah, sweet Jesus!

He lifted a boot and, using the banister for leverage, brought his heel into direct contact with the lock. It took five kicks before the mortise ripped from the jamb, only for the door to come up short against an obstruction. Jimmy lowered his head in exhaustion, then, with a deep breath, put his shoulder to the panel and thrust his whole two hundred and fifty pounds into shifting the door and whatever stood behind it.

9 HUMBERT STREET

It was with relief that Gaynor heard the news that exits were opening up all along Humbert Street. Although she didn't know it then, the story of how Friendship Calling used its network to recruit sons, daughters, nieces, nephews and friends to make passageways to the gardens on both sides became the silver lining to the awful trauma of the July riot. It spoke of a continuing sense of community in even the most fractured of societies, and sowed a seed of hope for the future.

At the time, since no one had told her differently, Gaynor assumed that Jimmy was responsible. "I said he was a good 'un," she told Ken Hewitt when he relayed the news. "So are you gonna let me go for Mel and Col? I'm that worried about them. My battery's almost out, and I reckon the lot around here have gotten the hang of what to do. There hasn't been any bargin' and shovin' for ages."

"We think we know where Melanie is," he said, repeating the information from the helicopter. "Jimmy said the description of the blond girl sounded like Melanie. There's a lad in the line as well. Holding her hand. Wearing a Saints T-shirt and blue jeans. Could that be Colin?"

"Oh, thank God, thank God," she said, her voice breaking with a sob. "Are they all night?"

"As far as I know," said Ken. "One of the officers monitoring the footage has been keeping me posted, and the last I heard they were putting a fire out at number twenty-three to stop it from spreading. They're brave kids, Gaynor. You should be proud of them."

She gave a joyful laugh as if a weight had dropped from her shoulders. "They're my babies, darlin'. 'Course I'm proud of them. Always have been. So where's Jimmy? Is he with them?"

There was a tiny hesitation. "We're not sure at the moment. His cell phone is dead, so we can't speak to him."

"What about the little ones? Where are they?"

"You mean Melanie's children?"

"Yeah. Rosie 'n' Ben. She had them with her when we started the march."

"We don't know. They're not with her, so we think she must have put them inside her house. It's pretty rough where they are, Gaynor."

Worry took an immediate hold again. "Oh, God!" She looked up the road but couldn't see through the crowd that was still thronging the tarmac. "What's going on? You said there was a fire."

"Some boys are trying to bomb the house. Your kids are standing in front of it to stop them," he told her. "I said they were brave, Gaynor."

There was a long silence. "I should've known the little bastard wasn't joyriding," she said obliquely before cutting the line.

INSIDE 23 HUMBERT STREET

There was blood on the floorboards and in splattered droplets on the walls. The sight of it brought back the nausea that Jimmy had felt in the Glebe Tower elevator. That and the terrible heat and smell of the room. Body odor and the muskiness of disuse. Out of the corner of his eye, he could see something human lying crumpled in a corner, but all his attention was focused on the man and woman facing him across the room.

He'd taken too long, he thought. Too long helping to put out the fire. Too long breaking through the door.

The woman was propped across the man's lap like a ventriloquist's dummy, eyes closed, face battered beyond belief, chin and chest saturated with gore. Jimmy couldn't even tell if she was alive except that blood and saliva bubbled from her lips like ectoplasm. She must have fought like a tigress. The old man's face was scratched and clawed as if two-inch talons had hooked into his skin and ripped it wide open.

"You want I should kill her?" Franek put one hand under Sophie's slack jaw and the other round the back of her head. "I snap her neck if

253

you make movement. She stay alive if you keep your friends away till policemen come."

Jimmy didn't move a muscle. He wanted to say something, but the only words that formed themselves in his mind were obscenities and recriminations. Hadn't he warned the fucking doctor? He remembered saying it. What's the fucking difference between one man and a thousand? You've got a fucking psycho bastard who's gonna kill her if I get it wrong. He'd fucking said it. *Jesus!* Even a fucking moron should've fucking known this would happen.

"You understand me, nigger? Or you too stupid?" demanded Franek angrily, fazed by the man's gaping mouth and look of blank incomprehension. "I kill her if you come close."

Jimmy watched a sliver of silver appear between Sophie's lids. He flicked a glance at the crumpled figure in the corner. "I understand," he said in a voice husky with dryness.

Franek nodded in satisfaction. "You stay scared," he instructed. "That way she live."

Jimmy did as Sophie had done several times, ran his tongue around the inside of his mouth to unglue it from his teeth. "You're a dead man unless you come with me, Mr. Hollis," he said.

A glimmer of humor twitched the man's eyes, as if he saw a threat and was amused by it. "The girl dead if you try and take me."

"No, you don't understand." He injected urgency into his voice. "There are barricades around the estate and the police can't get in. The whole place is rioting. There're guys in the street wanting to burn you alive with gasoline bombs. I've agreed to take you and your son out the back and get you to the police at the perimeter wall. You've got about thirty seconds to make up your mind."

More amusement. "You think Franek believe this? You think Franek a fool?"

Sophie's eyelids started to flutter with returning consciousness.

"Yeah," said Jimmy recklessly, itching to wipe the smile off his face. "I've never met a psycho bastard yet who had a brain. They're all sodding retards. What's so clever about smashing a woman's teeth in? Any fuckwit can do it."

Franek tightened his grip on Sophie's neck as she started to move. "We stay," he said. "You guard the door. Keep us safe."

It was Jimmy's turn to smile. "They're gonna fry you, Mr. Hollis. You got enough brains to understand that? Me standing here ain't gonna make a blind bit of difference 'cos the only way out'll be through the window, 'n' there's guys down below waiting with blades. They don't like sickos, and they're stoned out of their skulls. They'll cut you to pieces as soon as look at you."

Franek's gaze never wavered, but it wasn't clear to Jimmy if lack of fear or lack of comprehension was the cause of his imperturbability. He couldn't fail to hear the shouts from outside, which were louder and more persistent since the bedroom door had been opened. Jimmy could make out Wesley Barber among the rest and that worried him, because he guessed that Wesley was moving closer to the shattered downstairs window.

"You get the brother out, Mel, or we gonna burn him, too . . ."

"You call the wrong man dirty names, nigger. Do you ask if the son is sick? Do you ask if the son does this? No, you spit on the dada and say he must be the guilty man." He stared Jimmy down. "But it's me—Franek—who does nothing wicked and me—Franek—who does what he can to keep his life."

"He'll never blame himself . . ." Jimmy glanced at the body in the corner again. "Is that your son? Is he dead?"

"I knock him from the girl with a chair. He doesn't move since."

"Yeah, well, you can save all that for the cops, Mr. Hollis. There's no way I'm gonna believe your hands are clean. You have to be a really sick fucker if you're willing to break a woman's neck."

"You give me no choice. Without the threat, you would not listen. But Franek is not the one you want. It is Milosz who causes this trouble. Milosz who does bad things." The old man's eyes narrowed as Jimmy's expression changed. "Why you look like this?" he demanded. "What you thinking?"

"They told me your name was Hollis."

"So?"

"It's fucking Zelowski, isn't it?"

"What difference is a name?"

Jimmy's fists clenched at his sides. He knew now why there was a studio downstairs. "A hell of a fucking difference. Jesus! I know what you did. No wonder your son pisses on himself every time the door opens. You whipped a five-year-old kid, you bastard."

"This is lies."

"Don't bullshit me!" he said angrily. "I knew your son in jail. I liked him. Milosz Zelowski. Best fucking musician I ever met." His voice rose in wrath. "They broke his fingers because they heard he gave hand jobs, and there's only one bastard who could've taught him to do that. You're a real piece of work. Fucking brave when it's kids 'n' women." He spat on the floor. "No guts at all for taking on men."

The sound of his raised voice caused Sophie's eyes to open. Her face was turned toward Jimmy, but he couldn't judge if there was any understanding there except that she lay still, seemingly aware that movement might be dangerous. She stared at him unblinkingly, and he had the impression she was trying to tell him something. But he didn't know what it was.

Franek was unimpressed. "This is to fight me, yes? Do you think it so easy to make Franek forget why he hold this little white neck between his hands?"

"If you break it, I'll chuck you out of the window myself."

The old man's eyes lit with amusement again. "Maybe I don't care. Maybe I do it anyway. Maybe I say to myself, let's see if a nigger tell the truth for once." He watched Jimmy's face greedily. "Hah!" he said triumphantly. "Now you not so interested in fighting. Maybe you carry messages for Franek instead. Make your friends go home to their cages. Tell them if Franek is safe, the girl is safe. Go. Do what Franek say"—he stretched a finger to caress Sophie's cheek—"and the little miss live. Argue any more, and she don't."

Sophie's eyes widened immediately, and this time the message was clear. *Don't leave me.* She was more alert than she was pretending, thought Jimmy.

He had already calculated that he couldn't cross the gap between them before Franek twisted his hands. He could take a gamble that Sophie would strike out when he made his move, or that Franek wasn't experienced enough to get it right the first time. But the risk was too great. He held no cards because he didn't want her dead. Franek held them all.

"They won't listen to me," he said.

"Don't argue."

"I'm a nigger, 'n' niggers aren't welcome in Acid Row." He jerked his head toward the door. "Listen! They're saying they're gonna burn me, too, just 'cos I'm black."

This time a flicker of doubt did creep into Franek's gaze. It was unlikely he could make out individual words among the shouts, but the sentiments Jimmy expressed matched his own views on blacks so he believed them.

Jimmy nodded toward Sophie. "They'll listen to *her*. She's their doctor. If we take her into the front bedroom she can talk to them through the window."

Franek shook his head obstinately. "It give you chance to take her away from me. Go. Do what I say. Maybe they listen more than you think."

Jimmy's seething anger boiled over. He didn't have the time or the patience for negotiation, or the mindset that would allow a man like this to think he would tamely take orders. He slammed the side of his fist against the wardrobe. "Listen, motherfucker," he roared. "I've had it with you. You'd better believe I'm the only bastard in this street who doesn't wanna kill you. You've got one way to save your sodding life, 'n' that's with me. I'm coming in for Milosz, so let the lady go and get your fat ass off the floor."

Perhaps Sophie had been waiting for just such an ultimatum, perhaps she felt an easing of the hand under her jaw, because she gave a sudden lurch and twisted out of Franek's grip, scrabbling on hands and knees toward Jimmy. He was half a second slower off the mark than she was, but still a damn sight faster than a seventy-one-year-old.

"Gotcha," he said, lifting her around the waist and swinging her around behind him. He lowered his head and spread his arms wide, ready for the tackle. "How about it, motherfucker?" he taunted. "Fancy your chances against a nigger?"

"Don't trust him," said Sophie's voice in a rasp behind him. "He's mad. I think he killed his wife. He'll kill you if he can."

Franek chuckled. "She talk rubbish," he said. "She very stupid girl. Yack-yack all the time. Now you make good your promise. Keep Franek alive the way you say."

Jimmy straightened and dropped his hands invitingly to his side. "Sure thing, baas, but I'm not leaving without Milosz." He took a step toward the crumpled body of his friend, heard Sophie's anguished cry as Franek made a lunge at him, and planted his fist on the side of the old man's head. "Like I said," he murmured, massaging his knuckles, "I've never met a psycho yet who had a brain."

TWENTY-FOUR

Melanie wondered why Wesley and his friends didn't just rush them. All they had to do was charge the line and they'd be in through the window, quick as a wink. It was weird. Almost as if they knew that Mel and Col were in the right and they were in the wrong. In an exhausted, abstracted way, she played *Star Wars* films across her mind, picturing herself as Princess Leia and Col as Luke Skywalker. Brother and sister Jedi knights. The force was with them.

She felt Colin shake her arm. "Are you gonna faint?" he asked in alarm.

"No, I'm okay."

She didn't believe in good or evil. Just kindness when you felt like it; and idiocy when you were wasted. So maybe it was the black lady at her side who kept telling Wesley his mother would have his guts that made him hang back. Or the helicopter, hovering overhead. Or his friends, who were Colin's friends, too. Wesley was a fuck head whichever way you looked at it. Stoned on acid. Prancing around with a switchblade in his hand. Yelling insults. Telling her he was going to slice Jimmy's gonads the next time he saw him.

Well, who cared? What had Jimmy ever done for her except get his ass banged up and leave her to carry his baby on her own? He wouldn't come on the march . . . wasn't there to take care of the bairns when she needed him. Where was he now? *"Cleaning out the pervert's*

259

house," Col had said. *"There's a fortune in stereos in the back room."* Fucking bastard. He'd always thought more of money than he did of her.

Colin grabbed her by the arm again. "Jeez, Mel. You sure you're okay? You're swaying all over the place, Sis."

Her weary eyes filled with tears. "I don't reckon Jimmy loves me no more, Col. Where's he been all the time? Why didn't he answer his phone? Do you think he's messing with someone else?"

"'Course he isn't. He just had stuff to do."

"Like what? What's more important than me and the baby?"

"Just stuff," said Colin uneasily. But he, too, was plagued with doubts. He couldn't believe Jimmy would put stereos before Mel and him. They'd been family to him, and everyone knew you didn't desert family.

INSIDE 23 HUMBERT STREET

Jimmy used a tie from the wardrobe to bind Franek's hands in front of him, before slapping his face to bring him around and hauling him to his feet. "We're leaving," he told him. "I'm taking Milosz. You can stay or you can come. If you come, you do as you're told. One false move and I feed you to the crazies. *Capeesh?"*

"Untie me."

"No. You're a fucking psycho, and I don't trust you." He dragged Milosz into the center of the room, then knelt to hoist the limp body over his shoulder in a fireman's carry. He watched Franek all the while. "It's your call. You follow or you die. I'm not turning around for you, and I'm not gonna help you. You make a mistake . . . anyone notices you . . . I'm outta there with Milosz and Sophie. Get it?"

Franek's breathing started to be labored. "You put me in danger with my hands tied."

"I know. It sucks, doesn't it?" Jimmy headed for the door, putting

a hand behind Sophie to urge her through. "I'll bet that's what the hookers said before you beat the shit out of them."

▼

The old soldier retreated hurriedly from the bottom of the stairs when he heard Sophie's scurrying footsteps and Jimmy's heavier tread on the landing. He had heard voices in the room above, but hadn't been able to make out words because of the commotion outside. He was elderly and disoriented, and, as he freely admitted to himself, extremely frightened. He hadn't realized how large the crowd was in Humbert Street, or how angry it seemed to be.

On previous occasions when trouble had erupted—although never on such a scale as this—it was invariably in response to heavy-handed treatment by the police. Acid Row harbored strong resentments against the forces of law and order, believing itself to be singled out for brutal treatment. There had been running battles on several occasions after gangland leaders had been beaten because the police claimed they were resisting arrest. Like most of the older inhabitants of the estate, the soldier always believed the constabulary's version, but it occurred to him now that something very bad must have happened for such a large number of people to be so irate.

He regretted having followed the black man into a trap. Pride had brought him here. A determination to prove that he was still a man to be reckoned with. He cursed himself for his own stupidity. His wife had been fond of saying that he lost whatever sense he'd been born with when he donned the king's uniform. Toting a gun in the jungles of Borneo, she would snap crossly, hadn't given him the right to lecture everyone else on their faults. Fighting never achieved anything except the death of other women's children. It had been the cause of every row between them, because he couldn't bear to have his lifetime's single real achievement belittled.

He looked around desperately for a hiding place, but there was none in the hallway. Terror settled in his stomach like a millstone. The door to the back room was locked, and he hadn't the speed to reach the safety of the gardens before the black man caught him. It was Jimmy he feared—and the gang he had with him—not the louts in the road, who would recognize the "grumpy old sod" who took them to task every Saturday night for being drunk and disorderly outside his house. Clutching his machete to his chest, he sidled into the front room and hid behind the door . . .

GARDENS, HUMBERT STREET

Gaynor decided against trying to push through the crowd, recognizing that anyone who hadn't taken the chance to escape was sturdy enough and strong enough to hold their place. Instead, she ran through Mrs. Carthew's house and followed Jimmy's path behind the houses, reasoning that if exits were opening along the road she could bypass the crush and come out somewhere near her children.

It was eerily quiet in the back. She expected the gardens to be full of frightened people, and she couldn't understand why they weren't. Her pace slowed. The beat of the helicopter's blades in the sky above reminded her that the police were watching everything. *Should she be doing this . . . ?*

COMMAND CENTER— POLICE HELICOPTER FOOTAGE

The video camera caught her upturned face in the garden with its jungle gym, while it waited for Jimmy's withdrawal from 23. Ken Hewitt's instructions had been to confine the exits to the even side of the road until he received word that Sophie and the Zelowskis were out. There was a collective sigh of relief from the watchers when three figures emerged, with the big man in black leather carrying a fourth on his shoulder.

The lens tracked them toward Bassindale Row as Jimmy kicked down fences with a well-aimed boot, then panned back toward Humbert Street.

"What happened to the guy with the tin helmet?" asked one.

No one knew.

GARDENS, HUMBERT STREET

To Gaynor, three houses down, Jimmy was unmistakable as he came through the kitchen door. She had a fleeting sense that she knew the woman beside him, but there was too much blood on her face to be sure. She raised a hand in recognition but they turned left out of the door, heading for Bassindale Row, and never even glanced in her direction.

She called out: "JIMMY!" but he was intent on kicking down fences and running for the next one, and he didn't hear her.

Not for a second did she guess that she was watching the exodus of the pedophiles. She had barely thought about them since the riot started, except to blame herself for inciting the march, and she didn't know where she was in relation to Melanie's duplex as she had never been inside the gardens before. She could only interpret what she saw from what she thought she knew, which made this one of the exits Jimmy had been sent to establish.

It was obvious there had been an accident. Or something worse. *Another gasoline bomb? A stampede?* It was the only explanation for Jimmy's frantic haste, the body across his shoulder, the blood on the woman's face and the elderly man who followed behind them, holding his hands in front of him as if he were hurt. Jimmy was taking the injured out.

Her heart lurched with immediate fear for her children. She took tentative steps past the jungle gym, expecting to see other people come running out in Jimmy's wake, but it was strangely quiet. She raised her face to the helicopter again, shielding her eyes from the sun. What on *earth* was going on? Where *was* everyone?

▼

Jimmy lowered Milosz to the ground behind the six-foot fence that was the border between the garden of the end house on Bassett Road and Bassindale Row. He had tracked through to the Bassett gardens in the hope that the crowd spilling out of Humbert Street was thinner there, although the yelling and shouting were still far too close for comfort. They could hear feet pounding on the tarmac, people talking, even smell cigarette smoke as bystanders lit up to watch from a distance. He saw his own fear mirrored in the eyes of Sophie and Franek as he held a finger to his lips to keep them quiet.

It was an unnecessary instruction to Franek, whose face was as white and pasty as his son's. He slumped against the fence and covered his head with his hands as if hiding behind the flimsy paneling could somehow protect him from the terrifying reality of mob blood lust. Neither Sophie nor Jimmy paid any attention to him.

Jimmy knelt on the ground beside Milosz and took several deep breaths before he could speak. "I'm not sure I'm gonna be able to carry him the whole way out," he whispered in Sophie's ear. "He weighs a ton. Do you think he's dead?"

She was squatting next to him and pressed her fingertips to Milosz's neck before resting a hand on his chest to feel for movement. "He's out cold," she whispered, rolling an eyelid back with the ball of her thumb, "but his automatic responses are functioning—he's breathing and his pulse is strong. It's not a concussion, because he'd have come to by now, so I'm guessing he's turned off completely this time."

"What does that mean?"

"It's how he deals with fear," she murmured. "Retreats inside himself. His father's doing the same thing by covering his head." She stuck her fingernails into Milosz's nostrils and dug them into his septum. There was a flicker of his eyelids as his nervous system registered pain but no returning consciousness in the way the policewoman had responded to Eileen Hinkley's smelling salts. "Sorry," she whispered apologetically. "He needs more help than I can give him at the moment. Even if I *could* bring him out of it, he'd be too uncoordinated to walk for a while."

Jimmy jerked his head toward the fence. "We've gotta break out onto Bassindale and aim for the perimeter wall. It means pushing through the crowd coming the other way, and that's gonna be fucking hard with a dead weight on my back and a couple of cripples in tow. Sorry, lady, but you look like shit"—he nodded at Franek—"and he ain't much better. I don't see how we're gonna do this. Only one of us needs to fall and we're all up the fucking creek."

Sophie's own fear came back in a tidal wave. She hadn't realized he'd meant what he'd said to Franek in the upstairs room. She had assumed it was an excuse to get them out of the house. "Oh, God," she said, pulling herself away from both him and Milosz. "I can't do this. Truly, I can't. I'm not brave enough."

"The doc said you were."

"Which doc?"

"Harry . . . at the clinic . . . and someone called Jenny. Reckoned you were a fighter." He gripped hold of her hand to stop her from moving any farther away. "You're Sophie, right? My Mel's doctor. The lady who started Friendship Calling. The one whose wedding we're going to. Shit, girl! Mel's standing in front of that house stopping the fucking retards from throwing Molotovs. Are you telling me she's got bigger balls than you have?"

Sophie's eyes filled with tears. "Melanie Patterson? Are you Jimmy James?"

He nodded. "I gave my word I'd bring you and these fuckers out before I went back for Mel and the babes. But we've gotta get a move on and you've gotta help me. I can't do it on my own. A lady by my side'll make it look kosher."

She envied Nicholas his coma. Why couldn't she just lie down and refuse to make any more decisions? She wanted to say: *I'm hurting . . . I'm bleeding . . . I'm frightened . . .* Instead, she flicked a glance at Franek. "What are you going to do if he collapses? You can't carry two dead weights."

"He won't. He's scared shitless of being left behind. He'll be ripped apart if he doesn't keep up."

"He has asthma. He might not be able to."

"Then he's a dead man," said Jimmy unfeelingly.

Oh, God! Her imagination was in overdrive again. Nothing was that simple. Even in Acid Row you couldn't just abandon old men beside the road with their hands tied. People would ask questions. "You don't know what he's like. He'll call out . . . draw attention to himself . . . make you go back to stop us all from being killed. Someone will recognize him."

"Trust me," said Jimmy with more confidence than he felt. "Most of the guys out there don't even know what this fight's about, and even if they do, they won't reckon a black guy and a girl would be hanging around perverts. They'll just think we got caught in the middle of something." His face broke into a smile. "Tell them you're a doctor . . . talk medical stuff . . . give us credibility. Your friend Harry reckons you can take the steam out of anything."

Briefly, Sophie closed her eyes. She felt like screaming. Harry was an idiot. And she didn't trust anyone whose idea of credibility was for a battered and bloody woman to walk down the road talking "medical stuff." "Where are we exactly?" she said then, glancing toward the nearest house.

She was delirious, like the policewoman, thought Jimmy. "The end house on Bassett Road," he told her, "at the corner of Bassindale."

"Which number?"

"Dunno."

She looked toward the Humbert Street house behind them. "If that's the end of Bassindale Row, then it must have a higher number than Melanie's?"

"Yeah. Hers is the other side of twenty-three from here."

"Okay." Sophie pictured the layout of the streets in her mind, mapping them according to patients. "That makes this two"—she pointed at the neighboring garden—"that one's four and the one beyond six. I know the woman who lives in six."

"That doesn't help us. We'll be going the wrong way, and half of Bassett's out in the road, anyway. She probably won't even answer the door . . . but, let's say she does, we've still got to get back onto Bassindale. It'll just add time to the journey."

Sophie shook her head. "She only leaves the house to go to the hospital, and she won't have an appointment on a Saturday. We can take shelter there, and it'll give me a chance to bring Milosz around while you go back for Melanie and the kids." She made a wry face. "I feel like death warmed over at the moment, Jimmy, and you can't carry all of us. So get us to number six, then go back for Mel. *Please?*"

Jimmy nodded toward Franek. "What about him?"

"I'll tie him up so tight he'll wish he'd never set eyes on me."

"Okay." He hauled Milosz into a sitting position, then lowered his shoulder to hoist him up again. "So what's wrong with this patient of yours?" he asked, pushing himself upright with an effort and locking his knees. "Why won't she go out?"

"Squamous cell carcinoma," said Sophie succinctly. "They had to take off most of her nose to eradicate it. She's got a hole in the middle of her face."

Oh, shit . . . !

COMMAND CENTER—
POLICE HELICOPTER FOOTAGE

The camera picked up Jimmy and his group again when the spotter watching them said they'd moved away from Bassindale Row and were heading back into the Bassett Road gardens. The observers at headquarters pinpointed the house they entered as number 6, and a check of their records showed the occupant was a Ms. Frensham. This information was passed to Ken Hewitt at the Nightingale Health Center and verification came back immediately that Clara Frensham was a patient of Dr. Sophie Morrison's. The assumption, rightly, was that Sophie had opted to take shelter, and Jimmy's reappearance through the back door, alone, some two minutes later confirmed this.

It was clear from the way he headed straight back toward 23 that his intention was to extricate his girlfriend. A tentative identification of the woman who had stood irresolutely behind the house before suddenly making up her mind to go in had recorded her as Gaynor Patterson, although a question mark remained beside the name as the only description the health center had been able to furnish was Jenny Monroe's belief that she had blond hair like her daughter's. Attempts to raise her on her cell phone proved fruitless since, like Jimmy's, her battery had run out.

A similar question mark remained beside Melanie's name, because Jimmy's earlier observation to Harry Bonfield that the tall, blond, pregnant girl sounded like "his Mel" was hardly proof that she was the girl in front of the house. All attempts by Ken Hewitt and Jenny Monroe to reach Melanie had met with failure. From being constantly busy the phone was now disconnected, its innards smashed beyond repair beneath the heel of a rioter after Colin had dropped it when he ran to Melanie's aid. The identity of the man in the tin helmet, why he had entered number 23 in the first place and why he remained inside, continued to mystify the police.

Jimmy's beeline approach toward the rear of 23 allowed the camera's field of vision to cover events on both sides of the house. It caught the abrupt change of pace in Jimmy James's stride as he pounded across the garden to fling himself through the back door; the sudden wild charge of part of the crowd toward the broken front-room window; and the gut-churning disappearance of the blond girl as Wesley Barber punched her in her pregnant stomach and she fell beneath trampling feet.

A shout of horror rose from every throat in the command center.

TWENTY-FIVE

Townsend's BMW stood on its own in a corner of the Hilton parking lot. "Anything?" Tyler asked the officer beside it.

The man shook his head. "The trunk's clean as a whistle, sir. A pathologist might find something, but I wouldn't bet on it."

"Too clean? How did it smell?"

"Nothing unusual. I'd have noticed detergent."

"Any luggage? Video camera?"

"Just a laptop."

"Interesting." Tyler peered through the back window. "What about inside?"

"Aftershave. An expensive one, too. The guy reeks of it." He made a face. "He's quite a piece of work, sir. The birth date on his driver's license says he's forty-five . . . but he's doing his damnedest to look thirty. Phony as hell, if you ask me." A thoughtful expression crossed his face. "He's no pushover . . . didn't blink an eyelid when I opened the car door for him."

"Did he object to you searching the trunk?"

"No. Opened it himself."

"Did he ask what you were looking for?"

"No."

"Interesting," said Tyler again.

270

CONFERENCE ROOM, HILTON HOTEL

Phony or not, Tyler understood immediately why Laura had fallen for Edward Townsend. "A piece of work" was a good description of him. Tanned, clean-shaven skin. Muscular arms and shoulders. Close-cropped hair. Compared with Tyler's ruddy and rumpled St. Bernard look, he had the polished bronze sheen of Barbie's Ken. (Which might explain why an eighteen-year-old going on twelve like Franny found him attractive, thought Tyler acidly.) But he was too synthetic to hold anyone's attention for long. The eye yearned for something interesting to fasten upon—laugh lines, wrinkles of character—anything that didn't conform to a love-starved woman's idea of male beauty.

It was an image that worked better from a distance. Close up, Tyler wasn't surprised that the manager at the Bella Vista had been suspicious of the man's relationship with Franny. His hair looked dyed, the tan was almost certainly fake, and his restless, pale eyes never held a gaze for more than a second. Tyler made a determined attempt to look at him objectively—it was too easy to allow prejudice to color his view—but he still felt his hackles rise in response. Perhaps it was the aftershave.

Two uniformed constables stood stolidly by the doorway, arms folded, moving aside to let Tyler and Butler enter. A table ran down the center with notepads, drawn-up chairs and a coffee urn and cups at one end. Townsend, in rolled-up shirtsleeves, sat at the other end, suit jacket draped across his chair back, laptop open in front of him, a screen saver of clouds flickering across the monitor.

"D.C.I. Tyler and Detective Sergeant Butler . . . investigating the disappearance of Amy Biddulph," said Tyler as he pulled out a seat beside the man and sat down, crossing his legs and resting his elbow on the table. Butler took the chair on the other side. "Thank you for agreeing to talk to us, sir."

"No one told me I had a choice." It was the same voice that had spoken on the cell phone, although the London vowels were less obvious in person than over the phone. Was his background something else he wanted to hide? Tyler wondered. He certainly had the trappings of a self-made man: BMW, Rolex, Armani suit.

"It's always difficult in cases like this," said Tyler equivocally. "We need to guarantee immediate access to people who can help us."

"I don't have a problem answering questions. Amy's a sweet kid. I'd do anything to help her. All I asked of these men"—he gestured toward the uniformed constables—"was that I be allowed to explain the situation to the other people at my meeting. I don't believe that warrants detention, does it, Inspector?"

"We've explained on your behalf, sir," Tyler told him pleasantly. "They're happy to wait until we've finished. They all agree that a child's life is worth a short delay."

The eyes rested on him briefly. "What did you tell them?"

"That you have privileged information about Amy Biddulph, and it was important for us to talk to you as soon as possible."

"What sort of privileged information?"

"From the time she and her mother were living with you. I understand you made a number of videotapes of her. We'd appreciate those, sir. Film is more useful to us than the still photograph we're using at the moment. People find it easier to recognize a child from a moving image."

He looked amused. "They don't exist anymore. Laura cut them to shreds and left them lying on my living-room floor before she left. Didn't she tell you?"

Tyler's certainty wavered. There was never enough time in an investigation like this. Too many questions would always remain unasked. "No."

"Then I'm sorry to disappoint you."

Tyler nodded. "How do you know Laura found them all? Do you remember how many you made?"

"I do, as a matter of fact. I used the same three over and over again. The only reason I filmed Amy at all was because she liked performing and wanted to see herself on TV."

"Then why film her naked in the bath?"

He gave an easy laugh. "Good acoustics and a handy loofah for a microphone. She was doing 'Like a Virgin' at full blast. Pretty damn well, too. She's a great little singer."

"What happened to the tapes you made of Laura?"

Townsend laughed again, his eyes pouching into mischievous creases. He was very relaxed. Even charming. "Come on, Inspector. They won't help you find Amy. She wasn't in any of them. Laura must have told you that, at least. Frankly, they weren't the sort of movies you'd put a kid in."

"So I gather. From the way Laura describes them, they were a masturbation aid. Presumably you saved them?"

He spoke without hesitation. "I never save anything from dead relationships, Inspector. I reused them."

"What for?"

He thought for a moment. "Probably a development we're building in Guildford. We've had problems with materials being stolen so I put a camera on site. The workforce doesn't like it but there wasn't much else I could do if I didn't want to be robbed blind."

The construction workers Tyler knew were tough-talking homophobes who held a person's gaze when they spoke to him. It didn't make them any more truthful and honest than the next person, just more direct, and he wondered what Townsend's men thought of him. "How can you be so certain about Amy's tapes . . . and so uncertain about Laura's?"

"I made more of Laura . . . mostly before she moved in. With Amy, there were just the three. She wasn't interested in past performances . . . everything had to be very immediate or she became bored." He unstrapped his Rolex and put it on the table in front of him, betraying the same impatience to move on that Martin Rogerson had shown earlier. "As I said, I'm sorry to disappoint you, Inspector."

Tyler reminded himself that his M.O. was to persuade women to pose naked in front of a camera. He would certainly know how to fend off awkward questions about predecessors. The voice was still edgy with irritation, but he had it well under control.

Tyler leaned forward. "You seem very impatient," he murmured. "Why is that, sir? The child's in desperate trouble and you said you wanted to help her."

The reaction was stronger than he was expecting. A flash of steel. "Some of us have to generate our own salaries instead of relying on the state to pay us," he snapped. "You're delaying my meeting. I understand the reasons for it, and I've expressed my willingness to answer your questions, but I would appreciate some urgency. What can I tell you about Amy that Laura and Martin don't know?"

Tyler raised a placatory hand as if to admit fault. "We've been told Amy made a collect call to someone named 'Em' about two weeks ago. Do you know who that might have been, sir?"

"No."

"Would you mind taking a little time to think about it? Did she mention any friends while she was living with you called Em or Emma?"

"Not that I recall. She was a great little chatterbox, but I didn't often listen. If anyone knows, it'll be her mother."

Tyler gave a tired sigh. "It is important, Mr. Townsend."

The man steepled his fingers under his nose and took a deep breath. "I realize that, and I'm sorry. Amy came as a package with her mother. I was pleasant to her, spoke to her on the few occasions I found her still up, made one or two films of her singing and dancing, and, as far as I was able to, provided for her. Laura had some confused reasons about not accepting child-support payments from her husband . . . She talked about a clean break but, in reality, it had more to do with giving Martin a poke in the eye. I can manage without you. That sort of thing. After six months I recognized that I was just a convenient stepping-stone on her route out of marriage. We had a row about it, and by the next evening she and Amy were gone. I haven't seen or spoken to either of them since."

"Cutting up tapes of her daughter and leaving them scattered across your floor suggest there was a little bit more to it than that, sir."

Townsend tapped his forefingers against the sides of his nose and took another glance at the D.C.I. "What do you want me to do? Blacken the woman's name? She's just lost her kid, for Christ's sake."

"We've heard her version. I'd be interested in yours."

He lowered his head into his hands for a moment. "Okay, she was jealous," he said bluntly, looking up. "It was absurd. She'd come from a marriage where the child's father barely recognized his daughter, and she thought it was sweet to hook up with a man who treated Amy with kindness. That mindset lasted all of about four months. Laura had had the kid entirely to herself when she lived with Martin, and she didn't like it when Amy started to share her affection with me. She became thoroughly possessive, resented every bit of attention I showed Amy, particularly the videos, and started accusing me of liking the child more than her. We staggered on for another two months—with me giving Amy the cold shoulder in order not to antagonize her mother . . . and the poor little kid getting really upset about it—then I said I'd had enough. End of story. Laura took off the next day."

Tyler nodded. "Did the same thing happen in your two marriages?" he asked.

He'd caught the man off balance. There was a flicker of uncertainty. "What the hell have my marriages got to do with Amy?"

"Just interested. Neither of them lasted very long either."

Townsend moved his mouse to bring the clouds back onto his screen. "I played around," he said curtly. "Neither of my wives liked it. I'd have done the same to Laura if she hadn't left. I'm not husband material, as most of the women I know will tell you."

"Does Mr. Rogerson know that?"

"What's that got to do with anything?"

"It occurred to me that Laura and Amy were on loan till your infatuation ran its course."

Another flash of steel. "That's offensive."

Tyler shrugged and reverted to the subject of the telephone call. "Laura believes Amy said 'Ed' not 'Em,' which I'm told is what she called you, Mr. Townsend. The sounds are similar, and the children who were listening to the conversation weren't concentrating particularly well."

He shook his head. "I've already said I haven't spoken to Amy since she left."

"We've only your word for that, sit."

The man assessed Tyler for several seconds with a remarkably steady gaze. There was no liking in the pale eyes, but no mystery either. "Do you think I had something to do with Amy's disappearance?" he demanded. "Is that what these questions are about?"

"Why assume that a phone call two weeks ago had anything to do with what happened yesterday, Mr. Townsend? All we're trying to find out is what was in the child's mind. She was obviously unhappy, because she was crying throughout the conversation, and it was someone she knew well, because the collect charges were accepted."

"Well, it wasn't me. I'd certainly have accepted a call if she'd tried to contact me—God damn it, I felt sorry for the kid—she was completely at sea. Didn't know if her mother loved her . . . if her father loved her . . . no contact with any extended family because they all disapproved of the marriage. What kind of life is that for a ten-year-old?"

There were so many echoes of Tyler's own thoughts that he was inclined to call a halt to the questioning. He knew better than anyone that this was a fishing trip, and so far he'd come up with nothing. "Would you be willing to confirm that by giving us access to your telephone records?" he asked. "If no charges show, then it was some-one else and we'll leave you in peace."

Townsend nodded. "Sure. Whatever you want." He scribbled three telephone numbers on the notepad in front of him. "Those are my num-bers. Home. Work. Cell. I'm happy to authorize access to all three."

Tyler reached for the pad.

Gary Butler stirred himself. "You have five separate numbers attached to your house, Mr. Townsend. I ran a check last night to see if there was any way we could contact you. I hoped we might be able to patch through to your cell phone. No luck. One's a fax, one's a modem, the other three are dedicated call lines. We need authority to access them all."

Townsend's eyes slid toward him.

"We'll be happy to apply for a warrant," continued Gary without hostility. "Perhaps you'd like a solicitor present while we explain the procedure?"

"You don't have grounds for a warrant. I've already told you I haven't spoken to Amy since she left my house."

"A child matching her description was picked up by a car simi-lar to yours outside the Catholic church in Portisfield at lunchtime yesterday."

No hesitation at all. "Those aren't grounds," he said forcefully. "I wasn't in Portisfield yesterday."

Butler looked at Tyler, who gave him the nod to continue. "Can you prove that, sir?"

"I can certainly prove I was somewhere else at lunchtime." He felt in his jacket pocket for his wallet and produced a receipt from one of the flaps. "I bought lunch at the Fleet service station on the M-three." He looked undecidedly between the two men, then offered the slip of paper to Tyler.

Tyler placed it on the table and smoothed it out. "It was an early lunch. This is timed at eleven forty-three."

"I hadn't eaten since the previous evening. I was on my way to Guildford for a meeting with my foreman."

"What time was that?"

"As far as I remember it was about one-fifteen. His name's Steve Ablett. Address: Twelve Dock Way, Millbrook. His number's in the book."

It was what he'd been leading up to. The perfect alibi. Not even Michael Schumacher could drive from Fleet to Portisfield and up to Guildford in one and a quarter hours. "What did you order, Mr. Townsend?"

"Lasagna and coffee."

Correct, but hardly difficult to memorize. *"Lasagna, six pounds and twenty-five pence. Coffee, ninety-five pence."* There were faint lines on the surface of the paper as if it had been crumpled, then ironed. Tyler nodded to Butler, who took out his cell phone and left the room to make the call to Steve Ablett in the corridor.

"How did you know lunchtime was critical?" he asked Townsend. "The only time we've given out is ten o'clock, which is when Amy was seen leaving the Logans' house. Did Martin Rogerson tell you?"

The man shook his head. "I didn't know it was critical till the sergeant mentioned it."

"Do you keep all your receipts?"

"Anything I can deduct."

"Show me some others."

He made a pretense of searching through his wallet. "I emptied it recently. I don't have any with me. There might be some in the car."

"You can't deduct lunch, Mr. Townsend. Everyone has to eat. Why keep that receipt? Were you expecting to be asked for an alibi?"

"It's the last thing I bought. I tuck all receipts in here, then sort them out later."

"Were you driving south or north on the M-three?"

"South."

"Then why go to the Fleet service station? Your best route to Guildford was to leave at the Camberley turnoff . . . a good ten miles before Fleet. There are plenty of gas stations along that road, and they all sell sandwiches."

"I needed a break from the car." He looked amused again. "The development's on the Aldershot side of Guildford. It's almost as quick to come off at Hook . . . and it's a pleasanter drive."

Tyler gave an easy smile in response, then looked at the tracery of lines on the slip of paper again. It had clearly been crumpled up into a ball, then flattened out later. He thought of the litter that accumulated in the parking lots of service stations. It wasn't beyond the realm of possibility that Townsend had driven in on spec—*after* visiting Guildford—to see what he could pick up. Quite unprovable, though, unless Fleet had surveillance cameras. Even then the chances that Townsend's license plate had registered out of the thousands of vehicles that visited the site each day was unlikely.

"Fair enough." He leaned forward again. "So where did you stay last night, Mr. Townsend? You didn't spend it at your house, because we've had a police car parked outside since Martin Rogerson gave us your address at nine o'clock. We hoped Amy might have been heading your way."

"I was with a girlfriend."

"May I have her name?"

He shook his head. "Not without her permission. She's married, and I don't want her involved unless it's absolutely necessary. I've given you the proof you asked for, Inspector. If you want anything else, you'll have to go through my solicitor."

"Meaning Mr. Rogerson?"

"Of course."

"It's an interesting relationship, sir. Why does he continue to represent you? Most men in his position would bear a grudge against you for stealing his wife."

He didn't answer immediately. "I'm a good client. I put a lot of business Martin's way. Why would he cut off his nose to spite his face when Laura had left him anyway?"

Tyler chuckled. "Human nature isn't quite that civilized, though, is it? Particularly when passions are involved."

The man shrugged. "Any passion Martin had for Laura died a long time ago. She's not easy to live with, Inspector. Far too clingy for someone like Martin, who needs his space. It's attractive to begin with. Vulnerable women always are—they make men feel powerful. But it soon becomes wearing when the jealousy starts."

Tyler thought of his own failed marriage. The psychology of its breakdown wasn't so different. "So why did you continue to employ him?"

"I don't understand."

"You'd stolen his wife and daughter. Weren't you worried about that?"

"Why should I have been?"

"I wouldn't want an enemy for a lawyer."

He didn't answer.

"But perhaps he isn't an enemy? Perhaps you and he have too many common interests to have a falling out?"

Townsend smiled. "Perhaps we do."

"So what are they, sir? What's all this business that you keep putting his way?"

"Property development."

"You're talking about Etstone?"

"Yes."

"*Mmm.*" He studied the man for a moment. "Then why did Franny Gough tell me it wasn't in very good shape? She said someone was stealing from you, and you went ballistic every time the subject came up."

The eyes started to roam again, but whether at the mention of Franny Gough or the reference to the state of the company, Tyler couldn't tell. "It's no secret we're looking for new investment. That's what this meeting's about. My suspicion is that Steve Ablett and his crew have been skimming off the top. It's the reason I went to see him yesterday. I warned him there'd almost certainly be firings and prosecutions as soon as the company's position was stabilized."

Strange answer, thought Tyler. *"Suspicion . . . ?" "Almost certainly . . . ?"* "Did you leave your luggage and camcorder with your girlfriend, Mr. Townsend?"

The change of direction was so abrupt that the man was off balance again. It was another question he hadn't prepared for. Tyler could almost hear him debating between "Yes" and "No." "Yes."

"Won't her husband wonder who they belong to?"

"He's away," he said curtly.

"Then you must be planning to spend tonight with her as well. You'll be wanting your toothbrush and razor at the very least. Will you agree to one of my officers accompanying you? All we require is confirmation of where you were last night . . . and if her husband's away, there shouldn't be a problem."

He shook his head but didn't say anything.

"Perhaps you'd like to consult your lawyer?"

Again Townsend didn't answer, and this time the silence stretched interminably. Tyler was interested in why the man was so determined not to summon Martin Rogerson to the room. Did he know that Rogerson wasn't there? Had he guessed it wasn't his lawyer who'd phoned his mobile earlier? Or did he not want Rogerson to hear his answers? It was another five minutes before Butler returned, and it was arguable which of the two men at the table was more relieved to see him. Tyler knew his sergeant well enough to know he'd have given him the nod if there was no more mileage in questioning Townsend.

"Mr. Ablett remembers the time as one-thirty," Butler said without emphasis. Unhurriedly, he resumed his seat. "There's a message from the super," he told Tyler, pushing a folded piece of paper across the table. "He wants an answer PDQ."

Tyler held it up so Townsend couldn't read it. *"He's lying. I need a word outside."*

"I'm sorry, sir," he told Townsend, tucking the paper into his pocket. "This will only take a minute. I'll have to ask you to wait a little longer."

Townsend's law jutted angrily. "You're being unreasonable, Inspector. I'm fighting for my company's life here. I need this meeting. If any of those potential backers leave, Etstone could be done for."

Tyler remained seated. "Is that why you came home from Majorca in such a hurry?"

"Yes!" he snapped. "Martin phoned to tell me the bank's refusing to cover the wages. That's what this meeting's about. I've been busting a gut for the last twenty-four hours trying to hold things together."

"Why didn't you tell Mr. Rogerson you were back?"

"I didn't want to put him in a difficult position. There are laws about trading while insolvent, and he might have felt he had to act in the interest of creditors by closing us down yesterday."

Tyler glanced at his sergeant and saw him give a tiny inclination of his head toward the door. "Why did you leave Franny Gough behind?"

A spark of anger flared in the pale eyes. "She was drunk. I couldn't even get her to her feet, let alone to the airport."

"She was stranded there. You left without paying the bill."

"I didn't have much choice. After Martin called I was afraid the credit cards had been stopped. I told her to sneak out, take a taxi and change her flight when she reached the airport. She had enough money to cover that. It was the best I could do. If she was too drunk to take it in, that's her problem."

Tyler didn't try to hide his skepticism. "If things are as bad as you say, why were you in Majorca at all? Why didn't you stay at home and sort it out?"

He had an answer for everything. "I thought I had. This has been going on for weeks. I've spent every waking hour trying to keep the show on the road. By the end of last week, I had a promise from an investor that half a million would be transferred at the opening of business on Monday. I believed it was signed and sealed, and in the circumstances I thought a short holiday was reasonable. Martin phoned on Thursday to say the backer had failed to come through and the bank had withdrawn its overdraft. At the crack of dawn yesterday morning, I took the first flight out."

Tyler stood up, nodding at Butler. "I'm still going to have to ask you to wait, Mr. Townsend."

The jaw jutted more aggressively. "Why?"

"I'm not satisfied with your answers."

His frustration boiled over as he slammed his palm onto the table. "Then you'll have to wait till after the meeting, because I'm damned if I'll lose everything because of some fucking Woodentop with a power complex."

"Do you wish to consult a solicitor, sir?"

"Yes," he said abruptly, snapping down the lid of his laptop and reaching for his jacket. "I do. I'll talk to him outside."

"Please remain seated, sir. If you try to leave the room before the sergeant and I return, you will be detained for further questioning and almost certainly removed to the nearest police station. Meanwhile, these gentlemen"—he gestured toward the uniformed constables— "will assist you in finding a court-appointed lawyer."

"Don't play games with me, Inspector," he said furiously. "I want my own lawyer."

"I'm afraid Mr. Rogerson is unavailable, sir. He's under arrest."

▼

"This had better be good," Tyler told Gary Butler in the corridor outside, groping for his handkerchief and mopping the sweat from his brow. "I'm building castles in the sand here. So far he hasn't said a damn thing that disagrees with anything anyone else has said. What did Steve Ablett tell you that makes him a liar?"

Butler didn't look quite so confident now. "Nothing major," he admitted, "and, to be honest, he's just answered some of it."

Tyler stuffed the handkerchief back into his pocket with a sigh. "All right, give me what you've got."

The sergeant read from his notebook. "Re. the security cameras on site. The tapes are supplied by the company who installed the equipment. Re. the state of the business. Up shit's creek without a paddle. Almost the entire workforce was laid off two weeks ago. Steve Ablett and three others are bringing the half dozen houses that have already been sold up to spec in order to pass building codes. The unfinished shells and the rest of the plot are effectively up for auction. He thinks that's what this meeting is about, although he was told by the office staff that it was happening next Saturday." He jerked his head toward the conference room.

"Re. Townsend's visit to the site yesterday. It was unscheduled. As far as Ablett knew, Townsend was in Majorca till the end of next week." He turned a page. "The guy turned up out of the blue at approximately thirteen-thirty. Ablett himself had only just gotten back from Southampton headquarters after having been told that no one was going to be paid and the office would be locked from noon on. He pulled his three guys off the jobs they were doing and went back to the trailer to sort out his personal stuff and close the operation down at his end."

He moved his finger down the page. "Townsend arrived five minutes later. He started a fight. Called Ablett a thief . . . said it was his fault the development was on the skids. Ablett stormed out rather than hitting him. The reason the business has gone down the drain is because the bank's pulled the rug out and all the suppliers have withdrawn credit." He looked up. "Ablett was so fired up, I'm amazed you didn't hear him inside the room, Guv. According to him, it's Townsend's fault the bank caved because he paid too high a price for the land, and now he's trying to blame his workforce."

Tyler tugged out the handkerchief again and gave his face another wipe. "That's pretty much what Townsend himself told me—minus the bank details. All it proves is he's a bad businessman."

Butler returned to his notebook. "Ablett said there was no reason for Townsend to make the accusations. There was some minor thieving at the start of the project, which Ablett solved with the surveillance cameras. Two men were fired, and they've had no problems since. His view was that Townsend just wanted to make a scene—pick a fight with anyone he could find—because he's furious about losing the business. Ablett was the safest target because creditors were hanging around the office all morning, threatening to floor Townsend if they found him."

"*Mmm.*" Tyler stared along the corridor, brow furrowed in thought. "Does he know why Townsend went to Majorca? That's the part I can't figure out, Gary. Why go at all? And why not check that the half million was in the bank before he left?"

"I didn't ask, but he was pretty colorful with his counter-accusations about thieving." He moved his finger down his notes. "Townsend operates a load of fiddles to avoid VAT and tax. Plus he doesn't pay well, so he's not too choosy about whom he employs. A fair number are regular visitors to Winchester Jail and they're all gunning for him on the basis that the company's about to go under and they want their money before it happens." He looked up. "Perhaps he decided to make himself scarce till the new financing came through?"

Tyler frowned at him. "Ablett said this meeting was postponed for a week. Did he say why?"

"Because the bank refused to pay the wages."

"How did Townsend know it was being postponed? His return flight was booked for next Saturday."

"I guess Martin Rogerson told him."

"*Mmm.*" A long pause. "Townsend used another name on the phone. He said John Finch told him what was in the wind."

Butler flicked to another page of his notebook. "There's a John Finch on the list for this meeting. Described as a shareholder. Do you want me to see if he's arrived yet?"

"Not yet." Tyler clicked his tongue. "Townsend says he spent last night with a girlfriend. Claims he left the camcorder and luggage at her place. Why would he do that? Why not just leave them in his trunk?"

The sergeant tapped a knuckle against his teeth. "Because he was expecting to be questioned at some point?" he suggested. "Only an idiot would carry around compromising tapes of Franny Gough looking like Amy Biddulph. He's probably got props in his luggage . . . wigs . . . little-girl dresses . . . whatever."

"He wasn't fazed by questions about Franny Gough, so he must have guessed we'd talked to her . . . found out about the sort of thing he'd been filming. Where did he hear about Amy anyway? If it was the radio or television, the earliest he could have known was around nine or ten last night. So why was he so ready with an alibi for lunchtime?"

"Someone warned him. Rogerson called him on his mobile."

"He said he tried and couldn't get through."

"Assuming he was telling the truth."

"He must have been. When I asked Townsend where he was, he said, 'England.' He wouldn't have done that if Rogerson already knew he was back."

The sergeant shrugged. "Then it was the radio. I don't see the problem."

"The radio said she'd been missing since *ten* o'clock. Yet this guy's covered from eleven-thirty or thereabouts to a convenient 'scene' at one-thirty. He knew lunchtime was important." Tyler paused. "After that, instead of going back to his house to prepare for this meeting today, he vanishes off to some mysterious girlfriend and leaves his luggage. Why didn't he go home and leave it there?"

"Maybe he did. Our car wasn't there till nine o'clock."

"Then why not say so?" Tyler didn't expect an answer because he went off into a private deliberation. "Did Ablett say if he gave a reason for turning up out of the blue?"

"No. Just that Townsend launched in with the accusations of theft."

"Mmmm. Making a scene." Another pause for thought. "Did he take anything? Documents? Architect's drawings? Tapes?"

"I didn't ask. Do you want me to call him again?"

Tyler nodded. "Just for the record. I don't want egg on my face if he went there to empty a filing cabinet. Ask him about Townsend's car as well. Did he see it? Was there any luggage inside?"

He waited while Butler redialed and asked the first question, listening for a couple of minutes before muting the mouthpiece against the cloth of his jacket. "He says the trailer's pretty much empty. Plans and files were removed to the Southampton office a week ago so they'd be available to prospective investors. He says the only reason Townsend was there was so he could vent his spleen on someone. He says he upended the table and smashed the workmen's mugs. That's when Ablett walked out."

"Ask him about the car."

Another period of listening. "It was parked outside the trailer. He says a couple of briefcases were on the back seat."

Tyler's eyebrows corkscrewed up his forehead. "What sort of briefcases?"

"One black. One brown."

"Franny Gough said he only had one and it was black. How much of the backseat did they cover?"

"Most of it."

"So what was in the trunk? No, don't ask Ablett . . . just double-check that Townsend didn't open it in front of him." He pressed his lips together in concentration as Butler shook his head. "Did Townsend say where he was going afterward?"

This time the answer was longer and more heated—Tyler could hear the ire in the man's voice from where he was standing. Butler pressed the mobile to his jacket again. "He's still fired up about this fight they had. There was a lot of argy-bargy, apparently, with each one calling the other a thief. Ablett says Townsend's about as trustworthy as a rattlesnake. You can't believe anything he says. Re. where he was going . . . well, according to Ablett, it wasn't Southampton, because Townsend laughed when he heard that creditors were hanging around the office waiting to break his jaw. Townsend claimed he wasn't that stupid. He didn't plan to go to Southampton till tomorrow . . . i.e., today. Ablett guessed he was talking about this meeting." He frowned suddenly as if something had occurred to him.

He spoke into the mouthpiece again. "Who's in charge? Who postponed the meeting when the bank pulled the plug?" He looked surprised. "*Mr. Rogerson?* The solicitor?" He stared at the inspector while he repeated what he was being told. "The office was closed on his instructions . . . staff were advised of a possible rescue package today." A prolonged pause before Butler muted the mouthpiece again.

"Rogerson owns a major share of the business. It's his money that set Townsend up ten years ago. The company should have gone under two weeks ago, but he's been pulling strings to keep it afloat. Now the employees are shit-scared that, because of Amy's disappearance, Rogerson's taken his eye off the ball . . . and he's the only one who can save their jobs . . ."

TWENTY-SIX

Franek's powers of recovery were remarkable, thought Sophie, as she watched him struggle into a sitting position. He was bound hand and foot by assorted pairs of Clara Frensham's tights, but he still had the strength and agility to raise the top half of his body from the floor. When Clara first opened her door to them, he had staggered across the threshold—face dewy with sweat, mouth sucking for air—and the woman's instinctive reaction was to reach out a hand to support him. The words "poor man" were on her lips when Sophie's hurried shove knocked her out of the way.

"Stay away from him," she said menacingly.

The woman quailed. "But he's in trouble. He'll die if he can't brea—"

"Do as I say, Clara," she hissed through her still-bleeding lips, "if he dies, he dies. *Just—don't—go—near—him!*"

As a parting shot, Jimmy had winded him with a knee to the groin to keep him quiescent long enough for Sophie to tie him up. "Use anything nylon," he'd said. "The knots'll get tighter the harder he struggles."

Sophie was doing her best to bring Nicholas around, but it was like waking the dead. She wished Bob were there. He would know the triggers that would make a man feel safe enough to open his eyes. It had to be that, she thought, running her fingers around the back of his head. She could feel a lump where Franek had hit him with the chair, but no other injuries. Perhaps, subconsciously, he could hear the noise from Bassett Road, warning him that danger still existed.

The telephone had rung twice in the front room, but Clara Frensham seemed too shocked to answer it. She was barely into her forties and had always been a shy woman, but the devastating effects of radical surgery had killed off every last remnant of self-esteem. She sat huddled in a chair, a hand covering the plastic prosthesis that masked her ravaged nose, staring from Sophie to Franek in frightened ignorance of why their faces were so bruised and bloodied. Sophie's attempts to reassure her had met with silence and, with a sigh, Sophie had concentrated her efforts on Nicholas. She didn't want to answer the phone herself for fear of what Franek might do or say to Clara in her absence.

"Come on, Nicholas," she said loudly, smacking his cheeks, "everything's okay. We're out of the house and still in one piece. You can open your eyes now."

"Why not call police . . . tell them we need help?" demanded Franek.

"There is no help," she answered curtly. "We're on our own."

"Then call a different doctor. Find out what to do. I know Milosz. He stay like this for long time unless his dada cuddle him and talk to him."

"I'll stuff socks in your mouth if you don't shut up," she warned him. "He's more frightened of you than he is of anyone."

The old man addressed himself directly to Clara, his tone soft and pleading. "*You* make phone call, lady. *You* talk to police. Tell them this doctor no good. Tell them she want Franek to die. You witness. You hear what she say when you try to be kind. Tell them the nigger hit Franek. Tell them Franek can't breathe because he tied up, and Milosz unconscious because he frightened. Tell them to make Sophie untie Franek so he can help his son."

The woman stirred as if the gentle voice with its lyrical Polish accent was in some way alluring. "Maybe I should, Sophie?" she murmured behind her hand, using a pleading tone herself. "The police ought to know, don't you think? I mean . . . well . . . it's not *right* to tie people up . . . and that black man did hit him."

Sophie laughed hollowly as she sat back on her heels and looked at Franek. "You really are amazing," she said with reluctant admiration. "Is this your way of confusing the issue? Get Clara to allege brutality from me and Jimmy first in order to weaken my case against you."

There was a hint of admiration in his eyes, too—a gleam of a smile—or perhaps it was pleasure at her disfigurement. "What case you have against me?" He tilted his chin to display his own disfigurement. "You attack me first with broken glass. Franek frail old man. You strong young girl. Of course Franek defend himself. Milosz see it all. He tell exactly what happen when police ask."

She wondered if such a grotesque spin could work. "You're very sure of him," she said, lifting his son's wrist to check the pulse again. "Has he told lies for you before?"

"I tell only the truth of what happen," he said. "This lady my witness. She hear what you say . . . see what nigger do."

Sophie glanced at Clara. She didn't want to frighten the woman by telling her who the Zelowskis were, but neither did she want Franek's story to go unchallenged. "Is your phone a portable one, Clara?" The woman nodded. "Then why don't you bring it in here? I agree with you. The police *should* know what's going on, but I'd like to be able to speak to them as well, and I can't leave my patient."

Franek nodded approvingly. "This is good. We all talk. This way the police learn the truth."

They both watched the woman leave the room.

"Why she hold her hand like this?" the old man demanded. "What wrong with her?"

"None of your fucking business," said Sophie bluntly, "and if you even mention it to her I'll stick so much duct tape around your face it'll rip every cut wider when they peel it off of you."

He chuckled. "Now who sadist?"

"You'd better believe it where you're concerned. I don't care how much pain anyone inflicts on you. It'll make me laugh."

"Hah!" he said with another delighted chuckle. "You so fierce when Franek tied up . . . such little coward when he on top."

"And *you* were so brave tottering along in the gardens, I suppose," she snapped, dropping into mimicry of his guttural consonants. "Vranek gan't breathe . . . Vranek avraid . . . Vranek vrightened."

"You worse." He raised his voice to a falsetto. "Nicholas, help me . . . nasty man touch me . . . please . . . please . . . Nicholas . . . Nicholas."

It was on the tip of Sophie's tongue to wade in for another round, when it occurred to her that there was a terrible intimacy in what they were doing. It was like sparring with Bob. *You said . . . I said . . . you did . . . I did . . .* It was as if this dreadful oId man had released a side of her that had been locked in a box for years and years, a side that could hate with a passion—and, worse, enjoy the hating. What was wrong with her? He'd tried to rape her, for God's sake, and she was behaving as if she'd known him for years, talking to him in a way she couldn't talk to other people—and feeling comfortable with it!

"You're confusing me with your wife," she said unemotionally. "I imagine she called for Nicholas many times before you killed her."

His humor vanished like the sun behind a cloud. "You talk lies again."

"Then prove it to the police, Mr. Hollis, because I'm going to make sure they ask questions about her."

"Franek not the bad one," he said angrily. "It's not me they question . . . not me they put on sex register . . . not me that causes all this trouble."

"The fact that your son's been convicted and you haven't doesn't make you innocent," she told him.

"You shut up now," he said angrily.

"It makes you *more* guilty," she went on, ignoring him. "You're the worst kind of pedophile, the kind that uses his child for his own sick pleasure. First you treated your wife with unbelievable cruelty, then you did the same to your son because you knew he was too afraid of losing both his parents to tell anyone. You *made* him, Mr. Hollis. His crimes are the crimes you taught him."

He looked away. "Always you blame me. But do you ask what happen to Franek when he little boy? You think I invent cruelty?"

It was the obvious question, but Sophie's sympathies were on a low burner. "Then why didn't you break the cycle?" she asked coolly. "You keep saying you're not stupid, but even a moron can work out that patterns of cruelty and abuse are never cured by repeating them. It's hardly surprising you have panic attacks. All your life you must have been in fear of the consequences of what you do." She paused. "The only thing you've achieved in seventy-one years is to become a focus of hatred for thousands of people. You'll never be remembered for anything else. Is that what you wanted, Mr. Hollis?"

It was a moment or two before he turned back to her, and she was surprised to see dampness on his eyelashes. "At least they remember me. You, too, little girl. You think of Franek always."

NIGHTINGALE HEALTH CENTER

"Someone's picked up at last," announced Jenny Monroe breathlessly to Ken Hewitt. "Ms. Frensham? Yes, this is the Nightingale Health Center. We've been trying to get through to you. Is Dr. Morrison there? Oh, thank goodness!" She listened. "It's the riot, Ms. Frensham. No one's able to get through to the police at the moment . . . I understand, but we have an officer here. His name's P.C. Ken Hewitt. Let me put him on. He'll be able to advise you better than I can. Just one second."

She pressed the "mute" button and addressed Ken. "She wants to talk to the police. Sophie's got the father tied up, and he's pleading with Ms. Frensham to untie him. He says he's dying and Sophie's refusing to help him . . . and Ms. Frensham's worried about being involved in a murder." She handed the receiver to the policeman and pressed "mute" to release it. "She's all yours," she murmured, "but I'll have your guts if you pass the buck back to her. You're being paid to make a decision . . . *she* isn't."

"I'm not your enemy, Jenny," Ken said mildly. "I may be fallible . . . I may be useless . . . but I am on your side."

"Prove it."

He introduced himself, then listened patiently for several minutes. "Yes, I understand. You say Dr. Morrison's still bleeding, but is she able to speak? Good, then will you pass the phone to her, please? Hello, Dr. Morrison. Yes . . . we've a pretty good idea. I understand. You don't want to talk in front of Ms. Frensham. Right. I'll ask some questions. Answer 'Yes' or 'No.' First, we're assuming the threat of rape came from Mr. Zelowski senior? Yes. Second, did he—er?" His eyes widened reassuringly at Jenny Monroe. "Good. Ms. Frensham says you've been badly beaten? That presumably means he tried? Yes. You fought him off? Yes. Is that why he's bleeding? Right. We know Jimmy James brought you out—we've been monitoring it from the helicopter—but, just for the record, confirm for me that he had a good reason for hitting Mr. Zelowski. Good. Would you prefer if I asked Ms. Frensham to leave the room? Good. Could you give the phone back to her, please? I'll talk to you again in a minute."

INSIDE 6 BASSETT ROAD

Clara Frensham darted a frightened look at Franek, then handed the receiver to Sophie and hurried from the room. They heard her feet on the stairs, then the slam of a bedroom door. "She's gone," Sophie told

Ken. "No, it's better this way. She's very fragile at the moment. I'm amazed she even let us in." Her eyes turned to Franek. "No, there's nothing wrong with him except a few cuts to his face. It's his son who's in trouble. He's gone into a coma and I can't wake him."

"She tell you lies," shouted Franek. "Franek can't breathe . . . nigger hit him . . . Franek want to talk to police."

Sophie smiled slightly. "Just in case anything happens to me," she said slowly and clearly into the receiver, so that Franek would understand every word, "I want Bob—*my man*—to know that this bastard punched me at least twenty times but *still* couldn't get me to submit. There is *nothing* . . . in this *whole* world . . . that would have allowed me to give in to a worthless piece of *shit* who first *murdered* his wife . . . then *destroyed* his son." She lifted her middle finger and jabbed it into the air at Franek. "And if I remember anything—or *anyone*—from this experience, it'll be Mel's Jimmy bursting through the door and rescuing me before Mr. Zelowski *senior* could rape and murder me . . ."

NIGHTINGALE HEALTH CENTER

Fay Baldwin hovered on the periphery of the huddle around the telephone, listening to Sophie's voice and Franek's more distant, angry interjections over the speakerphone. She heard Sophie's precisely related narrative of what had happened, then listened to Harry giving a brief version of Milosz Zelowski's psychiatric report. "He wasn't considered a danger," he finished, "but some idiot thought better and leaked his whereabouts to the estate. We've already heard that one poor lad's died of burns. God knows how many others there are going to be."

They all heard Sophie's sigh, loud and clear, over the amplifier. "It was Fay Baldwin," she said, unaware that the woman was listening, "but I've no idea how she found out who the Zelowskis were or where they lived." Another sigh. "And it wasn't entirely Fay's fault either,

Harry. She tried to tell me there was a pedophile in the road, but she kept mouthing off about Melanie Patterson being a whore and I got the wrong end of the stick. I assumed she was accusing Mel and her men of being child abusers, so I gave her a piece of my mind and she went off in a huff and told Mel perverts were waiting to grab little Rosie. I think that's what must have sparked the riot. It's all so crazy . . . I keep thinking if only I'd listened to the stupid woman, none of this would be happening. Did you know that Jimmy James shared a cell with Milosz? He could have told Mel he was harmless if he'd known what his real name was." She fell silent.

"It's not your fault and it's not the Pattersons' either," Harry said firmly. "All Melanie and her mother did was organize a march. They happen every day of the week, and there was no reason to suppose that this would be any different. No one can be blamed if rioters jumped on the back of it to launch a war against the police . . . and this is too well organized to have been spontaneous." He glanced at Fay. "It would have happened anyway. It's a copycat of the gasoline-bomb riots that have been going on in Bradford and Belfast this last month. We're in a heat wave and youth is angry. It's a volatile mixture."

Sophie sighed again. "From what Jimmy James told me, it's Mel who's been trying to contain it. She's a great girl . . . always does her best, even if it doesn't work out right. Jimmy said we'd have been burned alive if she hadn't stopped people from throwing gasoline bombs. He's gone off to try to get her and the little ones out."

"We know," said Harry. "We're being kept informed by the officers monitoring video footage from the helicopter. That's how we knew you were at Ms. Frensham's. What we're going to do now is find someone to watch over Zelowski, senior, for you, while you concentrate on Milosz."

"Oh, God, be careful," she cried in alarm. "If word leaks out that they're here, then we'll end up imprisoned in this house. I can't go through that again, Harry. Wouldn't it be safer to wait till Jimmy gets back with Mel?"

Harry glanced at Ken Hewitt, who shook his head. "We think they might be in trouble," he admitted reluctantly. "Some of the crowd stormed the house, and Melanie was knocked over in the rush. At this point we're not sure exactly what's going on."

"Oh my God! She'll lose the baby, Harry. *Why* did you make Jimmy come for me? He should have gone for her. He's the father, for Christ's sake."

"We're hoping her mother's with her, also her brother. Jimmy certainly is. He was seen running in through the back door. He'll get her out, Sophie."

There was a pause. "I'm going back," she said with sudden decision. "I'm giving the phone to Franek. His hands are tied in front of him so he can hold it. You can talk to him, Harry. It'll be an education."

"No, Sophie, wait!"

But she was already gone, and the next voice on the line was a man's.

"Who I speak to?" Franek demanded.

Harry straightened and gestured to Ken to take over. "The police, Mr. Zelowski."

"Hah! This is good. Now I say what really happen."

Ken took out his notebook with a small smile. "That's your choice, sir, but I must warn you that Dr. Morrison has made some serious accusations against you . . . and there are several witnesses to this conversation. That means anything you say may be used against you in a court of law should arrest and prosecution follow. You might prefer to remain silent until you've had an opportunity to consult a solicitor. Do you understand what I've just told you?"

"I understand everything. You think Franek stupid? I tell it all so you know Franek old and frail and do what he can to save his Milosz's life . . ."

HILTON HOTEL, SOUTHAMPTON

Tyler borrowed the manager's office and put through a call to the custody sergeant at headquarters. "I want you to bring Martin Rogerson to the phone," he told him. "I need to talk to him."

"What the hell's going on, sir?" the other man demanded angrily. "I can't hold him much longer unless you substantiate the charges."

"I'll get back to you after I've spoken to him." He waited, drumming his fingers on the desk. "Yes, it's D.C.I. Tyler, Mr. Rogerson." He held the receiver away from his ear. "You'll be released quicker if you calm down and listen," he said when the storm finally blew itself out at the other end. "I'm calling from the Hilton Hotel in Southampton, and this time I'd appreciate your full cooperation with the questions I'm about to ask you. No, sir. It is not a threat. Mr. Townsend and a Mr. John Finch have made certain statements about why Mr. Townsend returned from Majorca yesterday morning. Some of them concern you. I would like to establish how truthful those statements are."

He consulted his notebook, which was open in front of him. "Is it true that you acted without Mr. Townsend's knowledge when you rescheduled this meeting for today?" He listened to the tirade at the other end. "You're saying you didn't have a choice? The bank was issuing ultimatums . . . *Mmm* . . . Then how come John Finch was able to contact him? . . . *Mmm* . . . Except Mr. Finch seems to think it was you who began the collapse in confidence." He stared at the wall as a bellow of sound from the other end hammered at his eardrums. "I don't know, Mr. Rogerson," he murmured into the silence that followed. "I suppose it depends on how vindictive you are . . . and how stupid he is. You're far better placed than anyone else to destroy him . . . You've been party to every dirty little secret he's ever had . . ."

NIGHTINGALE HEALTH CENTER

Bob Scudamore pushed through the door of the reception area and stopped in front of the bizarre tableau huddled around the telephone. Harry was the first to notice him. He raised a finger to his lips to stop him from saying anything, then beckoned him forward. *"The father,"* he wrote on a piece of paper. *"Sophie's safe. Bruised and battered but no rape. She fought him off. Father now justifying himself. Completely barking!"*

Bob closed his eyes in relief, then turned his attention to the self-congratulatory monologue on the speakerphone.

". . . she very arrogant girl . . . dress sexy to make men look at her. If I go talk to crowd, she say, they do what I tell them. Everyone know me . . . everyone like me. Men like me most of all. Me very pretty girl. She find Franek nice . . . say now in front of lady of house . . . you amazing, Franek. Franek say to her, you very pleased with yourself, little miss, and she get angry . . . break vase, slice Franek's face . . . try turn Milosz against his dada. She talk to son all the time . . . look at me, she say . . . take notice of me. But Milosz not interested . . . he say to her . . ."

Oh, fuck this!

Adrenaline had been sitting like a lump in Bob's stomach ever since Harry had phoned him. Release of tension set it roaring through his veins. He leaned forward to bring his mouth within two inches of the speaker. "I'm here," he said in a voice like sifted gravel.

A long pause. "Who is this?"

"Sophie's man."

"Where police?"

"It's just you and me, you twisted little sod."

"I don't talk to you."

Bob gave a low laugh. "You will when I come for you," he said. "You won't be able to stop yourself. That's what I do . . . take a man's brains and turn them inside out. I'll have one guess at what I'm going

to find in yours. A sniveling little runt who was so scared of his dada he wet the bed the first time he tried to make love to a woman. Am I right?"

The silence became oppressive. Jenny Monroe made a move as if she were about to speak, but Bob held a finger to his lips.

"I want police. Give me police."

"I'm still here, Mr. Zelowski," said Ken Hewitt.

"You hear that? Man threaten Franek."

"It must be your conscience," said the policeman calmly. "No one here heard anything."

DEVON & CORNWALL POLICE

➤ Missing person investigation—Amy Rogerson/Biddulph

➤ IMMEDIATE SEARCH OF PROPERTY REQUESTED

➤ Rose Cottage, Lower Burton, Devon

➤ Authorization received

➤ Full details to follow . . .

TWENTY-SEVEN

INSIDE 23 HUMBERT STREET

Like Sophie, Gaynor would have recurring dreams filled with blood. Jimmy, too. Post-trauma, they would lurch awake at night, sweat pouring down their backs, eyes staring widely into the darkness, fingers searching desperately for the light switch. They would all refuse counseling. Sophie, because she had Bob to take her patiently through it; Gaynor, because she couldn't bear to relive the terrible guilt and grief of that day; Jimmy, because he needed to relive it over and over again in case he forgot the lives that were lost.

Despite her unease, Gaynor finally made up her mind to approach the back of number 23. She wondered why the kitchen door was broken, but Jimmy wouldn't have come out of it if it wasn't an exit, she kept telling herself, and all she wanted was a route through to the front. Jimmy had used one earlier to materialize at her side. This was no different.

A quick glance through the window of the back room as she passed showed it to be unoccupied, as was the kitchen. She stepped through water on the floor and paused in the doorway to call out.

"Hello! Is anyone here? I'm trying to get through to Humbert Street. I'm looking for my kids."

She sensed only stillness in the house. If anyone was there, they were keeping their heads well down.

302

She tested the door of the back room, but it was locked—*the empty one*—looked up the stairs, then paused by the open door of the living room. She took in everything at a single glance. The shattered window. The blowing curtains. Broken furniture. Lamps knocked over like coconut shells. Bricks and stones, littering the floor. The damp, acrid smell of a fire extinguished with water.

. . . she was in the pedophiles' house . . .

Her instinctive reaction was to retreat but, through the window, she saw the tall, unmistakable figure of her daughter, standing with her back to the house. Next to her was Colin. As she watched, the shouts of the crowd resolved themselves into individual taunts. Gaynor recognized the first voice, but couldn't place it.

"We ain't gonna wait much longer, bitch!"

"What your man doing, Mel? Getting hisself jocked by perverts?"

"Maybe he don't fancy girls wiv' big bellies! You wanna cross your legs next time!"

The same voice, louder and wilder. A black voice. "He'd better not be helping 'em, bitch, or we'll fucking 'ave you and your bruvver. You talked right hard when you was making bombs, Col, but you never said you was too yellow to use 'em."

Wesley Barber, thought Gaynor in alarm. The idiot on crystal meth . . . and hyped to the eyeballs by the sound of it. *Oh, God!* What to do? Go and stand with Melanie and Colin? Tell the crowd Jimmy wasn't there anymore? *They wouldn't believe her.* Where had he gone, anyway? What was he doing? Who were the people with him? Her mind grasped for answers. Were they the pedophiles? But where was the girl? And what would the crowd do to Mel and Col if they thought Jimmy had helped the perverts escape?

She reined her thoughts in with determination. A solution was all she was interested in. There was no sense in Mel and Col guarding an empty house. Better to slip through the window and tell them to move aside and let Wesley enter. The smell of burning didn't register as a threat. The fire was out, and the consequences to the rest of the road if number 23 went up in flames were so far outside Gaynor's list of priorities at that moment that she never even considered it. With hurried tread, she ran upstairs to check the bedrooms.

She thought she was used to shock until she saw the blood in the back one. The smell of body odor—hot, rancid, disgusting—brought bile surging up her throat and she clamped her hand to her mouth and fled down the stairs, weeping in fear. Like her son earlier, she was physically unable to absorb any more adrenaline without her body protesting. She supported herself against the wall and bent forward, retching violently.

"Who are you?" asked a querulous voice.

Her head snapped up. A man with a machete was standing at the living-room door. She tried to say something . . . give her name . . . but all that came out was a scream . . .

▼

Everyone outside heard it.

Jimmy accelerated his pace across the garden at the back.

Melanie turned a white face to Colin.

Wesley let loose his dogs of war and charged.

"Bitch!" he snarled as he landed a punch in Melanie's stomach.

He stood over her as she fell, twirling his knife in his other hand. He was Wesley Snipes in *Blade*. Killer of vampire perverts. *White ones.* It was his destiny. He *was* Wesley Snipes . . . had been Wesley Snipes since he first saw *New Jack City*. A mean, black bastard who could rule the world. There *had* to be a reason for his name. Not his dad (Wesley Barber, Sr.). His dad was a loser. A two-bit thief who wandered in and out of prison like he was in a revolving door.

Somewhere in Wesley's confused, meth-shot mind, his mother's Christian voice resounded: *"Youse no good, boy. Youse your father's son. Only Jesus love you. Only Jesus make you worthy. Take the Lord to your heart and make your mamma proud."*

"NO-OO!" He whipped his knife in a backhand slash across Colin's cheek, straddling his legs and bringing his arms back into cruciform pattern in front of him. "MOTHER-FUCKER! I am BLADE!"

He vaulted the windowsill and padded across the living-room.

INSIDE 23 HUMBERT STREET

Jimmy came to a dead halt in the kitchen doorway. Ahead of him, Gaynor was cowering against the wall, trying to ward off his soldier friend, who was bending down to help her up. The old man's tin hat sat lopsidedly on his head and his legs protruded like knobby twigs from his Empire shorts. He looked like what he was. A daffy old idiot in Borneo fatigues.

It was the machete that was frightening. He was swinging it at his side like a counterbalance. It swished through the air, backward and forward, a blade so old and unused it was red with rust. *Or blood?* Even Jimmy wondered, and he'd spoken to the man. He called out reassuringly.

"It's okay, Gaynor, I know this geezer. Hey, mate! Do me a favor! Put the machete down. You're frightening her."

The soldier straightened. "Oh, it's you," he said. "I followed you. You came in here to steal."

Jimmy held out his hands in surrender. "You've got me dead to rights, sir. That's me. Jimmy James the thief. Always have been. Always will be. Do you wanna leave the lady and take me in?" He crossed his heart. "God's honor, I won't give you no trouble."

The old man took another puzzled look at Gaynor. "This woman needs help."

"No, she don't, mate. She's got kids outside. Show him you're okay, Gaynor. Get off your ass and open the door. Go tell Mel and Col to shift themselves into the house. I'll get to you soon as I can. Okay, darlin'?"

305

Gaynor nodded and scrabbled along the floor toward the door.

Jimmy turned his hands palms up and beckoned to the soldier with spread fingers. "Move yourself, my friend. This ain't healthy. There're guys out there on crystal meth gonna come through that door like Exocet missiles. I might be a nigger, but I know what I'm talking about. Trust me. You don't wanna be around when it happens."

The old eyes stared into his. Confused. Frightened. But *trusting . . .*

He took a step forward.

Too late . . .

Wesley came out of the living room.

"GO, GAYNOR!" Jimmy roared.

COMMAND CENTER—
POLICE HELICOPTER FOOTAGE

The police camera recorded the front door opening and the woman they believed to be Gaynor Patterson come tumbling out. She struggled to her feet and waved her arms in desperation, but her voice and gestures were lost against the trampling mob of youths who were climbing through the window to her left.

Did she hear something? See something she recognized on the ground? She made a sudden dart into the fray and began hitting and kicking like a street fighter. They saw the black woman who had stood beside Melanie wade in from the edge, plucking boys aside with her large hands, boxing their ears and shoving them away. She must have been calling for help, because a handful of people separated from the watching crowd and ran toward her.

Perhaps twenty youths made it through the window before a semicircle opened up to show Gaynor's son and daughter sprawled in tangled union on the grass in front of it. Even to the cold, unemotional eye of the camera lens, the attempt Colin had made to protect his sister was clear and heartbreaking. He lay half across her, his thin immature arms wrapped around her shoulders, his cheek pressed against hers.

Were they alive? Every head bent toward the monitors, willing, praying, urging, as Gaynor flung herself to her knees to lift their hands, stroke their faces, call them back. But there was no response. Just the awful relaxation of death.

INSIDE 23 HUMBERT STREET

Wesley herded the old soldier in front of him, allowing the youths behind him to enter the hallway. One of his friends kicked the front door shut to block out some of the noise. Others set off up the stairs. Wesley was more interested in his prize. He pricked the old soldier in the arm with his switchblade and giggled when he squeaked in terror.

"This the pervert?" he asked Jimmy, swinging the old man against the wall and thrusting his head forward to examine him.

Jimmy stayed where he was in the kitchen doorway, afraid that any movement would cause Wesley to use his knife again. "No. This guy lives in Bassett Road."

"So what's he doing here?"

The only answer Jimmy could think of was the truth. "He thought I was stealing . . . came in to stop me."

"Was you?"

"Yeah, why not? There's no one here, Wesley. The house is empty." He nodded toward the door of the back room.

"There's a whole studio in there, if you're interested. One of the perverts is a musician."

Wesley reached down to yank the machete from the man's grip. "What's he got this for?"

"I guess he didn't fancy tackling me without a weapon." Jimmy took a cautious step forward. "Let him go, Wesley. He's a harmless old geezer who was trying to stop kids from being trampled at the other end of the street. I'll do a swap. I've got the key to the back room in my pocket. I was planning to come back and empty it before anyone else got a chance." He unzipped his pocket and took out the key, placing it on his palm, where Wesley could see it. "I'll give it to you for the old guy. There's a fortune in sound equipment in there."

"He's conning you, Wes," jeered one of the other youths. "That key don't fit that door. He's got the hots for the nonce."

Jimmy's eyes narrowed immediately. "Do you wanna come closer and say that again, motherfucker?" he growled, bunching his fists and taking another step forward. He spread his lips as the boy retreated. "Okay, I'm gonna spell it out for you one more time. This guy ain't the one you want. The perverts legged it out the back. I've checked the house, and the only room that's got anything worth robbing in it is this one. There's about ten grand worth of gear in there. That's why I locked it up." He raised the fist with the key. "If Wesley's too fucking stupid to make a deal, then I'm gonna throw this in the air and whichever one of you gets it wins the jackpot."

Wesley's eyes rolled as his slow brain tried to follow the argument. He relaxed his hold on the old man and turned to glare at his friends to warn them off. Now less than a couple of feet away, Jimmy folded the soldier's frail, marbled hand inside his huge black one, ready to pull him away, when feet thundered on the stairs and a frightened voice shouted: "He's killed Amy. There's blood everywhere."

There was a brush of warm fingers, a glance of bafflement from faded eyes, before the machete sliced through the air and came down on Jimmy's head like a piledriver.

COMMAND CENTER—
POLICE HELICOPTER FOOTAGE

The footage of the old man's murder was too horrific to be shown in full, and only a few people outside the command center ever saw it uncut. Twelve of those were the jury members at Wesley Barber's trial, when the judge overruled his defense team's efforts to have it banned. There was no mistaking Wesley's face. He raised it to the helicopter as he smeared the blood of his victim on his cheeks, before strutting and prancing at the upstairs window and raising his fist in a Black Panther salute to the crowd.

The jury reached a guilty verdict in under half an hour. They, too, were offered counseling.

Drugs were cited in mitigation. Lysergic acid diethylamide—LSD, or acid. Methedrine—crystal meth—the drug of choice of Gianni Versace's murderer, Andrew Cunanan. Taken individually, each was a proven exaggerator of anxiety, aggression and paranoia. Taken together, it was axiomatic that anyone under their influence would lose touch with reality. Particularly someone as "socially damaged" and "educationally subnormal" as Wesley Barber. He was deprived. He was abused. He was black.

Blame the dealers. Blame his absent father. Blame his overly religious mother. Blame his school for allowing him to become a truant. Blame the climate of anger in Bassindale. Blame the crowd for inciting the mentally unstable to action. Blame the boy's accomplices for encouraging his madness before melting away into the hinterland of the gardens and never being identified.

The judge, unmoved, commended the jury on its decision before passing sentence. He reminded the court that Wesley Barber had been given numerous opportunities during that afternoon to reconsider his position. Various brave people had tried to reason with him, but he had chosen not to listen. Drugs may well have been a contributing factor to the appalling savagery he inflicted, but he could find no evidence that Wesley was any more "socially damaged" than his victims.

"No civilized person can understand," he said, "what led a vicious young man like you to think you could pass judgment on other human beings. Yours is a flawed and dangerous character. In your short life you have contributed nothing to society, and have learned nothing from it. It is my hope that a long period of incarceration will teach you wisdom."

▼

It had been a lynching by strangulation. The body was lowered on a rope from an upstairs window, blood streaming down its legs where the genitals had been hacked off with a blunt machete. It danced for several minutes while the noose tightened round the old man's neck.

Down below the crowd laughed as Wesley strutted his stuff.

Hell . . . ! It was funny . . . !

The black guy was gibbering like an ape . . .

The pedophile was wearing a hat that flopped from side to side as he jiggled in his noose . . .

TWENTY-EIGHT

The door opened a crack in response to the policeman's loud knocking and repeated warnings that he would break the door down if it wasn't opened. He and his colleague had caught a glimpse of movement in the living-room window as the car pulled up. A flash of blond hair as a head ducked out of sight.

"What do you want?" said a frightened voice.

"Are you Amy Biddulph?" he asked, pressing the door open wider. There was some similarity between this girl and the photograph, but it was very slight. This one looked like an older sister.

She tilted her law in defiance. "What if I am?"

"May I come in?"

"I'm not allowed to talk to anyone."

Surprise . . . surprise! "We're the police, Amy. We've been looking for you, sweetheart. Your mum's worried out of her mind."

She flounced her shoulders. "She's just saying that. If she cared, she wouldn't have left me with Barry and Kimberley."

"Come on, love. She's very upset. She was afraid something bad had happened to you."

"Don't see why. I can take care of myself."

The policeman's colleague came around from the back, where he'd stationed himself to block any attempted flight through the garden. Their first idea had been that some third party was involved, but he returned when he heard conversation at the front. He caught the tail end of it, took in the child's made-up face, peroxided hair, tight halter top and brief miniskirt, and raised an eyebrow. "I see you've been having a good time, Amy," he said. He was older than his partner and had daughters of his own. He recognized the symptoms of rebellious alienation immediately, though, at ten, the kid was pretty damn young for it.

"It's allowed," she said, pushing out her nonexistent breasts. "Children have rights, too, you know."

"Not to waste police time they don't," he said severely. "Haven't you been watching television? Don't you know that officers all over the country are looking for you?"

An odd little smile played across the painted lips. "I guess I'm pretty famous."

"You certainly are," said the officer cynically. "You'll be even more famous if the photographers get a shot of you looking like that. Is this what it's all been about, Amy? Fifteen minutes of fame? Never mind breaking your mum's heart."

She didn't understand fifteen minutes of fame. At ten, encouraged by the reactions she inspired with her dancing, she wanted a lifetime of adulation. She flounced her shoulders again. "She doesn't love me," she said. "She's jealous of me. She doesn't like it when men like me more than they like her."

If Tyler had been there, he'd have recognized an echo from Franny Gough, and he'd have asked himself what kind of people fed such ideas to children. The older officer gestured to her to come outside. "Time to go home, Amy."

She stepped behind the door. "I don't want to. I want to stay here."

The younger policeman shook his head. "You don't have a choice, sweetheart."

She pulled her arm away as he reached inside to catch it. "I'll say you touched my breasts," she warned.

"God almighty!" grumbled his colleague, reaching through the car window for the radio. "Where the hell do you girls learn this stuff?" He gave his call sign. "Yes, she's here. Alive . . . dressed up like a tart . . . and refusing to leave. She's threatening us with accusations of indecent assault. Yes . . . female officers and a social worker." He glanced at the child. "A real little madam . . . I don't envy her poor mother, that's for sure. The kid thinks she's Lolita . . . but she looks more like Macaulay Culkin in drag. You've got it . . . *Home Alone* . . . and reveling in it."

Telephone Message

For: D.C.I. Tyler
From: Mrs. Angela Gough
Taken by: P.C. Drew
Date: 28.07.01
Call timed at: 16:15

Mrs. Gough now wondering if blackmail was the reason for
Edward Townsend's interest in Francesca. During second
conversation with daughter in Majorca, Francesca explained the
trip in the following terms: "Ed said the best way to find out if
someone loves you is to see how much they're prepared to pay for
you." Francesca assumed he was talking about the plane fares to
and from Majorca and the hotel bill. Upset that he didn't love her
as much as she thought. On reflection, Mrs. Gough wonders if he
was planning a crude form of blackmail—i.e., pay up, or nude
photos of your daughter will appear in the *News of the World*.
Mrs. Gough describes herself as "reasonably wealthy."

                                              G. Drew

TWENTY-NINE

Rogerson was informed that his daughter was safe as soon as he reached the hotel. Tyler spoke to him in the manager's office, and waited while he composed himself. It was hard to say if his tears were genuine, but Tyler assumed so. The man's passions ran higher than anyone had realized.

He insisted he had not, and *could* not, have known that his daughter had been abducted by his client. He had cooperated fully once certain issues were brought to his attention, and had immediately revealed to D.C.I. Tyler the address of a second property owned by Edward Townsend. Rogerson agreed that he had capital invested in Etstone at the time his wife left him, but was unwilling to say how much. Certainly, it was a substantial amount, and it was in both his and Mr. Townsend's interests to remain on good terms following Laura's departure to Southampton.

Tyler was amused. On the Trojan horse principle? he asked. Bide your time, pretend to retreat, then take your revenge when your enemy is looking the other way?

Rogerson, equally amused, said that while he could not, of course, speak for his client, he had been surprised by Mr. Townsend's readiness to assume that he could take another man's wife with impunity. He referred to it as the Jeffrey Archer/Bill Clinton syndrome. Some men delude themselves into thinking they can get away with anything, he murmured.

However, he denied absolutely that he had engineered Etstone's collapse. Yes, as the company's legal adviser, he knew the local manager of the company's bank, but he refuted any suggestion that he had ever hinted to him that he was about to call in his loan under the agreement made with Townsend some ten years previously. He had no idea if the manager was a Freemason, and could not say if he had ever met him at a lodge meeting. The company's difficulties were of Townsend's making, not his.

In Rogerson's view, and the view of the majority of shareholders, the business could only be rescued if Townsend was bought out and the company restructured. It was Townsend's bad judgment that had led to a collapse of confidence in the Guildford development. He had paid too high a price for the land, and the planners had refused permission for an executive-style estate. The climate of opinion had changed in favor of cheaper properties to allow first-time buyers onto the housing market. Under these circumstances, Townsend's figures were no longer viable and the bank had gotten frightened and pulled the rug out from under him.

Clearly, Etstone's value was considerably less now than prior to the Guildford debacle, which made Townsend's future uncertain. Both his house in Southampton and his cottage in Devon had been put up as security for loans, and he faced imminent ruin. Rogerson took no pleasure in this. He was not a vengeful man, and had always kept his business and private affairs separate.

How vengeful did he believe Townsend to be? Was Amy a consolation prize or a ransom chip? But to that Rogerson had no answer. He merely repeated his strong denial that he'd ever had reason to think that Townsend was a pedophile.

▼

Laura Biddulph wept on the phone line. "Thank God . . . thank God . . . thank God" was all she could say.

Tyler explained that the child was unharmed, although she hadn't yet been examined by a doctor. "She's adamant that Edward's never touched her in a sexual way," he said, "and, for what it's worth, the Devon social worker thinks she's telling the truth. The woman says she's grown-up for her age and understands the difference between appropriate and inappropriate touching."

"Then why did he take her?"

"We haven't asked him yet." Tyler paused. "Amy says he came for her because she told him she was so unhappy she was going to kill herself."

More weeping. "Why didn't she tell me?"

"Perhaps because you were too frightened to ask the question," said Tyler gently, "and *he* wasn't."

POLICE CAR EN ROUTE FROM SOUTHAMPTON
HILTON TO HAMPSHIRE POLICE HEADQUARTERS

Despite being advised of his rights, Townsend was eager to justify himself He sat in the back of the police car and spoke earnestly to Tyler in the front passenger seat. Gary Butler, who was driving, watched the shifts of expression cross his face in the rearview mirror.

"I've never laid a finger on Amy," he said. "I'm not an abuser, Inspector. I would never force or coerce her to do anything she didn't want to do. I love her too much for that . . . unlike her parents, who treat her like a commodity. Her father uses her as a weapon. Her mother uses her to bolster her self-esteem."

Tyler turned to look at him. "And you just want to have sex with her?"

"I'm not some sleazy child molester. If I were, Amy would never have come with me. Everything I do is done with her consent. I wouldn't have it any other way."

Tyler wondered if there was some pedophile creed in existence that he'd learned by heart. *"I'm not an abuser" . . . "I'm not a molester . . ."* *"Everything is done with consent . . ."* "You'll tell me next that she initiates contact."

"She does. She's learned from her mother what pleases a man. It's hard to resist sometimes. She's curious about sex. Most children are."

Tyler shook his head and turned back to stare out of the window. "She's ten years old, Mr. Townsend. Of course she's curious. That doesn't mean she knows what she's doing. Consent has to be informed, and a child of Amy's age is incapable of understanding that when a pedophile touches her the feelings she arouses are different from the feelings that other men have."

"I am aware of—"

Tyler interrupted him. "Her mother put it to me rather well last night. Apparently Kimberley Logan accused her of trying to run Amy's life, and Laura replied that if Amy can't even decide between fish fingers and sausages for her tea, how can she make choices about her future?"

"I've never once attempted to exploit my feelings for her."

"You abducted her."

"I *rescued* her. She said she'd kill herself if I didn't take her away from the Logans."

Tyler watched a carful of children pass by, laughing and pushing one another in the backseat. "According to the officers who found her, she's dressed up like a tart with peroxided hair and full makeup. Whose idea was that?"

"Hers. I just bought the stuff. She wanted to look older. It wasn't my choice. I prefer her as she is."

"They said it was a good disguise, particularly the blond hair. They wouldn't have recognized her from her photograph if they'd passed her in the street." He shook his head. "What were you planning to do with her? Hide her in Devon for the rest of her life?"

"I never thought that far ahead. I just *did* it. I suppose I hoped we could lie low for a while, then start again somewhere else. I read about this teacher who took one of his pupils to Italy and lived with her for a year before they were found. It seemed worth a shot."

"You must have known you'd be caught."

"Not really." He stared past Butler to the horizon beyond the car. There was a faraway look in his eyes. "I thought it more likely she'd get bored and want to go home. I told her at the start that I'd return her to her mother the minute she changed her mind."

"What *was* the start, Mr. Townsend? How did you get into this position?"

"Are you asking me what makes an adult man fall in love with a ten-year-old?"

"No," said the D.C.I. with mild amusement. "I'm prepared to take that at face value. It's not something I will ever understand. I like women. If I can find one with brains, tits and a sense of humor who enjoys a career and my cooking, then I'll be in seventh heaven. A dependent ten-year-old stick figure with no conversation would bore me stiff . . . unless she was my daughter. In which case, I'd almost certainly find her stumbling advances toward adulthood fascinating. However, I would *not*—under *any* circumstances—wish to have sex with her."

Butler saw a gleam of humor spark in the pale eyes. "How would you know if you've never had a daughter? You might not put it into practice, Inspector, but you'd certainly think about it at least once in your life."

Tyler glanced at his sergeant, who was keeping his eyes firmly on the road. "You said Amy threatened to kill herself," he went on. "So why did you abandon her to go to Majorca with Franny?"

"I didn't abandon her. I bought her a mobile and programmed in my number so she could call me whenever she wanted to."

It was only half an answer, but for the moment Tyler let it go. "You were the 'Em' or 'Ed' that she called from the phone booth?"

"Yes."

"Why did she have to reverse the charges if she had a mobile?"

"She didn't have it then."

"Had she called you before?"

He nodded. "Every day on her way home from school."

"What about when she and Laura were in the hotel?"

"There was a phone booth round the corner. She used to sneak out when Laura was asleep."

"So what changed?"

"The holidays. She was in tears all the time . . . hated the Logans . . . hated the bullying . . . hated her mother for being a loser . . . hated her father. I saw her as often as I could, but it just became more and more upsetting."

"It's an interesting coincidence, wouldn't you say?"

"What is?"

"That around the time her father says he's going to withdraw his money, you start spending time with the daughter. Are you saying those two facts are unconnected?"

"From my end, certainly." Another wry shrug. "She never wanted to leave my house, Inspector. She needs to be loved. Children aren't stupid. They know what makes them happy."

"Where did you take her each day?"

"The downs. The seaside. The sort of places a father takes his child for fun. But it wasn't every day. Three or four . . . no more."

"Where did she go the other days?"

He gave a small laugh. "Nowhere, as far as I know. She phoned me several times from her bedroom . . . said the Logan kids were so stupid she could run rings around them. She used to hide under her bed and read books. It gave her a buzz to make them think she had a friend they knew nothing about. All she had to do was slip downstairs while they were watching television and slam the front door . . . they always assumed she'd been out . . . particularly when she acted angry or upset."

Tyler recalled Kimberley's words: *"I'll bet she's skulking in a hole somewhere so she can pretend she's got friends . . ."* Two sides of the same coin. "When did you buy the mobile?"

"After those calls the Logan children witnessed. I didn't want them telling Laura what she was doing. Amy kept saying she'd kill herself if she wasn't allowed to see . . ." His voice faltered to a halt.

Tyler found the emotion as fake as the tan. "I hope you're not planning to stand up in court and portray yourself as St. Eddy who saved a child from suicide?" he snapped. "Abduction's a very serious crime, Mr. Townsend."

"I know . . . but what else could I do?"

Tyler gave a snort of derision. "I can't see a jury being impressed by your sudden flight to Majorca for sex with an Amy look-alike when the child herself was begging you for help."

"I didn't have much choice. I had creditors on my back. I left John Finch to sort it out in my absence."

"Why take Franny with you?"

"She seemed like a good alternative."

"To Amy?"

"Yes . . . till she got drunk." He stared at his hands. "I'm not proud of any of this, Inspector."

Tyler turned his face to the passenger-side window so Townsend wouldn't see his expression. "Why didn't you tell Laura her daughter was suicidal?"

"She took Amy away because she was jealous of the closeness we had. What do you think she'd have done if I'd called her and said Amy wants to kill herself because she'd rather live with me? She'd have blocked every call, then had a nervous breakdown when she came home and found her daughter dangling from the banister." Butler watched him raise a hand as if to plead for belief, then drop it again. "She said she'd do it in the morning while Miss Piggy and Jabba were asleep, and she hoped everyone would cry when she was dead, because the only person who cried about her life was she."

"Children often talk like that."

"I believed her."

Tyler turned to look at him again. "Why didn't you speak to her father?" he asked cynically.

"He'd have taken her back immediately."

"Why? You keep telling me how indifferent he is to her."

"He is. It's Laura he wants—preferably on her knees—begging for her kid. He's that type. Dominating . . . possessive . . . He can't forgive her for finding the courage to leave. He'll punish her forever if he can. Look at what he's done to me."

Tyler nodded. Even without the evidence of the hatchet job Rogerson had done on Townsend's company, Tyler believed the man to be intensely vindictive. *But* . . . "Then why take his wife?" he said unfeelingly. "You must have known what would happen."

"I didn't. Not at the time. I used to listen to the way he talked to her . . . saw the way he treated Amy . . . like an irritating mosquito. It never occurred to me he'd be jealous if they left. In any case, it was Laura who did the running. I wouldn't have bothered if it hadn't been for Amy."

"You didn't find Laura attractive?"

"Not particularly."

"Then why make tapes of her? Why make tapes of any of the women whose children you liked?"

"It made them less suspicious."

Gary Butler glanced up to find Townsend looking at him in the mirror and, like the D.C.I., he began to wonder how truthful any of these answers were. They were certainly glib, although why any man should want to paint himself as a pedophile was beyond him.

"Did Laura know about the other tapes?" Tyler asked. "The ones you made of your wife and stepdaughter? Did Martin tell her?"

"I don't think so."

"Did Martin warn you to keep your hands off Amy?"

"No."

He turned again. "Did you ever discuss your pedophilia with him?"

"No." Another flicker of amusement. "He's not that type of man."

"Is he the type to download indecent images of children?"

Townsend shook his head. "Not children."

"Women?"

A nod. "You asked me earlier what happened to the tapes I made of Laura . . . Martin's got them. It was her parting present to him. Add them to your collection, she said. Make some other poor idiot watch *me* in order to work up enough enthusiasm to have sex with you."

Tyler smiled slightly. "You realize, of course, that we'll be searching your computers for evidence of pornography, Mr. Townsend—particularly child pornograpy—either downloaded by you or on Web sites operated by you. Do you want to save us time by telling us what to look for?"

"There's nothing to find. I'm not into Net pornography."

Tyler resumed his study of the passing countryside. He had a sneaking admiration for the man's cunning. Even the public would be on his side when they learned that the child was alive and hadn't been interfered with. They might even sympathize with his dilemma. To rescue or not to rescue? He might have sympathized with it himself if he could believe that Townsend was capable of loving anyone but himself.

"You're bullshitting me," he said after a moment. "I'm prepared to accept that you have an obsession with youth—I only have to look at you to see that—but I'm hard-pressed to believe that that obsession extends to sex with ten-year-olds. You're willing to exploit them—that I don't doubt for a moment—but I can't see you engaging in illegal intercourse. You're like a heroin dealer . . . happy to peddle filth but not stupid enough to become involved yourself."

"I don't deal in children."

"Of course you do. Women, too. You're an Internet pimp. We'll find it . . . It may take time . . . and we may not get all of it . . . but I *will* have you for it, Mr. Townsend. Off the top of my head, I'd guess it began with your first wife, who was probably as enthusiastic as you about performing on camera, which is why she went coy at the time of the divorce. After that, you sought out women and kids who were happy to show off. It made it easier."

"That's crazy," said the other man without heat. "Where's the money?"

"Anywhere you like. You can wire it all over the world these days." He turned with an inquiring expression. "Perhaps this errant half million represents part of it? What happened to that? Did someone else get to it first? Or did it never exist?"

Townsend put his head against the back of his seat and stared at the roof of the car.

Tyler chuckled. "You don't fancy children any more than I do. You just want us to think you do. A repentant, self-confessed pedophile with no previous convictions—who hasn't interfered with the child he's abducted—or any other child in his care—will receive a far lighter sentence than a man who kidnaps a child for extortion."

Townsend continued to stare at the ceiling. "You're pissing in the wind, Inspector."

"You were keeping Amy nicely on tap till you needed her. Presumably this little charade was set up for next weekend, then you got a message from John Finch to say Rogerson had postponed the meeting. So you hightailed it back for her. I'm betting there's an interesting video hidden in that laptop of yours of Rogerson's daughter acting the tart. I'm also betting you were going to show it to him before the meeting, which is why you were so shocked to hear he was under arrest. What was the threat going to be if he didn't back down? Sell her to the highest bidder? Plaster her across the Net?"

"All you'll find in my laptop is a spreadsheet on Etstone," he said evenly.

"No one's that good, Mr. Townsend. We'll find it eventually."

"There's nothing to find. Ask Amy. It was all very innocent."

"At the moment, she'll be saying whatever you've told her to say . . . but it won't last. You may not have touched her, but it won't take a professional long to find out if you persuaded her to take her panties down to show her father just how much control you have over her. I think you're a sick fucker, frankly, but you're not a pervert. Any more than Martin Rogerson is. As you say, he prefers women . . . which is what he says about you." He chuckled again at the man's expression. "I'd rather get you for kidnapping and extortion. That's a hell of a long sentence. You shouldn't exploit people's love for their children, Mr. Townsend."

"What love? What makes you think Martin would back down because of a video? Everyone knows he doesn't give a shit about Amy."

"So you keep saying," the D.C.I. murmured, "and if you repeat it often enough you might convince a jury. It won't work with Laura, though. No one will believe *she* didn't love her child." He leveled a finger at the man. "*That's* what I'm going to hound you for. Making an already insecure child believe that her mother didn't love her. I've sat with the woman . . . dragged her sad little secrets out of her . . . watched her pain . . . listened to her guilt. And, *by God,* I haven't enjoyed it. She knows she's imperfect . . . knows that Amy wishes she were different . . . but that doesn't give a prick like you the right to manipulate her child's affections."

THIRTY

Sophie knelt beside Jimmy's prone body. The top third of his ear had been severed from his scalp, but he was alive. He lay half in and half out of the kitchen, muttering to himself against the floor, saliva dribbling from his mouth. There was no one downstairs. The door of the back room stood open, but the only noise inside the house seemed to be coming from upstairs. Laughter and singing. Sophie could make out some words.

". . . *we* are the champions . . . **we** *are the champions* . . . **we** *are the champions of the* **WORLD** . . ."

Feet drummed on the floor like a tattoo. *In celebration? Coming downstairs?* She didn't know. She rolled Jimmy over and smacked him hard across the face. "Wake up, you bugger!" she said as loudly as she dared into his bleeding ear. "It's Sophie! Mel needs help."

He opened his eyes, and she slapped him again. "Go away," he mumbled. "I'm tired."

This time she grabbed him by the shoulders and shook him. "Mel's in trouble," she said urgently. "I need you to come with me. There are people upstairs. Do you understand?"

The movement hurt his head, and he clapped a hand to his torn ear. "Ah, *shi-i-it!* What the *fuck!*"

"Wake UP!" she snarled, smacking him again. "I'm SICK of men passing out on me!"

He sat up abruptly, recollection flooding back . . . Wesley . . . the machete . . . the soldier. He looked around. "Where's Wesley?"

"Upstairs," she said, grabbing his hand and urging him to his feet. "We have to go."

"What about the old man?"

"Safe," she said, thinking he meant Franek. "Come on . . . come on." She urged him down the hallway toward the front door. "Harry said Mel fell under the feet of the crowd. We need to get her out. I'm worried about the baby. You'll have to carry her."

She had an awful sense of foreboding as she reached for the latch. It reminded her of the last time she'd stood by that door—when she could have walked out—but didn't—because a patient's son had said thank you and she paused to smile at him. She turned painfully to Jimmy. "I'm frightened," she said.

"Yeah," he said, "me, too." He caught her arm and drew her behind him. "I've got a really bad feeling about this," he muttered. "It's too fucking quiet."

She clutched at his jacket. "What should we do?"

He took a deep breath and twisted the latch. "Get ready to run," he said, easing the door open.

COMMAND CENTER—
POLICE HELICOPTER FOOTAGE

The police could calculate to the second how long it took for the bestiality of the lynching to metamorphose from laughter to shock. Almost every face was turned upward toward the window as Wesley paraded his prize. An old man with his shorts around his ankles, blood running down his legs and a noose around his neck. Expressions were vivid. Eager. Amused. Did they understand what was happening? Did they approve? Had the movies inured them to reality?

Who knew?

The journey to shock was equally vivid. Perhaps they thought it was a mannequin that Wesley had tossed so carelessly from the window to dance on its rope, because a wave of laughter rippled across the faces. Soon after, the smiles turned to puzzlement. Some continued to watch Wesley strut his stuff, but most averted their eyes. There was a spontaneous push away from the center. A girl dropped to her knees and was sick on the pavement. On the fringes, the crowd began to melt away through the exits.

It wasn't their fault. They hadn't asked the black boy to behave like a maniac. It was pretty bad what he'd done, but, hell . . . it was only a fucking pedophile!

OUTSIDE 23 HUMBERT STREET

Gaynor lifted a sweat-drenched face to look at Jimmy but didn't pause in her attempts to revive Colin. Straight-armed, she was pumping his heart. "One—two—three—four—five." She bent to breathe air into his mouth. "We think Mel's alive—three—four—five." Another breath. "Please help—three—four—five."

Sophie dropped to her knees beside the black woman who was holding Melanie's wrist between her fingers. "We got her back," she said, tears rolling down her cheeks. "See. It's like on *Casualty*. She's breathing. She's got a pulse. Ain't that right?"

Sophie pressed her fingers to the girl's neck. "Yes," she said. "Oh God! Oh God! Thank you. Thank you." She raised her own tear-stained face to Jimmy's. "Talk to her, sweetheart. Tell her how much you love her. The quicker you can bring her back the better. Make her listen. It's your voice she hears all the time, Jimmy. Nobody else's. She's told me over and over again how much she loves you."

Jimmy sank to his knees and pressed his hand to his lady's face. "Help Gaynor," he said. "Col's her baby, too."

But Colin was dead.

MONDAY, 30 JULY 2001

MEMO

From: D.C.I. Tyler
To: Superintendent Hamilton
Date: 07.30.01
Re: Charges relating to the abduction of Amy Biddulph/Rogerson

Sir,
Updated information is as follows:
➤ No evidence of incest against Martin Rogerson. Both Laura and
  Amy deny any such intimacy took place. Laura has confirmed his
  interest in soft pornography.
➤ Rogerson admits that if Townsend had threatened to send tapes of
  his daughter "posing for the camera" to his colleagues and clients,
  he might have "been more amenable" to postponing Townsend's
  bankruptcy. "A man in my position can't afford scandal." Less
  concerned about the images being logged on the Net, interestingly.
  "No one would know who she was."
➤ Rogerson admits to being upset and angered by what Townsend
  persuaded Laura to do on camera. "I was jealous. She never did it for
  me." Laura agrees she gave the tapes to him. "I wanted to hurt him."
➤ It seems clear that Rogerson has always been more interested in his
  wife than his daughter.
Advise no further action in regard to Martin Rogerson.

Re. Edward Townsend
➤ Computers currently being searched—estimated time of
  investigation: 2–3 weeks.
➤ Denies filming Laura Biddulph/Franny Gough/women/children for
  pornography.
➤ Denies any involvement in Net pornography.
➤ Denies abducting Amy for purposes of extortion/blackmail/ransom.
Questioning continues.

D.C.I. Tyler

P.S. The bastard was lying. Watch this space!

THIRTY-ONE

It was twenty-four hours before the police could confirm the true identity of the hanged man—Corporal Arthur Miller, Second World War veteran and widower—but the press was surprisingly coy about reporting it. They had rushed into print in the hours after Bloody Saturday, taking official refusal to release a name as corroboration of what was being whispered on the streets of Acid Row. The victim was a pedophile.

However, even the tabloid editors balked at SOLDIER BUTCHERED IN ERROR FOR SEX PERVERT for the Monday editions, for fear of being seen to condone lynching as a method of dealing with deviants. Most preferred the more anodyne TRAGEDY OF OLD SOLDIER or MURDER VICTIM WAS RANDOM KILLING.

Headline writers leaped to their pens after the Home Office confirmed that a registered sex offender had been rehoused anonymously on Humbert Street to avoid vigilantism. An injunction was issued against the reporting of his name in the interests of public safety, but there was no such restriction on the details of his conviction because the Home Office was keen to emphasize that the local police had been right to say he wasn't dangerous.

Sections of the press seized on this as evidence that, had he been "outed" in line with Megan's Law in the U.S., the events of Bloody Saturday would not have happened. It was the secrecy surrounding

331

him that had led the mob to riot. If his name and the nature of his offense had been widely publicized, the inhabitants of Acid Row would have known that a reticent man, convicted of minor offenses against sixteen- and seventeen-year-old boys, was unlikely to pose a threat to their toddlers.

Others argued forcefully that to reveal any pedophile's identity or address was to court the sort of hatred seen on Bloody Saturday. The man in question had already been hounded from one estate, even though the details of his conviction had been printed beside his photograph. The problem was the word *pedophilia*. In most people's minds it was synonymous with evil, and few were ready to draw distinctions between inadequate men who sought only to touch and psychopaths who set out to hurt and kill children for pleasure.

Politicians tried to avoid the issue by blaming the riot on contemporary drug culture.

By contrast, the public—*democratic*—response was unequivocal. When they learned that a confused old soldier had been brutally murdered because he was mistaken for a pervert, people came from near and far to pile the entrances to Acid Row with flowers.

▼

But during the twenty-four hours when they had believed him to be a sex beast, not a single blossom was laid.

TUESDAY, 2 OCTOBER 2001
(TWO MONTHS LATER)

THIRTY-TWO

Eileen Hinkley said Jimmy was making a fuss when he produced a brightly colored throw from a shopping bag and tucked it around her knees in the wheelchair. "It's a present," he said, before vanishing into her bedroom and poking around in her cupboards.

"If you're looking for something to steal, you're wasting your time," she called out cheerfully. "The only thing I have of any value is my engagement ring . . . and you'll have to chop my finger off to get it."

He came back into the living room with a collection of hats in his hand. "I know," he said. "I worked that out the first time I met you." He held up a red beret. "What about this? No? This one." He discarded the others on the sofa, and placed a brown felt trilby at a jaunty angle across her limp white hair. "Perfect."

"Why do I have to wear a hat?" she asked suspiciously, as he spun the chair around and pushed her toward her front door.

"It's cold outside."

The lift had been cleaned and painted since W.P.C. Hanson had bled across its floor. It remained unpredictable and the local youths still emptied their bladders into it on weekends, but the tenants had formed a cleaning brigade and it smelled of disinfectant more often than it smelled of urine. There were other small changes. Someone had imported potted plants into the foyer, and the cigarette butts

were regularly swept up. It wouldn't be long, Jimmy often thought, before rugs and curtains started arriving.

He pushed Eileen out through the doors into the blustery October afternoon. "Where are we going?" she asked him, clinging to her hat.

"Not far."

She tucked the throw under her thighs. "Did I tell you Wendy Hanson came to see me the other day?"

"The policewoman?"

"Yes. She's gone back to college to train as a nursery-school teacher. Says she thinks she'll get on better with the under-fives."

"Will she?"

The old woman chuckled. "I shouldn't think so. They'll scare her stiff the minute they start fighting. She's been watching too many films. She's got it into her head that toddlers are little angels and that corruption doesn't begin till secondary school."

"Is she still seeing the old geezer who hit her?"

Eileen tut-tutted. "She's a glutton for punishment . . . says he's got full-blown Alzheimer's . . . hasn't a clue who she is . . . but she feels she owes it to him to waste an hour a week in the nursing home. Have you ever heard such nonsense? He nearly killed her, and she thinks it's her fault for upsetting him. She ought to have been a nun. Martyrdom and saintliness appeal to her."

Jimmy grinned. "She's being conned. The word is his lawyer got him committed to avoid prosecution. I mean, if he really did have Alzheimer's, he wouldn't have been able to get her into the lift and stick an 'Out of Order' notice on the door. Stands to reason."

They passed the co-op, also repainted and refurbished. Young trees had been planted in the newly pedestrianized area in front of it, and several more shops—grant assisted—had opened, giving a taste of upward mobility to the area that hadn't been there before. Eileen remarked on how pretty it was beginning to look before cocking her head to listen to the sound of bulldozers in the distance. "Have they started on Humbert Street yet?"

"Yup. First house came down yesterday."

"Is it really all going?"

"Every last brick. Bassett Road, too. They're clearing the whole site between Bassindale and Forest, and starting again."

"About time," she said bluntly, "even if it is akin to closing the barn door after the horse has bolted. Are you happy in your new house, Jimmy?"

"Sure am. It's a palace compared with the last one. We've got a real garden this time, plus we've been given the choice of staying there or taking one of the new ones when they're built. We're waiting to see what they look like before we decide."

She twisted around to look at him. "Is that where we're going?"

"I'm not telling you."

"Are there going to be people there? Is that why you've covered me with a blanket and put a hat on my head? Are you ashamed of me, Jimmy?"

He squeezed her shoulder. "I'm proud of you. Everyone is. You're the most famous old lady in Acid Row. They reckon you saved more lives than anyone else by persuading your friends and their relations to open their doors."

"Not enough, though," she said sadly. "I still think about poor Arthur Miller and young Colin. Such a terrible waste, Jimmy. Will Gaynor ever get over it, do you think?"

"No," he said honestly, "but she doesn't have so much time to think about him since you made her your Friendship Calling visitor. She takes Johnnie, Ben and Rosie with her and the oldies get a real buzz out of it. Half of them are so confused they think they're their own grandchildren . . . but at least it makes them feel part of a family again."

"And what about you, Jimmy? Will you ever get over it?"

"I guess," he said grimly. "When I stop wanting to murder Wesley Barber and that bitch of a health visitor. She's still trying to claim she told Mel Milosz wasn't dangerous . . . says it's not her fault if Mel's so thick she got the wrong end of the stick."

She twisted her head again. "No one believes her, my dear. People are judged by their actions, and Miss Baldwin's been spiteful all her life. Everyone around here knows that. She's a silly woman. You reap what you sow in life, and she's reaping a lot of animosity. Wendy Hanson says ex-colleagues are fed up to the back teeth with her whining excuses, and they're looking to charge her with incitement."

"It'll never stick," said Jimmy.

"Maybe not, but it might make her face up to what she did. There are too many rabble-rousers in this world, and too few peacemakers." She folded her ancient claw over her shoulder to pat his hand. "Whatever your other sins, Jimmy, you're a peacemaker. It's a rare breed, and a fine one. Never let anger persuade you otherwise."

He dropped a kiss onto the gnarled fingers. "What other sins? I'm Big J., remember. The Main Man. Hero of the bloody hour. Going straight for the first time in his life."

She gave another chuckle. "How's that working out?"

"What you'd expect when you pay a guy peanuts to run a ramshackle youth center. I spend most of my time doing my Cetshawayo impression to stop the various gangs from killing each other. There are some good musicians, though."

"Is that where all the sound equipment went?"

"What sound equipment?"

"The stuff that vanished mysteriously from number twenty-three."

He gave a grunt of amusement. "There was no mystery about it. Milosz signed it over to me for saving his life. I've got the paper to prove it."

"Sophie said he was unconscious for three days."

Jimmy grinned. "I looked in on him a few times in the hospital while they were operating on Mel. He had a rare moment of lucidity at two o'clock in the morning. He sat up and signed the document. Take it all, he said, with my blessings."

Eileen clucked her tongue busily. "Fuck that for a load of bananas," she said happily. "You grabbed it before anyone else could. Dolly Carthew said you smuggled it out the back while the police were guarding the front, and stashed it in one of her empty rooms for a week."

"Language, Mrs. H."

"You've been a very bad influence on me, Jimmy. I'm swearing . . . I'm party to crimes . . . and I haven't felt so useful in years."

His infectious laughter bellied out above her head. "I still think I'd have done better to hightail it out of here with Mel and the babes. I'd be making a fucking sight more money selling drugs to kids in London than knocking heads together in Acid Row."

"You'd never be able to do it," she said comfortably. "It's just another form of child abuse. You care too much, that's your trouble. If you didn't, you wouldn't have told Milosz to get lost."

"How do you know I did?"

"Sophie told me." There was a twinkle in her eye, though he couldn't see it. "There were several references to Armageddon, apparently. Something along the lines of . . . next time good and evil wage a war outside your door, find some guts and pick the side of the angels instead of taking the coward's way out . . . or words to that effect."

"Yeah, well, I'd had time to think about it by then, and I reckoned it sucked that a guy'd let his father beat a woman black and blue because he was afraid of him. Okay, he had a lousy childhood, but then so did a lot of us. You have to make choices in life . . . and all he ever chose was to make his father worse. He said it would have been different if he'd known his dad had killed his mum"—he shrugged—"but I reckon he's lying about that. That's why he closes down and never mentions her. He knew she was dead, may even have witnessed it . . . but what did he ever do about it?"

Which was more or less what Sophie had said, but it was interesting that neither she nor Jimmy felt any compassion for Milosz because of it. "It would have been a terrifying experience for a little boy," Eileen pointed out.

"Sure," said Jimmy, "but he grew up, didn't he? It's never too late to change your mind. He should have turned his bastard father in years ago instead of going back to live with him. That makes him a real motherfucker even if his statement does support Sophie's version of events. He shouldn't have let it happen . . . shouldn't have let his dad smack the whores around. I don't care how frightened a geezer is . . . beating up on women's wrong."

He was a true gentle giant, thought Eileen. Hard as rock on the outside, soft as marshmallow inside. Love for him threatened to burst from her chest. "You and Sophie are two of a kind," she said gruffly. "Hearts as big as mountains . . . tolerance for sinners zero."

"It depends on what the sin is," he said. "Our Col was a thief . . . but I loved him. And Sophie's got more balls than I'll ever have. I couldn't've walked up the aisle looking like Elephant Man. That takes real class. She is who she is, and fuck anyone who says differently . . . that's her style. Me, I'm vain. The day I marry I want the world to say: 'WOW! There goes a dude.'"

Eileen laughed. "They'd say it whatever you looked like. It's behavior that makes a man, Jimmy, not the beauty of his face."

He turned the corner onto Carpenter Road and slowed to a halt in front of the third house. He squatted down in front of her and rested his palms on her knees. "Ready?" he asked.

"What for?"

He nodded toward the door. "To meet my daughter. Sophie delivered her, at home, in our bed, at three o'clock this morning. She's the prettiest babe you ever saw."

Eileen's old eyes lit up with excitement. "Oh, Jimmy, how wonderful!" she said, clapping her hands. "What's her name?"

He grinned. "Colinna Gaynor Eileen Sophie Melanie James."

She chuckled. "Will she remember them all?"

"She'd better," he said, grabbing the handles and spinning her up the path. "They're the first words of her story."